DEATH OF ROYALTY

By Rashon Burnett

35-11B Farrington St Ste 121
Flushing, NY 11354
Ordering Information:
Quantity sales. Special discounts are available on quantity purchases by corporations, associations, and others. For details, contact the publisher at the address above.
Orders by US trade bookstores and wholesalers. Please contact Rashon Burnett by phone or e-mail: 707-646-9106, rashonantwonburnett@gmail.com.
Printed by CreateSpace, an Amazon company
Rashon Burnett, 2015
Rashonburnett.com
ISBN: 0692441425
ISBN 13: 9780692441428

Chapter 1

Mating season on Aries: always a time filled with lust and love. Sometimes the two are indistinguishable from each other. This year would be no different in that regard.

A prince and a princess from two different kingdoms prepared for copulation.

"What will we do if my father finds out, or your father, for that matter?" the princess asked.

Princess Diantha of Taurus toyed nervously with her long, jet-black hair. A beauty with an earth-toned complexion, delicate features, high cheekbones, and small black horns, her well-sculpted face was shadowed with concern. She had been told to stay away from the prince of Aries, Mar, by her father.

The prince replied, "No need to worry, we will be fine, I never get caught doing anything, unless I want to." The orange-complexioned, handsome, and well-built prince of Aries was confident, as he always was that things would go his way.

Prince Mar had also been told various times by his father to stay away from the young princess.

The young prince would have ordinarily been right. Normally, he wouldn't have had anything to worry about with his mother and father gone and the servants away. But this time was different because the fact was at that very moment members of the royal Cancer Elite were infiltrating his father's castle.

***

"Maestro, don't you think it's strange we've been spying on all the royal houses so much lately?"

"There is nothing strange about it. Our king said a lot of things are supposed to be happening soon. He needs to know everything and keep tabs on everyone.

The two males were of the royal Cancer Elite. They could be anywhere, undetected, because they were invisible; in other words, the perfect spies. King Cancer utilized his spies often, especially after the large-scale Battle of Orion, a conflict that pitted all twelve kingdoms, against giants bent on dominating the twelve planets. The final conflict being laid to rest less than a year ago it was still fresh in all the kings' memories. The two light-blue men had heat vision so they were able to see each other.

Maestro, while shorter than Gregorio, was slightly more menacing, possibly because he had more experience than his protégé, and more weight, most of it muscle, aside from the slight gut he had.

Gregorio was more than a few inches taller than his mentor but might have weighed half as much.

The hallway they walked through was simple but plush, with red leather on the walls and windows on the ceiling.

The two men continued through the castle of the king of fire, King Aries, and finally made it to the king's quarters.

The room was made out of some sort of soft stone that seemed both rigid and yet malleable and was colored black, and the room was enormous. While the room was large, it was also simple, with a few cages that had an assortment of lizards from Aries that came in the widest spectrum of colors imaginable, from white, to red, blue, yellow, everything in between, all the way to black. There was also a massive bed, and a motion painting on the roof. The two regarded the painting and examined it for a moment. Maestro didn't care for motion paintings, so he spent less time looking at it than Gregorio. Supposedly, they told a story, but the characters in the story would only repeat one or two simple actions over and over again. In the case of Aries's painting, that action was him slicing four trolls in half with a sword rapidly, and smiling and flexing afterward. They quickly realized the room had nothing of interest. No one was there, and nothing looked out of the ordinary.

Suddenly, they heard a woman moan, a very…particular moan. The two then began to search for the origins of the interesting noise. Gregorio and Maestro were so close that they didn't need to speak, which was important because speaking too much would blow their cover; just because they were invisible didn't mean others couldn't hear them.

The Cancer Elites reached the room where the sound originated. Pushing the door open quietly and slowly, they saw Mar and Diantha, both naked and engaged in coitus. Mar was mounting her from the back. Gregorio smiled at his mentor, who nodded at him, and the two backed out of the room, having found some useful information to report back to their king.

***

"I'm telling you, that is not how we do things here on planet Aquarius," King Aquarius said through the aqua communicator. He continued, "I know you have your worries, King Pisces, and your visions, although lacking detail, sound troubling, but the diplomatic approach is always most beneficial. I honestly still don't agree with the treatment of half bloods. I even find addressing them in that manner distasteful, by the way." Aquarius ran his fingers through his naturally blue hair as he spoke to Pisces (all Aquarius have blue hair), Aquarius's was cut short except for the top, which was parted to the side, his blue eyes were trying to gaze into the future, not the real future, but rather the future he wanted to see. Milky skin-toned, pure emerald crown atop his head, Aquarius was a handsome man by most tastes, and he had a gentle pushiness to him that usually gave him the ability to get his way without even ruffling any feathers.

Aqua communicators had only recently been created, but they were all the rage. They were the only way that royals communicated anymore. Golden frames surrounded clear yet bluish screens that projected the face of the person you were talking to and allowed them to physically step directly where you were, or vice versa. The technology was very advanced.

King Pisces wanted to interrupt, but realized it was a bad idea. He could tell by judging Aquarius's expression that he was far from done. *Apparently King Aquarius has a lot on his mind,* he thought. Pisces tried to look as unmoved as possible by Aquarius's speech so far. His silver skin was as shiny as always, but his face was solemn. Pisces, a thin, silver skinned, handsome man. He had two fish-shaped birthmarks, one per arm, common of all Pisces, even half bloods. He was beginning to feel the weight of his red coral crown heavy on his head as he spoke with Aquarius, who was apparently very zealous about the half-blood cause.

Aquarius continued. "In fact, I would like to call a meeting of the council to discuss the future of the half bloods. I have a lot to prepare for, including a presentation, so I would prefer if you contact everyone for me." Aquarius stood up from his seat that was in front of the aqua communicator. "Would you mind telling them all that I would like to meet on planet Libra? I have a proposal to make."

Pisces contacted the other kings.

***

5

Planet Libra, the most balanced planet in all the area, was the accepted meeting place of all kings and other royalty, if needed. Green acres of land, beautiful trees abundantly scattered, and oceans that stretched for miles, this was the part of planet Libra that royalty from all the kingdoms would see.

In the giant hall with twelve chairs made of pristine wood, the kings began to sit. King Aries first, followed by King Taurus, King Gemini, and all the others, except for King Cancer.

Aries looked around and asked, "Is everyone here?" Shorter and stockier than his son, he had the same orange firelike skin tone, but with much more muscle. Aries demanded attention with his black diamond crown, armor fashioned in the same manner, and his robust build and facial hair.

Gemini replied, "It appears as if everyone is here, save for King Cancer." Gemini, an ebony-skinned male with one blue eye, one yellow eye, a crystal blue crown, and an impressive physique, demanded even more attention. He was thought to be one of the strongest and most intelligent of the twelve. His clothing was light and regal and matched his crown color.

"Maybe he's here, but he's just hiding, he can turn invisible after all," King Leo said. The king's mane looked extra shiny during this council meeting. His orange-brown fur also looked as if it had just been polished. Despite the beauty of his fur, he was still fearsome to behold because of his huge head and fangs. He dressed in simple leathers, and his orange sapphire crown loosely fit on top of his mane.

Sagittarius stood from his chair and called out, "Come out, Cancer, we don't have time for this, and you're boring me with these hiding games." The spiky golden-haired, golden-eyed male had perhaps the shortest attention span of all the kings. His golden attire matched the color of his hair and eyes.

King Pisces chimed in, "I'm pretty sure he's not here."

"Perhaps we should meet again at some other time," King Scorpio lightly suggested with a shrug. The bronze-skinned king was considered one of the most attractive because of his chiseled muscles, which he showed off frequently by choosing a wardrobe that allowed for it, at times abandoning a shirt entirely, as was the case at the council meeting. His physical appearance was also fear inspiring however, because of his large black scorpion tail that hovered just above his head.

"We shouldn't have to put up with his disappearing acts, he comes and goes as he pleases, but that doesn't mean our lives have to be put on hold," Aries said, standing up. "I say we make the decision without him."

"Wasn't he off the council last year?" Virgo asked. Dark-skinned, handsome, with strong facial features, he had a V engraved in his forehead. Virgo also stood out among his fellow kings in terms of looks, and because he wore a white diamond crown, with brilliant white garb. "In fact, shouldn't it be Leo to sit off the council this time and for the rest of this year?" Each year a member of the twelve on the council must sit out so that there is no chance for a tie with important council decisions.

Aries replied, "I understand that, but this is only one decision. We can just hear Aquarius out and make a decision, and the next time the council meets Leo will sit it out, like he's supposed to."

All the lords of their respective planets nodded their heads in agreement. They were all fed up. This sort of thing happened too often, because King Cancer would have his mood swings and was nearly impossible to find, unless he wanted to be found.

Libra brought up another perspective. "I think we should contact the Cancer Elite first, before we make such a rash decision. Perhaps Adeline, his closest servant, has heard something of his whereabouts."

With his see-through skin, King Libra had no real complexion and was basically transparent. In fact, you could even see some of his organs. Unless, of course, he wore clothing with strong colors or was exposed to certain conditions and environments; then he would take the appearance of his surroundings. For the council meeting, he wore opal-colored garb, and so his skin appeared in a variety of hues, and reflected and changed colors, depending on how he stood or what he was facing. Ordinarily, even his big angel-like wings would be see-through, but were a mixture of colors in this case. Of course, his clear skin wasn't uncommon. All Libras, save for half bloods, had naturally transparent skin. They say the transparency also bled over into all their decisions, which they tried to keep as fair as possible.

Using the aqua communicator, Libra first attempted to look for King Cancer, just in case he could be found, but of course, he couldn't be reached. Immediately after, Adeline appeared before them all on the aqua communicator. The water screen displayed a crisp image of the king of Cancer's favorite servant and confidant.

The green-skinned Gemini-Cancer woman known as Adeline appeared before them. With her cutting, catlike eyes, perfectly structured high cheekbones, and razor-thin eyebrows, she looked disappointed as she gazed back at Libra. Her ruby-red eyes appeared tired, and her stick-straight hair was in a lazy bun.

Libra asked her, "Do you by chance know the whereabouts of your master?"

Adeline replied, "I'm unsure of where he is at this moment. I don't believe he is in the kingdom right now, or even on planet Cancer for that matter, but I would be happy to relay any message you have for him." She looked a little past Libra to see the others who stood before the water screen. "Seeing as you all are requesting his presence, I imagine it must be quite urgent."

"Just tell him Aquarius called a council meeting, and he should get to Libra as soon as possible," Libra answered.

"Very well, I will try my best to locate him, and let him know that the great kings seek his company." She smiled.

Libra gave a partial smile. "Thank you, please do all that you can."

"But of course." Adeline nodded her head just before disappearing from the water screen, which shrank back to the smaller size that it maintained when not in use.

Aries laughed and sat back down. "You see. It's just as I said, we shouldn't waste our time waiting for him."

Leo immediately turned toward Aquarius. "I believe it is time you told us all why you asked us to come here."

Aquarius pulled out a metal square. He placed it in the center of the table that the council sat at, pressed a button. The square lit up, and a holographic image came up and threw itself on the largest centralized wall. The image displayed a scene of violence against different half-blood groups, and the violence perpetrated was coming from different common citizens from all of the twelve planets.

Capricorn was instantly curious. "What exactly are we looking at here?" Built like a tank, the only things small on Capricorn were his horns; aside from that, everything was big about his appearance. He wasn't the tallest necessarily, but looked as though he lifted boulders in his sleep. However, he wasn't the most attractive, his gray skin was nothing exceptional to look at.

"I'll tell you exactly what this is." Aquarius fought back tears. "This is all the pain and suffering of the so-called half bloods ever since the last uprising."

Leo sneered. "It serves them right, they had the nerve to plot against and try to kill us. They're lucky I haven't annihilated all of them. As are you. I think I'm finished here."

Scorpio stopped him. "Calm yourself, Leo, we haven't even let him get to his point yet."

Aquarius looked to Scorpio first. "Thank you." Then he looked to address all the others, standing with his palms held firmly on the table. "I have called you all here today because I would like to propose that all the half bloods, as we call them, come to live on my planet. You all have half bloods on your planets that I'm sure you can't nor want to deal with. They can stay on my planet, in my kingdom. The Aquarian people will be more than hospitable, resulting in a more pleasant standard for the half bloods than their current living conditions. I have set up an area just for them especially, and I have given my royal guardians strict orders to protect any half bloods who need help. I wanted a vote from each of you for your support. Also, I would like to vote on having a different name for these people. I feel the term *half blood* is derogatory and implies that they don't have loyalty to their home planet."

Aries laughed. "It's clear they don't have loyalty to their home planet, as Leo said earlier, they plotted against us, all of us, yourself included."

Aquarius replied, "I know that." Pausing, he closed his eyes and continued. "We all know that." He opened his eyes again after regaining his composure and looked Aries directly in his eyes. "They made mistakes, but that shouldn't mean they all suffer for the rest of their lives. All I'm asking is that you consider my proposal. If none of you trust them, it shouldn't be a problem for them all to live on my planet."

"I actually find some of the half bloods to be quite useful. In fact, some work for me in my castle, personally, side by side with my royals," Gemini said.

"That's fine, I'm sure some of the others would agree that having certain half bloods in their employ has proven useful. I only ask that you send any half bloods that don't work for you personally," Aquarius offered. "Of course the same goes for you all." His eyes swept the planet leaders.

Everyone at the table fell silent as they sat there contemplating his proposal.

***

"Adeline, I trust you must have something of utmost importance to say. I recall repeatedly telling you I wished to not be disturbed."

She bowed gracefully and deeply. "Master, I have been contacted by Libra." She stood up straight and found his gaze. "He tells me that there is a meeting of the council taking place at this very moment to make a decision."

"You two are free to go. Thank you for your report." King Cancer dismissed Gregorio and Maestro, the last two of his elites to report their findings for the day. "Interesting," he replied, turning his attention back to her. "Did they tell you what they were meeting about?"

Blue and bald, King Cancer kept his appearance simple but refined, and always dressed in the finest garb. He enjoyed deep, almost black purples, and his crown was colored likewise. His intense ruby-red, glowing eyes intimidated some, but not his servant.

"They said nothing about the reason for the meeting, my liege." She gave another submissive bow.

"It's no matter, they must wait for me to make a decision because this year, I'm one of the eleven on the council, as last year I was out. I suppose I made them wait long enough." He stood up from his throne. "I will head over there now," and with that he disappeared.

***

Prince Mar and princess Diantha laid in his bed for a while and talked. Prince Mar usually had a good sense about how long his dad was going to be gone, and he felt like it would be some time yet.

Princess Diantha was worried. "Are you sure we should just be relaxing like this?"

He gave a carefree laugh. "Yes, we should be fine. My father always spends a very long time out whenever he leaves for his council meetings. I suppose it's because he loves all the splendor Libra has to offer, but if you feel uncomfortable, maybe you should be on your way, just in case. I'll see you out."

The two young people reached the door, and she looked at him and said, "This has to be our secret."

"Of course, our secret until death," he replied. The two parted ways with a quick kiss.

***

"Leon, are you sure that your plan will work?" the hornless, red-skinned, tall and slender Aries-Piscean asked his friend. Most Aries-Pisces didn't have horns, and Arkin was no different.

"I have made all the proper preparations, and if my calculations are correct, there is at least a ninety-four percent chance that everything will go perfectly according to my plan," the furry-faced half blood said. He didn't have the usual V imprint in his forehead that most Virgos had. Not Leon; even his Leo features weren't very prominent, which made it hard for some to tell what race the reddish, slightly furry, Leo-Virgo male was.

"In fact," Leon continued, "I'm sure that our plan's goal will be reached soon. In no time at all, we should be living on planet Aquarius, with the way we stacked everything."

The two lived together on Aries in a tiny one room shack, just outside a small village once most of the smoke caused by the Battle of Orion cleared. The two half bloods had planned to reach this day for quite some time, well, Leon planned it mostly, he was an expert tactician, after all, despite the fact that his plan had failed at the Battle of Orion.

Leon, was the brilliant mind behind almost every move the half bloods of most worlds made, even though he had the brains, he still wasn't really a leader as much as Arkin. Arkin would often lead for the both of them and would only occasionally seek advice from Leon, but often times would not even listen to what was suggested, which could have been an additional factor that caused the plan at the Battle of Orion to fail.

The half bloods were an interesting lot; they had some of the abilities of two different types of people, but on rare occasions, they would have the physical characteristics of neither, as was the case for Leon. While Arkin was a different story entirely; it was said that the blood of an Aries was very strong, even when it coursed through a half blood's veins, and judging by Arkin's skin color that statement was most definitely true. Arkin also took after his Pisces side, for he bore the mark of the Pisces, two birth marks, one per arm, in the shape of a fish.

"If my analysis is correct, then Aquarius will try his best to keep us safe. I'm almost one hundred percent sure that Virgo is working on countermeasures for our next operation already."

"How could you possibly know that?" Arkin asked.

"If my analysis of Virgo and the situation is correct, I'm sure that after the last incident, one of the members of their council must have asked Virgo to come up with countermeasures, as he is essentially the smartest." Leon said.

"I thought King Aquarius was the smartest." Arkin said.

"There are multiple definitions and categories of intelligence. In the case of Virgo, I actually mean the most meticulous, technically. If there is anything that requires great, painstaking detail and refinement, which I would say countermeasures against us would be the very definition of that, Virgo would be the one to rise to the task, happily, I should add. Aquarius is better with more original and innovative creations, generally speaking." Leon said.

"You got all that information from your analysis of them? Where do you get your information from, exactly?" Arkin asked.

"I have my sources, but that's neither here nor there. I have something more important to discuss with you at the moment."

***

The great men had finally reached a satisfactory conclusion.

Pisces happily stated, "So it's settled then, the majority of half bloods will be living on Aquarius." He stood up with a smile. "Indefinitely, for the time being."

With glee Aquarius replied, "Indeed it is settled. I will need all of you to transport your dyads to my planet as soon as you can. Speaking of, thank you for the name idea, Gemini." He gave Gemini a firm clap on his shoulder. "I feel nobody else could have come up with such a clever name."

"You're welcome, and since the people of my planet are naturally dual in nature, I have a ton of names for them. I just suggested the one we use the least."

Libra excitedly came around with a bottle of univine, opened it, and poured a glass. "Let's all have libations in celebration of our accordance."

"I see festivities have begun without me." Cancer appeared from out of nowhere.

"You always come and go as you please, and often you delay our meetings," King Sagittarius answered. "Aries suggested we go on without you, and everyone else agreed."

"How dare you, Aries!" Cancer screamed at the top of his lungs. "I sat off the council for a whole year. Rules say that I am only to sit out decisions for my year off. And every year I'm on, I'm supposed to be involved in each and every decision. And yet you just bring it upon yourself to decide not to include me in this one."

"Hold on now, Cancer, calm down. I merely did what I thought was best so we could all get on with our lives, we are all busy."

"Apparently not too busy to partake in festivities along with food and drink." Cancer crossed his arms over his chest.

"It's true we were about to enjoy libations, but I assure you I have already thought of how to make it up to you. Eleven years from now, when it is your turn to sit off the council, I, King Aries, will sit out all decisions for that year instead. Are you happy now?"

"No! Something so simple cannot appease me. I'm not a child. Plus, everything you just said is still against the rules. What is right is right, and wrong is wrong, and it's wrong to not include me in a decision the council makes. You have all most likely been looking for this chance to betray me." He unfolded his arms and looked around. "Scorpio, I'm mostly shocked that you were OK with this, and Taurus, too. You two are supposed to be my allies."

"We all waited for you. Libra even contacted Adeline to inquire about your whereabouts, and then we waited some more. I honestly feel that you're just overreacting. You should calm down," Scorpio replied.

Taurus attempted to empathize with Cancer. "I don't think he's overreacting. It kind of makes sense for him to feel betrayed. After all, this is the first time a member of the council who was sitting in for the year has been left out of a decision."

Scorpio directed all his attention to Taurus at once and said, "It may be events like this and discussions like this that make Cancer feel as though he can come and go as he pleases. We should not cater to his every whim. After all, we are all kings, with busy schedules. In fact, I think I'll be taking my leave."

And with that, Scorpio left, and as soon as he did a few others left as well. Sagittarius had grown bored quite a while ago and slipped out when no one was looking.

In the end, only Libra, Aries, Cancer, Taurus and Pisces were left around.

"Pisces, are you sure you can see into the future? Why didn't you see this one coming?" Libra joked.

Pisces became a little bit upset. "I cannot always see Cancer and the places he goes, or where he's at. It's most likely an effect of his powers and, for some reason, it even blocks me from seeing his future location and actions."

"I think that everything will be OK, Cancer. No one is trying to betray you, and you have Aries's word that he will sit out your next year to be off the council." Taurus stood a few inches over Cancer.

"Irrelevant." Cancer shook his head. "Everything Aries has promised is inconsequential. I've already moved on from the issue. I just want to know what the decision was regarding, and what conclusion you all came to," Cancer intoned.

Taurus gave Cancer the whole rundown while Aries took his leave.

After Taurus thoroughly explained the situation to Cancer, they left, leaving only Pisces and Libra.

Pisces said to Libra, "I think we should be a little bit worried about the things that Cancer is doing behind our backs." Pisces sounded concerned.

"I'm sure it will be fine. I trust him. Well, not really, but I mean what can we do, he is a king like us, after all." Libra shrugged.

"This is true, but very often I feel that in the game of subterfuge and backhanded politics his powers give him an absolute advantage."

"Is that how you truly see what we kings do here Pisces, as backhanded politics?" Libra regarded Pisces for a moment and paused before continuing. "Further his abilities don't always give him an advantage, just a moment ago we made a decision without him. I guess overall I'm not worried about that yet, Pisces. I'm sure it will work out in the end, and if there's anything wrong with what Cancer is doing, it will come out. I'm more concerned about the fate of the half bloods."

"You mean the dyads?" Pisces corrected him.

"Oh yes, that's right, I'm sorry, I meant the dyads. I mean, it seems a little too risky to have them all on one planet. Won't it upset the balance of everything?"

"You may be right in some ways, but I have had visions of the future, and things are going the way they are supposed to. Glorious things are to come to all kingdoms." Pisces gestured toward the walls of the council room on which paintings of the original kings hung.

"If you say so." Libra was confused. He could have sworn Pisces had just questioned the cohabitation of all dyads on one planet, which to him also implied uncertainty and danger in the future. "Can I ask you something?" Libra looked Pisces in his silver eyes to get his full attention.

"Sure, by all means."

"How does your ability work? I mean, specifically seeing the future."

"Honestly, it depends on the situation." Pisces looked away and stared at the ground. "I would say it starts with me focusing on someone or something, and usually I see the most likely alternative that will happen to them, but sometimes I see multiple possibilities. I can more or less filter through the decisions and actions that lead to the best case scenario happening, but if I'm being honest"—Pisces finally looked back up at Libra—"I have been wrong about one or two of my predictions before, even after I went through all the possibilities and alternatives. I still don't understand how I was wrong. Perhaps there are things that even I can't predict."

"Clearly there are, not to be rude, but a few moments ago you said that you can't always track Cancer himself. I do find what you just said very interesting, though. Maybe one day you'll tell me about some of the times where your predictions were wrong."

"Yes, maybe I will someday."

Chapter 2

The kingdom of Aquarius was one of the biggest within the twelve planets. It was entirely underwater, with pipelines that allowed citizens to travel about with ease.

Aquarius had a special portion of his kingdom sectioned off for the dyads. He, of course, didn't want them to be separate from all the other people of his kingdom, but he wasn't sure if he wanted them with the general populace right away, either.

He wanted to do what he felt was right, but even he had his doubts in terms of how everything would work out. Luckily for him, the dyads were not set to be integrated into his kingdom for a little while. They were to be given time by all their kings to tie up loose ends, as well as say all their goodbyes to their homelands. Aquarius also felt that it was important that all the kings take time to think on the gravity of the decision they had made. He felt as though some of them may have sided with him because of the nice trade deals he cut them. Aquarius was a planet rich with resources, and the king did not mind sharing resources with the rest of the kingdoms, but only for the right reasons and to those deserving.

Aquarius sat in his amethyst-colored throne and reflected for a moment. He thought back to the events that transpired at the last battle he and the other kings had to fight in. The more he thought about it, the more it made sense that the dyads, still known as half bloods at the time of the last battle, would try to overthrow them. It actually made Aquarius a little sick and disgusted with himself as he thought about how the dyads were sent into battle first. In particular the Battle of Orion came to mind and he could not remember when it was decided that half bloods would be the first to enter large scale battles.

He knew that it must have been a decision agreed upon by the council, but he could not remember how it came about. It was not very often that the twelve kings had to join forces. Their powers were so great that it usually only required one or two of them to handle a problem. However, Orion was a different story, it was one of the most gruesome battles that any of them had fought, especially on planet

Bellatrix. It was an exhausting multi planet spanning experience for most of them that took—Aquarius had his thoughts interrupted by the appearance of his subordinate.

"Sire, I have returned. I just wanted to inform you that all the preparations have been made. The living quarters for the half bloods are fully prepared for their arrival," Linden said with a quick bow.

"Very good, Linden, I'm pleased to hear the news. I would like you to refer to the half bloods as dyads from now on."

Long blue hair that went straight back to his shoulders, Linden was just as good-looking as his cousin the king, with an icier blue pierce to his eyes and all the grace that one man could yield.

"Sire?" Linden raised an eyebrow and his head to make eye contact with his king.

"It has been decided that from now on the half bloods will be known as dyads. We discussed it during the council meeting and came to that conclusion."

"Very well, my lord." Linden bowed again, deeper this time, before departing.

***

Capricorn, a planet with lots of rocky, mountainous terrain and plenty of green grass. The rocky surfaces had few water sources, but the ones it did have were beautiful and surrounded by nice plants and healthy grass, such as the river Serpens. The largest river on planet Capricorn, said to span the entire planet, it was shaped like a serpent and had a glow to it. According to legend, drinking the water would give the drinker powers similar to King Capricorn, who was said to be immortal.

It must be a rumor. The boy silently stared at his own reflection in the water of the river. King Capricorn's immortality and the river's effects both had to be rumors. If it were the case, almost all Capricorns would never die.

The Capricorn boy had always been told stories as a child about how the king was his father. None of that mattered, because he still lived a life of squalor. He had a father who had raised him and took care of him, but now that man was gone. If the king was his real father, then the king did not care about him and was worthless in the fatherly capacity. None of that mattered to the boy, though. Whether the king was his real father or not, the boy's true concern was for a better life. *I want to live like the royals do.* He threw a small rock into the water.

Suddenly, he heard a woman scream. He got up and raced in the direction of the scream. When he arrived at the scene, he saw a giant spider assaulting a woman. Quickly, he picked up the biggest rock nearby. Gripping the rock with two hands, he spun around to get some momentum going. Swinging the rock as hard as he could, he released it in the direction of the spider just shy of its head. The spider stopped what it was doing and turned to the boy, but the boy had already picked up smaller rocks and was flinging them at the spider. The spider must have felt it wasn't worth it to attack, because it slowly left the area.

"Hello," the boy said to the young woman. "Are you OK?" he asked, holding his hand out to help her up.

Regaining her composure on her own, she looked at him and gave a weak smile. "Yes, I'm fine."

"Can I ask what brings you here?" he said to her.

"I don't understand what you mean by that." She dusted off her dress a little, then briefly made eye contact and began to look over the person who had saved her. Staring at the brown- skinned, short, scrawny Capricorn boy, with his small orange-yellowish spiral horns, she tried to ascertain who he was. What he lacked in size, he made up for in looks. The same could not be said of his dark brown clothing, however, she concluded.

He said, "I can tell you're not one of my people, you don't even have any horns. Even babies have horns, all our horns may be smaller than those of Taurus and Aries, even the king's, but we all have horns. In fact, I know what you are. You're a Virgo, aren't you? What brings you here?"

"It's a long story," she said as she began to tell him why she had come there.

While she told her story, the boy couldn't help but realize how beautiful she was. She had fair skin with light brown hair, so curly it was as if she had dozens of long springs in her hair that were ready to burst. She was petite, with a small waist and a lovely black dress that opened at her left and right side. The boy felt as though there was something regal about the beauty with the V engraved in her forehead.

After that, he saw it: the bracelet that appeared to contain the entire cosmos within itself. This bracelet was the keepsake of some female Virgo royals. The boy couldn't remember the crown his king wore, and for some reason couldn't think of what the other royals wore to signify their royalty, but he recognized that the bracelet she had was designed to let others know at a glance that she was royalty.

"Are you some sort of princess?" he asked, while still staring at her bracelet.

She laughed lightly. "Close, nice try, but I'm a queen actually."

The boy's eyes widened. "Wow, what brings you here to this part of Capricorn, where it is unsafe? Why don't you have anyone to chaperone you?"

"I most certainly don't need anyone to look after me. I can hold my own quite well." She began stretching. "Although my abilities are more suited for dealing with the twelve peoples of our twelve planets, I always have some sort of trick up my sleeve for dealing with brutish creatures. The giant spider you saw me contending with"—she made eye contact—"merely caught me off guard." She stopped stretching, stood up straight, and looked around. "Not to mention, I'm surveying this area, along with less popular areas on the other planets, unbeknownst to my love. I don't really want to be a bother to him or the royal force. I'm gathering information and seeing how I can be of better use to the peoples of the planets, and what use and purposes each planet serves."

"If that's all, my lady, couldn't you have just as easily spoken with the great administrator, Lord Viscount? As I understand it, he's an expert in all things of all kingdoms, and even from your kingdom, if I'm not mistaken."

"Yes, of course," she answered, lackadaisical, some wind coming out from her sails, "but hearing something from someone and seeing it in person are two vastly different things." She stared at her sandals. "I have grown bored as of late and seek to be stimulated through my actual physical exploration of the different cultures." Her gaze met his. "Now, if you would kindly show me around and give me a tour, I would be deeply obliged. But first, what is your name?"

"My name is Callum." He extended his hand toward her.

"My name is Valera, it is nice to meet you," she said as she shook his hand.

"The pleasure is all mine, Your Highness." He added an awkward bow. "I will try my best to ensure that this is the grandest tour you will ever receive in all the lands."

***

"No means no, and that's final," King Aries told his son.

"Father, hear me out, I will not do as you command just because you command it. I am in love, and I should be free to do as I wish, just like you always do."

"It may appear as though I always do as I desire, Mar." Aries stopped in front of a family portrait in the dining area where they spoke. "But I actually think of everyone in our family, even our kingdom, before I ever make a decision. I told you before, my hands are tied. I can't have you marrying the princess of Taurus when I have already promised that you will marry the Capricorn princess."

"I have never even met her before. I don't even know what she looks like," Mar said.

"I already told you. You can meet her whenever you want, just give me the word and I will set everything up with the goat-man," Aries said with an overly zealous smile.

"You don't even like the Capricorns, you just called the king a goat-man. Why should I have to marry the goat-man's daughter?"

The prince of Aries couldn't stand how his father always tried to force his will upon him.

"I don't like the Capricorns, and that's exactly the point. The marriage was arranged in an attempt to maintain peace between the two nations and to improve relations between our kingdom and theirs." His tone became even more fatherly as he continued. "Your brother Ram accepted his duty when he married the Libra princess, which has been profitable for our kingdom as well. You need to accept your responsibilities to this family, the same way your brother accepted his."

"That's easy for you to say." Mar distanced himself from his father, almost walking out of the room. "This isn't your life, it's my life, and I don't understand why my brother would let you dictate how to live his life, but I'm not having it."

"You don't have to love the woman, son." Aries put his hand on his son's shoulder. "It's mostly just a formality. You could always bed whomever you want while you're wed to her. Nobody can stop you from that, because you're my son. Nobody ever stops any king from doing whatever they want. I assure you that you will take over in my place, as my heir." Mar finally made eye contact with his father, which made the king smile. "I love your brother, too, but you remind me more of myself and how I used to be. Don't tell your brother I told you that." He whispered the last part to his son, winked, and added a friendly nudge.

It was true that King Aries was going to pass the kingdom to his younger son. But in truth, part of the reason for that was, Ram, his elder son, was already off exploring uncharted planets and galaxies, expanding the Aries Empire.

Mar's disposition instantly changed. "I understand your position, Father, and I'm honored that you're going to pass the kingdom down to me, and I can see a little better where you're coming from. I will meet the Capricorn girl and make a decision from there. After all, it's not like Diantha's father would approve of us being together anyway. "

"I'm happy to hear you have finally come to your senses, my boy." He briskly patted his son on his back. "I will set the meeting up at once."

***

Croix could barely hear his shiny orange flesh sear as the cattle brand was shoved onto his right arm. His skin got red for a second and then black around the area where he was being branded. Croix was a tall and handsome Aries man, with a sharp jawline and deep brown eyes. His long horns went straight back behind his head and looked a little frayed, and he had brown horns, like all Aries. Pain from the heat was nothing to an Aries, because they couldn't feel it. He still thought it was a silly initiation, but he had wanted to be in the brotherhood for as long as he could remember.

This rite of passage was reserved for those born into royalty on Aries. Not only that, but one had to be of age to go through the process. Luckily, he was born a male, he was now of age, and he was born into the right family.

The sun had long since set, but there still was a strong amount of red in the night sky. It was a special time of the year. The woods were alive with all sorts of action from creatures and Croix and the others.

His father was the king's brother. If only his father had been born at the right time, with the right alignment of the planets, under the right moon, then Croix would have been the prince, as opposed to just a member of the Aries royals. He knew he should be grateful, but he found himself thinking for a few moments about how great things would be if he was the prince of the planet, not just cousin to the prince.

"Croix, Croix." The pale orange-yellow skinned Aries male called to him, who, with his fellow brothers from the brotherhood wore red robes and surrounded Croix.

"Sorry, I was lost in thought."

"That's understandable, after all, now is the hard part. You have to partake in a mating ritual, with a woman. We all know how shy you are, but this is a part of the tradition that you must do all by yourself. Don't worry, though, brother. I'm sure they are all in heat, this should be easy. After all, you're one of us, one of the royals. Make us proud," the hooded Aries man said as he disappeared from Croix's sight.

With that they all disappeared, almost as if they were part of the Cancer Elite. The only ones left were Croix and two Aries females doing a dance before a fire, they seemed so close and yet so far away. Croix hoped they were far enough away that they couldn't hear him and the other royal males speaking, but he was sure that as Aries royal females, they knew about the rite, and that they had even been encouraged to be a part of it by their fathers.

Croix figured there were two of them so he could have a choice rather than have one chosen for him. At his level the marriages were still somewhat arranged, but with a lot more free reign than at the level of his cousin, the prince.

The two women danced around the fire as if they and it were one. Their merger with the fire would end briefly for a few seconds, only for them to join the flames again, or rather, that's what it looked like. It shouldn't have been a surprise, given the fact that they were women of the fire people and of similar skin tone to the flames. It took a little while for him to notice, but watching one of the two made his heart dance and race more than watching the other woman. They were both beautiful, and didn't look that different from each other; in fact, he was convinced they were sisters, but one just made him feel a little more in his chest than the other did.

He immediately approached her. The young woman stopped dancing around the flames in the dirt patch near the grass and, without a word, grabbed his hand, and they walked away.

***

The crown can be very heavy sometimes, King Leo reasoned with himself as he sat in his wooden throne, which was made in his image with multiple carvings of him. His crown was literally heavy from all the orange sapphires it held.

His kingdom, while not the largest, was generally known as the most entertaining due to the fights in the gladiator-style lion's den. His castle was massive and made from red brick and hidden away in a forest surrounded by trees. The king did enjoy nature greatly.

It was not all fun and games on planet Leo, though. There had long been talks that a commoner who referred to himself as Crimson was rallying other commoners behind his cause, which was, foolishly enough, to attempt to overthrow the king. Recently these talks manifested themselves into a small riot in which minor property was destroyed. The royals of King Leo, the royal pride, the king's warriors, had given him word that Crimson was inciting even more anarchy and disobedience among the people, and had a band of followers, whom started a full blown rebellion at a work factory, but King Leo and all his arrogance didn't care. He hadn't cared and didn't act for a time, which may have been how the situation escalated into a rebellion in the first place. But with Crimson's influence increasing Leo began having some interest.

King Leo in part wanted a conflict, he was actually itching for a battle in which he could show all of them just how powerful he was. In most conflicts, he allowed his royal pride to destroy his opponents, and most of the common people had never even seen a fraction of his power as there had never been a need for him to flex. So a part of him really wanted to kill some of them so they would complain less about their working conditions, and they would know just how different he was from them.

While the king of Leo could easily destroy thousands, if not all common people of his planet, his royal pride convinced him that it would not be for the best. After all, the weaker lions of common blood worked hard to produce crude polumb, a useful liquid found naturally on planet Leo, which was then refined by Virgos and used in mostly all the technology that the Aquarians had created. In other words, the common Leos had some use, and it would be counterproductive for King Leo to destroy them. But the king needed entertainment, and so gave his pride specific orders to make an example of the most influential of all the rebels.

Crimson and his followers were easily captured. The king's royal pride were light-years ahead in strength when compared to the average Leo. The pride captured twenty of Crimson's lieutenants as well. Some of the weaker rebel lions were allowed to go back to work immediately. Some of the others, who were stronger than average, were deemed a threat, and detained and locked away. They were going to be forced to fight in the lion's den for their right to exist.

Leos were an ambitious lot, commoner or royal born, and examples needed to be made to crush dreams and ambitions. It was unclear why Crimson had actually started the uprising, and King Leo did not one hundred percent care what his motivations were, but he figured he would hear him out tomorrow. The sentence was going to be carried out tomorrow in the lion's den. The more the king thought about it, the more interested he was in hearing what the rebel leader had to say so he could better understand Crimson's motives, he was curious. Maybe he would personally destroy Crimson himself. He still wasn't sure yet, it all depended on how he felt the next day.

***

King Gemini had his royal shadows gather all the dyads so they could be brought to the planet of Aquarius, which was to be their new home. It seemed like it was mere minutes before his shadow warriors returned with the dyads.

He had them all meet in one of the training rooms for his royals. The room was massive and could easily fit over three hundred men. It was important that the room be so large so it could hold all the royal shadows of Gemini. Every portion of the room was set up to mimic one of the other kingdoms, in a basic way. For example, there was a desert area to mimic Scorpio, volcanic area for Aries, amphibious area for Aquarius, rocky mountain area for Capricorn, a forest for Leo, a sort of island oasis to represent Pisces, and so forth.

"They all came with you without incident?" Gemini stopped pacing to ask his servant when he entered.

"A few of them tried to put up a fight, but of course, they were no match for us." Grinald pushed one of them forward.

"You have gathered both of the peoples then, those of Gemini-Cancer descent and those of Gemini-Taurus blood?" King Gemini looked at the dyads inquisitively.

"Yes, of course, Your Majesty."

"Very well, escort them personally to planet Aquarius. You can use any ship that will accommodate the large group, or you can even use this aqua communicator in this room."

"Understood, sir, thank you. Grendel! Bring them in at once," the paper thin, male called to his twin brother.

"You can't do this to us," one of the red-eyed, green-skinned Gemini-Cancer dyads called out.

"We have done nothing to deserve this," an olive-skinned Gemini-Taurus said. There weren't a lot of them, only a group of about one hundred-seventy-five, with most being Gemini-Cancer. Dyads were rare in any kingdom, rarer still on Gemini. Beyond that, the fact remained that King Gemini found his dyads to be useful, and thus all the rest of them born into the kingdom were going to stay.

The king thought about ignoring the dyads, but explained the situation instead. He looked to the center of the green- and olive-colored crowd so that he could have all their attention. "Supposedly, this is for your own good. You will all get to be with others who are of two peoples. I have heard that some of you faced hostility here, and while I did not do anything to stop it, I also did not necessarily agree with it. I think you will have an easier time and fewer problems in the designated area that Aquarius has picked for you all to live. I understand some of you may miss some things about our planet, but perhaps you can all come back if things don't work for you on Aquarius, or maybe you could even live somewhere else. Remember, nothing is permanent, and try to make the best of your situations. Grendel. Grinald. Please take them away."

The twin royal shadows stepped through the aqua communicator to bring the dyad people of Gemini to their new home on Aquarius.

As soon as they stepped through, they saw him, blue-haired as all Aquarius are, tall, and blue-eyed: Linden, Aquarius's right-hand man. The dyads felt like prisoners, as they wearily arrived at their new home.

***

The prince of Aries was amazed when he saw how beautiful the princess of Capricorn was. He thought he'd feel contempt or disgust when he saw her, but instead he felt butterflies. He was expecting for her to be nothing special to look at but instead, what stood before him was a gorgeous young woman. She had beautiful dark hair that had such a shine to it that it looked like it was glowing; long and flowing, it came down to the middle of her back. And even though she wasn't of planet Aries, her skin had a slight tinge of pink and was lightly complimented by her dark red, garnet-colored dress. He wasn't sure how exactly he could describe her complexion but he knew he liked it, and he felt as though he had never seen a woman like her before.

The little orange-yellow spiral horns on her head were the only way he could tell she was a Capricorn.

"King Aries, Prince Mar, I'm glad you're finally here." Capricorn stood up next to his daughter. His red garnet-colored armor matched his daughter's dress color. "This is my lovely daughter, Catalina. I know you two are supposed to be joined to one another at the end of the season, but there's no need to rush or think about that. Take your time and get to know each other. See how you like each other for now. Catalina, please give the young prince a tour of our castle."

"Yes, Father." She gave a slight bow. "Salutations, King Aries," to whom she gave a deeper bow. "I will show you around as soon as you're ready," she said, finally looking at the prince.

Prince Mar realized that he hadn't said anything since seeing her. He'd been too awestruck.

"I'm ready. Let us see this castle posthaste," he said excitedly, partially hoping to make her laugh. He thought it would be a clever joke, because they were already in the castle and could already see it. Whatever the case she didn't laugh, but he was also being somewhat serious as he was excited to see the rest of the castle for the first time.

After all, he had never been on planet Capricorn before today. Of all the kingdoms he had toured so far, Gemini was his favorite, but he still hadn't seen Capricorn, Virgo, Scorpio, or Cancer. At least he could mark one off his list today.

Catalina began walking and talking as if she were a tour guide. She was hard to read. He wasn't sure if she was interested in him at all. It could have been that maybe she just took castle tours very seriously, or maybe that she was excited to have a new visitor there as well and wanted to make a great impression. At any rate, she spoke on the history of the castle.

On the inside, the castle had a surprisingly elaborate design with all sort of creatures painted on the background of the walls. The whole thing was surprisingly vibrant. On the walls, there were paintings hanging up of Capricorn royals.

"My father, the first born of the tenth generation of royal lineage to the planet of Capricorn, had this painting made in his honor." Capricorn looked regal in the portrait and was adorned in the same armor Mar had just seen him in. "And here is a painting of his heir, my eldest brother, Cicero."

Cicero, while handsome, looked nothing like his sister Catalina. Immediately, he wondered if they had the same mom, or if they were even actually brother and sister. Cicero had bronzed skin, golden hair, and a chin that appeared to be made of steel. Odder still, his eyes appeared to be golden, too. Mar wanted to ask her about her brother, but figured he shouldn't. It was probably too personal for a first encounter.

As they walked through the hall of King Capricorn's castle, Mar began to realize that the royal Capricorns had a lot more paintings than he did at his castle; perhaps his father didn't care for the same things this king did. He began to wonder what sort of king he would be. His focus momentarily drifted from her.

She could tell right away; she stopped and asked, "Hello, are you listening?" She waved her hand slowly in his face.

"Yes, of course."

"Then tell me what I just said, repeat it verbatim," she commanded him, folding her arms over her chest and impatiently tapping her feet.

He laughed and recounted her words with ease.

***

"Are we all set here, Capricorn?" Aries put his cup down on the dark blue table that Capricorn kept in his chambers and stood up. The two had drank together.

"We are indeed, Aries. You can leave if you want. After she gives him a tour of the castle, if the boy wants to leave, I'll have some of my men escort him back." He set his drink down on the table as well. "If my daughter wants, I'll have her escorted back to your kingdom, and your son can give her a tour of your castle. Either way, feel free to take your leave." Capricorn stood up, reached out his hand, and the two shook briefly.

"If this marriage happens, are all the conditions we agreed upon going to be met?" Aries looked him in the eyes.

"I would have it no other way. I'm a man of my word. As long as nothing is awry on your end, I will deliver on my end as well. This venture will be profitable for my people also."

"I'm looking forward to the two becoming better acquainted, then. Thank you for your hospitality. The ale of Capricorn is just as good as I remembered. I'll be off then."

Aries instantly disappeared from Capricorn's chambers. Capricorn's room was large and simple with an extensive bar that had a vast assortment of drinks, a massive bed, a table with various kingdom and planetary maps, and military diagrams and lists on his walls of all his soldiers, lieutenants, and so forth, and the blue table where they had both just sat.

Aries seemed to disappear because he left Capricorn's castle so fast and even though neither he nor his royals, the brotherhood, could vanish in thin air, it seemed like it sometimes because they were so fast. King Aries of course was the fastest. The great men who were the kings of the twelve planets would not be able to hold their positions if they weren't the strongest of all their people.

***

No one knew how or why the planets, stars, sun, and moons aligned perfectly to make the outrageously powerful twelve kings, or even if that had anything to do with their abilities, but one of their number, King Virgo, intended to find out.

"I am so glad you're here, Scorpio." Virgo spun around in his chair to look up at him. "I really want to show you something. Look at that glass slide." Virgo pointed to the microscope right next to him. "What do you see?"

"I see DNA of some sort."

Brown DNA was displayed in the microscope.

"Yes, that's a DNA blood sample of a commoner from your world. Now watch this."

King Virgo placed a dropper-worth of blue fluid onto the slide with the Scorpio commoner DNA.

"Now what do you see happening?" Light brown DNA was now on display, and the two different samples were becoming one as Scorpio looked again.

"It looks like the two are mixing. Why do you ask? What is so important about this?"

"Don't you see? "The second sample is that of a commoner from planet Cancer."

Scorpio looked at him, confused for a second. He was used to being confused while in Virgo's lab. The only thing simple about the lab was the setup. The room was all white; Scorpio imagined that was so colors of fluids and experiments would stand out. All the equipment was silver. *Simple* was definitely the word to describe the layout, but that was where simplicity stopped, because all of Virgo's experiments were complex. "So what you're trying to show me is that commoners of any planet can mix with the commoners of any other planet, and the two will become one?"

"Not exactly."

Virgo removed the slide of the commoner DNA, slid in his chair to a different table, grabbed another slide, and placed a different DNA droplet beneath the microscope.

"Look at that, and tell me what you see."

"I see what looks like two different types of DNA again." This time Scorpio saw a blue-gray color sample.

"What you're looking at now is the DNA of a dyad. Do you see the difference between the two?"

"I'm not sure, but I think the difference is that in the first sample you showed me, the blood was mostly one type or the other, even though it was mixed. But with the dyads, it's spread a little more equitably." Scorpio lifted his eyes from the microscope and looked toward Virgo.

"Wow, that's exactly right, good job. Now I have one last thing to show you."

He reached to his immediate left and grabbed another slide from his table and put it on. Dark brown DNA was on this slide.

"Give it a close look," Virgo insisted as Scorpio glanced at him briefly.

Scorpio stared through the viewer of the microscope. "Now look at it again." Virgo said, adding a green drop of DNA on the slide. The dark brown got even darker, almost black, and the original DNA engulfed the whole of the second.

"What do you believe just happened?" Virgo excitedly questioned him.

"It looks like whatever was originally on the slide consumed or overtook all the blood you put on after."

"Guess whose blood that was." Virgo had a pretentious smirk on his face.

"How could I possibly know that? Please just tell me." Scorpio lifted his gaze from the microscope again.

"That was your blood, like actually one hundred percent your blood, well, just the first DNA on the slide."

"How could you possibly have my blood?"

"I was able to gather some of the blood of all the kings during the Battle of Orion on Bellatrix, even Cancer's. In fact, if you recall, I told you I was working on antivenom for the fatal poison your tail produces. If I didn't have your blood, then I wouldn't have been able to do that. Your blood was the first blood that was on the sample. The other blood on the sample that I added later was mine, believe it or not."

"Okay I do recall you mentioning working on the antivenom. But I'm more curious in your current experiment. Does what happened on the blood slide mean that my blood is stronger than yours?" Scorpio was more and more fascinated as the conversation developed.

"That's what I thought at first, too, but I tried the test multiple times, and the interesting thing is that it doesn't always go the same. Some of the time my blood would be more dominant, and other times your blood, like just now, would be more prevalent.

"Do you know what this means?" Virgo's eyes got larger as he continued and stood up from his chair. "It explains why whenever a king has a child with a woman of a different race, the child ends up taking after the male in most respects. Of course, only recently have royalty begun breeding out of their race, so there aren't many examples, but as of now, it seems to be the case. If you study the sample closer, you see that even though your blood overtook mine, there are still some faint traces of my DNA in there." Virgo walked around a bit.

"I don't understand. How can this," Scorpio gestured toward the slide, "possibly be the same thing as when a king mates with a woman? Wouldn't the blood mix more naturally with a king and any female?" Scorpio returned his stare to the slide of the microscope.

"Easy. I took out certain membranes from the cells that we have before us and gave them preservatives to keep them alive. I then added a catalyst to ensure that they multiply and function normally. Lastly, I added a gene to trick the cells into thinking they are all alike. If the cells think they are similar because they have a common strand, this allows them to attach to one another and form bonds. Basically, this is the closest simulation I could possibly make for the conception of a child and the way their genes are dispersed, using only DNA and slides."

"OK, so in other words, the reason that any child I have will become a Scorpio like me is because my blood is stronger than any woman I can have a kid with?" Scorpio was still puzzled. He lifted his gaze from the microscope and looked at Virgo.

Virgo walked back near the microscope and continued explaining. "That is a factor, but if it's her mating season and she's of a different race, there's a chance the offspring will take more after her, whether she's royalty or not. Not only that, but this experiment shows that all commoners are compatible with each other. You and I and all the other kings are almost like a different species entirely. It's almost like we aren't even genetically the same as our own people."

"Wow, that's crazy." Scorpio let the weight of Virgo's words sink in. "I guess that explains why we are so much more powerful than commoners."

"Yes, exactly, that's exactly why we have abilities that the commoners don't. There are still a few things I don't understand, though." He scratched his head and stared off into nothingness. "I don't understand how the royals of all the planets work yet. Furthermore, I'm unsure why my wife has similar powers to me. I believe she's capable of all the things I am." He looked around his lab as if the answer was in a past experiment. "I don't know if she is as powerful as I am, but if she isn't, then she's at least very close."

"That's fairly interesting. Is she your sister or something?" Scorpio joked.

"Disgusting, you're terrible." He laughed off the matter with his friend. "But it does make me wonder about our own origins. Also about the origins of all the kings, and their fathers before them, and their fathers."

"Me, too, I'm very curious about all the origins of all the great races now, and the royals and the other kings and myself. I've heard the legends, as I'm sure you have, but maybe there's more to it than that. Keep up the research." He clapped Virgo on the shoulder. "Let me know how it turns out, or if you find anything new or interesting."

"Will do."

"All right, I'll see you later, old friend, take care of yourself."

"Of course, you do the same." Virgo finished with a nod.

***

The time had finally arrived. King Leo was ready to see a show; his men versus the rebellious commoners. The king sat in a huge throne just above the gladiator stadium with his crown atop his furry mane and his beautiful Lioness by his side.

He had a goblet of his favorite Libran-brewed ale. Green in appearance, it didn't look palatable, but it was, and he finished it quickly and signaled for a servant to refill his goblet. He was growing impatient as he waited for the entertainment to begin. Finally, the speaker arrived. The golden stadium known as the lion's den was spectacular and grand in size, seating was multitiered, with a box area for the king and queen that was above it all. The stadium was circular in shape, enclosed around itself, and one of the crown jewels of planet Leo.

The speaker was a short Leo, probably the runt of his family. He wore a suit and tie to cover his upper body but no pants, and he had his small mane slicked back. However, he was certainly full-blooded Leo, and his lion-like features appeared stronger than his body. His appearance was perfect for his function, as his king would sometimes have him perform to entertain him and other royalty.

"We are all gathered here today to see the guilty sentence of the accused carried out. If the guilty party wins the fight, however, they will win freedom according to the rules of battle in the arena. On my left side we have the royal pride of Leo!"

The pride stormed out from behind the battle gates, beautifully forged leather and metal armor partially covering their bodies. The royal pride was varied in color, but all members had the same menacing stance and demeanor, which somehow gave them an even more uniform appearance.

A lot of Leos cheered. Brown, red, orange; the crowd was a mixture of all sorts of fur types as well, a diverse group of lions. Even some half bloods were mixed throughout.

"And on the right side we have Crimson and his band of rebels. These interlopers caused quite a ruckus with the insurrection that happened yesterday, and today they face judgment!" The ragtag group of rebels had makeshift leather armor that wasn't very well put together, and were as varied in color and size as the crowd. Their entrance wasn't as grand, and some of their number seemed hesitant.

The announcer looked up at the king, who gestured for him to get on with it.

"For the kingdom!" The announcer Leo immediately made his way out of the center of the stadium.

There were fifteen total rebels in the arena, and nine members of the royal pride. However, despite having a greater amount of Leos on their side, the rebels were no match for royalty.

The pride moved together as a team, coordinated, synchronized, and swift as they approached the rebels and surrounded them and attacked at once. The fact that the pride was much stronger than the rebels made it easy for them to kill two Leos who were defending themselves. The rebels formed a tight circle among themselves and tried to fight back. One rebel even landed a significant strike on a royal.

It was at that time that Crimson must have felt bold because he then pushed his luck, stepped out of the rebel circle, looked up at the king, and said, "Your royals are stronger than us as a group, but I still don't think they have what it takes to defeat us all. Why don't you come down here and face me, you coward!" Spitting on the ground at the end of his statement enhanced the disrespect.

The king writhed in his seat, the words seemed to physically injure him. He leaped down from his throne at once, his crown nearly falling from his head. His royal pride must have figured he was going to do that, because they had already scattered by the time he was in the arena.

The king walked toward the disrespectful commoner slowly, and on his way, some of the other commoners rushed him. He didn't even fight back. One, two, three, four, five, six, seven lions total had pounced on the king, and they began to attack with all they had. Clawing and scratching and biting ferociously. Their attack was relentless, and it looked like it was having an effect, as the king's body swayed, and his head moved back and forth.

"Hahahahaha!" The king's laugh grew in loudness and intensity. Until his laugh sounded completely insane. "Weaklings!" he exclaimed. And his body rapidly grew tenfold, and he roared, exhaled fire as they began falling off him. It seemed as if his fire breath wasn't aimed at anyone in general, almost as if it were for show, because none of the rebels were hit directly by it, but they were visibly terrified from seeing it.

All except for one. Crimson still had the same facial expression as when he audaciously called him out. The king noticed that and made his way toward Crimson. Now the king was intrigued, he wasn't going to kill him right away, he needed to at least ask him a question first. He shrunk back in size to talk to the bold rebel.

"Why do you hate me so much? How is it that you could have possibly thought that you, someone nowhere near my strength or caliber, could have taken me on?" the king queried once he was in closer proximity to Crimson.

"I know you're strong," the dark-red furred rebel said. "I know that you're much stronger than me, but I wanted to see it with my own two eyes. I thought, why would someone as evil as you be gifted enough to be the strongest? Also, I wasn't sure if your strength was just a rumor. Before today I had never seen you fight, only your pride, so I just had to see it. As far as why I hate you, well, that really comes down to the very place we are standing in right now." Crimson looked around the stadium and pointed to the ground. "This arena. The arena in which you make weaker Leos face off to the death for your own enjoyment."

"Those I have made fight in this arena were not without sin. I only chose criminals to fight," Leo defended himself.

"Really, those who stole food for their families, for example, right? Is that really the sort of crime that deserves a death sentence? You know what, I've had enough of talking to you. Someone such as you would never understand. That is why you must die."

Crimson swung his arm with all the might and force that he could muster, but the king just caught it, snapped it where it connected to the shoulder, breaking it as hard as he could, and then ripped the arm off. Crimson screamed in pain, but not for long, because in a millisecond the king lopped his head off his shoulders, and held it in his hand. He began displaying the head before the audience.

Crimson's expression was frozen on his face. It was a face of agony, of pain, his dark-red fur sagging on all sides.

"Do you all see this? This is what happens when you go against your king." Leo walked around the arena. Displaying the head. Holding it high. He wanted them all to see it. "This is what happens when little lions forget their place and try to contend with the alpha male! Let that be a lesson to all of you."

Once the head no longer served a purpose, he tossed it at the frightened rebel lions. Leaped back to his throne and called his pride to him, the few who hadn't fought.

"Let all the living rebels go free with no further punishment, but follow them. This is the third uprising since the spring solstice. I want you all to look into this. This may be deeper than the headless one would have me think." His men quickly disbursed with no words, only a nod.

"My strong lion," his wife purred as she rubbed his face and brought it toward her for a kiss. She flirted a little. "I love when you make everyone get in line and show them all your strength. I wish you would have killed them with your flames."

He laughed, staring out at the lion's den audience. "Next time, my queen, their flesh will burn.

Chapter 3

Croix was brought into a special area in the kingdom that he had never been to, but then again, he had never been in the chambers of a royal female. The room he was taken to was beautiful; it had a heart-shaped door and a heart-shaped bed, and the bed had a blood-red blanket that was draped on the burgundy-red bed in such a way that it appeared as though the heart bed was bleeding. The parts of the room that weren't red were pink or white; she had various flowers all over her room, and ornaments that covered her walls, and a painting of herself on the wall farthest from the bed.

"Have a seat," the young woman offered him. "Would you like something to drink?"

"Ambrosia, if you have any." He sat and tried to get comfortable.

She went into her kitchen area and brought back glasses full of very fine ambrosia for him and her. The liquid was clear with no real color, with a little white foam toward the bottom of the beverage and mist emanating from the cup that held it. Croix had never smelled anything as lovely as this beverage.

She sat down next to him, and he quickly realized that she smelled even better. She smelled even more divine than the beverage they were to consume. He was unsure of what to say, but figured he had to say something, since so far she had done all the talking.

"Is this the first mating ritual you are going to partake in?" Croix asked seriously, not looking at her.

She laughed. "I should hope so. Would you want a woman who has been touched by another man? If I'm not mistaken, isn't it forbidden for a woman to take place in more than one mating ritual with more than one lover?" She asked the question rhetorically and began softly kicking her legs up off the edge of the bed, and she stared at them. "I don't know if I'm even going to partake in this one right now." She steadied her legs, but kept staring at them. "I know there are a lot of women running off to find a mate to have offspring with, but that shouldn't mean that I have to rush off and mate myself. My father had a long talk with me about legacy earlier, but I'm not sure if any of that matters to me, not right now anyway. I really would rather get to know someone first, and get to choose if I want to be with them, and after that, give my body to them." She gazed at Croix. "I have heard a lot about you. Your name is Croix, correct? I would like for you to tell me about yourself in your own words."

"If you heard a lot about me, then I don't understand why that's necessary."

"Well, maybe some of it's rumors or lies. Maybe I only heard bad, and you should want to clear it up. For example, is it true that you have extra toes to make you faster?"

"Don't be silly. I have the same number of toes as anyone else."

"See, I already learned something. I heard that all Aries men closely related to the king had extra toes, and that's what made you all so fast."

"Did you really hear that from someone?"

"Maybe I did, maybe I didn't, either way, that's not really the point."

Croix was finding this woman vexatious. He wasn't sure how this process was supposed to work, but he was pretty sure this wasn't how mating rituals usually went. He felt it would be crude to force himself on her, but he did want to try intercourse. He heard it was enjoyable whether or not the woman became impregnated.

She was the image of beauty. Her raspberry-red skin shined brilliantly and looked amazing against her yellow topaz-lined dress that exuded a princess-like elegance. Given how beautiful she was, he figured maybe he should just keep quiet and see how things played out with her. *Maybe this is what all males have to deal with* he figured. No, he couldn't just let things meander, so he got it in his mind that he should say something in order to guide their discussion to something more meaningful.

He placed the empty cup down on a red end table not far from her bed. "I don't mean to be rude, but do you intend to mate or not? Today is the day I am to officially become a member of the brotherhood. I cannot without your help. If you didn't intend to mate with me, then why did you bring me back to your quarters? Couldn't you have let the other woman from earlier take me back to her quarters instead?"

"Can't we just lay here, and you tell them all we did it, and not do it?" She laid on her back on the bed dramatically, her head nearly spilling off the edge. "I mean, after all, if the only point is for you to get initiated into the royal brotherhood, then you and I can just say that we mated when we didn't." She brought her head back up, and her green eyes met his. "Wouldn't that be interesting? Aren't you the least bit curious to see if we can get away with that?"

"A lie. I'm not sure if it would work. I'm not good at lying. Also, don't they have ways to detect whether I'm a virgin or not? There may be a punishment for me if they find out I'm lying."

"Don't worry, I would take full responsibility." Her voice became lighter and sweeter, almost a purr, and she sat up again. "After all, isn't it the woman's duty to bed the male in this tradition on your special night? As far as lying goes, you can learn how to lie, I can teach you. Look me in my eyes."

Croix stared deeply into her intense, grass-green eyes.

She drew him in deeper, staring intently with a passionate look and told him, "I love you."

He didn't know what to say. He didn't know what to do. This seemed like a lot all of a sudden. Then, to make matters worse, it didn't seem as though she was finished. He tried to pull his head away from hers, the stare she had was so intense, and it had multiple connotations attached to it. She pulled his head back and stared at him again with the same stare.

She asked him, "Don't you love me, too?"

Before he could answer, she burst into laughter. She laughed so hard that eventually she began rolling on the bed.

Croix didn't know how to react. And here he thought this was going to be easy. He should have known this woman was trouble when she first grabbed his hand. *But that doesn't make any sense, he thought right back to himself. How could that have been any indication?* That seemed like a standard way for a woman to accept her place in a mating ritual.

He didn't know what to do. He was sure that the other woman by the fire was no longer there, but he still thought maybe he should go back.

"What are you going to do, Croix?" she taunted him. Sitting back up straight, no longer laughing, she challenged him.

He wasn't sure how she could think it was OK for her not to take part in the mating ritual. Fact was, she had a better chance of being punished than he for not fulfilling her duty, but she still seemed dead set on not doing it. *She's insane. This woman*—he just realized he didn't know her name—*is insane.*

"What is your name? I just realized I never caught your name." Croix felt he needed to ask at this point.

"My name is Ava." She offered a light smile upon saying her name, and her hand briefly, but he seemed to ignore it. She wasn't fazed, though, and she just resumed her original position. "You see, you didn't even know my name, and you thought I was going to mate with you." She waved her finger in his face a little, as if to say tsk-tsk.

He registered that her name was Ava, but he didn't see a need to respond to her right away. At that point, it was more important for him to think of his next move. He could tell everyone the truth about what happened, and that she wouldn't do the mating ritual with him.

She seemed to be an experienced liar though, so much so that maybe she could tell a lie better than he could tell the truth. It would be her word against his. As ridiculous as the thought was, he thought that maybe she would be more believable telling her lie than he would be telling the truth. To add to his problems, he didn't know who to tell or complain to, exactly.

He wasn't sure but as far as he could tell, Aries women weren't especially known for telling lies, so odds were low that they would believe him. He had never heard of a royal woman refusing the mating ritual, which probably meant that nobody had ever been in the position he was in right then.

Croix sat there speechless, immobilized by shock. Ava finally spoke up again, as if she felt that he'd run over all the options in his head and needed her help making a decision.

"Here's what you should do." She sat down with her back perfectly straight, crossed her legs, and made eye contact. "Go back and tell them all that we mated as intended. I'll corroborate your story. I'll even say that you're the best." She did a long blink as she said it. "Whatever you want me to say, I'll say it. You can get into the brotherhood as you planned, and we don't have to mate when we don't love or even know each other." She squeezed his arm gently as she continued. "At the end of this mating season, I'll actually give you all of me; mind, body, and soul." She leaned into him more. "If you can impress me five times"—she paused—"shock me five times, and thusly make me fall in love with you. By this time tomorrow, you'll be a part of the brotherhood so you should have much more means at your disposal, so all you have to do is be creative. I'm sure you can do it, Croix." She rubbed his back. "I'll be your wife, and a good one at that, if you meet my conditions." She let go of him completely, backed away a little, and began standing over him. "If you tell my father or anyone else in the kingdom I did not do my duty, I will lie, and I'm quite sure I can tell a better fictional story than you can tell a truthful one."

His suspicions were right, but that was nonsense. It had to be nonsense, his uncle was the king of the planet. Of course he had more credibility than her. Also, what did being the best mean? In truth, he had not known that mating was a competition.

As if she could read his mind, she leaned a little toward him, put a hand over her mouth as if telling a secret, and whispered, "If you're not the prince or the actual king himself, it is said that all royalty is equal." She stood up straight again. "In other words, you and I are indistinguishable. Of course, except for the fact that I'm a woman, but we are equivalent in terms of credibility."

He wasn't really sure how she could read his mind. Maybe that was one of her abilities, but he couldn't be sure. He had never heard of Aries women having the ability to read minds. Maybe he should be happy with just being able to say that he had intercourse with her, and go along with the story. Even though it would be through lying, he would at least become a man of the brotherhood by tomorrow. No, that shouldn't be where it ended. He needed to do this for himself, to actually experience it. Croix wanted to make all his new compatriots in the brotherhood proud. Not have a lie as his crowning achievement.

He lifted his head toward her and said, "What will it take to impress and shock you?"

She laughed, clearly pleased, clapped her hands together, and said, "That's the tricky part. I'm not going to tell you. At all. Not even a clue. You'll have to figure it out on your own. Call it getting to know me better."

Croix loved challenges as much as the next man, ever since he was a child he did, but he felt a little uneasy about this one, mainly because he wasn't even sure what he was supposed to do, but he felt like the prize might just be worth it, so he reluctantly agreed to her terms. With that, she began preparing for sleep. It was almost like he wasn't even there anymore.

She only looked in his direction for a moment to say, "You should sleep in the other bed in the room right next door. That room is also mine, and it is much more comfy. It should also help you to control any urges you may have."

He wasn't sure if she was trying to humiliate him on purpose, or if this whole thing was just a test or some sort of sick joke. All he knew was that for now, at least, he would play along. He laid himself down in the black satin bed of her other room, a little bit upset, but mostly confused. This was not at all how he expected his night to end. *Oh well, at least the bed is comfy*, he reconciled with himself as he began to doze off.

***

Planet Aquarius, aside from Libra and Pisces, was the most livable environment of all the planets. In a way, it was more inviting than the other two due to the vast array of Aquarian technology that facilitated and enhanced life.

It was somewhat odd, Leon considered, to have a city entirely surrounded by water. He wasn't entirely sure, as he usually was with most of his analyses of situations, but he felt as though it would one day be thought of as a mistake to have enclosed one of the largest kingdoms of all the twelve in a glass bubble of sorts underwater.

Of course, it wasn't simply glass that covered the kingdom. It was a much tougher polymer. Aquarian technology was fascinating. Leon mentally reviewed all the possible reasons King Aquarius could have had for designing his kingdom this way, but that didn't last long for he was distracted on the way to his destination as he got a brief look at an area submerged in water. This area was underwater but was still sectioned off from the great seas of Aquarius.

The two half bloods, Arkin and Leon both looked the room over and pondered what purpose it could serve. *The Aquarians were a strange people, but maybe they love the water so much that being surrounded by it is not enough. Apparently, they need to also have an outlet to actually fully submerge themselves in the water without actually being in the water that was outside of the kingdom.*

Ridiculous, Leon laughed to himself quietly. He hadn't appreciated much about any kingdom so far, and thought that he could run any one of them better, and in a way that was fairer to all people rather than just celebrating royalty. The unguided tour of Aquarius was over as they abruptly stopped in front of a huge amber-colored hall area that sectioned off into rooms with various styles and types of living quarters. Finally, the royal that led Leon, Arkin, and their group spoke.

The Aries man wore simple leather garments and an iron helmet that fit snugly on his head and didn't obstruct his horns.

"This is where you all will be staying. King Aquarius has prepared multiple styles of living quarters to accommodate the lifestyles of the various half bloods who will be living here," the Aries royal stated emotionlessly, as if reading a script. "A member of the Aquarius royals will be meeting with you all shortly to tell you more about your new life here. This is a temporary thing. Negotiations have been done so that you all can live here peacefully, rather than on our own planet Aries. If things go wrong, negotiations will likely be reopened for you all to go back. If things go well or you like it here, it may become more permanent. Wait here until you are given further instructions by the Aquarian representative."

The Aries royal who never named himself disappeared in a flash back to Aries. Perhaps the idea of being surrounded by water didn't appeal to him.

"I'm not sure, but I think it's a little irresponsible for him to leave us here alone." Leon looked around as he said it. While he didn't like taking orders necessarily, he did like order, and felt that the royal leaving them unattended like that wasn't an act of order.

Leon had been able to stay on planet Aries ever since the final Battle of Orion at Bellatrix. He lied to the great council, or rather their henchmen, when all the dyads were being deported after the battle, telling them that he was of planet Aries. He wasn't really sure how the lie worked so well, but it could have been because most people had limited knowledge of dyads, and to some degree, they could turn out different than others of the same mix. Or it could have been the red-orange tint of his fur.

He knew it was necessary for him to have the proper time and space to plan and strategize, and he had been able to do that on planet Aries with his friend Arkin, who was still with him, and now they would be in an even better position to make moves on planet Aquarius.

It wasn't long before six additional distinct groups of dyad peoples from other planets arrived in the great hall. He wasn't really sure if all the twelve races would show up in strong numbers, because some of mixed bloods were still thought to be great negotiators between two planets and were used as liaisons. The Tauruan dyads showed up in all their bulk and horns, then the green Cancer dyads.

Next to show up were the Sagittarian dyads, then the Gemini dyads and their royal escorts, followed by the Virgo dyads and their escort, and lastly the Scorpio dyads.

Leon had the feeling that some of the other groups were late for a reason, rather than simply not being punctual. With perfect timing Linden, King Aquarius's most trusted advisor and right-hand man, arrived.

"Royals of the kingdoms and planets." Linden bowed ever so slightly. "You may take your leave if you're ready." He straightened all the way up and stood with his arms behind his back. "I will see to it at once that your people are welcomed graciously to our kingdom from here on, and I apologize for not meeting you all as soon as you arrived. It seems that my master has been having some trouble figuring out the arrival of some of the other groups. I assure you all that there is no need for you to worry about such matters."

Nobody moved, so Linden cleared his throat and spoke further. He moved his hands together in front of him again.

"Gentlemen, I will see to my new guests, as I said before. You are free to go, or you can partake in the feast that is taking place in the common area. I suggest you all eat, try some of our delicacies, before you leave. Today is a day for great celebration, as we move forward, hopefully improving relations between all the peoples of all the planets. I will communicate to my master the success we have had so far in bringing these peoples here peacefully."

Some royals of the multiple races took their leave, some went to the common area. None of them replied back to Linden directly in any way.

Linden turned to the large group that was before him and addressed them. "I will give you all a brief tour of the living quarters where you will sleep, and the common area where you will eat. There also are a few areas for you all to take part in recreational activities. Nothing too extravagant, but all the preparations were made to simulate your home planets as closely as possible. Please let me know if you have any questions. Although, because you are a large group, please raise your hand.

Despite the enormity of the group and the possibility of personality clashes, given that they were all of different peoples, and even more complex than the average because they were of two races, Linden did not seem the least bit worried by the huge group of dyads from various planets. They all seemed calm. Maybe it was the shock of it all or wonder, or adjustment, and they were all taking it in.

"Let's begin the tour." He nodded his head to the group.

Many of them were wondering if this new living situation would in fact improve their lives. It didn't take long before they arrived at the first destination.

"This is the common area. Free food is served here every single day. On special occasions, such as today, there are great feasts, with food prepared by professionals to meet a higher standard than usual. However, the food is very good even on regular days. I eat here myself sometimes."

The common area was massive, it appeared as though it could seat thousands. Oddly enough, it did not appear as big from the outside. Even as he spoke, at least two hundred people were eating in the dining area, most of whom were Aquarians.

Aquarian designs were very efficient. Not only that, but the common area was much cleaner than the mess halls or other areas that the dyads were used to on their respective planets. The rooftop was so high that a fifty-foot creature could fit comfortably in the room and not disturb anyone, the ceiling was concave with the same glass that the Aquarians had spread throughout their entire kingdom. Even the tables and chairs were colorful, made from an upbeat green metal.

"Moving right along, here we have one of the recreation areas. This is the nearest to the dyad living quarters. Inside, there is the game One King Left, which you all should enjoy because you are from different kingdoms, and would likely play different and use diverse strategies and way of thinking. Of course, there are other games present as well here, but they are games that Aquarians play. I'm unsure if you all would be familiar with them." The recreation area was massive, not as large as the common area, of course, but large enough to fit more than a couple hundred easily, and seemed to have duplicates of all the games and plenty of tables, so multiple groups could play at once.

Leon and Arkin were both familiar with One King Left. It was one of their favorite games. It actually helped them develop strategies they hoped would defeat the kings in real life. Of course they could never fully utilize the strategies, but the game's plans would often lead them to thinking of some sort of approach they could use in a practical way.

In the game, players each assumed the role of the king of any one of the twelve kingdoms, from Aries, all the way to Pisces, except for Cancer. Your player would have all the powers of the kings, theoretically, but it wouldn't matter, since you would be facing off against other kings who also had powers. Your powers were mostly effective in fighting off other minor royals from rival kingdoms.

The real objective of the game was to destroy the other player's kingdoms from the inside, through sabotage and other sorts of trickery. Players were also able to form alliances between amiable kingdoms and ones they generally traded with.

Of course, in any game of duplicity Cancer would have the advantage, due to his power to turn invisible, so to get rid of his inherit upper-hand, players were only able to hire Cancers for services. As an additional caveat, players were only able to hire Cancers for their services if and only if they were already in the lead. The game was all the rage because everybody in the kingdoms wanted to be king.

"Keep in mind that restrooms are abundantly located here, so there should be one in every hallway you pass through. Here we have an institution of higher learning." The building was a thin triangular shape that seemed to get thinner toward the top. It was hard to tell, though, because the structure was over fifty feet high and in a narrow corridor. "I don't feel that now is the time to show you that, however, so now I will be showing you to your living quarters. Rather I and some of the other Aquarian royals will show you to your living quarters."

Other Aquarians of both sexes appeared in fine light-green royal garb on queue and began leading some groups to their dorms.

The Aries dyads were with Linden still.

"Right this way," he continued.

Finally the tour was over, *what a relief*, Leon and Arkin thought. The living quarters were nicer than their homes on Aries. A modern Aquarian lighting system was available in all the rooms. Also in the room were posters of their home planet, which was a nice gesture, but not very helpful. The red fire rock that was Aries was missed maybe, but not that much. Each room had a pet, the one from Aries was a fire dragon. Fire dragons were little lizards with red-and-black skin, similar in appearance to magma; they were born near volcanoes. The walls of their rooms were painted in a similar black and red manner.

Also there was a small aquarium, a personal bathroom, and holographic display for memories, and any other assortment of entertainment that was in holographic display format. King Aquarius had pulled out all the stops. It made Leon and Arkin both wonder how it was possible for Aquarius to afford to put them up in such luxury.

The next thought that ran through their heads was whether all the other dyads from the other planets had equal accommodations. There would always be a time in the future for them to look into that. Linden let them all choose their rooms they chose their rooms almost at random since all the rooms were exactly the same. After they chose their rooms Leon and Arkin simply parted ways with each other, both too exhausted to plot anything.

***

"I'm sure my son and the princess of that rock planet must be hitting it off. Hopefully, I have nothing to worry about now. That boy sure is hardheaded, though." Aries scratched his chin hair.

"Still talking to yourself, huh, Aries?" The blue man's voice was behind him.

"Cancer, where did you come from?"

"It really doesn't matter now, does it? What does matter is that your dear son, Mar, doesn't seem to be keeping things on the up and up with you or the Capricorns."

"I really don't know what you mean." Aries stood from his throne and stared the man right in his red eyes.

"That's why I'm here. I know something you don't." Cancer grinned.

"So just spit it out already. Or are you not planning on sharing this secret with me?"

"That depends, how much does it mean to you?"

"I'm not sure. I would have to know how devastating the secret is before I could appraise its value."

"It's no big deal," Cancer said playfully, looking away and playing with a tiny Aries figure on a board in the room. "It's only a secret big enough to ruin the unification of your dear prince and the Capricorn girl." Cancer returned Aries's stare, but his had more intensity and he watched for a reaction.

Aries sighed deeply, shoulders slumped. "What will it cost me? Furthermore"—his tone picked up—"I want your word that whatever it is, you keep it from the Capricorns at all costs."

"Negotiations have just opened up, there's no way I'll agree to something like that so soon." He looked away quickly. "I am open for bargaining, though." He walked around Aries's throne room for a bit, looking at the board that held small figures in the likeness of the all the twelve races and was useful for battle simulations. While standing over the board, he looked up for eye contact again. "All I want is for you to let me borrow a few of your brotherhood men. I hear the Aries royals are the fastest in all the galaxy."

"What possible use could you have for my men when yours can be any and everywhere without anyone so much as noticing their presence?" Aries tried to look through Cancer to the deeper meaning of his request.

"What I want is my business and none of yours. Either you agree to the terms or you don't. I'll sweeten the deal, because I'm feeling generous. I'll give you my word that this secret that I'm about to share, as soon as we come to an agreement, will never be uttered from my lips or the lips of any of my subordinates to the Capricorns or the Taurus."

"This even involves the Taurus. Wow, it sounds far worse than I suspected." Aries's eyes widened in worry.

"I say three of your fastest scouts from the brotherhood should suffice for an equal exchange. I need them to follow my direct orders to the T until I am done with them." Cancer struck deftly, seeing the flash of fear in Aries's face.

Aries regained a bit of his composure, and took his time answering. He almost had half a mind to ask Cancer for some sort of proof. But there was no need. Cancer's reputation was flawless. Any knowledge that Cancer dealt around the kingdoms was considered fact among kings. Cancer was an information dealer. Aries trusted Cancer's word himself. Usually Cancer's information would confirm something you had already suspected. "I can't say I like the sound of this, but I really want to keep relations good with the Taurus, and I would like to improve things with the Capricorns if possible. Mar seems to have been keeping a few things secret from me as of late, so I don't think he would tell me, otherwise he would have already done so. Very well, I will tell three of my royal men to take direct orders from you until further notice. If I suspect any foul play or that you're playing me for a fool, I will relinquish your command over them at once."

"You have my word that you won't hear of any foul play," Cancer said with a slight smirk. He quickly shifted to serious business. "This should not come as a great surprise to you, but your son, Mar, is quite familiar with Princess Diantha of the house of Taurus, in an intimate way. My men reported that the couple seemed to have done the deed before. Maybe even that they had been meeting up in that way for a while." He shrugged. "Or so it seemed. I suppose things like that are hard to confirm exactly, since you can't ask your son about it, and Diantha would rather not divulge the truth, I'm sure. I'm actually even doing Taurus a favor by keeping this secret, as his daughter is engaged to be wed to the Sagittarian prince, Ranger."

"I had my suspicions, and I'm somewhat relieved to finally know the truth. Thank you for coming to me first with this information. I don't know how it would have gone over with Capricorn, but I imagine that it wouldn't have been good. I appreciate the early notice."

"Discretion has its merits, I suppose." Cancer cleaned his thumbnail with his index finger before finally looking up again. "Remember our deal and have your men report to my castle as soon as they can. I expect I will see them within the next few days, or the deal is off, and so is my oath of the secrecy."

"I understand, I will send them over as soon as possible."

As soon as Aries finished his last sentence, Cancer was gone. Cancer wasn't technically the strongest of all the kings, but sometimes Aries and the others felt like he was, or at least that he had the most advantages. Not only was he able to turn invisible like his men, but he could teleport, which Aries had seen with his own two eyes, and rumor had it that he could project force fields around his body and travel through other dimensions.

The truth was, even though they fought together, the need never really arose for them all to unleash their full power, not even at the final Battle of Orion at Bellatrix. Not to mention, Aries didn't get to spend an equal amount of time with all the other kings. The only time everyone met up was for council decisions or other important matters.

Aries let those thoughts go quickly. Cancer's powers didn't matter. What mattered was Cancer's plans for the Aries royals.

"I shouldn't have been so quick to agree to such terms," Aries said to himself. Although Mar had hidden many things from him, he began thinking that he still should have confronted him properly before he made the decision to give three of his men to Cancer to command. He never did trust Cancer, who he always felt was too quick to blow up and was always plotting something nefarious.

Whatever Cancer's plans were, it was too late at that point. Aries had so very imprudently signed up three of his men to aid him. Now the problem was who to send. He knew none of his men would want to go.

The most important thing was to send someone he could trust to deliver information back as to what being under Cancer's command entailed. He would have to pick the most obedient and loyal men that he had. Choosing anybody else could otherwise lead to trouble. He called for his men, using the great horn. A legendary item on Aries, it was said to be the left horn of a great Aries man, the first Aries man ever, his ancestor, who was said to have discovered all the other planets and met with all the kings of old, the ancestors of the other kings, and have slain a number of legendary creatures.

"Master," he heard at that instant, as one of his most loyal, Magnus, kneeled before him. Titus and Bartholomew kneeled as well.

Magnus, Titus, and Bartholomew, as the fastest scouts of Aries, had to stand out, so the three wore black-and-blue garb that was lighter on the blue, sleeveless, and a red belt to divide the pants from their shirts, which were tucked in. The three had an even bell-pepper-yellow skin tone, horns that curved out to the sides, rectangular faces, and brown eyes, and were identical in every aspect save for their facial hair. Magnus sported a simple gentleman's finely groomed mustache, Titus had a nice goatee, and Bartholomew had a full beard, but it was neatly trimmed.

"Magnus, I need you, Titus, and Bartholomew to report directly to King Cancer at once. From now on you will be taking his orders directly until further notice." Aries stared down at his men.

"I don't understand. What are you saying?" Magnus stood up.

Aries sat down in his diamond throne. "I'm saying exactly what I just said. I want you to keep me posted on everything he's having you do when you're under his employ. Update me daily. If you shoot a star beacon, I'll see it and open a line on the communicators between that planet and ours, and you all can brief me. I'm sure you probably already figured this out, but I can't have Cancer know. I want him to think I know nothing, so be sure to only send the star beacon when you're absolutely sure that you can speak without being noticed. You all don't have to report there right away, but be there within at least two days from now. Otherwise, it will be a waste for you to go." Aries was quite sure that Cancer wouldn't keep the secret to himself for free for any longer than that.

"I have sworn my allegiance to you, my king, but I don't know if I can do this. I despise the Cancers." Magnus's disgust was written on his face. Bartholomew and Titus looked somehow unmoved, and they finally stood up straight as well.

"I'm not too fond of them either," Aries said, "but you really shouldn't talk so badly about them. They could be watching us at this very moment, even as we speak. Things will be fine. Just watch yourselves. If he asks for you to do anything that would violate any of the peace terms we have with other nation-planets, don't obey it. I will see you gentlemen later. I'm going to my chambers. Do not disturb me. Go to Cancer as soon as you can and report to me that very first night when it is safe for you to do so."

He walked away slowly, mentally and emotionally exhausted with what had just transpired. He had a bad feeling about everything that was happening, but he wasn't really sure of a better way to handle it.

Chapter 4

"**P**isces, you need to explain what you are trying to say to me because I don't understand it at all. I'm mostly confused because you didn't bring any of this up when we had our council meeting a few days ago?" Aquarius said, clearly frustrated, given the look on his face visible through the aqua communicator.

"Aquarius, please calm down. I have told you and everybody else that my abilities don't always work the way I want them to, sometimes my visions come to me only after a decision has been made. It may be problematic to have all the dyads living on one planet, in one area. I had a bad vision in which all of them lived on the same planet together."

"If you didn't agree to this, or think it was a good idea, you should have made your point earlier, during the last council meeting. By now it's already done. I really don't understand what your visions are telling you or not telling you, because you're never specific, but what I do know is that at this point, whatever will happen, will happen. I ask that you either quit hiding your visions from me and tell me everything in great detail so that you may convince me that it's a bad idea, or that you let your dyads go and have the others send all theirs as well, aside from those that may stay behind to be liaisons between two peoples or work directly under royalty."

"OK, Aquarius, you win. I will talk to the others and have them send theirs and send my own. Which groups are missing?" Pisces pulled out fancy parchment and a writing utensil.

"Libra, Capricorn, yours, of course, and Leo are all missing."

Pisces was writing until Leo was mentioned, and then he looked back up at Aquarius.

"I have not spoken with Leo at all, so more than likely he has his own reasons for not sending them. You should contact him yourself personally. As far as the other groups, I will speak with them as soon as I can."

"I appreciate it, thank you for cooperating with me," Aquarius said, and then he disengaged contact with Pisces.

Aquarius wasn't the type to worry. He was an optimist overall, but his conversation with Pisces left him a little unnerved. For a few moments, he went over the conversation again in his mind to try to find the source of his unease.

All of a sudden it came to him. *The visions. Pisces never shares details of his visions with anybody. It could be that he doesn't have specific visions, maybe he just uses intuition or gut instinct. That would explain why he doesn't know everything before it happens. Then again, he carefully and precisely predicted the births of princes and princesses of the current generation, even letting each of the kings now exactly how, when, and where their children would be born and the gender.*

Aquarius feared that rather than Pisces lacking precision in his art of premonition, that the case was instead that Pisces merely did not like to disclose his visions with the others. The more Aquarius thought about it, the stranger it was that no one, questioned Pisces.

He continued to mull over the situation and remembered that Pisces could and often did divulge a lot when he wanted to, especially when it was something important, during conflicts his future-telling abilities had aided everyone in combat. There must have been a specific reason why Pisces did not go into details with Aquarius.

He wondered what Pisces was hiding. What incentive did he have for being so cryptic? What could Pisces have told the other kings? Maybe Pisces told each king different things than what he told the next. A scary thought. What could King Pisces possibly be hiding? Aquarius was not sure, but he figured that he could not trust him fully.

After all the contemplation, he nearly forgot to contact King Leo. Using the aqua communicator, he tried to reach out to Leo. There was no response, until finally a much smaller lion bearing a strong resemblance to the king answered him.

"Yes, Aquarius, my father is fully aware that you have not received our planets half bloods yet," said Aleser, the smallest and youngest of all of King Leo's heirs. "Right now, my father and the pride are preoccupied trying to quell a rebellion." Aleser's brow furrowed. The little one seemed worried.

"Don't worry, if anybody is strong, it's your father. He'll be fine. Ask him to send them when he gets a chance. You look more and more like him each day. I'm sure you'll be king one day, and then it will be your time to worry about matters such as these. For now, though, you should relax, you're safe. Make sure you tell your father I called as soon as you see him."

There was a lot going on, Aquarius was still thinking about all the events that were taking place after speaking with the Leo prince and trying to see if he could piece together something significant that connected them all, but he couldn't. Everything seemed to be chaotic and unrelated. If there was a connection between the events happening, he could not deduce it. Time would tell. Aquarius came to the realization that whether or not something was going on, he wasn't going to be able to figure it out at the moment, so he moved on.

***

Arkin and Leon were sitting at a green metal table in the common area, enjoying their food and getting ready to plot their next move.

"How are things going on planet Leo?"

"Things are going swimmingly. My contact just told me those royal fools and silly lion king have no idea what is going on." Leon smiled, thoroughly pleased. "Although"—his expression changed to a frown and he stared at his food tray—"Crimson and a few of the others were killed."

"That's the price of war. They were all good soldiers and will be honored. When should we stir things up on Aries?"

"I'm not sure we should." Leon looked up from his tray of green-colored food. "Especially not at this time. I'm curious to see how this all turns out. We should keep things manageable. If we have too many things going on at once, it may be hard to keep up with everything. Besides, there is a reason that I chose planet Leo. I—"

Before Leon could continue, a large Aries-Taurus male slammed his food tray down as hard as he could on their table. The Aries-Taurus was a bull-horned, brown-red-skinned man, with black chest hair that covered his entire torso like a sweater. He had a bald head, no shirt, huge arms, and black, slightly tattered pants with no shoes to speak of, only hooves. He hovered over Leon in an aggressive manner and breathed very hard out of his mouth and nose. Aries-Taurus were known to have very dense skin, that some said was impenetrable, and horns that could conceivably penetrate through anything. The horns of an Aries-Taurus were harder than the average Aries or Taurus horns put together.

Once he had their attention the bull man spoke. "I always see you two together, plotting. I don't like it. I have it on good authority that it is your fault that we are all here now. I don't like change, and I miss my planet. If I have you two weaklings to blame, why should I not kill you both right now? Talk me out of it," he said through bared teeth. "Otherwise, I will drive my horn so far down both of your skulls that your entire family will have brain damage." Around that time, everybody who sat at that table with Leon and Arkin walked away.

Leon immediately attempted to reason with the angry man. "I assure you we had nothing to do with all of us getting transferred here. Whoever told you that we did must have been mistaken."

"There's no mistake. After hearing you talk, I think I remember you guys. You guys were somehow involved in the rebellion at the Battle of Orion on planet Bellatrix."

Arkin looked up at him and finally spoke up. "Yes, that was us, we seek to free all half bloods from the tyranny and oppression of the twelve kingdoms."

"It's because of you bastards that many of my brethren were slain by the kings during that very battle," the bull man said, spitting mad.

"No need to be angry. We lost a lot of good friends during that battle as well," Leon said.

"Well, don't worry because you're about to join them," the Aries-Taurus man said before he flung the table to the side as hard as he could.

Leon ran away from the Aries-Taurus man, knowing that neither he nor Arkin would be powerful enough to stop him physically. But it didn't seem to matter because he had Arkin as his target, most likely because of his previous statement.

Arkin didn't back down. "If it's a fight you're after, you got it, but you might not be as happy with the results as you think."

Arkin dashed directly in front of his opponent, appearing as if he were going to give the man a clear shot at him, but he disappeared in an instant, using his superior Aries speed to give a quick thrust to the bull's ribs. Luckily for Arkin, those of the Aries-Taurus mix do not possess the Aries speed, rather they only inherit immunity to fire from their Aries side. Arkin didn't know all these things, but he did assume that he would be faster than the other man.

He dashed back at the bull again, striking him in his face, then another time striking him in his side. Arkin's attacks, as fast as they were, didn't appear to be having any effect on the hulking Aries-Taurus man.

Leon could see that Arkin's strikes weren't doing much damage, so he figured his only option was to get help from an enhancer. The Gemini-Cancer dyads were able to enhance or decrease the powers of others. If Leon could convince just one of them to help his friend, it could save his life. Arkin was using too much energy, so Leon knew he didn't have much time.

Unlike the full-blooded Aries, Aries royals, or the king of Aries, Arkin could only expend so much energy before he would grow weary. Knowing that his friend's stamina was wearing down, Leon desperately searched for a Gemini-Cancer.

He found a table full of the green-skinned, silver-haired, amber-red-eyed women and men who were quietly sitting down, still eating, trying their best to look as though they weren't watching the fight. It wasn't as though they didn't care. They just didn't want to get involved and weren't even sure who, if anybody, to help.

"I need your help," Leon pleaded to everyone at the table. Only one or two even looked up at him.

"Why should I help you?" a Gemini-Cancer woman said and looked Leon in his eyes.

"If you don't help, I'm afraid my friend will die."

Leon and the Gemini-Cancer both began paying more attention to the fight. Arkin was hitting the bull slower and slower, until finally the bull saw Arkin sprinting at him and clotheslined him and began laughing. "I knew you would run out of energy eventually."

He picked up Arkin by his throat and lifted him, then let him go and punched his face. Arkin slid across the floor.

"I know I told you I was going to pierce you with my horns," the bull man said as he walked past the spectators and tables toward the downed Arkin, "but I'm not really sure if you're worthy to be skewered. You're such a weakling, I may kill you with my hands."

"I promise you, Arkin and I never wanted any harm to befall any people born of two. I know you don't know me or him, but I would be indebted to you if you saved his life," Leon earnestly implored her with the most humble tone and facial expression he could imagine.

The Gemini-Cancer, finally won over by Leon's words, looked to all her comrades for them to help as well, but they never looked back at her or focused on Leon or the situation.

The bull picked up Arkin by his neck again. "You did attempt to fight me like a man, so I suppose you do deserve to die by my horns after all. You should be honored." He smirked. "Goodbye."

The Aries-Taurus tossed Arkin in the air, and prepared for the finishing blow by cocking his head to the side and crouching, then he jumped as high as he could and twisted his head back the opposite direction to destroy Arkin with his horns and everything he had, but his horns didn't even penetrate Arkin's flesh instead he merely knocked the wind from Arkin.

"What? Impossible! You should be dead!" he yelled at Arkin.

As soon as Arkin fell to the ground he found his balance as quickly as he could and figured he would capitalize on the bull man's consternation, so got up to give him his best last shot. He charged toward the bull man directly then used his super speed and charged toward his back, but changed courses again and hit the bull man directly in the chest headfirst as fast and as hard as he could.

The bull man was paralyzed in shock.

Wooo! Eh! Eh! Eh! The alarm sounded, and Aquarian royal guardians showed up in battle gear. The color of light blue water.

"This is the Aquarian royal guard." They took aim with long, see-through guns. "All dyads stand down at once. I repeat, all dyads stand down at once."

Arkin felt himself losing consciousness by the time the Aquarian royal guardians showed up, and before they converged on his location, he passed out.

When Arkin finally came to, the first thing he saw was Leon's fuzzy face standing over him.

"You're finally awake, you had us worried there." Leon's concern was not only on his face, but in his tone, and he patted Arkin's shoulder.

He scanned the sky blue room for a second, trying to make sense of everything. He looked up at the ceiling, which was translucent and had water on the other side, then he looked at the machine that was next to him, which had a display of his body and readouts of his condition. It didn't take long for Arkin to realize that he was in an Aquarian healing center; he continued to look around, and then he saw the same Aries-Taurus who had just tried to kill him.

"What is he doing here?" Arkin asked, and he pulled back a little as if to hide.

"Now calm down, Arkin," Leon said. "He was actually worried about you when he saw you pass out earlier. He said he was so impressed by the fact that you survived his ultimate piercing attack that he wanted to meet you."

"It was his fault that I passed out in the first place."

"My name is Pierce," the bull said.

"Pierce?" Arkin repeated.

"Yes, Pierce. My mom figured she had to give me a name like that so the Aries of our planet and the other breeds such as yourself wouldn't mess with me. They would all be afraid of being pierced by my horns. At least, that's what she used to tell me. Anyway, I'm sorry we got off on the wrong foot. I would like very much to be your friend, Arkin."

"How do you know my name?"

"Leon just said it out loud a few seconds ago." He shrugged.

"And who is she?" Arkin said as he looked at the woman that stood before him in the room with Leon and Pierce.

"My name is Gwendolyn, but you can call me Gwen."

"You're a Gemini-Cancer right?"

"Yes, but how did you know?"

"It was either that or Cancer-Leo, because of the red iris of your eyes, and as of now there are no Leo hybrids on this planet. In addition, I think your kind may be the only race of green people that I know. Not to mention the facts that you're here and that I'm alive most likely means that you used your powers to keep his horns from penetrating my flesh and gave me that last burst of energy I used before I passed out."

"That's why my horns did not tear through your flesh." Pierce felt the tip of one of his horns, he must have doubted the sharpness ever since the incident. "Ha, interesting, this is going to be fun, being friends with you all. I feel a lot better. I thought that maybe you were just stronger than me, Arkin."

Pierce walked closer and began patting Arkin hard on his back.

"By no means am I stronger than you. I think I may still have a set of broken ribs. Where is the healer at, anyway?"

"The Aquarian healer left a little while ago, said to let you sleep," Gwen answered. "He said you should be fully healed in a little while, but that your body healed so fast, that your brain may still send signals of residual pain. And as far as your energy, since we told him about the fight and how you were zipping around, he said that may take longer, and you can only recover your energy by resting and taking it easy, and over time it will slowly come back to you."

He laughed. "Are you trying to be funny? I didn't expect for him to help me get my energy back."

"I don't know," she said, looking around at the technology in the room and touching the holographic readout of Arkin's vitals. "Aquarius is said to be one of the most medically advanced of all the kingdoms and is a mecca of technology. Compare this kingdom to any other, aside from Virgo, and the other kingdoms almost look uncivilized."

"If you say so. Anyway, I'm starting to feel a little bit better. I think I'm ready to go."

"Good, we have already lost out on some precious time," Leon agreed. "I don't like when we deviate from schedule." Leon smiled and backed away from the healing bed Arkin lay on.

"Have you told these two our plans?" Arkin held his hand to his ribs and began getting up. It certainly didn't feel like his ribs were already healed.

"Not yet, I wasn't sure if it was the right time."

"They seem as though they want to help, and we could certainly use it. In fact, I think we could use a couple more varieties of half bloods to help us reach our goals."

"What are these plans?" Gwen asked.

"I think Leon is right, now probably isn't the time. Let me check out of the healing center, and then we will have a full discussion as soon as possible." Arkin walked toward the door.

They all made their way out of the front door of the center. The entire facility was mostly sky blue, some rooms being translucent and some rooms completely transparent.

"For some reason, I honestly thought that it would be harder to leave the healing center than it was."

"I don't even think the healer was going to come back to check up on you, actually. I'm pretty sure they knew that you were OK, you are pretty strong after all," Pierce said.

They all walked back to their living quarters. The only problem was that since they were from different worlds, they were going to be split up to their respective areas. Arkin thought it might be a good idea to ask if they could all live together, so once he got changed into his standard clothing he decided to ask.

"Is there any way that my friends and I can room together, even though we are different species?" Arkin asked the tall, blue-haired, gray-skinned, Aquarian-Capricorn male who spoke with him at the doorway of the office of dyad management. The office had been established because of the living quarters, and was there for all the dyads to ask as many questions as they needed or for help. He could tell the man was part Capricorn because of his tiny horns, which were smaller even than the average Capricorn.

"I will look into it for you tomorrow. Unfortunately, as of now, there are no clear rules as to whether different dyads can live in the same area. I cannot get anyone to address nonemergency issues tonight because it is too late. The royals wish to be left alone at this time of night. For now, I would say your safest bet is to simply room with people of your own mix. If you must, then you probably could get away with rooming with a different mix from your planet, for example the Aries-Taurus. I think any other sort of other mixing would likely be frowned upon."

"I understand, thank you," Arkin said.

It wasn't the answer he was looking for. The Aquarians were such a kind and easygoing people, and he figured they would easily give in to a simple request such as freedom of living arrangements. Perhaps the Aquarius-Capricorn hybrid wasn't as easy going or kind as the standard Aquarius, or even the Aquarius-Pisces hybrid, for that matter. Maybe still, the head of dyad management wasn't at liberty to make such decisions on his own, which seemed a bit strange as he was the only one working in his office. *Oh well,* he thought as he made his way back to his friends.

"The head of dyad management said that as of now, it is not a good idea to try to room with each other. There are no clear rules or regulations regarding whether we can or can't, but he advises against us staying together for the time being."

"That's OK by me. I'm just fine with my people, and I don't want to be the only girl surrounded by a bunch of guys," Gwen said with her arms folded over her chest.

"Don't be silly, nobody would try anything. It's not even mating season," Arkin dismissively responded.

"Yes, it is, actually, for both you and Pierce," Leon quickly corrected him.

"I knew I couldn't trust you two." Gwen walked away briskly.

"Wow, you totally blew it," Pierce said, and he shook his head and walked away as well.

"What did I do?" Arkin asked.

"Don't worry about those two. Right at this moment, we need to worry about our next move."

"Eventually, it will be important for us to be able to room with others from different planets and breeds in order for us to organize and grow strong the way we need to. And I really think we should focus on that for now." Arkin sat down.

"I understand that, but you can always just keep trying and keep asking them to let us room together. The Aquarians are an empathetic sort of people. I'm sure that if you stay diligent, they eventually will let us all live together. Now let's discuss some other things."

***

"And here we have a water tree, my lady. They are native only to planet Capricorn, I believe."

Valera and Callum stood before a gunmetal-colored tree that seemed to be dripping water from everywhere. It only had about ten leaves, and they were all big and tilted downward from the water they held.

"Interesting, why are they called water trees?" She examined the tree, slowly walking around it.

"They are called such because they absorb extra amounts of water, which is then readily available for anyone to drink from the leaves of the tree, and if we were to cut open the tree it would release a stockpile of water that is stored inside. These trees hold up to two gallons of drinkable water in their center, and that's why they are called water trees." Callum patted the tree with his right hand and stared up at the dangling leaves.

"Very fascinating, you're a very good guide. Thank you for all the details, so far this has been the best tour I've ever had, Callum." She stopped pacing the tree and stood in front of him with a smile.

"My queen." He bowed. "I appreciate the compliment, but I haven't earned such kind words yet. I still have plenty to show you." They began walking again.

"I'm looking forward to it all, then." She paused for a second, and then looked directly at him. "Callum, my curiosity is eating away at me. May I ask you a personal question?"

"Of course, my lady." He nodded his head.

"Why are you so far outside of the kingdom? I've noticed that a few planets have been cultivated in such a way that the entire planet is useful for all the people of that world, providing great utility, but Capricorn does not appear to be one of those. Why is it that you venture so far from the kingdom?"

He looked away from her entirely. "I couldn't trouble you with my reasons for wandering the wild areas of Capricorn instead of touring the kingdom. Nothing good can come of it"

"Nothing good? Maybe you're right, but it will settle my curiosity. Tell me. I'm commanding you as the queen of Virgo, it is an order, young man." The two stopped briefly, and she glanced at him.

"It's really no big deal." He looked away from her again, and they kept walking. "I just like to be out of the kingdom so I can forget who I am. I love being out of the kingdom so I can dream great dreams and not face the reality I am stuck with." He stooped to pick up a small rock and tossed it forward.

"What do you dream of, Callum?" Valera already had an idea of what Callum dreamed of because she read his thoughts, one of her abilities. But she never liked to pry too deep into people's minds unless the need arose, and so she didn't know everything. Callum would be very excited to talk about his ideas she knew and so she wanted to ask.

"I mean no offense by this, my lady." He lowered his eyes before glancing up at her for a brief moment. "Never mind." He looked away. "In fact, I probably shouldn't even tell you this."

"You're still under my orders, so you absolutely must tell me," Valera said playfully.

"OK, again, I just want to say I mean no offense or harm to anyone by wanting this or dreaming about this, but I want to be a royal. I actually want to be the king of Capricorn someday, if possible." His eyes sparkled as he spoke.

She laughed as if she just heard a great joke. She couldn't continue walking. She had to stop and enjoy her laugh.

"I should have expected that you would react like this." He stopped walking as well. "Go ahead and laugh, but I don't think it's so impossible."

"I'm not laughing because of what you said. I'm laughing because you thought you needed to hide it." She stifled her amusement a bit and straightened back up. "Everyone wants to be a royal, live the life, be the king or queen of the kingdom they are born into. I'm not really sure it works like that though, Callum. I believe that most of those things are decided when you're born, or so I'm told." The two began walking along the path through the grass that surrounded the river Serpens.

"I know that's how everything appears," Callum said, "but I'm sure if I can be of some value to the king, then I can at least become a member of the Capricorn Royal Cavalry. From there, if I lead well for long enough, I'm sure I could become a commander, and from there if I'm effective, I'm sure I could become an honorary member of the royals. I hear not all royals of Capricorn are from royal bloodlines. I hear some just have certain abilities that led others to notice them, and from there they are appointed royal status."

"You certainly have a plan, and that's good to hear. It sounds very practical and realistic, too. Do watch yourself, though, others may become envious of your ambitions, or even want to steal your dreams from you. Be sure not to tell everyone about your dreams. I'm happy they are so lofty. Don't ever quit until you accomplish them."

"I won't ever quit. Never. I will accomplish all my goals. All things are possible, they just take time, and I have all the time in the world, because I'm young, and I'm going to age well."

She laughed again. "I do so enjoy your outlook. Maybe you're right, all things take time." She stopped and looked toward the beautiful sky with its sun and clouds.

"May I ask you something?" Callum ventured.

"I don't see any harm in it, after all, I have asked so much of you."

"What do you know about not accomplishing goals? I don't mean to be rude or too inquisitive. Forgive me for my insolence"—he bowed apologetically—"but I'm very curious as to how you can know the ramifications of one not accomplishing his or her goals."

"Very well, I shall tell you my secret. I know full well because I was not always a royal. It is not well known outside of Virgo, but at one point in time, they had difficulty matching up the king with a female mate.

"All the royals born this generation on Virgo, as few as they were, turned out to be male, all of them. Not only that, but the king was the only royal born from the first bloodline. All the other males born were second, third, or fourth cousins, barely related to the king. Nobody could figure out why. Perhaps it was just bad timing, but whatever the case, there were no suitable mates for the current King Virgo.

"The royal family gave up entirely on finding a bride for him on Virgo and were going to seek to mate him with a foreign wife. The king himself did not give up. He scoured the entire planet. I myself was born to a commoner family, on the same day and time as the king but twelve years later. My bloodline was not royal, but all other conditions of my birth were the same as his. I was found capable of doing things that only the royals of Virgo were supposed to be able to do. The king found me and tested me and saw my abilities himself with his own eyes. I demonstrated what I could do before him, and he chose me to be his bride at that instant. I was quite young at the time, so we did not consummate the marriage, not that I need to tell you that, but ever since then I have been queen of Virgo."

"Wow, amazing. That means that maybe there is a chance that I could become king one day. Well, it's not the same thing exactly, your story is very different than mine, but I just want to say that I find your story very inspirational. Thank you for sharing that with me. Although"—he paused and placed his hand on chin—"now that I think about it, that story technically still doesn't tell me how you know about someone not accomplishing their goals."

"I'm sorry, but I feel any more stories would be far too personal for our first encounter. I must take my leave, actually. I have rather enjoyed my stay on your planet, but I have a variety of other things that I wish to see and do. I will tell you a different story next time that will involve failure."

"I understand, my lady, I will walk you back to your ship." Callum was disappointed that he didn't get to finish giving her a tour, but he didn't want to push the issue.

"Very well, young man, I will feel much safer with you, my guide, continuing to watch over me." She smiled at him and locked her arm into his.

The two began walking to her ship, away from the beautiful stream, water trees, and other shrubbery.

Chapter 5

Croix woke up, still confused about what happened last night. He believed that a woman named Ava took his hand and brought him back to her place, only to not partake in the mating ritual with him.

"I cooked some food," Ava said as she entered the room. "You can have some before you go. I think it will make our little secret more convincing." She winked playfully at Croix.

He was startled by her presence and by the rude awakening that it wasn't a dream. He really had missed out on the mating ritual entirely.

"Thank you, I would appreciate that very much," he answered, and walked out of the bedroom and into the dining area. He was trying to sound as polite as possible. Croix figured at this point it did not matter, but he enjoyed being cordial.

They sat down to an elaborate spread that had an assortment of fruits and meats found only on Aries, along with some items from other planets such as Sagittarius, like the doe meat he saw lying before him. It is said that the best doe is one that never sees the arrow coming. Sagittarians take pride in their hunting, so they only sell doe meat that way.

He sat down on the tall plush leather seat that was made from the bovine creatures of Libra. Croix could tell, because his parents had the exact same set of chairs.

The table was huge and sturdy, it appeared to be made out of galvanized titanium, a metal found only on Aries, which was used to forge most things, but yet the table was somehow soft in parts. He didn't know for certain, but he had his suspicions that there was something special about the table, which made him think for a second that perhaps her family was wealthier, or had more prestige, or knew more important people, but that was impossible. He was the king's nephew, his family was the most important on all of Aries. *There must just be some things my family doesn't care for, or that other Aries royals have that we don't,* he reconciled to get over the issue.

"Here, let me feed you." She sat near him with a spoonful of mushy black stuff that she held near his face.

"I am perfectly capable of feeding myself," he said, but then he thought about how cool it would be to have her feed him. "I suppose it can't hurt with the way things went last night, right?"

She looked at him with shock in her eyes for a second and then said, "Yes, of course not, it is said that Aries women usually feed their men in the morning after the mating ritual is performed." She lowered her voice significantly and earnestly asked him, "Have you thought about what I said earlier?"

He looked back at her and brought his face closer to hers and lowered his voice to her level and said, "Well, I have no other choice, do I? I have to become a man of the brotherhood, no matter what it takes, just back me up please."

She laughed. "No, not that, silly. Of course I already figured that part." She began whispering again. "I meant the part of making this a little more real."

His head popped back almost reflexively, and he said, "Why are we whispering, anyway? I don't think I want to play along with your games." He was visibly irritated, and tired of being toyed with. He stood up.

"Very well, my lord," she replied, it was custom for female royals to address their beloved as their lord. "I hope you enjoyed your meal," she added, her disappointment carried by her tone.

"The food wasn't bad, and I appreciate your hospitality," he said. In reality, it was some of the best-tasting food he had ever had. It made him wonder if her parents had sent her away to Libra to learn to cook. The chefs on Libra were said to be the best in all the kingdoms.

"May I continue to feed you?" she asked him.

"Sorry," he said, and sat back down and returned to the same relaxed position he had before.

She continued to feed him, and it seemed as if she knew exactly what his tastes were and how much of each thing he wanted without him having to stop her and ask for anything else. He had his fill, and she stopped; maybe she could tell that he didn't want anymore. She seemed to be a completely different woman from the one he met last night, in his opinion.

Ava had either warmed up to him, or had a purpose for acting so differently. The cooking was amazing, she was beautiful, and there was something peaceful in the ambiance once he finished eating, and they both sat there quietly. All that, combined with the way she was acting that morning, almost made Croix want to stay, but instead he figured it was time to go.

"Thank you again for the meal," Croix said. That was the only compliment Croix gave her.

"Goodbye," she said with a wave and a seemingly genuine smile.

"I just don't understand that woman. It doesn't make any sense. What was different between last night and this morning that made her act so different?" He sighed deeply. "It doesn't matter. I can't get caught up in that. I have to face the brotherhood," he said to himself just outside of her house.

The young Aries man walked with zest to the house of the brotherhood. It was near all the castles of the lords of Aries, but it was its own separate building. The building seemed rather modest to be the operating location of the Aries royal men. It was about half the size of the smallest castle, was composed entirely of black wood, and had simple designs on the door, including an off-white ram's head with flames coming out of its nostrils, which lay on the siding between the first floor and the second floor facing anybody who would enter.

On the second level of the building, high up but still easily visible from below, were white letters that read: "House of the Royal Brotherhood, Only Enter If You Have Permission." He walked up the wooden stairs that led to the first floor and the front door, and then knocked. He wasn't sure of the proper etiquette. Within seconds, somebody rushed to the door.

It was the tall and lanky Rowen. He seemed goofier than the usual royal Aries male. He wore an azure blue sweater that matched his skin tone, and sort of made Croix think, what's the point? Blue was a rare color for Aries royals, but some came in that variety. He had wild hair all over his head, and his horns were crazily curved out just the same as his hair. *It really is all about your family and circumstances that you're born into*, Croix thought as he looked at the other male.

"Brother Croix, you're early, we have been expecting you. Come right in. I will show you the way," Rowen said as he led him upstairs. It was time to face reality. Croix wasn't sure if the lie would work, but he was ready to try. It was time to become one of their number, the men of the brotherhood.

***

King Aries did not want to fight with his wife, Ember, but he knew it was coming when he sent out three of his best men from the brotherhood.

"Husband," his wife said, as she always liked to call him instead of any other number of stronger titles she could use to address him. "Why is it that three of our men are missing?"

"Well, wife"—which the king called his wife to match the way she addressed him, only he did it sarcastically—"I needed the men to do a special job for me." His wife was as beautiful as she was troublesome, deep green eyes, strawberry-red skin and smell, long eyelashes, petite features, and shoulder-length black hair with a silver streak straight down the middle. She wore a diamond gown that hugged her body in the right spots and was yet somehow loose.

"Special job? Why didn't you tell me anything about this?"

"It came up suddenly. Besides, I don't need to consult with you before I make any decisions."

"That is true, but we both know that usually when we talk things out, we come to better conclusions together than alone."

"I don't have the patience nor desire to talk things out all day. Neither do I have the need to do so."

"Fair enough, OK, just tell me what special job you sent the men on, and I will drop the whole subject."

Aries wasn't sure if he should tell her the truth, so he figured he would go with the lie he had thought of for this situation. He had anticipated something like this would happen.

"They are away scouting new planets for resources. They are somewhere in the Cancer region. It is terrible to deal with those pesky Cancers." He shook his head heartily. "I figured if they could find a natural source of aluminum, then we would be less dependent on their kingdom-planet."

"If you say so." She stared at him, but eventually lifted her gaze and shrugged. "That sounds like a reasonable plan. I guess I'll look forward to seeing more aluminum around here soon, then." She walked away.

"Yes," he said, a little uneasy, still unsure if she really bought his story, but in the end, he figured it didn't matter.

He was the king and could do whatever he wanted, but he didn't want everything to blow up in his face, so he figured the fewer people knew the truth about the deal he made with Cancer, the better. The good news was that for the very moment, he didn't have to worry about his wife prying.

Croix finally made it to the room upstairs; it was huge and shaped like a perfect square. A big table made of white wood stood in the middle of the room and a lot of chairs made of the same, many of which were nowhere near the table. A variety of glowing glyphs covered the left and right walls, the glyphs stored power that the Aries men would use to replenish their own or increase their power before they left to complete their missions.

The glyphs had a beautiful glow to them, and they were like decorations, adding life to the room. Not only that, but the room also had a holograph display in one corner, and in another corner of the room, there were monuments erected to some of the leaders.

There was a sort of organized neatness about the room, despite the fact that some odds and ends were strewn about here and there. There were two other young Aries males sitting in chairs, and given their demeanor, they were joining the brotherhood just like Croix was.

Aside from those men, there were seven members of the brotherhood sitting around the room and two standing; one of those was Rowen, who had got the door for Croix earlier. Croix was sure that there were more men in the brotherhood, and he wondered where the others were, but then thought that they couldn't all have the time to engage in these sort of ceremonies. Most likely, the others were busy, off handling business for the king or doing any other number of things.

One of the brotherhood, a shirtless and chiseled Aries, finally spoke up. "Gentleman, my name is Briccio, and I'm the leader of the brotherhood," Briccio said. His body looked as though it didn't have any fat at all; his abdominal muscles were the most impressive part. He must have known, hence his lack of a shirt.

"I thought the king was the leader of the brotherhood," one of the other recruits said.

"The next person to say something else like that is a dead man," Briccio announced with the most serious face that Croix had ever seen. "Officially, as in on record, the king runs the brotherhood, but you all have to get through me"—he poked his own chest—"before you ever even get to work under the king. From now on, until I deem you worthy of the brotherhood, I'm in control of you guys."

"I thought we were already finished with all the trials and were just going to have a ceremony to welcome us into the ranks."

"Hahahaha, oh no, no, no, no. Poor guys, you don't even know what's ahead of you. I'm glad you all got to enjoy your first night with an actual woman. Transcending the realm of virgin and crossing over into the territory of real men is a noteworthy feat."

Croix had an uneasy smile while Briccio spoke. Luckily, there were two other recruits in the room, so all the attention wasn't focused on him.

"Yes, that really was just a way to get you motivated. A tool to give you strength." Briccio flexed his bicep. "The point of that ritual is to give you power." He clenched his fists and flexed both arms before continuing. "Energy for you to accomplish the next set of real tasks that lie ahead of you. Also, a bonus is that you will have an heir to live on in case you die during the tasks." He shrugged.

They all swallowed very hard when they thought about dying just for a chance to join the brotherhood.

"No need to worry, though, that only happened once to one recruit, and that was a long time ago."

One of the brothers stepped up and whispered in Briccio's ear, but he didn't do a good job because the recruits could still hear him. "I thought we agreed not to tell them about the death during the trials."

"What am I supposed to do, lie to them?" Briccio somewhat whispered back and gave a massive shrug.

"They're staring right at us. I think they can hear us."

"Well, it's your fault for talking to me." Briccio lightly pushed the other man away before returning his attention to them. "Anyway, recruits, it will all be fine. You have to do ten trials that will shock and amaze. I mean, you yourself will be shocked and amazed if you manage to pull these trials off." When Briccio finished his speech he lit a torch.

Croix had a flashback to what Ava had told him last night. That's right, all he had to do was shock her five times and amaze her five times. Maybe Ava knew more about the brotherhood than he had initially thought. Furthermore, and more importantly, maybe through these trials he could kill two birds with one stone, and actually participate in a real mating ritual with her

What if it was a coincidence? Croix considered for a moment. *No, there's no way, there has to be some connection between the ten trials he had to complete in order to become one of the brothers and between the lovely woman's requests.* I guess Ava wasn't being as difficult as I thought. He suddenly snapped back into listening to Briccio.

"These quests are tailor-made to test your abilities in order to see if you're fit to be a member of the brotherhood." Briccio passed the torch to his other hand, the orange red flame matched his skin tone and gave him an even more commanding aura. "Only the powerful will make it, but I must warn you gentlemen that it won't be as simple as, gather this here"—he pointed toward the left side of the ground in front of him—"or fight this thing over there." He pointed to the right side of the ground in front of him. "Rather, this set of tasks will be life-altering, legendary, I-have-to-tell-all-my-descendants-because-it's-so-interesting, multiple world spanning, epic level quests. I hope that you all have glory on your minds, because that's all a real Aries royal man should think about.

"Brother Eames here will give you all your tasks." He nodded to a member of the brotherhood that was still seated. "Not all of your tasks will be completely the same, and while team work is not always illegal, it could be counterproductive, because some of the items on your task list may be rare." Briccio gestured to the man. "Eames. Give it to them." A serious looking fellow, Eames had the appearance of someone who would seek out work before fun. His horns curved backward and straight down toward the middle of his back. His black piercing eyes stared into the souls of the recruits.

Croix thought back to what his supposed Aries mate said one more time and thought it had to be more than a coincidence. He became excited, thinking that he would get to have intercourse with the woman while actually getting to join the brotherhood, since he still wasn't an official member. That day combined with the day before it, reminded Croix that even when you're royalty, things don't always go your way. The decision was made, he was definitely going to try to win over the heart of Ava. He might as well, since he already had quite a few things that he needed to do in order to join the brotherhood.

Eames was suddenly in front of him and the other recruits. "Your first assignment will be on planet Scorpio."

"In order to be successful, you must behead a sand dragon. You will be able to keep the head as a trophy. All we need is to see you with the dragon head in your hand, and we will take that as proof." He began pacing in front of the recruits with his arms behind his back. "We don't need a bunch of sand dragon heads in the lovely brotherhood house." He gestured toward all corners of the room. "I'm fairly sure that none of you have ever seen a sand dragon. Some of you may have never even been on planet Scorpio as of yet.

"I want to assure you that the legends and rumors are real. The sand dragon can be as elusive as it is deadly. But usually, if you find one, the complicated part is over. There are a few ways to kill them. Unfortunately"—he smiled at the recruits—"I myself will not be telling you any of those ways."

A few members of the brotherhood laughed at that.

In an instant, he was right back into serious mode. "Actually, the reason that the trials are kept secret, and are even changed sometimes, is to prevent those who have already passed the trials and become full-fledged members of brotherhood, past or present, from helping recruits cheat. That would defeat the point. We need to know that you're smart, tough, and have what it takes to get the job done.

"I will be watching all of you and your progress while you're on Scorpio. But make no mistake: I will merely be there to ensure that none of you die. I am not there to make sure that you pass this trial or any other."

"Nobody cares if your uncle is the king." He didn't look at Croix, but he might as well have been talking directly to him because everybody knew that Croix was the king's nephew.

"Nobody cares about your bloodline or lineage because that's not how we do it on planet Aries. Men of the brotherhood earn their keep. As you all shall. I expect great things out of you. Please do not let me down."

"We understand, we will not fail you," the other two recruits declared in unplanned unison.

"Tomorrow, I will give you more details. Tonight, I suggest you all pack your things and prepare to spend at least a full day on Scorpio. I have here a list of recommended supplies to survive the planet's harsh desert environment. None of you is allowed to go to any vaults or to the knowledge center for assistance. If you are caught reading or watching any material pertaining to sand dragons or planet Scorpio, you will be disqualified. The point of this exercise will be to see how you think and react on your feet. I have nothing more to say to you. You're dismissed."

With nothing but the list of recommended supplies, the three recruits left.

"Do you want to team up?" one of the candidates asked the others as they all walked away from the brotherhood house and back toward their homes. The one who asked had big arms and a big stomach, with horns that curled into themselves and lemon-colored skin.

"I'm not sure that's allowed. Let's wait for tomorrow for Eames to brief us on the rules," Croix said back to the recruit.

"Don't you remember? He said that teaming up is allowed," the other recruit said. This recruit had golden eyes, semi-common of Sagittarius, curly horns, well-kempt black hair, carrot-orange-colored skin, and was standard in all other manners.

"Technically, Briccio said that, and it may still not be a bright idea, especially when we don't know everything yet. It may really be best to go at this task alone," Croix said.

"I'm not really sure there is ever a time when going at a difficult task is better by yourself, but maybe you're right. We should wait until tomorrow when we have a better idea of what we are dealing with. My name is Archer, by the way." The golden eyed recruit said and extended his hand toward the other two men. They all slowed down their walking pace to shake hands.

"Archer?" the big recruit asked when he shook the other recruit's hand.

"My dad was a royal from Sagittarius." Archer pretended to shoot an arrow into the sky, "and my mom is Aries, so my dad figured since I looked more like my mom, I could take after him, by name at least," he explained after shaking hands with them.

"Oh, OK, I see that's a good name when you put it that way. My name is Ronan," the one with the big stomach said. "I'm not really sure why my parents named me that, but it is what it is."

"My name is—"

"We know who you are, Croix. I'm pretty sure everybody there did, too. You're the only one that Eames could have been talking about earlier." Ronan looked back at the brotherhood house briefly.

"Well, he was wrong about me," Croix defended himself. "I would never expect nor would I want any special recognition or treatment just because my uncle is the king. Like he said, that's not the point of becoming a man of the brotherhood."

"That's good, because it seems like we are going in as equals, and performance is the most important determining factor," Archer said with a quick head nod.

"Yes, that's true, at least it seems so. It was nice meeting you guys, I have to go." Croix, generally a man of few words, disappeared in an instant, dashing back home. Not running back anywhere near his top speed, but still fast enough that he got there instantaneously.

He arrived back to his lavish home. It wasn't as big as his cousin the prince's house, but it was very close. He had all the amenities he could possibly want, and nobody was home, so he could really relax. The castle was square-shaped on the outside, with four round pillars in each corner of the square. Croix stuck mostly with the pillar that was his designated area, which was the right side, furthest from the front door.

In his particular area, everything was simple, all furniture being black, soft and easy to the touch, walk-in closets in each room except for the bathroom and kitchen, and holographic displays in every room so he could watch whatever he wanted to, whenever he wanted to.

Both of his parents were away for business on planet Taurus, last he remembered. His father wasn't the king, but he still had a lot of pull and was one of the most important faces of the Aries Empire, second only to the king, as he was in some ways more popular than the queen, even.

Croix's mom just wanted to tag along because King Taurus always had exquisite jewelry not found on any other planets. The king and queen of Taurus had a thing for possessions, and they had a lot more than most, if not all the other planets.

Croix fixed himself a simple stew and then sat on his bed in his room and packed all his belongings in a long black sack. He had to be ready for tomorrow. He had never even heard of a sand dragon before, so he was a little worried. Not to mention the fact that Scorpio was completely foreign to him; for some reason, he remembered thinking that it was an ice planet, but he must have been mistaken, or maybe it was just because of the season. Either way, word was that Scorpio had one of the toughest terrains of all the twelve planets, which was part of the reason that the people born on the planet were so tough, or at least that's what was believed.

It didn't take long for Croix to finish his packing, and once finished he went straight to bed.

When morning came, he ate his breakfast quickly, grabbed his belongings, and headed for the brotherhood house. Immediately at arrival to the front yard, he saw that brother Eames had prepared a vessel to transport them all to Scorpio. Eames stood on the black grass while he waited for Croix in the front of the brotherhood house.

"Why can't we just use an aqua communicator to get there?" Croix's face displayed his puzzlement, and he stared at the lightning bolt-shaped ship.

"We aren't going anywhere near the kingdom of Scorpio. As you know, aqua communicators can only be used if both sides have them, and both are turned on and in use. The part of the planet Scorpio we are going to is rarely even occupied by the Scorpios themselves during this time of the year. We have to fly you in using this craft."

Croix continued examining the craft. It appeared to be the latest model of the Lightning Ship 5000. The ship was called such because it was literally shaped like a lightning bolt. It could extend itself to a diamond shape or contract and conceal parts of itself, depending on the flying or battle conditions. Originally created by the Aquarius, lightning ships were the best at transporting large groups of people long distances no matter the conditions, which gave it a slight advantage over aqua communicators. The Virgos had consistently improved upon the technology the Aquarius created, until the Lightning Ship 5000 was made. They all boarded.

Croix felt ready. He had brought everything Eames had told him, and a few other items he thought would be useful like some boots his uncle gave him. The boots were a special make, so light and snug it became one with your foot. Yet the boots were dense enough to protect the feet from most dangerous objects. Light brown in color, he figured it would be a good idea to dress as close to the color of sand as possible. Therefore, his whole outfit was light sandy brown in color, even the frames of his googles and his face scarf. Unfortunately, the only part he couldn't get sand-colored were the lenses of the goggles, they were a greenish hue.

The candidates strapped themselves into their soft fabric seats and prepared themselves mentally.

Eames stood before the candidates, unshaken by turbulence and intense warp speeds. "I will now give you all a few minor details about planet Scorpio. Scorpio hosts some of the most extreme weather and terrain of all the planets. The part we are going to is desert-like all year round. During this season in particular, it's even more unbearable because of constant sand storms.

"I will now tell you how you will know when you're looking at a sand dragon.

"There are a few ways to spot a sand dragon. One, when the sand is overly uneven in a certain area, that is one indicator. Two, when the sand has a lot more empty spots in it than you think it should have, that usually means you are looking at a sand dragon's face, in particular its eyes. Notice that these techniques can only be used when it is probably too late.

"However, they are important to know and keep in mind, just in case you need them. How do you hunt a sand dragon? You begin by finding its nest. You will know that you have stumbled upon a sand dragon's nest when you see its eggs." Eames put his hand just below his pocket to indicate the size of the eggs. "They're about this tall. And in fact, the eggs are actually the easiest things to spot, because unlike the dragons themselves, the eggs stand out because they are a greenish-black color.

"It is important that you all have the goggles and some sort of scarf, like I asked you to bring on that list I gave you. You will need them to protect your eyes and mouth. Quite frankly, sand dragons are usually so hard for newbies to spot that the next piece of advice I'm going to give you all will probably sound crazy.

"You want to grab the eggs of the sand dragon and move them away from the nest and lair and into a location of your own choosing, particularly a moist, wet, or humid area, which are pretty scarce on Scorpio, but there are still a few. The thing you should be thinking now is, 'How will we know when to steal the dragon egg if the dragon is so hard to spot that they could be watching us while we're infiltrating their layer?' The answer is very simple, the dragons sleep during the same time of the day each day. Which is our estimated time of arrival.

"Once you're finished stealing the egg from the beast's lair to lure them out, you're going to want to set up the tent, sleeping bag, blanket, and portable room that I told you all to bring, in the area you chose." A hatch opened up near where he was standing, bringing in lots of noise, causing him to raise his voice. "Next you must put the egg down, and you sleep on it like it's a pillow. You don't have to actually sleep on it, but you should lay on it in such a way that the dragon can't hurt you without hurting its unborn child.

"Unfortunately, this ends our tutorial. I will not be telling you anything else. You may still have a hard time finding their lairs after my explanation just now, but, oh well." He shrugged nonchalantly. "Like I said before, some of this should be difficult. I just hate when too much time is wasted on luring the sand dragon out. Now you can worry about finding its lair and also killing it, which are the most difficult parts for recruits, we found. We are here at our location." Eames looked down through the opening in the lightning ship toward the ground as if to confirm with himself.

His gaze fell back upon the recruits and he continued. "I know Briccio said that teamwork is allowed, and that's true for some of the later tasks, but it doesn't really apply for the first five missions.

So I'm going to drop each one of you off in a different area." He called for each recruit to stand near him, by the opening.

"You're first," Eames said, seemingly picking at random, and then he pushed Archer off the ship before yelling, "Good luck!" The ship was designed to automatically cushion someone's fall so a protective bubble surrounded Archer as he fell and only disappeared when he was a safe distance to the ground, allowing him to land on his feet.

Eames waited for a little while and did a count with his lips, not saying anything, and then looked at the pilot who gave him thumbs up. He came behind Ronan and pushed him next, and again said, "Good luck!" Ronan landed the same way Archer did.

Last was Croix, maybe it was because he had the farthest position from Eames when Eames began ejecting them. Eames repeated the same routine before finally pushing Croix out and yelling, "Good luck!"

Croix felt an intense amount of wind, sand, and air surround him after he landed out of his bubble. The air was so hot and thick he felt as though he could drown in the heat. The humidity felt unbearable to him. He almost felt as though he might pass out right away. At that point, he realized the task was going to be hard for a multitude of reasons, starting with the weather.

"Aries men fear nothing, least of all the weather," he said out loud to himself with a chuckle, in order to feel better. "It's time to slay a dragon," he added, and put on his googles and scarf and made his way through the sand storm.

Not even knowing where to start was the worst part of the mission; to make matters worse, he wasn't even sure of how he was supposed to kill a sand dragon. Eames practically told him nothing. Furthermore, he did not even know what they were capable of. Croix figured that they must be powerful, after all they were dragons, even if they did live in the desert. He began sifting through his backpack and looking through his supplies, trying to make a plan. *That's it!* Everything might be easier than he thought; he had a life detector device.

A small, silver-and-white box the life detector could detect any multicellular organism within five hundred kilometers. It sent out a frequency in the form of a pulse. The pulse picked up heartbeats and sent the information back to the box.

Firing up the device, he sent out the frequency, and it picked up two strong pulses and a few weak ones. The stronger the pulse, the closer the life-form. There were two life-forms not too far from his location.

Of course, he had no way of telling whether either life-form was the sand dragon he was trying to hunt, but there was a chance that one was the baby dragon and the other was the momma dragon. Luckily, the life detector delivered the pulse in the same direction it came from.

There was even a simple diagnostic screen on the life detector with generic information about the organism such as the approximate height and weight of the creature, its current heart rate, and an estimate of the how far the creature was. It must have been his lucky day, because it wouldn't take him long to walk to the location. He wasn't really sure what he would need to slay the dragon, so he figured he would just do reconnaissance, check out the lair, and try to take in everything he could as fast as he could, and then come back the next day.

That is, if it's the case that the dragon is actually asleep when he got there. He wanted to try to handle this as stealthily as possible.

He made it to his intended location. The cave was a light, almost pink, color, and at the base of a mountain.

The cave was very big, definitely big enough to hold a few dragons.

This must be the place, he believed as he looked over the inside of the dark, damp, stalagmite- and rock-infested, jagged cave through the green lenses of his goggles, which served as both protection for his eyes from sand and doubled as night vision goggles.

He had a few options for checking out the cave. He could take his time and ease his way in, or he could dash through and check out everything he could see in seconds. Instantly, he disregarded his stealth plan and settled on a quick dash, and rather than gathering information, he would search directly for the eggs of the dragon, so he could lure the beast out as Eames had told him to.

At lightning-fast speed, he dashed through the entire cave and simultaneously looked around and took in everything in with his superior eyesight. Carcasses were strewn all over the entire cave, ranging in size from inferior smaller creatures all the way up to the size of a typical Aries male. The cave had even more stalagmites the further he traveled in, a few had huge water drops falling from them, but at his speed, no drop could touch him.

Croix was amazed with how large the cave actually was, and was surprised not to find more creatures living there.

When he finally reached the end of the cave, which closed off into a large fresh water pool, he finally saw the cave's actual occupants, two gigantic scorpions, sable in color, and both as big as a house.

The momentum of his run almost caused him to crash into one of them, but he caught himself and ran on the wall to avoid running into either. The two scorpions noticed him and one tried to sting him as he sprinted back out of the cave.

Plan A did not work, so now it was onto plan B to find the other nearby life-forms, which hopefully would include the sand dragon.

He took a break outside to refocus his efforts and set up his device again, but he could hear the sounds of one, at least one, maybe both of the scorpions making their way out of the cave. A part of him thought that once he ran out of the cave, the scorpions would give up, but it seemed they really wanted to add him to their prey. They had such a lovely collection of bones, after all, of course they wanted a fresh addition.

Sprinting further from the cave in the direction he thought the other pulses had come from, he watched the cave entrance to see what the scorpion would do. The scorpion walked to the front of the cave and out through the entrance, walked left a few feet, right a few feet, stopped, looked around, and then went back into the cave.

Breathing became easy to him again, it was such a relief that he made it away safely from those creatures. After activating the life detector, he felt the other pulses, and he had in fact been going the right way. This time, he paid more attention and realized that only one of the pulses was strong enough to be that of an adult creature; the rest could only be children, and this time the display on the life detector confirmed that. Not sure of how long it would take to get to the cave, and not wanting to arrive at a time when the sand dragon was actually awake, the thought crossed his mind to go back to where he set up camp, but he quickly disregarded it. Continuing on was the best option, he decided.

Finding the lair was a more difficult task than he would have thought, despite the life detector. Truth be told he still wasn't even sure if he had the right place, maybe another creature lived in this lair with its children.

Can't afford to lose the momentum, he thought in order to drive himself forward and pushed the notion of retreating until another day out of his mind completely. Not to mention the new lair seemed to be very close to his current location.

This lair was very different than the scorpion cave, at least from the outside. It was near impossible to tell where the entrance was, or where the cave began or ended. It just looked like a huge mound of sand at first.

However, this was the location the life detector indicated. He made his way through sand until he found an entrance that he pushed open by accident, almost falling through. This was definitely the right place, this time he knew it. No doubts were in his mind. This was the cave of the sand dragon. The entrance was underground, but not that far beneath the surface. It was sand on top of sand, but the sand of the cave was a bit moister, which made it a darker color than the sand that was outside. The second cave was much smoother than the scorpion's den.

After this mission, I'll be an expert on sand, he smirked to himself. This lair was a lot different from that of the scorpions, on the inside, too. It didn't even feel like a cave, more like a giant sand ball, and it was actually a much larger area than the scorpions lived in. At times, he felt as though he was going to slip into the sand. It was then that he noticed that some of it felt different under his feet.

One thing was for certain, he was not going to be able to sprint through this cave. Slowly, trying to take all proper precautions, he traversed the massive lair, the huge damp cave. While it wasn't as obvious as when he was in the scorpions' den, there was still a lot of bones.

Crunch, crunch, crunch…he felt bones crack under his boots.

The further he got in the cave, the more he wished the cave had been like the scorpions' den. Visually, almost all of this cave looked the same, with no significant landmarks. But on instinct he stopped and began studying a new area that somehow felt different to him. After staring at the new sand a memory came back to him. He had heard legends of a type of sand that could swallow men of Taurus size whole for them to never be seen again.

Taking heed to the legends, Croix took out a short sword he had from his backpack, it was extra because he had other larger weapons he planned to fight with. He threw it into the different-looking sand and saw that it sunk a little, but he weighed more than the sword, and if it sunk he would most likely sink even more. Figuring it would be best to avoid that area just in case his suspicions were right, he dashed along the wall until he reached another patch that looked more like the sand near the entrance, and then he resumed his previous cautious walking speed.

As he crunched on another skeleton, he heard a low grumble. He dropped into a crouch and weighed his options: keep going, or sprint down the wall or the ceiling.

He opted for the ceiling, after thinking about what almost happened in the scorpions den. He began building momentum by sprinting forward several steps and then up the side of the wall, and then he made his way up to the top. He didn't need to run his fastest, just fast enough to stay on the roof, so he toned down his speed quite a bit. Making his way through seemed less worrisome, as the ceiling of the cave was much quieter to run on than the floor was.

After a while he came to a dead end, with nothing but a large pool of water similar to the scorpion's den. And there he finally saw the dragon eggs. There were five of them, dark green in color, each the size of a six-year-old.

How am I supposed to carry one of these all the way out of here, or even do the plan that Eames told me to do?

Additionally, it began troubling him that he could not see the mother of these babies. The thought crossed his mind that maybe she was right in front of him at that very moment, or that maybe he had already passed her. There was no time to worry about that. For now, he just had to make an attempt to grab one of the eggs and dash off with it.

It was then that he noticed sand moving with a lot of empty pockets in it. She was on to him. Before he had a chance to react, the cave he was just inside was gone.

Impossible, there was no way a huge cavernous lair could have disappeared in an instant and yet it had. Looking all around in every direction, he tried to make sense of it. It seemed as though he was back outside in an area he had just walked through. Suddenly he heard Eames call out to him.

Eames was off in the distance and looked extremely far away, but it was hard to tell with the sand storm still going strong. Either way, Eames managed to reach him in an extraordinarily short amount of time. However, it made sense for him to be extremely fast, he was one of the brothers after all. Croix resolved the issue mentally.

"Good job, recruit, your work here is done." Eames gave him a quick salute.

"Are you serious? But I never even killed the sand dragon."

Eames laughed. "Nobody can kill the sand dragon, that's impossible. We were really testing your resolve, and you passed. Are you ready to go?"

"What do you mean?" Croix remained confused.

"I mean the fact that you found the sand dragon is good enough alone. I suggest we get going soon, before this sand storm gets any worse."

"I still don't understand."

"Look, I'm going to break this down for you really slowly, because you're not getting it for some reason. The sand dragon is un—stop—a—ble. Do you understand now? We don't want you to get yourself killed. Therefore, the test is just to see if you're able to find the sand dragon and actually have the determination to take it on. I see that you took on the dragon, and I'm impressed, and your work here is done." Eames gestured for Croix to go with him.

"But I never even took on the sand dragon at all. All I did was find where its lair was at. I attempted to take one of the eggs, and then the cave disappeared, and I ended up out here somehow. It was like the cave disappeared, and then suddenly, you appeared." Croix said the last part of his statement slowly, and his eyes darted while he tried to make sense of things.

"None of that matters. What does matter is that you come with me right now."

Croix no longer believed any of it.

"I'm not sure what's going on, but I'm not going anywhere with you."

Eames looked at Croix with clear disappointment, then a flash of anger, and suddenly, a diabolical grin covered his face, and he began laughing maniacally. "Very well then, it looks like you shall die here. I gave you a chance to live and to save your own life."

After he finished speaking, Eames became frozen in place, a sand statue of himself that quickly faded into the wind.

Croix woke up in the familiar setting of the desert. The very desert he had been in before he found the sand dragon's lair, to be exact. None of it made sense.

"Where was I just a moment ago?" he said out loud, and looked around the rough sandy terrain. The sand storm was so disorienting that he didn't have the slightest clue of his bearing.

"You still don't get it, do you?" A high pitched voice in his head demanded his attention. Croix realized it was most likely the dragon. "I am everywhere and everything out here, and yet nothing and nowhere if I want to be. You have so boldly stepped into my world and from here, there is no escape, if I so wish. I could kill you simply by making it so you never find your way out of here, and the irony is that some of your friends aren't very far from here, but you will never see them again, if I so desire. You know, I saw your meeting with the scorpions. It's quite brave how you ran from them," the dragon laughed. "I have them as my prey regularly, if you're afraid of them. What makes you think there is any chance for you to face me, or are you so eager to prove something that you would put your life on the line to face one much more powerful than you?"

"I am perfectly capable of destroying those scorpions. I merely wanted to save myself the time and did not want to unnecessarily take their lives."

"Ha. Are you trying to convince me of that, or yourself? If you're so powerful, bring me the two you just encountered. I long for scorpion meat, the giant ones are the only ones worth killing. No, no, I actually have a task far more suited for someone of your abilities. Your speed is undeniably impressive. I have seen a few of your kind before, and I think I know of a way in which you can be useful to me."

"Why would I do anything for you? I've come here to kill you."

"Because, boy," the dragon snarled, "I still haven't decided if I'm going to kill you yet. If you do me a favor, I may be persuaded to spare your life. More than that, I may even help you accomplish your goal of bringing back a sand dragon's head. Now, what do you say? Would you like to hear my proposal, or will your silly ego get you killed here and now?"

"I'm listening," Croix retorted. He was curious about the deal the dragon was making with him, but wasn't sure if he could trust him. What did he mean, he could help with his goal? Another problem was that Croix wasn't even sure what the dragon's head actually looked like. When he caught a glimpse of the dragon back in its lair, all he saw were some spots that weren't completely saturated in sand and appeared as though they could have been the eyes, but there was so much sand everywhere, it was really hard to say.

Even as he spoke to the dragon, he wasn't sure where it was at. It didn't help that he was talking to the dragon because the dragon's voice seemed to only be in his head. For that matter, he didn't even remember actually saying a lot of his responses out loud. After he thought about it, he had no doubts in his mind. The dragon was using telepathy. It seemed as though this dragon was more powerful than he had anticipated. It was a horrible mission to send someone on, especially on their first mission. *Brotherhood men are crazy.*

The sand dragon began detailing his request. "There is a magical item that is said to exist in this desert. I will guide you to it, but I need you to retrieve the item. If you bring it to me, I will not only spare your life, but I will also assist you in pleasing those brutish friends of yours that you're so desperately trying to impress."

"What does the item do?"

"That is none of your concern at this moment. I will be watching you, and I will tell you what the item is capable of, if I feel the need to."

"If you're so powerful, why don't you get the item yourself?"

"I have already told you, this task is better suited for *your* abilities. I can still kill you, if you prefer."

"I was just asking because you seem to be very powerful, and I was confused as to why you need me."

"Indeed, a reasonable question when you put it forth with that manner of thinking. Regardless, I grow weary of this back and forth, and would like to get on with this."

"Wait, but you still haven't even told me what the item is."

"Don't worry, you'll know it when you see it."

"OK then, we have a deal." Croix responded in his mind.

Croix really felt as though he had no other choice. Maybe the item would help him kill the dragon. Whatever the case was, he had no way to even know where the dragon was or how to even hunt it anymore, so he figured that it would be a good idea to follow the dragon's instructions, at least for the time being. Right away the sand storm cleared up some, especially in the path that Croix suddenly stood in. The sand before him was now laid out as if it were a sidewalk. The sand on which he stood was raised above the other sand and had no wind or sand kicking around. The dragon had cleared a passage for him.

A layer of sand glowed and floated about chest level a few inches in front of Croix, and was enticing him. This sand stretched the entire path as far as Croix could see. The dragon really did not want Croix to get lost.

He jetted down the path. There was no need to waste time running an errand for someone else, especially when that somebody else was an enemy. He had no idea how long it would take to sort out this whole ordeal with the dragon. What he did know was that it was going to take him a long time to get to his destination; he realized the path was really long, once he bent a few corners and looked forward to see the length of the bending path.

***

The princess was finally ready to show the prince her quarters. "And here we have my room," Catalina said to Mar. Her room was elegantly decorated with plush furniture everywhere. Everything in her room seemed old-fashioned and wooden or made from stone, aside from the furniture, of course, which was made from some sort of soft dark blue cloth. Old-fashioned was the way most Capricorns liked it, from what Mar had heard.

She had a simple holographic display in her room along with a multicolored bird and temperature regulator system. She also had a lot of artwork including actual busts of her and her father, a machine that appeared to be capable of producing sculptures, and a blank canvas with some paint. She had an enormous bookshelf with quite possibly the most holobooks Mar had ever seen in his life, and a lovely square bed the size of a small room.

"Is that a Piscean Mantico?" Mar asked. Giving his full attention to the caged bird, he began examining it. The bird had a smirk on both of its faces, the bird was two headed but only had three eyes because the fourth was sealed shut, it was said to be common among their breed. It was said that the sealed eye was used to look into the past, present, and future simultaneously. The bird's colors were interesting, it was gray around the chest region, blue around the nose, red around the sealed eye, and black across the rest of its body. It was a strange- looking bird indeed.

"Yes, of course. It was given to me by King Pisces himself," she said proudly, standing near the birdcage as well.

"You should get rid of it," he said, aggressively flicking a finger at the bird. "Not to be rude, but it is believed that those birds are bad luck. You've heard the rumors, right?" He looked up at her, paused, and made sure he got eye contact. "You heard that they can tell the future, haven't you?"

"Yes, of course, everyone knows that." Catalina nodded in agreement with the statement.

"Well, it is said that they eventually start feeding their masters bad predictions until their master ends up dead, and they gain their freedom." Mar's eyes landed on the bird once again.

"It is not a rumor that they can tell the future. I assure you that it is very much true. However, I would like to know who you heard that from, that they kill their masters using their ability?"

"I heard it from King Taurus. Aside from that, it's an old tale that all children are told on my planet, even the commoners of Aries have heard the tale." He stood up straight and looked up at her again.

"I don't think I'm familiar with it. Please tell me."

"Story goes that one of the original kings of the twelve from the first generation would always seek out the bird's advice. It stands to reason that Pisces isn't the king from the story because he could predict the future himself.

"As I was saying, one of the kings would always seek advice from the bird. The bird would tell the king who to war with and how, and help the king devise great strategies. It was during a different time, when the twelve kingdoms were not at peace. Before the great truce, which, according to my father, was established somewhat recently.

"The man plotted against the other kings and was always successful in battle. Until one day, the bird told the king to bring his wife with him to a conflict. The king thought it was odd to bring his wife with him. After all, his wife wasn't particularly experienced with combat, and he didn't feel that she would bring any good luck or anything, but the bird had never led him astray. With that said, he felt he had no reason to distrust the bird.

"The bird also gave him two more bits of advice for the battle. One, don't use his archers, because in a long distance skirmish the rival king would defeat him. He was instead to creep on the enemy, and his soldiers were only to engage in close quarters. Two, not to surrender or give up, no matter what. As it turns out, the king's forces were slaughtered. Once his forces were decimated, the king was asked to surrender by the rival king. Of course, he refused, as the bird told him to, and was forced to see his wife killed before his very eyes. The next part of the story gets a bit blurry. I've heard it told multiple ways, but it is commonly believed that after seeing his wife die, he surrendered and had planned to work under his new king and plot his revenge as the other king's captive, but was still killed eventually by the rival king anyway."

"Another version of the story goes that he still was unwilling to surrender and was beheaded right after seeing his wife get her throat slit. And yet another version says that the other king granted him the chance to prove himself by working for him, and that he lived a coward's life from then onward, and still died a year or so after, during a battle fought under the rule of his new king. Either way, the last part of the story is usually the same. The king and his wife were dead and his only heirs, his one daughter and two sons, were too young to do much, and they were supposedly also killed by the guile and cunning of the devious bird. 'The bird only sought freedom,' some say, 'so how can you blame it.' I myself would never be caught dead having one of those birds. I actually find it quite odd that the bird hasn't spoken even once since I have been bad-mouthing its kind right in front of it."

Mar continued staring directly at the bird even after he finished with his story. The bird stared back with all three eyes, unflinching.

"As far as I can tell, the bird only talks to me. It won't speak to anyone else, or even in front of another person. Pisces told me that the best thing that could happen is for these birds to talk to their master and nobody else. Also, I don't understand how all the heirs could have died. If that were the case, one of the twelve wouldn't have a king, right?"

"Judging by your speech, you still seem intent on keeping the foul beast." Mar pushed his statement forward, completely ignoring her logic, stepped away from its cage, and eyed her aggressively.

"But of course I do. I don't believe in folktales. I have never and won't ever." She looked as though she were ready to laugh. "Besides, the king and the queen from the story were clearly fools. I will never blindly follow the advice of the bird or anyone else for that matter, regardless of whether or not I trust them, or they have the ability to tell the future."

"I understand that, and that's reasonable, but with you, the bird might not be as obvious as it was with the king. Clearly, the bird would have to find some other way to get you, since you're not going to lead an army into battle, and the truce between the kingdoms is still in effect, anyway. All I'm saying is that folktales have some purpose to them, otherwise people wouldn't tell them." Mar calmed himself a little toward the end of the disagreement but had moved closer to her to continue the conversation.

"If you say so. I believe that you should continue to believe in the things that you believe in, and I shall continue to keep to my beliefs, kind prince. Thank you for the story."

Mar, a little frustrated after their verbal exchange, couldn't decide if he liked her beyond her looks. Maybe it was too early to tell.

Everyone is entitled to their own opinions, especially royals from different kingdoms who have entirely different customs and beliefs.

"Would you like to go to planet Leo with me, Catalina?" He flashed a smile at her when he changed the subject. "I hear King Leo's birthday is approaching, and that the feasts during this time are exquisite."

"Isn't there a rebellion in the kingdom of Leo at this very moment?" The concern in her voice seemed genuine.

"This is true. I suppose we will have to go some other time, then."

"How about we go to Libra instead and see a performance?" She smiled back at him.

"That could be interesting."

"Let's go then," Catalina finished with an even bigger smile.

Chapter 6

"**S**ire, I wanted to let you know that there was a fight among the dyads in the common area," Linden said, and bowed immediately upon entering Aquarius's throne room.

"Unfortunate, well, I suppose they are all from different planets and don't possess the refinement of those of the royal class. It can't be helped. As long as the confrontation was ended peacefully, that's all that really matters," King Aquarius decided thoughtfully.

"Do you wish to have the guilty parties punished, to set an example?" Linden took a standing position and asked.

"No, not yet, that seems a bit rash." He dismissed the thought with his hand. "If only one quarrel happens between the multitude of races that now belong on our planet, then punishment of the responsible parties is an uncalled-for action. Rather, let's make them feel at home as much as possible. We brought them here to offer sanctuary from the tyranny of their old worlds. It is not good for us to offer them the same sort of life they could have had where they came from. However"—Aquarius paused, leaned forward in his amethyst colored sparkling throne, and made very pointed eye contact—"I would like for you to keep an eye on those who were involved in the altercation."

"Sire?" Linden raised an eyebrow.

"Just watch them closer than the rest. You don't need to report back to me their actions unless you feel they are noteworthy. I just want you to keep a steady eye on them. Pisces was trying to warn me about something, and while he didn't give me any of the details, he did say that it had something to do with the dyads. Not to mention, planet Leo still has the rebellion going on, it's hard to gauge the severity and interconnectedness of everything." He looked away, seemingly for answers.

"One more thing." His gaze fell back on Linden once more. "Just for curiosity's sake. What planets were the guilty parties from?"

"The two involved in the fight were both from Aries, actually."

"Interesting, do you have anything else to add?"

"I have word from one of our men that the two who fought seem to be on more amicable terms now, and further, that a female who appears to be a Gemini-Cancer mix and some other whose breed I'm unsure of, seem to have all taken up together."

"Very interesting." Aquarius stroked his chin softly in thought. Hanging nearly toward the edge of his throne. "I would say forget what I said about watching them closely, then." He stood up and smiled. "I want them to feel comfortable making friends. Maybe things are going better than I thought a moment ago. This could even be the first and last fight among the people. Thank you for your report. You can take it easy. Remember, I have Stone as my primary to watch over them. In fact, he's supposed to bring matters to me of this nature, but I still appreciate your efforts, Linden. I'll see you later." Aquarius dismissed him with a salutatory gesture.

"Understood, sire," Linden said, partially bowing then gracefully walking out.

Linden had the most grace and elegance of any royal from any planet, or so it seemed most of the time. He was the king's cousin and was ordained to serve his cousin for the rest of his life. It wasn't bad, though. Linden was second only to the king on his planet, and actually gave orders directly to the rest of the Aquarius royals, not all the time, but a large portion of the time.

***

Back in the common area for dinner, Leon, Arkin, Pierce, and Gwen plotted their next move.

"I suggest we wait until we get our request denied or accepted to dorm near each other before we make any drastic moves or decisions," Leon stated.

"An understandable thought, but the next move I'm planning won't make any waves," Arkin revealed. "I think we should try to increase our number. Strengthen our group. The four of us can get a lot done, but imagine if we had three more or even four more in our group. I was hoping that the two of you would get some others to join us if possible, as well." He glanced toward Gwen and Pierce.

"I can ask," Gwen said. Her green face tightened and became serious when she said it, and her demeanor instantly became less easygoing. "But there is no guarantee. I will go back and speak with my people. I will see you all later; before nightfall, I will try to have an answer for you."

As soon as she finished speaking, she went back to the area where her people were seated in the common area.

"I don't really think I need to ask any of them. I'm sure they all still want you dead," Pierce said.

Arkin, Pierce, and Leon looked over at the Aries-Taurus-dyads, who all sat at the same table, except for Pierce and one other Aries-Taurus male who appeared to be flirting with a Scorpio-Sagittarius female, who didn't look the least bit interested in him. Indeed, the Aries-Taurus who looked over at Leon and Arkin still wanted them dead. Either that, or the biggest one at the table wanted to eat them, that's what his stare said.

"That's fine, maybe it's better to get a more diverse team anyway. I have an idea of how we can do so," Arkin suggested.

He immediately stood on top of their table and began speaking for all mixed blood peoples around to hear him.

"I know we all have different cultures and different planets that we hail from. I also know that we all have different thoughts and feelings about living here on Aquarius." His eyes scanned the crowd, trying to make eye contact with all who paid him attention. "Some may be upset about living here, and some others may appreciate the hospitality of the Aquarians. Either way, I feel it's important that we all give each other a chance to get to know one another better. If any of you, from any other planet, or even from planet Aries like me, would like to join us, please come on over. My group would be more than happy to welcome you."

Arkin noticed that a lot of people in the crowd did not even look up at him. He was certain that they could hear him, though, because for the most part, everyone got quiet when he spoke, which was a lot nicer than he would have given them all credit for. It must have been sheer curiosity that made the hundreds of different peoples from different planets give him their attention for that short amount of time. Whatever the case, not a single dyad from any planet made their way to their table.

"Well, it was worth a shot, I suppose," Arkin conceded, stepping down from the top of the table to stand near Pierce and Leon, who were now standing, visibly hurt by the lack of acceptance from his fellow mixed race peoples. "I guess we can still hope that everything goes well with our query as to living in the same dormitory." He gave a weak shrug.

"Indeed, in fact I am going to look into our future living situation right now." Leon hastily walked away.

"He sure is in a hurry," Pierce observed.

"Yes, he probably feels embarrassed by the speech I just made." Arkin dug his toe at the floor.

"I thought your speech was very rousing. If I hadn't already fought you, I would have fought you here and now after hearing you talk."

"That wasn't the goal at all," Arkin replied.

"Either way, good speech." Pierce looked at him with big smile on his face and gave him a hard pat on the back.

"I guess we should just go. I am no longer hungry, and you seemed to have already had your fair share of food. I think we should leave."

"No, I am merely taking a break so I can gorge myself some more." Pierce patted his stomach. "I eat five large meals a day. Perhaps if you ate more like me, you would not have gotten tired so early during our fight." The two sat down so Pierce could finish talking to him.

While Pierce was explaining the finer points of eating extremely large amounts of food daily, two males approached their table. One was a tall, slim, square-faced male and the other was short, stocky, with a rounded face and beady eyes. They both appeared to be Scorpio-Sagittarius from the look of their veins.

All Scorpio-Sagittarius had black veins that stood out against their pale skin, and their blood was said to be poisonous. Rumor had it that they were excellent archers, second only to full-blooded royals in the Sagittarian Royal Army. The tall slim male had long black hair that was slicked back. His hair looked like it naturally went back like that. Whereas the shorter male had a low haircut, and his hair stood up like the stems of a cactus.

"We found your speech to be interesting," the short one said. "My name is Rudolph and his name is Sage. We would like to join your group to get to know you all better." Arkin and Pierce stood up to greet the two Scorpio-Sagittarius.

"Why doesn't Sage just introduce himself?" Arkin stared at the taller man.

"His tongue was cut out for back talking a royal from our home planet Sagittarius. I have grown able to understand him over time, and I will always express his feelings to the best of my abilities to you."

Sage nudged him with his arm.

Rudolph sighed. "I mean, I will try my best to express his thoughts, desires, wishes, and feelings to the best of my abilities to you."

He corrected his sentence appropriately, it seemed, because Sage didn't nudge him anymore.

"Wow, this is getting interesting," Arkin said. "Let's go and meet up with our other friend. We can talk on the way there. Hopefully, he will have some good news for us."

They all walked toward the meet-up spot. The hallway between the dorms and common area was vastly wide, with lots of long windows that took up almost the entirety of the walls, only separated by metal dividers between the windows. In other words, it was another place where the water could easily be seen.

***

"So you're saying that some of the dyads are asking if they can live with each other already, despite the fact that they are from different races. Well, that is what this whole thing is about. Increasing peaceful interactions and fostering friendships among the myriad of peoples. I say let them go for it," King Aquarius proposed enthusiastically. "However, put them in a separate part of the living quarters from the rest of them. It may be for their best interest, anyway. Oh, and please do check on them personally, as often as possible, Stone. I know you do so hate to do things such as this, but I would really appreciate it if you also served as the ambassador of all the dyad people." Aquarius sat leaned back in his throne and eyed the other man, waiting for a response.

"Since when am I the ambassador of the dyads?" the Capricorn-Aquarius man asked.

"Since now. You've always been really good at every task you've been charged with thus far, and now you just have to take an interest in some extra happenings of the dyads. You're already head of dyad management, and you yourself are a dyad. Who better to bond with them? An increase in your responsibility and title will of course mean an increase in your benefits as well, but we will talk about that later. Please report to me regularly. It doesn't have to be every day, or even every other day. I expect you to report to me weekly at least, or more frequently if you have important news on how things are progressing with the special group of friendly dyads, and even with the larger groups who haven't decided to comingle yet."

"Your wish is my command," the dyad man said, and he bowed as unenthusiastically as he possibly could.

"Thank you again, Stone." King Aquarius smiled as he concluded speaking to his dyad management officer, who was now also the ambassador to the dyads, whatever that meant.

Although it couldn't be all that bad, he said there would be benefits involved. Stone didn't care for the way Aquarius made up job titles and responsibilities on the fly.

As soon as Stone reached the amethyst-colored door to his office, he had a visitor.

"Hello, how are you doing? Any word on our living situation and the rooming of multiple races together?" Leon greeted him.

"The king said yes, he even went as far as to say that the whole plan was for you all to join and become fast friends from all over the planets, and room together."

Leon couldn't tell if Stone was being sarcastic or not, because Stone's monotone delivery seemed to be dripping sarcasm to Leon. Leon paused for a moment, unsure of how to react.

"That's good, very good, I'll have to go tell the others," Leon responded.

"One more thing." Stone's voice stopped Leon cold, and he stopped walking and gave Stone his full attention. "He said that you all will have to live in a separate area from the others. He doesn't want anything to happen, and he fears that if you all live in the same living quarters as others who are only of any one type of hybrid, that things may be thrown into a state of discordance. Therefore, in order to avoid any fracas of any sort, you and all your friends will be moved to a different area with no other groups of dyads."

Leon almost got too excited. He wanted to jump for joy. How was it possible that things worked out so perfectly, exactly how he had wanted, without any manipulation or trickery or plotting of any sort?

In order to not arouse suspicion, or jinx the good luck they were having, Leon held all his joy in. Besides, he wasn't generally the type for big, loud, or overly joyous outbursts or celebrations. A lot of his celebrations and his victories were relished in his mind. All that mattered at the moment, though, was for him to tell Arkin and the others the good news.

"Who are these two guys?" Leon asked when he saw Rudolph and Sage waiting with his friends in the hall.

"They joined us right after you walked out. The tall one is Sage and the shorter one is Rudolph," Arkin said.

"Nice to meet you," Rudolph said, and Sage just looked him in his eyes and nodded.

"Why didn't the tall one say anything?" Leon asked Arkin, but stared at Sage.

"The tall guy can't talk. Apparently, he got his tongue cut out by a Sagittarius royal," Arkin answered.

"It was God awful, it was," Rudolph exclaimed, and Sage started to tell the story with his motions while Rudolph verbalized.

"I know it's extremely rude to interrupt, but I would prefer if you told me that story later. I have important news to tell you all. So I spoke with Stone, the Aquarius-Capricorn head of dyad management or whatever they call him, and he said that we can all live together. It worked out so perfectly; in fact, he even said we will be given our own area, so we shouldn't have to worry about anyone meddling in our affairs. He said for us to just pack up our stuff and meet him back at his office."

"Sounds great, I guess we can all meet back here after we get our stuff," Arkin said excitedly.

"Wait, I almost forgot, what happened to Gwen?" Leon asked.

"She never met back up with us." Arkin shrugged lightly.

"Maybe one or two of us could wait for her while the rest of us begin the transition into the new living area," Leon said.

So, Pierce eagerly volunteered to wait with Arkin while Leon and Rudolph and Sage went to gather their belongings.

Not long after the three returned, Sage and Rudolph with deep red bags, and Leon with a long, golden-colored bag.

"All right, I have all my things and so do these two, or so they tell me. She still hasn't shown up yet?"

"No, but it's no big deal. We can just speak with her tomorrow in the common area. I'm sure we will see her there."

"True, there's no need to worry. OK, we will wait here. You and Pierce should get your stuff."

"Are you sure you guys really need to wait here? I'm pretty sure she's not going to show up tonight."

"It doesn't matter. At this point, we might as well wait here, because there's a chance that she might. Not to mention we all need a place to meet up at, anyway, before we go to see that Aquarius-Capricorn guy, Stone, who's going to be showing us to our new room. His office isn't far from here, so it's an ideal location."

Arkin shrugged and left with Pierce to get their belongings. Leon started up some small talk with the two other men.

"So, how are you guys liking it on planet Aquarius so far?"

"It's not bad really, but probably anything is better than living on planet Sagittarius, I think, at least with the way the royals used to treat us."

"Why is it that you had so much contact with the royals of your planet, anyway?"

"Oh, on Sagittarius, the Sagittarius-Scorpio dyads are viewed as assets, vital to military operations. We are naturally good archers, and our bodies produce poison through our saliva, sweat, and blood. Our poison is used for a lot more things that most people would even think. Sometimes the king would even send some the best archers out as his own personal assassins.

"Further, we are forced to try different types of fruits and berries and plants in the wilderness to see if they are poisonous or not, because we are immune to most poisons, and that's just one example of our many functions. And because of that we were basically always surrounded by royals who would talk down to us and do all sorts of other vile things I'd rather not get into.

"So you always had to work directly with the Sagittarian Royal Army all the time?"

"Yes, we actually always took direct orders from high- and even low-ranking royals of the army on a daily basis."

"And yet they were willing to send you off to planet Aquarius? That's fairly interesting. I suppose King Aquarius must be very good at sealing a deal."

Arkin and Pierce were back, each with multiple long red bags in tow, but there was still no sign of Gwen.

"I guess we will just see her tomorrow," Arkin said, swinging a bag of his possessions on both his shoulders at the same time, and Leon simply nodded his head.

The group of five made their way to the office of dyad management to get situated in their new living space.

***

"My king, I have a lot of news for you." Maestro said to Cancer as soon as he saw him on the aqua communicator.

"I'm sure you do. You have yet to fail me, Maestro. Please, tell me everything."

"I've been following the events of rebellion on planet Leo, like you told me to." Maestro paused.

"OK, yes, and--?" the blue king prompted.

"I have been watching an interesting bunch. And from everything I've witnessed, I believe that I know the ones who are the leading this revolt."

"Ha, very good. Keep the information from King Leo for now."

"Of course, do you want me to come back to planet Cancer?" Maestro said, practically leaning into the aqua communicator's screen.

"No, there's no need for you to come back yet. You still have plenty of work to do, but I think I'm actually going to pay Leo a visit personally."

"I'm not sure if that's such a good idea, Your Highness. The revolt has actually gotten so bad that King Leo himself may eventually need to get his hands dirty, at this rate. I hear that even his elder son may have already been caught up in the fighting."

"What do you mean, *hear*? You haven't been watching it yourself, personally?" Cancer was outraged, it was clear from his tone.

"I have been watching the rebel leaders and their transmissions," Maestro restated.

"Good, keep up the good work." Cancer dismissively waved. "That's very good, Maestro, you and Gregorio have done pretty well." He became more serious and looked his henchman in the eye. "Just stay on Leo for the time being. I will make contact with you as soon as I arrive. This may be the opportunity I've been looking for."

Cancer ended the aqua communicator transmission immediately. The watery, mirrorlike display vanished instantly.

If Pisces was telling the truth, which it looks like so far, then I have to capitalize on this event.

King Cancer was the king of information in all twelve of the kingdoms. The most important aspect of having information was knowing how and when to use it, and Cancer was good at that as well.

***

"Sire, we cannot kill everyone who is rebelling. In all honesty, I'm unsure if we are even capable of such an act, even with all your strength. Further, it is the greater portion of the population at this point. If we kill them all, we may put ourselves in a predicament where we are weak against other kingdoms."

Llewellyn was nervous about the entire situation.

"I already know that, but you're leaving me with no choice." Leo growled from his throne to his subordinate. "I told you to find out who specifically incited this rebellion. In fact, I even asked you to look into the situation before it got this bad." Leo clenched his fists angrily. He loosened his hands and calmed down to finish giving his commands. "If we can take out their leaders, we can stop them all."

"I'm not sure it's that simple. This seems to be well thought out, my lord. I have never seen the common folk and the half-beasts work so closely together. I didn't even know they got along so well. We have already lost some of our lions. The pride is being worn thin." The dark brown Leo pleaded with his king, as if asking for another solution or suggestion.

"Then I guess you know what you must do. Your only choice is to find out who is responsible for this. You can't possibly not know anything after all this time, can you? Have they made any demands?"

"They have demanded that we pay for the injustice against Crimson and all other Leos who were carelessly slain or forced into combat in the lion's den."

Leo sighed deeply, his orange sapphire crown leaning as he held his head down briefly.

"I don't care how you do it, but you need to set up communication with one of the leaders of this rebellion. Don't come back until you do," the king said, and he gazed out the window, viewing a fire that was just outside of his forest castle, on the outskirts between the urban area of commoners and his royal area.

Llewellyn knew he was dismissed without his king even saying it, and he left the castle, which was one of the only places left in the kingdom that felt safe.

For the most part, the rebels seem to only be destroying their own property, but they no longer work and they are ruining my chances of getting anything done. I was supposed to have delivered the half-beasts to the Aquarius kingdom by now. King Leo reflected on a few things as he looked out the window. Unsure of whether or not he would even get to celebrate his natal day, which was fast approaching. The fires, while far from his castle, were spreading, many buildings were destroyed. Out his window, it looked like his world was ending.

"You seem worried, my dear friend Leo."

"Cancer, what are you doing here? Why didn't you send a liaison or one of your men? I don't have the time to deal with you right now." Leo glared at him.

"Oh, is that right? I figured, why send one of my men. It has been quite a while since I've been to planet Leo personally. I figured I would check up on you and see how things are going."

"Don't lie to me. Seriously, please get to the point that has brought you here."

"I have information that can assist you in ending the rebellion transpiring on your fair land."

"That figures. What is the catch? What do you want in return, you sniveling little worm? I know how you are you. You never do anything unless it's in your best interest."

Cancer laughed heartily. "I beg to differ! I actually only do things if it's not only in my best interest, but I also consider the interests of my family, my royals, and even my kingdom. After all, I'm not the one who has a rebellion on his hands, so perhaps you are more selfish than I. What do I want in return?" He tapped his chin. "Let's see." He scratched his head. "Let me think. I have a question." He met Leo's gaze and raised his index finger. "How competent would you say that your men are?"

"The men of my pride are second only to me in fighting prowess. I don't mean to brag, but in terms of strength, they are capable of taking out one or two members of the council."

"You truly believe your men are able to take out one of our fellow kings? Impressive, that sounds really good. How about you let me borrow three of your finest?"

"Are you insane? I can't afford to take such a loss to my forces, especially not during this rebellion, that doesn't make any sense." Leo stood up, insulted by the proposition

"Fair enough." Cancer immediately attempted to console him and avoided eye contact by looking away, and moved further from Leo. "OK, I suppose I can take any three of your men that you feel you can spare."

"Why? What game are you playing at with this, Cancer? I know you do so love your games."

"Any games that I play, I play to win, and part of winning is keeping secrets. Obviously, I don't have to tell you anything, including who is responsible for the rebellion or how to stop them."

"How do I even know that you have such privileged information?"

"You don't and you won't until you give me what I want. That's all a part of the game that I'm playing." Cancer laughed as he used Leo's words for his entertainment.

His expression changed in an instant he went back to serious. He glided closer to Leo's throne and continued. "In all seriousness, though, I grow weary of this. Your kingdom will be quite weak by the time this is all over." He stared at Leo. "I hope that you're prepared to face all the ramifications that a decision like letting the great kingdom of Leo fall can have with it. I know I'm prepared to accept the consequences of such a calamity," he concluded with a grin.

"Give me some time." King Leo plopped back in his throne, defeated. "I will need to gather my men to me. Some of them are so loyal I'm sure they would rather die than fight by your side."

"Let's hope that you're wrong about that, but please take all the time in the world. I have nothing but time as of now. In fact, I don't need to be here while you talk to your men, just send them when you're ready. I'll be in my castle."

Cancer disappeared right after he finished his sentence.

Leo, terribly troubled, could think of no other options but to loan out the services of his men to Cancer. *I wonder what he could possibly be up to.* Leo pondered and tried to figure out what he was going to say to his men.

***

"Maestro, I'm pleased to tell you the information that you gave me has already proved invaluable. You and Gregorio always do what you're supposed to do in the most efficient and useful way, and I appreciate that. Now I would like to hear any more details that you may have regarding this rebellion."

"Well, first I want to say welcome to Leo, Master. I hope that your stay so far has been as pleasant as it could be." Maestro bowed deeply. Maestro welcomed Cancer to the temporary headquarters Gregorio and he had set up. Extremely basic, the room was small with only necessities, really: an aqua communicator, food, a few chairs to sit, and two beds.

"Of course, everything is stupendous." Cancer physically stood Maestro up straight, annoyed by his bowing. "Just explain to me everything you know about the rebellion."

"I told you earlier that the commoners and half bloods have been working together, right?"

"Yes, you informed me." Cancer crossed his arms impatiently.

"Yes, but what I didn't tell you yet is that one of the lions pulling the strings behind everything is a half blood named Leon. He was sent away to Aquarius." Maestro smiled, pleased with himself.

"Aquarius? But that doesn't make sense, aren't all the half-blooded lions still on this planet? Speaking of which, did you do as I told you to with our half bloods?"

"I did just as you instructed. And as far as how he's on Aquarius already, I'm not sure how, but perhaps he is from Virgo."

"Hm, OK, that's fine. Please continue with your report."

"Recently, King Leo killed one of the faces of the rebellion personally, with his own hands. A man who was known as Crimson." Maestro pulled up a holographic display of the event to show Cancer. "Once Crimson died, he became a martyr for their cause. He was well liked among both the commoner population and the half bloods of this planet. It is believed that he even had some involvement in the minor revolt during the final Battle of Orion at Bellatrix."

"Very interesting, I wonder if Leo has put any of this together yet. What was his role in the Battle of Orion?" Cancer stared at the frozen image of the red-orange lion, who sported flimsy leather armor, and a look of contempt across his furry face on the holographic display.

"I'm unsure of what role he played there, but I know that recently he banded together with twenty other Leos and started a small uprising. With his death, a surge of believers began to act out against King Leo, their 'unfair and unjust king.' Now the number of commoners involved in the rebellion is said to be in the thousands, not including the people of half blood." Maestro turned off the holographic display.

"Do you know how to stop this revolt?" Cancer gave his subordinate eye contact.

"The way I see it, it could be done one or two different ways—"

"I have an idea," Gregorio interjected.

"OK, speak your mind, young one." Cancer's focus shifted to Gregorio.

"I think we can personally speak with the Leo on Aquarius named Leon, and threaten to expose him to King Aquarius if he doesn't tell his forces to back down."

"No, I don't want to handle it that way." Cancer stood up and took a step to the side. "I want for it to be something more along the lines where I just point Leo in the direction that he wants to go and he goes that way, whether it's right or wrong. That's too hands-on, what you're talking about." He looked at Gregorio briefly to make his point. "Additionally, even if he has been pulling the strings, who knows if it will stop when and where he wants. Once things of this nature get momentum, they usually keep going. I want for there to be a chance for something like this to happen again. Therefore, it's important that the key players on Aquarius aren't made conscious of what we know about them." He took another step to the side. "In fact, I'm not even going to tell Leo. Neither of you tell Leo either." Cancer got eye contact and a nod of the head from both of them.

"Instead, I want for you two to look deeper into the ones who are having direct contact with Leon. Follow them, their every move, and watch them for any weaknesses. I will feed Leo some of the information you discover when he gives me what I want. I need to know more by tomorrow. For now, I will return to Cancer." He turned his back to both of them and faced the entrance. "Contact me only when you have more to tell. Information always gives the upper hand, and I need to keep it over Leo. I'm taking my leave."

"We shall remain vigilant until we reach our goals," Gregorio said excitedly.

Cancer had already disappeared before Gregorio finished his last sentence.

"Sometimes it is tiresome being king," Cancer said as he stretched in the hallway of his modest castle.

His castle wasn't the flashiest of all the kings. In fact, it was probably the least flashy, but it was the most secure. It started with very thick castle walls that were made out of refined polumb mixed with rabidicus. When the two were mixed, they formed some of the toughest, most durable metal in all the kingdoms. That metal gave the castle a simple black exterior.

The castle wasn't that big, either, only about twenty feet tall at the highest point. The top of each part of the three story, three-sectioned castle was shaped like a key with vertical ridges.

The inside was nothing special. It mostly contained paintings, a few permanently fixed holograms of creatures he found interesting, a painted battlefield that spread across the entire floor, and paintings of each one of the twelve kingdoms on each wall in the bedrooms. There was the board game one king left set up on a table in the master quarters, along with a huge bathroom and a large bed with violet sheets, violet blankets, and violet pillows.

"Welcome home, Master. Can I do anything for you?" Adeline greeted him in a violet- colored silk long blouse that stopped just above her knees, her hair in a tight bun, and she bowed deeply.

"Yes, Adeline, please run my bath for me and bring me some of our best Univine. You can have some yourself also. Bring the bottle from Libra, they always have the finest and best aged." Cancer sat on the edge of his bed. Adeline returned quickly with two silver chalices and began pouring him a cup. The red beverage from Libra filled his cup; once it was full, he set it down on a small table near him and disrobed until he only had on his undergarments and a thin shirt.

Cancer relaxed, enjoyed himself, celebrated with his lady servant, but did not take part in her body. He had done so once but it had been quite some time ago. Now wasn't the time. In truth, he missed his wife. Maybe he was being overdramatic; after all, she had only been gone for a few days, which somehow felt like a lifetime. And they both agreed it would be for the best, given all the things that he had been planning and doing. Soon, nowhere would be safe, if everything Pisces was saying was true. He stared at his ceiling while contemplating all the decisions he had made recently and all the things that were happening. Was everything he was doing and planning the actual right thing to do?

He dozed off a little, but only to dream of one of his many conversations with Pisces.

***

"What I'm about to tell you is very important. Everyone, from commoner to king from all over the kingdoms, is in danger. You're the only one who can save us. However, you will have to do some distasteful things to save everyone," Pisces implored him. The dreamscape was simple, nothing but clouds surrounding the silver King Pisces.

"Why should I trust you?" Cancer questioned everything Pisces just said.

"Have I ever lied to you?" Pisces replied.

Cancer gave Pisces a skeptical look; a look that said, that's not a good enough reason.

"OK, how about if I tell you a series of things that are going to happen and will precede all the trouble, and when you see these things happen, you will be able to believe me," Pisces said.

"I'm not really sure. You could still be making those things up to manipulate me," Cancer replied, giving Pisces a cold glare.

"Humor me and hear me out."

"I guess it can't hurt." Cancer shrugged.

"Number one," Pisces began.

"Your Majesty, Your Highness, Master, Master..."

He was suddenly woken up from his sleep. Adeline stared down at him.

"Why have you disturbed my slumber?" he cried, half asleep, rolling over, prepared to go back to sleep.

"Your men said that the Leos have arrived and are ready to take your commands. They are downstairs in the study, waiting for you."

"Have you heard anything from the Aries men that I sent out?" He rubbed his eyes vigorously, still waking up.

"It's been a few days since they last made contact. The last time they did, they left a message saying they were about forty-five percent complete with the list you gave them."

Cancer smiled a winner's smile, became alert and embraced the new day. He got dressed and headed toward his study to meet the Leos. He was a little surprised that King Leo was willing to give up his men before Cancer even began solving his problem. *Leo must really be desperate,* he reasoned to himself as he walked toward his study, mentally preparing for his next move.

***

Croix finally reached the end of the path. He had no idea what the item was capable of, but he imagined it must be powerful for the dragon to want it. All around him was dry sand, plus more sand blowing around as the storm started kicking up again. He was no longer insulated by whatever the dragon had used to protect him.

All that stood before him was more sand, of course, and a large structure that was shaped like a giant square, perfectly even on all sides. There was only one door, dead in the center, or at least from what Croix could tell. There might have been doors on the other sides, but he didn't feel it would be necessary to find out. He didn't think there would be any harm in entering through the front door, otherwise the dragon would have told him, most likely. Then again, he had no real reason to trust the dragon. The whole thing could be a trap. That didn't make much sense, though. The dragon could have easily killed Croix near its lair.

The outside of the giant square was made out of black, moist-looking sand, and was the darkest sand he had ever seen. Overall, it appeared to have the exact same color all the way around. A large shadow, cast at an angle to the right side because of the sun's positioning, gave the square a slightly more intimidating look.

"Here goes nothing." He walked to the black sand door and attempted to open it by simply pushing against it. There was no doorknob or opening mechanism on the door of any sort, so he figured it just required a nudge forward. The door actually opened, to his surprise, and with that he was in. Inside, the square had a really high ceiling, which made sense, given the size of the structure. The walls were a lighter color than the rest of the square, and the entire interior was lighter than the outside of the square. The walls looked as if they were painted a light gold color, as opposed to the mixed colors of sand on the floor. The floor was clean, immaculate, made of solid dark brown, tan, and golden sand the same consistency as rock.

Croix was looking around as he walked, then heard a sudden noise from below him. Catching himself just in time, he barely avoided falling down into a trap floor. Whoever made the trap must have anticipated that the person in this room wouldn't suspect it was there until it was too late. He was starting to form some ideas of why the dragon may have sent him.

In order to avoid unnecessary risk, he figured it would be best to speed through the rest of the cube. He ran lightning fast, past a large statue and then he heard a whistling noise from behind him. It must have been another trap. The cave was set up to keep any and everybody out.

Further in, he saw, off in the distance, a giant axe swinging back and forth.

"I'm not sure if I should try to sprint past it, or time my run just right by watching it, or if I should just run up the wall."

Not wanting to take any chances, he darted back some to get some distance. Then he raced forward to build some momentum, and then bolted across the wall. Finally he took to the ceiling as fast as he could, that way he only had to maneuver around the skinny part from which the pendulum swung. The ceiling around the pendulum was much lower and the hallway containing the pendulum was much narrower than the rest of the square.

As he continued through, he ran back down to the floor again.

He saw a few sets of eyes that glowed yellow as he ran, and figured there were also some monsters that lived here in this cube who were supposed to protect it from intruders. But he didn't need to fight them, nor did he have the desire to, and given their slow reaction time they probably weren't even prepared for him, or sure of what he was.

Croix could see the light at the end of the tunnel. In a few more seconds, he would be at the end of the square and reach his goal.

Suddenly he heard something snap at his feet. He was lucky it didn't trip him, he figured, but then he saw that it was a trap set to throw acid. Thanks to his superior speed and reflexes, he dashed right past it without a drop getting on him.

"Perhaps I should have sprinted faster," he said out loud, dusting himself off.

"I think you ran quite fast enough, after all, you're alive," he heard from an unknown voice.

"Show yourself right now," Croix said, and visually scanned the entire room.

In the large room, there were only four walls, and an opening in the roof to let sunlight in, a display case that held a ring, which must have been the magical item he was sent to fetch, and a few steps that led down to a another area. From one of the four corners, he saw a sand-colored, humanoid-size creature walking toward him. He only realized that's what he was looking at because of the deliberately slow pace of the being. The creature finally showed his true form and appeared out of thin air. He had green scaly skin, wide-set, beady eyes, and a long tail, and he was dressed terribly, wearing a tattered shirt, shorts, and a pair of reading glasses.

"Who are you?" Croix had never seen a humanoid like him before.

"I'm obviously one who is in charge of safeguarding this temple." He took the glasses off and put them in his pocket.

"This is a temple?" Croix looked around the room a bit, expecting to see more signs of religion.

"Yes, it was once a temple of worship for the God of the desert, Sandara, but now it merely holds this ring of might." The lizard man stood near the display case and placed his hand on it.

"What does the ring do?" Croix stared at the display case.

"That's really a complicated question to answer. The ring does different things for different people. It is said to give the wearer a gift that they truly need. If the wearer does not truly need a gift, it gives them what they truly desire. I suppose it's open to your interpretation," he offered with a shrug.

"How does such a ring exist, and who are you guarding it from?"

"It is said that the ring has the very essence of Sandara, the sand god's actual soul, trapped inside of it. I'm unsure of how that's possible or if that's even the case, but it's the only story I have ever heard of it. As far as who I'm guarding it from, I'm guarding it from everyone on Scorpio who wants it. Specifically, anyone who is a Scorpion who wants it."

"Why is that?"

"Long ago, when the ring's power was first discovered, before I was even born, my ancestors held the ring. Word got to the first King Scorpio of the ring's power. He figured even someone as powerful as him could use the ring, so he sought it.

"My ancestors fought him back, as well as they could. He slaughtered many of them in order to get the ring, believing it would give him immortality. Through magic, my ancestors forged this square in order to protect the ring from the former King Scorpio. He sent many of his soldiers here, but all of them failed. It even seemed as if he had given up, but with your arrival, I can see that now the new King Scorpio is after it just like his ancestor was. He was even smart enough to bring in someone from a different world. I'm sure you're not like any of the people of this planet."

"No, I'm not," Croix agreed with a hearty nod for good measure, "but I'm also not here on King Scorpio's behest. I'm actually here for a dragon."

"Dragon? You mean, like a sand dragon?" The temple guardian's eyes widened, and he walked away from the display case.

"Yes, that's exactly it. How did you know?"

"Well, I've had to deal with him personally before, because he wants the ring also. He's just as evil and greedy as Scorpio, in my mind." His face twisted briefly in anger, but he quickly composed himself and hid his rage. "I will most definitely not be letting someone such as you take the ring."

"That may be fine. I don't necessarily need the ring if I can find a way to defeat the dragon."

"What do you mean? I just heard you say that you're working for the dragon." The guardian was truly astonished, and again gave Croix his undivided attention.

"Yes, I am, but only because I don't know how to defeat her." Croix's stare landed on the floor. "You see, I've been dropped off on this planet by my people to bring back the head of the dragon. When I encountered her, I was overwhelmed by her powers and realized she was too much for me. She had me right where she wanted, and said she would kill me if I didn't bring her the ring." He finally looked up.

"Intriguing, if what you say is true, then you and I may have a common interest." The temple guardian began pacing around in a circle around Croix, his green arms folded over each other behind his back.

"Yes, I believe we do. Please tell me, how did you defeat the dragon?"

"I can only tell you that I was able to do it with the help of the ring, and I didn't do a very good job of it, clearly, because he's still around."

"Maybe you did slay the dragon you fought. Isn't there more than one dragon? The dragon I'm talking about is a female. At least I think so, she was watching over some dragon eggs."

"No, it's a male dragon, the females merely lay the eggs. The males guard the eggs and nurture the baby dragons." He stopped pacing and stood in front of Croix, looking about thoughtfully. "I'm not positive that it's the same dragon, but it most likely is, if he wanted the ring of might. I have only run into one dragon that sought it. I feel like the dragon I am speaking of is the same one you were in contact with. A reason for this is that a large portion of sand dragons have gone from this area."

"Why would they have gone, and where to?"

"The desert is vast on this planet. Most likely, they went to other areas that have more resources and more prey, but the dragon who tried to steal the ring may have stayed in the area, waiting for another chance, and then he met you and saw the perfect opportunity." His beady eyes fixed on Croix again.

"I'm telling you, I owe no allegiance to the dragon and would just as soon bring you his head as proof that I killed him, if you help me find a way to eliminate him."

"I suppose it could be beneficial for me to help you. I would rather not fight you if I don't have to. You seem quite capable. You promise that your only goal here is to get the dragon's head?" The lizard man's beady eyes tried to spot a lie or inconsistency in Croix as they bore into him.

"I assure you that is the one and only reason I'm even on this planet."

"Fine, I will let you borrow the ring. I'm sure it will give you more than enough power to defeat the dragon yourself. You already seem quite competent."

He went down the stairs that Croix had noticed earlier, and a few seconds later the glass was lifted from over the ring. Croix walked closer to the display case and stood over the ring. The ring didn't look special at all. It had a gemstone in the middle, but the stone was very dull and a grayish almost black color.

"Go on, I'm giving you permission to wear it." The lizard man gave an affirmative nod.

He put the ring on his right ring finger, and suddenly the ring became an intense bright red, almost as if the ring was burning. Croix's eyes burned with orange-red fire coming out of the corners, and it hurt for a few seconds.

He couldn't see, so he closed his eyes, and when he closed his eyes, he saw images of himself wielding fire from his hands. He saw himself absorbing energy, running so fast that he swore he was faster than his uncle. He opened his eyes, which no longer burned.

"Did you see the vision of your new powers? The ring gives any new wearer visions of their new abilities."

"Yes, I believe I now have all the same powers of my uncle, Aries, and I think I'm faster."

"Aries? Is he one of your kind?

"He is one like me but much stronger than me. Correction, was stronger than me." Croix finished his statement with a smile.

The lizard became grave and straightened his back completely; his eyes began to bore into Croix again. "I know you're excited about the power the ring has given you, but I'm only going to tell you this once. You cannot keep the ring. The ring does not belong to anyone. Power and ambition on the level the ring inspires only leads to bloodshed and heartache. You are to bring the ring back as soon as you're finished killing the dragon."

"I understand," Croix said, smiling and staring at his hands.

"I hope you do. Don't make me regret my decision."

"Don't worry, you won't." Croix looked up, grinning from ear to ear. "I have to go now. I have a dragon to slay," Croix said as he dashed back the way he'd come, twice as fast as when he came in. Croix never felt so alive, he ran so fast it was like teleportation, leaving the temple.

This time I'm going to have the dragon right where I want him.

***

"Are you pleased with the food?" Mar looked up from his plate to ask his lovely companion.

"I sort of always feel like Libran food is overrated," Catalina said. "No, I'm joking, I'm really enjoying it."

Her plate was nearly clean, with only a few crumbs and morsels left over that she most likely wasn't going to eat.

This restaurant enjoyed catering to peoples of all types from all over, because when the royals visited Libra, they all went here. It was one large room with one centralized area. A few doors were located on both of the far ends, which led to restrooms, exits, and areas for workers and staff.

Ordinarily, a royal could request to be served by a commoner or a half blood from their own planet, if they so desired. Given everything that was going on, it was unclear whether that was the case at the time. There was a massive stage at the back end of the restaurant, for performances, some of which were done by half bloods, and some were done by commoners. The walls were multicolored with some parts blue, some parts green, red, yellow, purple, brown, orange, and streaks of white and black. The vast array of colors was designed to make the royals of each kingdom feel at home. For example, red was the color of choice for the Aries side. Of course, nobody was required to sit in the section reserved for their planet's royals.

There were two tables closest to the stage, one to the left of the stage and one to the right of the stage, which had all shades of colors along the walls behind and on the floor below. The left side's colors were arranged in a circle that stretched and curled outward so the floor had all the colors that were in the rest of the restaurant all together, alternating starting with white, red, blue, then green, all the way until black, arranged in lightest to darkest. Not only did the floor have this exact design, but the wall behind the left table did as well. The right table had the same colors in opposite order along the wall and across the floor under the table. The colorful circle on that right side appeared to be curling inward.

The ceiling had two parts. There was a ceiling that most of the tables that the patrons sat under. This roof was high, and had beautiful chandeliers hanging about six feet above each table. The ceiling was about twelve feet higher than all the tables, and had sections painted to correspond to all the kingdoms. For example, the Taurus section had a painting of the king of Taurus painted above it, along with a glistening chain around his neck, which was to represent the riches of Taurus, a planet known for its beautiful trinkets and wealth of diverse stones.

The other part of the ceiling, above the two stage tables, had paintings of all of the kings charging toward combat together at once. Because the two tables had opposing images, it appeared as if the kings were charging into combat to face themselves. The stage was simple, with a holographic monitor at the far back end for watching recorded performances. However, the live entertainment was what really drew the crowds.

On stage was a band. The band was a small group of Libras. The singer was a pink-clad female. A man who played the harp was dressed in dark yellow from head to toe, and the one who played the flute was in rich purple. It was all very harmonious. Mar and his lovely date had the best seat in the house, the table to the left. Sitting at the table to the right were some Gemini royals Mar was unfamiliar with.

"The servant sure is taking a long time to come back," Catalina commented.

"Relax, if anything it's my fault, I told him to take his time coming back, and that we were trying to get to know each other better." He leaned forward, closer to her side of the table. Putting some of his body weight on the white tablecloth as he leaned in toward her. "What do you need?"

"Nothing, I just saw you finished your plate and thought you might be prepared to order some more." Catalina played with some of the leftovers on her plate for a second before looking back at him.

"Very considerate of you, but I have had my fill, and shall not eat anymore here." He sat back in his seat and slouched a little. "Although I could go for dessert. I just want to sit here and take in the ambiance. I do enjoy the music that the Librans play. Also, the painting above us intrigues me."

"Oh, you don't say. Why is that?" she asked, turning her attention to the painting above them.

"It's just…it's just that it seems interesting that all the kings are in the image together rather than Libra deciding to pick himself or one king to take center stage in the painting. They all appear with equal positioning. I can't say I feel it's an accurate depiction. What would you say?" His eyes dropped from the ceiling and landed back on her.

"I'm unsure of whether they are equal, but I know that some kings scare me more than some of the others," Catalina remarked, bringing her eyes to meet his gaze.

"Do tell."

"Take, for example, King Scorpio. I heard that he has such an intense stare that it's filled with poison, along with his tail for that matter. I even heard that his arms were chopped off before, only for him to grow new ones immediately."

"I do hear that Scorpio is quite formidable," Mar said lightly. "But I'm sure that his stare is not filled with poison. That sounds like a baseless rumor." He smiled.

She laughed. "I'm sure you're right, most likely it comes from a silly story a commoner exaggerated, which made its way to one of our servants and got to my ears somehow. Most of my bedtime stories were told by our servants, come to think of it. I mostly had commoner servants until I became older and started having half bloods as servants, well, that is, until now, at this time, with the bulk of the half bloods having been shipped away to Aquarius. What do you make of them all being on one planet?"

"I'm unsure if it's a good idea, but hopefully they do well there. If I'm being honest, I don't blame them for trying to kill my father and the other kings. It's not always particularly nice, the way they are treated. However, I personally feel better with them not being on Aries. They are a force to be reckoned with and may surprise people someday if they ever mount a more successful rebellion. How about you? What is your take on them?"

"I feel they are traitorous and deserve to die. I guess that's not practical, however, and not all of them were involved with the rebellion. I hope that the responsible parties all suffer, at least." She finished her statement, hiding her anger from her tone as much as possible.

"I'm not so sure that they have or will. The rebellion going on right now on planet Leo may very well be tied with the past rebellion on Bellatrix." Mar shrugged and glanced into his glass briefly.

"One thing is for certain, I'm glad we aren't caught up in that," she said as a relief.

Chapter 7

Fire was spread throughout the gravelly streets of Leo. Llewellyn wasn't sure whether he should give up for the night or continue to pursue the rebels. The ones he was after were a particularly fearsome bunch. He had already killed three of them, after they ambushed him. They retreated, but he wasn't sure if it was a trap. It was odd, despite the fact that so much was going on, the area that Llewellyn was in was quiet, too quiet.

The fire did not scare him. However, he was not immune to it. He heard rumors that his King was, but he was sure that he wasn't. Walking down an alley he was sure some rebels would pass, he stopped and looked for a place to hide in order to pounce on them, once they let their guard down. Off to the side of the alley, there was a large, navy-blue trash sorter machine. He decided to hide behind it after he saw a flicker of torches that indicated rebels passing.

Without warning, he felt something hot and sharp slide into his side. Someone had stabbed him. It was then that he saw about twenty rebel lions, most with torches, rushing toward him, along with four Leo-Virgo half-beasts. He was stunned for a moment. Then he struck backward, hoping to hit whoever stabbed him, only for him to feel the knife slip in and out on his other side. He was briefly overwhelmed by the horror of the situation.

Finally, he regained his senses and delivered a spinning elbow to the backstabber with all his might. His great strength smashed the head of his attacker wide open with the one blow, leaving the half-beast dead.

"Come on, I'll take on all of you," he yelled at the oncoming crowd.

The lions rushed at him, about half from the front, four or five from the side, and some began flanking him. He tried to focus on the ones who were flanking him first, because he could hear them moving the fastest toward him to attack.

Swinging, he scratched one with his paw. With that strike, he snapped that one's neck causing his opponent's eyes to go dim. Then he picked up another of them and flung him as far and hard as he could. Even with his impressive combat prowess and power, he could not take on twenty-four lions at one time. Whether they were commoners or not.

That's when he felt the familiar hot, sharp, intense pain in his side again. He immediately turned around to face the one who did it and snapped his neck. Then he felt a flurry of sharp claws that struck him from all sides. It felt like a thousand claws were striking him all at once.

None of this would have happened if he hadn't lost two of his companions, both killed earlier by the rebels. This was the worst battle he had ever been in. Disheartened for a moment, he thought briefly of his fallen comrades, and let all the claws fall on him. He snapped out of it quickly, however, and threw all his attackers off him at once.

"You will have to try harder than that. Don't you realize this is an elite you're dealing with? I'm part of the royal pride," he roared and took a loose battle stance. "Also, just so you know, the knives to the back don't bother me, but the cowardice angers me. The next one of you cowards who attempts to stab me will be have the honor of dying the most painful and slowest death." There were only twenty-one lions left to deal with. Unsure if he was even going to make it out of alive, he resolved to try.

Today, if he died, it was going to be a glorious death with a high body count. Laughing, he braced himself for his attackers. Today he was alive.

All the remaining Leos charged at him again.

***

Callum sat in the grass near where Valera's ship had taken off, still excited about what had just happened. What were the chances that he, a commoner from Capricorn, would get the chance to meet a royal, personally, even get to talk to her, a Virgo at that, the queen of Virgo, even?

He was ecstatic. Never had he thought of himself as a lucky person, but he thought that maybe, just maybe, his luck was turning around and that things were going to start going in his favor. It would be very fortunate if that were the case. After all, he wanted a lot.

It was often said that on Pisces an item existed that could bring back the dead. This meant a lot to Callum, because his old man, his father who actually raised him, not the king (his supposed father), had died in one of the battles in which even commoners were forced to fight. It was so long ago, Callum could barely remember it, and it wasn't really a big deal to the king or the people of the planet, so nobody ever really talked about it.

Not only that, but his little sister was gone, kidnapped, it was believed that she was dead. Commoners sometimes committed terrible crimes against other people without status. Capricorn wasn't an especially poor planet, but it wasn't as rich as some of the other ones.

The king didn't take big risks very often. Capricorn only believed in the safe bet. Therefore, it was always slow expansion of the kingdom. Which is why the planet had a lot of areas with wild beasts and other nondomestic portions. It could also have been that Capricorn favored nature somewhat.

Callum jumped up, startled, as he noticed some men of the Capricorn Royal Cavalry approaching. He wasn't sure what they wanted, since the area he was in wasn't all that special, so he became curious. He wasn't the only person in the area though; there were a lot of women, children, and older Capricorns around. Perhaps the common people of the area needed to be addressed for some reason. There were only about three of the Calvary men, which seemed strange because the Cavalry was supposed to be the largest group of royals of all the twelve kingdoms. Apparently, they didn't need any more than three men for this assignment, whatever it was.

The royal men wore selindium armor, which was a very tough and durable substance that was mined near the center of Capricorn. The selindium was not only tough but was also beautiful; it was silver in color but much shinier than normal silver, it also had traces of gold running through it in the form of little gold flakes scattered unevenly on the breastplate.

One of the men, the only one of the three who was on a horse, had the most beautiful armor of the group. His armor shined and glistened as if all the sunlight was directed at him. He was on a fire horse. The breed of horse was found only on Aries and was said to be the fastest breed of all the twelve kingdoms, so some royals from each planet generally had at least one or two.

The fire horse that he rode had crimson-red skin and a black mane; it was a big horse. It seemed to be twice the size of a regular horse from Capricorn, to Callum's eyes.

One of the three men was tall with sandy brown hair, a square-cut jaw, handsome, with a thin moustache, and light-brown skin. Another of the men was a little darker with jet-black hair, tall as well but shorter than the other Capricorn who was on foot like him, and a clean-shaven face. The one on the horse had a rectangular face, golden hair, golden eyes, a defined, slightly pointed chin, and a sturdy jawline.

The Capricorn on the horse began speaking.

"I am here before you today, people of common blood, to offer a great opportunity. My father, your great lord of this planet and kingdom, has decreed that the Capricorn Royal Cavalry begin enlisting the help of common folk such as yourselves. You can work your way up the ranks and may even someday become an honorary member of the royal family. Tell me, does honor await any of you?" The young man spoke in the most inviting tone he could, smiling, with his right hand extended in a downward angle after his speech.

The crowd didn't seem like the best venue for the prince to make his speech, as a lot of people in the crowd were either women, too young, or too small. Callum was the only person in the whole group excited about the opportunity. In reality, to say he was excited would be an understatement. He felt as though his heart would burst through his chest he was so anxious. For a moment or two he was speechless.

The prince was a handsome man, much better looking than his father. His golden hair seemed to glow in the light. It was long, not extremely long, but longer than the way most Capricorn men wore it. It went down to his shoulders and seemed to have no split ends or tangles.

Callum looked up at the people nearby who were not even remotely interested in this opportunity. Most of them just looked up at the man on the horse and kept walking. Some were scurrying away and moving on with their lives.

One balding, gray-colored older male spoke up. He was standing up perfectly straight in his worn out navy-blue one piece. He was partially covered in sweat and dirt, as was his clothing.

"Why do you want us to go join you? So we can be fodder and forced to fight first, just like the half bloods? Move up the ranks? What a bunch of hogwash. I don't believe a word you're saying, and any man that does is a fool."

"Do you call me liar?" The prince returned the man's gaze equally.

"You are never to speak to the prince like that!" The taller royal on foot closed some distance between himself and the old man. "You are lucky to be alive even now. The very fact that he has not struck you down is a testimony to the fact that he is merciful."

"Thank you for your mercy, oh, gracious prince," the older man said and even added a bow mockingly. Glaring at the prince still.

The clean-shaven royal, the one who hadn't yet spoken, drew his sword, and moved toward the old man.

The prince got off his horse and physically stopped him.

"No, let him say whatever he wants. All people are entitled to their own opinions, whether we agree with them or not."

"But, my prince, his insolence should not be tolerated. Respect should always be shown to royals from everyone, at all times. If others see or hear this, they may get bad ideas." He tightened his grip on his sword.

"I'm telling you that it's OK to let it go for now. We are out for recruitment. Unnecessary bloodshed is not what my father wants."

The royal sheathed his sword and turned to the old man and lightened his tone just a bit. "Go on about your day."

The old man stared at the royal who had drawn his sword for a little while, but eventually just walked away.

"I think we can all agree this was a waste of time," the tall one said. "We should get out of here my lord."

"Wait, I want to join!" Callum finally spoke up, causing them to turn back around.

"You want to join our ranks and become a member of the Capricorn Royal Cavalry, do you?" the prince asked in a lighthearted tone.

Callum nodded his head.

"Splendid choice, my friend," the prince said with a friendly laugh. "What is your name?"

"My name is Callum, and I am one of the toughest men I know."

"Very impressive," the prince said ambiguously with an incomprehensible smile. "I assure you that you will receive proper training in order to become the best asset to our planet as you can possibly be. My name is Cicero, this is Caleb"—he pointed to the man who drew his sword earlier—"and this is Cassius." He pointed to the taller Capricorn. "It is nice to meet you. May I ask, how long ago did you come into being?"

"You mean how old am I?"

"Yes."

"I am sixteen years old."

"I think he's too young," Cassius whispered in the prince's ear immediately.

"Nonsense, it's going to be fine. A year younger than that and I would agree with you, but he's at the perfect age. Callum, my dear boy, I would like to start you with our training program as soon as possible. Feel free to go to your residence and collect your belongings. My men here will escort you to your place and then back to mine. Take your time."

Callum was excited. This was the opportunity that he had been waiting for his entire life. He had to tell his mom about how fortunate he was on this blessed day. Not only had he met a queen, but he also was recruited into the Capricorn Royal Cavalry. He was convinced that none of this was a coincidence. This had to be fate.

The prince got back on his horse and looked to his men.

"Wait for the boy to gather his belongings and bring him back to the palace when he's finished. I grow weary, and I'm heading back."

He rode off, not the least bit thrilled. He was sure that his dad was doing this as a safety precaution in order to prevent rebellion on Capricorn or any other large-scale calamities from happening. All the kings were worried about similar things happening to their kingdoms as what was happening on Leo.

Capricorn's plan to prevent rebellion was to give the commoners a higher stake in the kingdom, or at least allow them to feel more important so that they themselves would quell a rebellion among their own fellow commoners. In fact, he was hoping that the commoners he allowed to join his cavalry would nip a rebellion in the bud before it even became anything noteworthy.

It was his way of feeling safe. Also, he was going to send away his half bloods. To hell with what Pisces had told him. At least that's what he told his eldest son Cicero. Cicero had all these things on his mind as he rode back for home and wondered for a second what his sister was up to.

He did so despise those Aries. He felt that they were too arrogant and self-centered. It didn't matter to him that it would be good for the kingdom to unify the two. He still didn't like the idea of having one of them as his future brother-in-law. The ride home wasn't long, but with all the thinking he did, it wasn't enjoyable.

***

Valera hovered over Pisces, a very beautiful planet made of eighty-five percent water and blue all the way around. She intentionally landed somewhere not as obvious as the capital in the kingdom. After all, she wasn't sure if she wanted King Pisces to know that she was there, but if he was as good as people said he was, he would have known she was coming a long time ago.

She landed in a grass field not far from an area that had various open huts where people appeared to be trading goods and wares. Some of the other Pisces had tables with a large variety of items ranging from foods, jewelry, animals, and everything else in between.

Apparently, the area she landed in was run by merchants, and it had consumers from all the twelve. Luckily, she didn't see too many Virgo customers. She was certain that the majority of these people buying goods on this planet were royals. The others were probably all royal servants who were acquiring items for their masters.

The servants were varied. Some kingdoms used commoner servants and others had half-blood servants still, even after the vast majority of half bloods were supposed to have been moved to Aquarius. In particular, she felt as though she saw a lot of Taurus, Gemini, and Sagittarius half bloods.

She saw various trinkets with signage that read Only Available on Pisces, and a variety of animals.

One of the animals was a two-headed, three-eyed, multicolored bird. The bird's fourth eye was sealed shut. Caught in all the excitement and hustle and bustle of the multiracial environment, she almost felt like she was spinning. There was so much motion, so much going on. For a second, she even lost her balance. An older, bearded Piscean man caught her.

"My dear, please do not fall. Try your best to not get lost in all this energy, it can be quite overwhelming," he said to her.

The bluish-silver-colored Piscean man was dressed in a semiexpensive sea-green robe that covered his entire body, but he had his sleeves rolled up for some reason, which revealed the two fish birthmarks, one per arm. And he had a see-through cane, which he leaned on while holding Valera's weight until she regained her composure.

The robe had a hood that covered the entirety of the top of his head and hair. His ears were not even visible. All Valera could see was his beard, nose, and mouth. His nose was longer than most and stuck out like a bone. His lips were small and chapped. His beard big and bulky. In other words, he wasn't pleasant to look at.

She looked at the cane for a moment, it seemed different, not like a normal cane. Thoughts of touching the cane ran through her head.

"Perhaps it is true," he began.

"Perhaps what is true?"

"That Virgos think a lot more than they speak, and keep the greater portion of their thoughts to themselves," the old man speculated.

Queen Virgo chuckled, dusted herself off, and stood a little straighter. Finally she felt a bit more comfortable, recovering fully from her fall, realizing that she had been analyzing the man the whole time without saying a single word.

She extended her hand toward him. "I apologize, my name is—"

"I know full well what your name is, Valera." He took off his hood, revealing his smooth, but dull head and silver eyes. "Some think that the king is the only one on this planet capable of seeing the future, but I assure you just as sure as I stand here before you today, that is not true. Many on my planet have similar gifts, but some of these gifts come with a price. Did you know that Pisces is said to be the most magical planet of all the twelve? Of course there is magic on all the other planets, but it is said that an abundance of magical energy is focused here on Pisces. In fact, it is said that much of the magical items and creatures of this planet have yet to be discovered."

She put her hand away. "Thank you for that information, but what does that have to do with—"

"You have come here for a tour, correct? Seeking knowledge of this planet, as you are on a quest to learn more about all the twelve in person. Am I not correct?"

"Yes, and how did you—"

"I have already told you that I can see things that most cannot see." He cut her off again, somewhat curtly. "My name is Pascal, it is a pleasure to make your acquaintance, Queen Valera of Virgo." He gave her a quick bow.

She looked at him, unsure of what to say.

"I think we should get out of this marketplace and go somewhere more private, so I can tell you a thing or two that may be helpful to you in your travels. Wouldn't you agree? Can't have Cancer spies watching our every move. I won't allow it." He was already moving before he finished his last statement.

Being that Cancers could be everywhere and nowhere, Valera began to wonder if Cancer spies had seen her on Capricorn earlier, or if they would report it back to anyone from Virgo. The chances were slim, she rationalized, because it wasn't scintillating information. Even if her journey was to be discovered, she would not be punished. She just knew that a servant would be sent to watch over her and escort her the rest of the way, and she didn't want that. Her journey so far was going exactly the way she wanted.

Pascal led her through the crowds of people and the marketplace to a set of brown stairs that lead down to a sea-green door.

"After you, my lady," he said as he gestured with an open hand for her to go ahead of him into the door.

The thought crossed her mind to not trust the man at all. Part of it was because she couldn't read his mind. She hadn't met a ton of Pisceans, but she was sure that most she had met had open minds for her to read, but this man must have had a mental wall of some sort keeping her out of his head. He was old and feebler than most men, even by Piscean standards, so she figured she didn't have anything to worry about. Her powers would be enough to take him out if the need arose.

She looked back up at him as he descended the stairs behind her, and it looked like he wanted to say something, but he closed his mouth instead. The brown stone stairs were longer than she expected, so it felt like a while before she reached the bottom.

She reached for the door and tried the knob; it was unlocked. She turned the silver knob and pushed it open. *Cccrreeeaaakkk.*

The room was filled with dust. This probably meant nobody came in the room that often. Not even the old man.

"Please have a seat," the man said to her. "I am going to tell you your future, or at least some of it," he said with a light smile.

Valera didn't want to sit because the mauve table was extremely dusty and dirty. She quickly changed her mind, however, figuring this would be one of the things on her journey that was going to help her build character. Being a good queen meant that sometimes, she would have to make hard decisions and do things she didn't want to do. *This is one of those times,* she thought to herself as she reluctantly sat down.

"I apologize for the mess. Give me a second and I will clean the table. Stand up for a moment, please."

Right after she had just sat, too. Maybe it was her fault for sitting too early, but he had asked for her to have a seat. Sitting in a little dirt for a couple of seconds surely couldn't hurt. There would come a time in the future where she would need to do things such as sit at dirty tables to speak with common folk, or at least she figured that would be the case. In fact, it wasn't a big deal at all, considering where she came from. Perhaps she had gotten too used to being queen and had already forgotten what being a commoner was like.

Pascal simply used a washcloth and some water from a bucket that was right next to him. Valera felt that neither the washcloth nor bucket of water had been there the entire time, but it didn't matter, even if it was magic, it wasn't anything special.

"Please sit down again. I'm sorry you sat at the table when it was all dusty and dirty, that was my fault for asking you prematurely. A thousand pardons, my queen," he said with a slight bow.

He then sat down himself, opposite of her, and stared at her. "Let's get started. Please hand me that deck of cards next to you."

Again, Valera felt that the item in use, this time the cards, hadn't always been there. However, it could have been that she was too focused on watching him. She still didn't trust him.

"What sort of cards are these?" She frowned, looking at the large cards before she picked them up and handed them to him.

"They are special cards that look into the past, present, and future of one's life. However, it requires a certain special sort of…touch," he said as he paused to look her in her eyes. "This is the reason why you could look at the cards personally and not see a thing. With me here, you should be able to see everything you need to see and much more."

He shuffled the cards rapidly. It was as if his fingers were dexterous creatures with minds of their own, far younger than the rest of the man's body. He finished shuffling the cards and handed them to her. "Now you do the same."

She shuffled the cards much more slowly than he had. She wasn't accustomed to cards.

"Don't worry about shuffling the same way I did. You can simply move cards about the deck in whatever way you find is easiest for you. It's more important that you don't look at any of the cards yet, and that you move the cards around so that no card is in the same place as it was when I handed you the deck. Try your best to touch every card, not looking at any of them and moving them over at least one card space," he said to really drive the point home.

She took her time, no longer in a rush, and slowly shuffled the cards, mostly by cutting them, and moving them to different spots in the deck at random. The cards were very large, so it wasn't always easy to move them and not look. But she knew that he must have given her that advice for a reason, and so she continued to move the cards around, trying to focus on the multitude of colors on the back to distract her from her urge to look. The cards were quite colorful. She recognized many of the colors on the back of the cards and figured they must symbolize the various royal houses of the twelve kingdoms.

After quite a while of her slow shuffle, Pascal eventually said, "Stop: that should be sufficient enough. Now both of our energies are mixed into these cards temporarily. Please hand back the deck. Clear your mind as best as you can. I am going to hand you exactly nine cards. Do not do anything with the cards yet, until I say so. I will also have nine cards."

Valera was extremely nervous.

"Don't worry, this will be painless, I promise," he said with a big toothy smile. He began setting cards for himself and passing some to her side of the table. It was the first time Valera had seen him smile genuinely, and it made her a little calmer, despite his lack of a few teeth.

"Let the time-traveling adventures begin," he said jokingly with a smirk, as he began the ritual with her.

"OK, what I want you to do is, without looking, pull the first card that is on top of your deck and place it directly in the spot farthest to the left in front of you."

There were nine yellow imprints on the table that were aligned from left to right. They were aligned so that five imprints were up and four were down. The arrangement went one up, next one down, then the next one was up again. All the upward imprints were parallel to one another, the downward imprints were also parallel to one another. This was the design for the side of the table that Valera sat on. As far as she could tell, the other side of the table had nine yellow imprints as well, but they were all in even positions, none were lower or higher.

Valera did as instructed and put the topmost card from her deck into the left yellow imprint. It was Aries. The card was red on both the front and back and had black letters that simply said *Aries*. The center of the card had a yellow frame that surrounded a portrait of King Aries, who appeared to be running through space, as there was nothing but stars and him in his portrait.

"OK, you have Aries in the upward position."

"What does that mean?"

"Hold on, patience, my dear." He set his hand out toward her as if to calm her even as he stared at his side of the table. "It doesn't mean anything until I put my card in the spot that corresponds with it." His hand lowered.

He pulled his leftmost card, which was also Aries, and he placed it in the slot parallel to hers.

"Very interesting. The Aries in this position on both sides means that you will be experiencing a first that will be very important in your life really soon. Your first will be pioneering and will likely be a first for others, too. I'm guessing it will have something to do with the kings because you are royalty."

"Is there any more detail you can give me than that?"

"Not just yet, we have to keep going with this for a little while. I may have a better understanding of what your situation is later, but these readings take time, and we must continue. Now, please pull the very next card in your deck, again without looking, and place it in the lower spot right next to the card you just set down."

Valera followed his instructions. This time it was Taurus. The card was silver on both the front and the back, but again, had the same yellow trim around the center portrait and had only one word written toward the bottom under the picture of King Taurus, who was standing on a mountain of gold. The word was *Taurus*, written in black letters.

Pascal then pulled his parallel card that was in equal position to her Taurus card. The card he laid down was Sagittarius. The card had a well-built Sagittarian stallion. The man was shirtless with a black lower body juxtaposed against his fair upper body, and he had his bow and arrow pointed with a target in his sights. It was a light blue card on the front and the back, and in black letters toward the bottom, it simply read *Sagittarius*.

"This is a good combination. The two together mean good luck and an abundance of opportunities for you. Since the Taurus is in the downward position, it means that there will be a small window of time for you to capitalize on these opportunities. However, the Sagittarius should mean long lasting good luck for you."

"Is this giving you a better picture of my entire future?"

"Yes, it is"—again he raised his hand toward her as if to stop her from asking questions—"but I still need to see more."

"Is this the same way that King Pisces's powers work?" She ignored the raised hand.

After a time, he lowered his hand and considered the question thoughtfully, playing with cards on the table they weren't going to use. "No, he has no need for any items such as these, but I do, and most likely any others who predict the future who aren't the king himself or from his bloodline do, too." Returning to business, he sat back straight in his chair. "Now, please pull your next card."

This time she pulled the Capricorn in the upward position. The card was dark green on the front and back, and had a gray-skinned Capricorn male standing atop a mountain, looking out at the horizon seemingly to greater heights. In black letters toward the bottom the card read, *Capricorn.*

He then pulled his card, which was a Virgo. Brown on the front, brown on the back, the Virgo card had the image of King Virgo standing steady on green grass with layers of brown earth visible below.

"Very good, this should be good for you. This means that you shall make a friend for life not long from now. The Virgo, as in the card on my side, can be taken literally here, as in you are the Virgo, and in this case the Capricorn represents friendship, a lifelong bond of friendship and this will be in the near future."

"Friends for life, that's interesting. How do you get that from those two cards together? I usually prefer to be alone." Valera looked down at the floor.

"Virgo and Capricorn are both alike in many ways. The two signs are compatible, but these two cards in this position doesn't imply a sexual relationship but rather one of friendship. Capricorns being steadfast in their decisions including whom they make friends with can be counted as life-long friends once they decide to become that. And as far as you enjoying to be alone, everybody feels that way until they find somebody who truly understands them. Let's move on to the next card."

She drew her next card and placed it to the right in the downward slot next to her Capricorn card.

This time it was Leo. Leo had an orange-red hue on the back and front of the card. Same as the other cards, it said *Leo* in black letters and had a picture of the powerful king, but he had no background or border around him like the other kings. His card merely had a portrait of him, as if he was larger than life itself.

He drew his next card and placed it in his slot. It was also Leo.

"That's not really that good," he uttered, slowly staring at the card he just laid down.

"What does it mean?" She hung on the edge of her seat, waiting for an answer.

"Whenever two Leos are pulled from both decks at the same time, regardless of position, it always means war," he said plainly. "In this case, it most likely means a battle or battles because your Leo is in the downward position."

"Who is going to war? Does this mean that I will have a direct influence in this war?" Valera asked.

"No, that can't be what it means." He looked up calmly and caught her gaze. "You are a royal lady, a queen at that, and being involved in war is not what ladies do. I am sure it merely means that your husband, the king will be involved in the war.

"I want you to relax." He breathed in deeply to signal for her to do the same. "Remain calm, the cards that I described to you earlier and told you to take literally, you should take literally, but this one you just pulled doesn't need to be interpreted literally. It makes perfect sense for your husband to be in a battle or two, doesn't it? The twelve kings have to protect all the rest of us, so it should not be uncommon to see something such as that in the cards. Let's move on to the next card. At least let me finish before you get irate," he said half-jokingly.

Again he repeated the instructions to her for the pulling of the card. This time it was Pisces.

He pulled a Pisces as well. The card was sea green on the front and back, yellow trim around the edges, and had a portrait of King Pisces standing on a brilliant white surface on his right side, this side of his face was also illuminated. On his left side, he stood in darkness, and his face was shrouded and obscure. It was hard to make out his features on the left side.

"OK, well, this one is an interesting combination." He folded his hands together and stared at the cards.

"How's that?" Valera was curious, but decided to wait for his explanation.

"The two of these together represent death," he said emotionlessly, still looking at his cards.

"Death?" She quickly stood up, bumped into the table and nearly knocked everything over.

Pascal held the table in place, so nothing moved. "Well, not death in that sense, I'm sorry to have startled you." He gave a smile with his apology and held out his hand to gesture for her to sit back down. "I mean, death in the sense that a great sacrifice was made. The two of them here represent the past, so a past sacrifice was said to have gotten you to where you are now." He paused. "One decision or one life road being chosen means the death of all alternate roads." He looked away for a second.

She slowly sat back down. Grave, but silent and calm. "Is that right?" She analyzed him again briefly, but continued speaking shortly after, mostly recomposed. "I suppose my mother and family did sacrifice a lot for me to be where I am now. Also, the king was willing to sacrifice the continuation of the bloodline with a traditional royal, and chose to be with me." She finally shifted her gaze from him to the cards before her.

"What do you mean by that?" Seemingly shocked for once, he finally looked up from his cards.

"I was sure that everybody already knew this. Oh yes, I forgot, you're not a royal. Perhaps this isn't common knowledge, but I'm not from a royal bloodline. I was born a commoner but because there were no female royals suitable for the current king to marry, he searched all over Virgo for a mate and found me the only one worthy, in his opinion, of course."

"I'm pleased that you felt comfortable enough to share that information with me. I feel a little bit privileged now. Thank you for that. Let's move onto the next card."

"OK, before we do that, I just want to make sure that I'm understanding you clearly." She lightly tapped the mauve table. Waiting for his eye contact. "You're saying that the two Pisces together means that there was a sacrifice made in the past? It has nothing to do with the future or present even, and certainly nothing to do with death. Right?" She paused, her stare and tone very pointed.

"Yes, that's exactly what I'm saying. Don't you remember?" He smiled. "I told you that these cards tell the past, present, and future. Some of these cards have to tell the past. Now, are you ready to go to the next card?"

She pulled her next card without responding directly to his question. This time it was Scorpio. Scorpio was on a card that was icy blue on the back and a realistic sand brown on the front. The sand looked and felt real, like it was fresh from the desert. This card had a bright red frame. *Scorpio* was written in black letters at the bottom of the card, just like all the other cards. The portrait was of a male Scorpio stinging a small creature in the desert. His card was Libra. He more or less dismissed his card, by saying it merely amplifies the nature of the card she had pulled from her hand in that position.

"Very good, that's the summer Scorpio. There are actually two or three different Scorpio cards. In fact, there are multiple iterations of most images. Some even have portraits of queens. Oddly enough, yours have been all male, not only male, but all kings. The Scorpio you just pulled symbolizes victory over a great challenge."

"Great, the cards are working in my favor again." She clapped her hands together.

"Yes, indeed. OK, now for the last three cards, I need you to do this differently," he pointed to the main deck. "Instead of pulling one at a time, I want you to keep your eyes closed"—he demonstrated by closing his eyes and pulling three random cards from the deck himself and placing them face down in three slots—"and pull three cards from this deck. However, I don't want them to all be from the top of the deck. Instead, pick three cards from random spots throughout the deck."

Valera followed his instructions.

"Keep your eyes closed. The next thing I want you to do is flip over your three remaining cards, one by one. Don't open your eyes until I tell you to. Just so you know these cards represent past, present, future from left to right in that order. OK, please begin turning over your cards."

One by one, she slowly began rolling her cards over. And sat there waiting for his signal.

"Open your eyes." Around the same time as she opened her eyes, he flicked over all his cards at once.

This last time the cards were vastly different from anything she had seen before. All three new cards were planets. Not a single one of her last cards was a king or any other royalty.

"Why are the cards planets now?"

"The last three cards are supposed to be planets."

"That's so strange. Do you have planets as well?"

"No, my cards are actually minor royals." He quickly dismissed his cards. "Mine actually aren't even important for this. Mine just correspond to the planets you have." He stood and leaned toward her side of the table. "Now, let's see, so you have Aquarius, that's very good, it means progress. Unfortunately, it's in the past position, so it may just mean that you have progressed a lot before you got here, but it also could mean that you are progressing, and will continue to progress. The Aquarius card revealed here usually means a long-lasting effect.

"And in general, the card that is in the past position has a continuing effect, otherwise it wouldn't be all that useful." He smirked. "In the present, it seems that you have Libra. Libra is very good for the present." His smirk became a full-blown smile as he continued. "It means that currently you are at peace. You're fulfilled emotionally, mentally, and physically, and you're at balance." He nodded his head to himself, still staring at the card. "The problem with the present is"—his smile lightened a bit as he continued—"that it could mean literally the present, as in it doesn't have to last for very long. The present can mean this very moment only, it could mean now all the way until a week later. Overall, it is the most fleeting of all the cards and has the shortest-lived effect."

He moved on quickly. "Lastly, we have the planet of Aries. Aries is known to be a fiery planet, and as such, it means that you're going to go through some fires, as in trials and tribulations, but you will be able to overcome them just like the Aries are able to withstand and even welcome the fire to their bodies. If you put all these things together, then you're in a very good position, young lady. A lot of things are going to be coming your way. You have to try your best to seize all the opportunities that come to you and not compromise on your goals. Whatever they may be." He offered the last part with a shrug.

"Don't compromise on my goals?" She said the statement out loud as if a question.

"Yes, stay committed, stay positive, and do what you feel is right in your heart." He moved from her side of the table back to his own.

"You got all of that last part from reading the cards, too?" Skepticism was written on her face.

"Yes, of course. I haven't made up anything I have said to you at all." His expression said he was offended. "What kind of seer would I be if I had?"

Valera was still unconvinced. Something he'd said toward the end was so generic it made her question the entire reading. She sat there, brow furrowed, thinking back to everything that he had said that she could remember. It wasn't that the last comment sounded like bad advice, or even that Pascal had said something wrong. It was the fact that he said it so casually and pretended as though it was psychic advice, when it was more so just a friendly thing to say, in her opinion, much less personal than the rest of the reading. For some reason, she couldn't shake the feeling that he was lying about something else, too.

I haven't made up anything I have said to you at all. That was a strange sentence.

"I understand that you may not be happy with all the results of this reading here today. However, there is nothing I can do." He unrolled his sleeves quickly and hid his hands inside them and crossed his hands in front of him "I merely interpret what the cards are trying to tell you."

"Yes, I understand, there are no problems," she said, but her tone said that she wasn't sure whether she was trying to convince him or herself.

"I appreciate the time that you have spent with me here." In an instant, he picked up all his cards from their slots, shuffled them, and placed them back on the table.

"I enjoyed it, too. I did not expect to spend all of my time on Pisces getting my fortune told, but it was quite interesting, and I appreciate your efforts." She stood up.

"The pleasure was all mine. I am going to say this to you as lightly as I can. I have not seen a queen with such grace and beauty as you in all the kingdoms." He bowed before her slightly. "I feel like you will only grow more beautiful with age. In fact, I can guarantee that you will without even looking at the cards."

She laughed modestly at his comment.

"Shall I walk you to your ship?"

"No, I couldn't trouble you further. I believe I remember how to get back from here. I appreciate all that you have done," she said.

"I insist, my lady."

"Well, if you insist, then I suppose I have no choice."

Pascal locked up his shop, and they walked back through the marketplace to her ship.

"Are you sure that you need to leave? Pisces is beautiful during the summer. I can show you around more," he offered with a sweeping gesture.

"Actually, I've seen quite a lot through your card reading. I have to go now. I actually hadn't figured I would have stayed here this long."

"In that case, I'm glad I got to spend all of your time on Pisces with you. Farewell, it's been a pleasure."

Pascal turned away from her and walked off before he even saw if she entered her ship or not.

She was slightly confused after her encounter with him. Something didn't seem right, but she didn't want to pursue it further, and she didn't feel comfortable anymore on Pisces, so she got on her ship and headed off.

***

Pascal was finally in a safe, secure location, and the time was right. The aqua-blue room was simple, only containing a kitchen to prepare food, a bed to sleep on, a closet, clothes, a mirror, and an aqua communicator. He took out the fake eye that he had in his right eye socket. His king had made the fake eye that was painstakingly detailed. Unfortunately, Pascal couldn't see a thing out of the eye so it really was just a part of his disguise. He also removed the beard, the fake nose, and some of the old skin that he wore as part of the disguise and took his hood down. Finally, he could relax and get comfortable. He began to contact his king through the communicator, but as if King Pisces knew that Pim was done with the deception, a bird showed up, a small raven, and began speaking to him.

"Master, I see that you have chosen a lowly life-form as means to communicate again rather than seeing me personally." Pim looked at the bird and didn't try to hide his disappointment.

"You and I both know that I don't have time to see you right now, Pim. On to the matter at hand, did you meet her?"

"Oh, yes, and she was just as beautiful and naïve as you said she would be." Pim stroked at the air as it were her face.

"How did the reading go? Did you learn anything about her that we didn't already know?"

"Yes, I learned a few things. Namely, that you were right, she's not of royal blood, but rather she's a commoner who exhibited useful abilities to King Virgo."

"Fascinating. Spare me any additional details for now, if there are any. We will talk further in person. I do have to ask now, however, if you took all the proper precautions I told you to?"

"Yes, I left out a lot of important details from her reading, and I even wore the disguise you told me to wear."

"Very good." The raven seemed to smile. "A job well done indeed. I hope you also told her your name is Pascal, Pim."

"Of course, Your Highness. I put on a full show"—he bowed like an actor on stage poised to receive applause—"just as you told me to." He straightened back up. "Shall I return to your side now?"

"No, I have another thing that I need you to do for me. If you complete this next task just as well as you completed the last one, then

I shall prepare something special for you. Good work deserves a reward. I will have something for you when you get here. Do not disappoint me."

The bird flew away immediately.

***

Virgo was getting frustrated with his servant. "I don't care what King Leo is saying. I need commoners and half bloods from Leo for my experiments. Do you not work under me as my servant? Am I not ruler of this planet?"

"Of course, my lord, but with the rebellion—"

"I have finally begun seeing useful results and learning useful facts, reaching a pivotal point in my research. And I'm not about to let you, or King Leo, or anyone else ruin that!" King Virgo yelled at one of his royal servants, who immediately scampered away.

"Good help is so hard to find." He shook his head, physically pained from the conversation. "I work tirelessly day and night, trying to unlock the mysteries of life, and the imbeciles I am surrounded by can't do something as simple as procure the things that I need. Good thing I had Aries and Cancers retrieve everything else I needed, otherwise it would have been impossible to have even made it this far.

"Bring in some commoners from Aries," he demanded while standing over one of his silver worktables.

A member of the Virgo royal guard, Vernon, an overly strapping male especially by Virgo standards, brought in both a male and a female Aries specimen. The two people were shaking, trembling with fear in their leather restraints.

Virgo had an insincere smile on his face. "Don't worry, I'm not going to hurt you." He leaned in, his face close to theirs. "I just wish to see something. This is a simple experiment. I have only had one or two deaths so far, and they all pertained directly to King Scorpio's blood. I'm not going to use his blood on either of you two, so this should go just fine. Please remain calm."

He then began staring them in the eyes one by one until they were both unconscious.

"Wow, I didn't know you could do that, master."

"Of course. I usually don't have to because the specimens are supposed to be given a sedative before they get to me. But I imagine your oversight had some logic behind it. Perhaps you wanted to see how I would handle two conscious, scared subjects. I assure you that if it happens again next time. I will be showing you personally what I am capable of, and I won't be merely putting you to sleep."

"Understood, sire, my apologies." To show remorse his servant bowed his head low and gazed at the floor.

Virgo picked up a scalpel and continued talking. "Don't apologize, just bring me my tools. Bring in some Gemini samples: the king's own blood, the blood of the royals, and the blood of some of the commoners. Be extremely careful with bringing the king's blood here." Eye contact really drove his point home.

"I had to obtain that during combat, just like all the other kings', and it's invaluable to me. Needless to say, I would like for you to be careful with the other two specimens, but they are more easily replaced. In fact, I would like for you to bring over the blood samples one at a time, while I prep the subjects. After you have retrieved them, place them in this machine."

He indicated a shiny, silver machine that had slots to hold up to six blood samples.

"Understood, sir," Vernon said before shuffling to retrieve the samples.

Vernon looked similar to his cousin, King Virgo, save for he was much taller and sturdier and a little less handsome. Of course, on Virgo, being sturdy didn't matter much. King Virgo's most able man had always been Vernon. One born with blood ties close to his own. As far as he understood, Vernon was his only first cousin. It bothered Virgo that Vernon wasn't as capable and powerful as he was. Not because he wanted Vernon to be his equal, but because it didn't make sense to him. The king's wife had been born under relatively similar circumstances to him, but he didn't understand why that made her almost as powerful as him.

He had thought originally it was all about bloodlines, and birth facts were only somewhat important, things such as how the planets were aligned at the time, and things of that nature. However, the way he saw it, apparently the circumstances for the birth must be very important since his wife, the queen, had no royal ancestors that he knew of, and yet was so powerful. It made him wonder if all the royalty, kings and queens, were just constructs created by those in power, held to keep commoners from realizing their true potential. Perhaps not, though. All things considered, royalty had to mean something. Valera was probably just an odd fluke of nature.

He had never heard of a nonroyal being powerful except for his wife, so maybe there were just special circumstances behind her own birth and powers. He found himself yearning to experiment on her, but it was a shameful thing for him to do. In all honesty, he didn't even feel it would be wise to experiment on any other royals directly. No, he would have to be happy with the blood samples. For now, it was the best that he could do.

He was so lost in thought that he forgot he was supposed to be prepping the unconscious Aries specimens. He decided to begin with the female, because she was lighter and easier to lift. Using his mind, he set up an operating bed for her. Then he picked her up telekinetically.

"No," he suddenly said aloud to himself. "I have to remember to be physical sometimes, I don't want to end up like my father."

Rather than picking up the woman with his mind and setting her in the bed, he went over to her and lifted her up. She was a little bit heavy, especially because she was unconscious, but he was up to the task. He hoisted her body over his shoulder and carried her over to the operating bed. He strapped her in at the waist and around both wrists and around the feet. Next, he strapped in her head and her neck. The restraints were made of powerful leather. For a moment, the thought crossed his head to lift the male and place him in his operating bed. Tempting as the thought of more strenuous physical exercise was, he decided against it. Manual labor was never really his thing. He just did not want for his body to become useless and atrophy from him using his mind for everything, but at the same time, he did not need to do back-breaking physical work to keep his body active.

He lifted the young Aries male with his mind and put him on his operating bed and restrained him as he had the female. The beds were cold and made of steel, so it was probably quite uncomfortable. Luckily for the patients, they were both unconscious.

He had to make this experiment successful. If he could, it would mean great things for everyone in all twelve of the kingdoms. It would be beneficial for all, from commoner, to hybrid, even to the royals. Experimenting on commoners was not a thing he was proud of, but it was only a means to an end. He had no intent on doing any unnecessary harm to anyone.

He thought on what his experiment could achieve for a moment, until he remembered that he still didn't have his Gemini blood yet, and the thought of waiting longer made him upset.

"Vernon, I understand that I told you to be careful, but please don't keep me waiting forever," he yelled toward the door of his lab.

Vernon finally walked into his sight with the first vial. He was walking very slowly. It annoyed the king for a moment as he watched him walk so slowly it was almost like he wasn't moving. *Tiptoeing has never made any act safer*, he thought as he saw Vernon begin tiptoeing even.

He simply rolled his eyes, feeling that showing Vernon the error of his ways might lead to more severe mistakes. If Vernon could safely deliver the vials, albeit while walking in such a ridiculous manner, why should he stop him? Quite a bit of time went by, and Vernon finally reached the machine to place the vial in it. He then hastily headed back toward the area where the rest of the blood samples were kept.

At least he walked fast when he was not carrying the blood samples. Vernon repeated the same process for the next vial. Virgo reasoned that the two he just delivered must have been royal blood, and blood of the king of Gemini. Virgo thought for a moment; and was sad that he hadn't been able to collect the blood of the queen of Gemini. He was further saddened by the fact that he hadn't been able to collect the blood of any of the queens. The opportunity simply never presented itself. No matter, he had female royal blood from all the different races, and that would have to suffice. The thought did irk him a tad, though, because he was not going to be able to see the fundamental differences between the queens and the standard female royals. He got lost in his thoughts long enough for Vernon to actually finish delivering the vials to his machine.

"About time," he said. "I can finally begin to bring my work to new levels. The two subjects before me will thank me some day."

Chapter 8

Croix made it out of the temple where the ring was hidden, but he had lost his place. Even though his speed had more than doubled, it still didn't help him. He could zoom around the desert all he wanted, but for some reason he was having a hard time finding where he had left the dragon. A moment of inspiration caused him to remember about the life detector machine and how it was really the only reason he was able to find the dragon in the first place. One or two options were available to him. He could continue to search for the dragon, or he could find the life detector machine first and look for the dragon from there. The ubiquitous sand storm surrounding him didn't help him make heads or tails of his location in the desert. *It's a wonder anybody can ever find their way around here,* Croix thought.

"I wonder why the dragon got rid of the trail that led directly to the front of the temple," he actually pondered out loud.

It was foolish for him to have relied so heavily on the dragon. He should have mapped out his escape when he entered and plotted a way back to the lair so he could've easily remembered. It was his original goal to kill the dragon in the first place, so he should have created a way back for himself. Clearly, he had lost sight of his goal, even if only for a little while, but it didn't matter how long it was. What did matter, was that it was a mistake.

"Maybe some new power I just gained from the ring can help me find the dragon," he said. "There has to be something I can do that will help. Come to think of it, I'm not entirely sure how to use the powers of the ring anyway. I always knew how to run, so becoming faster was easy to get used to, but how am I supposed to use fire, or absorb energy?"

He brought his mind back to the images he saw of himself using the ring. In one of the images, he had his right palm extended and fire was coming out of his hand. Imitating that image he extended his right palm. Nothing happened.

"OK, maybe I have to think about fire or something."

He thought of fire and all its beauty. He had the image of Ava dancing around the orange-red fire stuck in his head for a second. Still nothing happened.

"I still don't get it. In the vision I had of myself earlier in the temple, it looked like this," he said as he closed his eyes, held out his hand, and focused on the image of him wielding fire.

He heard the sound of flames nearby. Immediately, he opened his eyes and saw a white-blue jet shooting from his hands.

When he got adjusted to the sight of flames coming from his hand, he realized that some sand around and under him was melting and becoming glass, and he wasn't even aiming directly in any particular direction.

"Now I know how to use continuous flames, but I wonder how I project fireballs. I hear my uncle can throw fireballs from his hands."

He closed his eyes and repeated a similar process to the flame stream and he was able to bring forth fireballs from his hands. He opened his eyes and watched as his fireballs flew through the air, creating small glass shards and glass balls as they flew.

"This is really cool. I wonder if I ever run out of energy," he said.

"I see that you have you have been successful in retrieving the ring," a familiar voice intruded upon his mind.

The sand dragon had finally returned out of nowhere, as it were.

Can he read everything I'm thinking, or just thoughts I project? Croix wasn't sure. He wasn't even sure where the dragon was. *He could be right next to me or a mile away.*

Buying himself some time was the only logical option he felt he had at that moment, so he decided to delay the dragon and try to think of a plan.

"I met an interesting person in the temple," he said, responding verbally as opposed to using thought. "He said he fought and defeated you in the past. How interesting, and here I thought you were such a powerful creature."

That's it, if he could just make the dragon angry, the dragon would possibly make a mistake that would leave him wide open for Croix to attack, or at the very least give up his location. And if he spoke out loud, that would probably keep the dragon out of his head.

"You truly are a fool if you believe that I couldn't have easily destroyed him. He got lucky and put the ring on before I finished him off, and with it, he expelled me from the temple and banished me. All it did was increase my resolve for finding the ring. I needed someone fast and foolish enough to retrieve it for me, and with great luck, I found you. I have tried to have others fetch me the ring, but they all have failed before you. Most impressive. You can die knowing that you accomplished something that many before you were incapable of doing."

The dragon still intended to kill him, of course. It was all a lie about letting him live and helping Croix accomplish his task, but Croix was not about to take the dragon's treachery lying down. He was going to make him pay for betraying him. Plus, he was supposed to bring his head back, anyway, and he promised the man in the temple that he would in exchange for use of the ring.

"Goodbye, fool," the dragon said.

Croix began to float against his own will, and before he knew it, he was in a sand tornado.

"I could just crush you, but I'd rather kill you by dehydrating your body slowly in this sand tornado. There is so much sand around you that it will get into your pores and into your mouth and all through you. Especially at the speed it's traveling."

The sand was everywhere and was everything and it was moving so fast. Sand enveloped Croix's entire body, running into his nose, maybe even getting into his brain.

In an act of desperation, he began using his flamethrower technique, but it was no use. The sand tornado was infinite, and to make matters worse, now it had glass shards floating around, grazing Croix's flesh. Maybe he truly was going to die here. No, he couldn't give up that easy.

He continued using the flamethrower technique, and for a second, the sand cleared up in front of him and formed a solid glass wall that was encased in sand. In that short moment, he saw a large body of sand moving up and down. The dragon was laughing. Croix finally had an idea of where the dragon was. So he put his flamethrower on again, and while the sand was becoming glass, he shot a fireball through the glass in the dragon's direction. Instantly, the tornado stopped, and he saw a glass tail and a glass lower belly of a large creature. He was finally getting a glimpse of the dragon's body. Croix fell to the ground, no longer trapped.

"Insolent fool, you will pay."

Croix, no longer caught in the sand storm, sprinted toward the sand dragon's tail. As he ran, the sand all around him kicked up in the air, and multiple small sand tornadoes popped up around and behind him.

He ignored all of it and closed the distance within a second. He began walking toward the dragon, who must have been stunned by how close he was to him, and he threw another fireball. This one hit the dragon in his stomach, making even more of his body glass.

The earth trembled below him, and suddenly he was in the clutches of a giant hand made of sand, it clenched him tight. He could barely breathe, but immediately he started a flame stream from his hand that caused the hand to turn into glass.

"You should already be dead!" the dragon roared in anger.

Croix shot another fireball with his right hand, which was still free; this one revealed the dragon's chest and neck. At this point, the dragon was mostly glass. No longer was he able to blend in with the sand. Croix melted the glass hand that held him.

"I guess it's actually your turn to die." Croix smiled artfully at the dragon. It was the wittiest thing that came to mind at the time.

He unleashed one final fireball at the dragon just as two giant slabs of sand surrounded him, about to smash him. The final fireball revealed the dragon's head, and at this point the entire body of the dragon was glass, save for a few of his spots in between his belly and chest. The dragon was frozen with a shocked expression on its face. He was a giant glass statue.

"That looks very interesting, actually. Maybe I should bring the whole body with me," Croix joked to himself.

He was unsure how to disconnect the glass head of the dragon from the rest of its body, so he decided to melt off the parts he didn't need. It seemed like a real waste to destroy the entire glass body, so he began to separate it at the neck.

The glass head of the dragon fell off after he blew flames on the neck for a little while. For the most part, the body was still intact. It even looked more fascinating because there were some grains of sand that weren't quite melted that were mixed in the glass on the head and throughout the body. It may have been because he did a rush job killing the dragon and because the fireballs he sent were spotty, unlike the flame stream.

He still felt great and had a ton of energy, so he imagined that using his new powers in the future wouldn't leave him feeling fatigued. The ring seemed to be the best thing to ever happen to him. He was so excited about his new powers that he forgot that he promised to bring the ring back to the lizard man in the temple. Now, the only problem was finding all his tools and his old campsite and where Eames and the other recruits were. Figuring the coolest idea would be to make everything glass, he sprinted, jumped, and began turning the desert into a glass path he could slide on as he glided through. After some time, he found his life detector device and eventually saw the cave where the scorpions lived. From there, he was able to plot his way back to his tent.

"I have defeated the dragon and am ready to go back to Aries," he said confidently to Eames from his side of the mobile communicator. Mobile communicators were mini aqua communicators, you could still see the face of the person you were talking to but you couldn't travel through to the other side.

"Wow, already? That was fast, a lot faster than I thought it would be. Impressive. I will be there to pick you up shortly,"

The other recruits were still working on the task, Eames told him when he picked him up.

Eames and Croix went straight to the brotherhood house, so that from there Eames could verify that Croix did everything properly. Eames merely looked at the head to verify that it was a sand dragon and then he gave it right back to Croix. He felt it was weird that it was a glass head, but he believed the story that Croix made up as to why it was glass as opposed to simply sand. Croix made up something about the dragon trying to use a certain magic against him, but it backfiring because of Croix's speed, causing the beast to get frozen solid in glass.

"Please enjoy some free time to yourself. You will not be able to move onto the next task until the other two recruits are finished," Eames said after he accepted Croix's story and departed. As soon as Croix was free he knew exactly where he wanted to spend his free time. So he headed directly to Ava's place.

"Back so soon? Have you already completed all of your tasks and became a man of the brotherhood?" Ava asked when she answered the front door.

"Can I come in?" He smiled big at her. Her statement revealed that she knew about the trials.

"Yes, of course," she said, turning her back to him, walking past the simply furnished living room and dining room, straight to the kitchen. "Would you like something to drink?"

"No, I don't imagine I'll be staying long. I just wanted to show you this." He went right back out the door to bring the glass head into the kitchen.

"Whoa, what is that?" Her eyes got big. She stared at the glass.

"It's the head of a sand dragon." Croix placed the glass head on a marble counter in her kitchen and leaned on it with a smirk.

"Why is it so glassy?" Ava reached her hand out to touch it.

"It's my secret, I will tell you one day after I win you over."

"What makes you so certain that you will ever win me over?" she asked playfully, finally meeting his gaze and looking away from the dragon's head.

"I think I have what it takes and I'm willing to try, so I believe it will happen. How am I doing so far?" He winked.

She laughed. "You are a fascinating man." She was smiling broadly at this point. "I find it rather strange that you thought it was a good seduction tactic to bring me a glass dragon head. I will give you one point for shocking me. And I will give you a point for amazing me. I have heard it is quite difficult to slay any dragon, let alone a sand dragon, and you seem to have done so in a short period of time."

The smile vanished quickly from her face, in an instant she turned serious. "However, I want you to know that the other points won't be so easily obtained. I'm sure the thought must have crossed your mind that shocking and amazing me was related to the tasks the brotherhood have given you to fulfill. But I assure you it's not going to be as simple as you completing the goals they set for you, and then showing me proof that you accomplished the goals, and I then become yours. That's not how you get a woman to fall for you. But no worries, I'm sure you will figure something out. You seem resourceful. Good job this time. I am truly impressed. I'm happy for you. I'm sure you left a good impression in the minds of the brotherhood recruiters."

"Thank you, I do love praise. I will continue to accomplish the goals that the brotherhood sets for me, and I hope that you will appreciate my efforts, but if you don't, I am willing to try to figure out other methods. As you have said before, I am resourceful." He stood up straight and gave her a light smile.

Ava could tell that Croix was finally warming up to the idea of winning her heart. She hadn't expected him to even come back, let alone to try to impress her. It made her a little bit happy, simply for the fact that his attitude changed.

Croix himself also felt happy because he had made big progress as a recruit, and because he felt he made good progress with this woman.

"If you don't mind, my lady, I think I'll be going. I'm sorry to have come to you so early with no notice."

"It's OK, I suppose it shows that you were thinking of me." She shrugged.

He was walking out, and then she cleared her throat. "Ahem, please take the dragon's head with you," she said, pointing at it.

He laughed. Yes, OK, I'm sorry about that."

He picked up the head and left her house. He had to celebrate his good victory. It was too bad his father was away on business. He was sure his father would be at least a little bit impressed by his son killing the creature. His father had most likely destroyed beasts far mightier than the dragon, but he would have still been proud of his son. It would have been nice to at least have gotten to show the head to his mother. *Oh well, they'll get to see it when they return.* At least he could relax, because he had the mansion all to himself.

***

"I wish the rebellion on Leo was laid to rest already, so I could show you the lion's den, where they fight to the death." Mar's eyes lit up as he spoke of the lion's den. And he was ready to leave Libra at once to go there.

"No thank you, I have never cared for the thought of seeing Leos fight to the death, commoner or not." She frowned.

"Does your morality hold you back? I hear King Leo only has criminals fight in the arena. There is even potential for them to be pardoned of their crimes if they can defeat one of the royal pride. However, it seems not a single commoner has won freedom even once yet, or so I'm told."

"I suppose it doesn't matter anyway," the prince said, changing the subject, adding a smile for good measure. "Where would you like to go?"

"How about Taurus? I have never been, and I hear it's full of treasure." Catalina's eyes glowed with excitement at the thought.

"Taurus is horrible this season," Mar blatantly lied.

He couldn't afford to risk it. It was likely he would run into Diantha. The princess was involved enough that she would greet practically everyone who came to the Taurus royal palace.

"I think Gemini would be a wonderful place." Mar sat up when he made the suggestion. "They have wonders not seen on any of the other planets there that I can show you. My father gets along well with King Gemini, so I'm sure we will be shown great hospitality as well."

"Fair enough, I haven't been to Gemini in many seasons, since I was a little girl, actually. I barely remember the place, come to think of it."

Mar felt great having the situation resolved, he sat there for a moment, thinking about how clever he was, smiling to himself. He had easily talked his way out of a disaster.

"I have to go to the ladies' room."

Mar simply nodded at his date, still reveling in his easy sidestep of an incident. The waiter finally arrived to take their empty plates. This waiter was different from the one from earlier. Mar was pretty sure without even looking up at him.

He rarely gave much notice to the help, and this time was no different. But somehow, he still noticed the stark difference in voice between the one from earlier and the waiter at his table now. They had to be two different people.

The waiter said something about taking their plates and asked if they were done, but there was something strange about it.

Something seemed harsh and abrasive about the current waiter's voice. Further, it had a slightly mocking undertone to it, almost as if the waiter would burst out into laughter after humiliating Mar. It didn't matter. His gaze was focused on the stage, a new show was about to begin. He had already left the money on the table, so he had no further need to give any attention to the waiter. He left a tip large enough to compensate the band and kitchen staff. It was what was expected of royalty. Especially the prince. All the trays were gone, all that was left were the half-full glasses and something else. Out of the corner of his eye, he saw something that seemed out of place, something new.

He finally looked down at the table and noticed a black, unopened envelope with fancy white writing sitting there. He was going to call someone over to ask about it, but before he could, he noticed it had his name written on it.

To be exact, it actually read: "To the Prince of Aries, Young Prince Mar." He could not recall telling anyone in advance that he would be visiting Libra. He hadn't even known himself not so long ago. It was really a spur of the moment sort of thing. He could feel his stomach churn a little. This wasn't good. His instinct was telling him that. He wasn't even sure if he wanted to read the letter, but he knew he had to. He figured he didn't want Catalina to see the letter, so he began watching his back to be prepared for her return. As soon as he looked up, she was on her way and was even close to the table. He barely had time to shove the letter in his pocket at the last minute before she got back.

"What was that?" she asked, standing near her white vinyl seat for a moment.

"Oh, it's nothing, a letter of gratitude for my father from the king of Libra himself." Mar gave the best smile he could.

"I have never known King Libra to do such a thing, that's very nice." She finally sat down. "I'm not sure I understand why he didn't simply tell your father thanks in person, though, instead."

"Yes, well, he's a busy man, I'm sure. Much too busy to make a trip to Aries." His eyes darted around the restaurant, looking for the waiter or some sort of clue. But he couldn't even remember what the man looked like. He quickly gave up his visual search and looked back at her. "And he must have felt so indebted to my father that he felt the compulsion to write this letter, even if it's something he normally doesn't do." He told his lie with a nervous laugh.

"Are you OK?" she asked, giving even more attention to him.

"Yes, no problem. I just want to get out of here."

Maybe he was overreacting. He should try his best to remain calm, he thought to himself.

He was unsure of whether or not it was time to panic, but he was sure that he wanted to get out of there. He had to get out of there. It was certain that Gemini would host better experiences for him, and he would read the letter once he got the chance. If there was nothing to it, or it turned out to be something small or good even, then it wouldn't hurt to read the letter later. And if it was in fact something bad, he would be better off not reading it right away, he reasoned. Especially when it could very well be something he didn't want Catalina to know.

"Let's take our leave before they attempt a grand gesture or begin giving gifts for me to bring back home." Mar stood up and waited for her. However, he did momentarily contemplate making up a lie for his date and trying to find the waiter immediately. But he would look foolish if he was worried about a letter he had not even read yet. He would have to look into it later.

"OK." Catalina got out of her seat slowly.

The two made their way back to the lightning ship and their escort, and began heading to Gemini.

Maybe it was all in his head. He stared out at the black night sky and the bright stars quietly. There was still a chance that the letter contained good news. A flashback suddenly came to him of his father, from his childhood. Mar made a lot of mistakes as a child, as any child is prone to, but interestingly enough, his father did not always punish him, but would sometimes force him to deal with the consequences all by himself. This made Mar somewhat independent, and was one of the customs Aries royals traditionally kept with their young ones so they learned directly from their actions.

Life was far better at punishing than any person could ever be. After he made a particular mistake, which oddly enough, he couldn't remember at the moment what the mistake was, but he did remember what his dad told him after. His father sat him down and pointed at Mar's stomach. "Gut instinct is even more important than the thoughts in your head." He gently tapped Mar's head. Then he grabbed his son's belly. "Your gut is closer to your soul and can tell you things that your conscious won't ever know." Thinking of that only made him all the more sure that the letter was bad, and that he couldn't let anyone see it. The ominous feeling he had in his gut spoke volumes. It was too bad he hadn't paid more attention to who the waiter was.

"What are you thinking about? You're acting differently than you were on Libra." Catalina's full attention was directed toward Mar.

"I'm fine, I just was thinking of something my father told me as a young boy, some advice he gave me." Mar finally lifted his eyes from the night sky to meet hers.

"Oh, OK, wisdom. I love wisdom. Do you mind sharing?" She smiled.

"My father would always talk to me about the importance of trusting your gut instinct, and would say that your instincts know more than your conscious mind does sometimes, about certain situations."

"Wow, fascinating, that's interesting. I've never heard that before, but that makes sense, we all have our instincts for a reason." She nodded her head in agreement at the advice.

Shortly after, she grew silent, which was good, he could finish thinking about what he needed to do. If he could track the waiter down, then the waiter would probably be able to tell him who wrote the letter. The thought had crossed his mind on Libra, but he did not want to cause a scene or worry his date. Additionally, he had let too much time pass from when the waiter walked away from his table to when he actually noticed the letter.

This made him think of another clue that the letter was bad news. The waiter had put it on the table after he took their plates. He hadn't noticed the letter until right after Catalina left. It could not have been a coincidence. Whoever took the plates did not want Catalina to know about the letter.

"Mar, Mar? Are you listening?" Mar was so lost in thought that he hadn't realized that Catalina had started talking to him again. "We are here at Gemini."

"Ahh, about time," he said to Catalina with a forced smile.

He looked out of his window, and saw large buildings and structures of various sizes that were juxtaposed against a vast forest. This was the kingdom of Gemini. The king loved the urban look against the background of nature.

"I know I asked this before, but are you absolutely sure you are all right? I really do feel like you have been acting strange since the restaurant." Her concern and attention were once again focused on him.

"Yes, yes, I'm fine. I just came to something of a revelation."

"Would you care to share it with me?" She wrapped an arm around one of his and paused, stared at him, and waited for eye contact.

Mar looked at her, unsure of what to say, but luckily for him the twins Grinald and Grendel, who served as the hands of the king of Gemini, met them right at their ship and interrupted their conversation. The twins' yellow skin shined in the sunlight.

"Right this way. King Gemini would like to see you," Grinald said with a bow.

"He's very pleased that you have decided to come and visit," Grendel said with a bow.

"You're just in time for dessert. The queen will be there as well," both of the twins said in unison, raising from their bows.

They made their way to one of the castles of King Gemini. He had two, which were exact opposites in color and appearance. He claimed that one was impenetrable and designed for holding off any enemy forces, and the other was practically impenetrable, but also had a few advantages that the other castle didn't have. Gemini never cared to divulge the differences between the two castles with anyone. They were "military secrets."

The main castle was pearl-colored, massive, and had at least forty windows for the forty bedrooms, and had towers that came to spiky points on the top.

The king of Gemini was always as hospitable as possible, especially to Mar since Aries was a lifelong friend of his, so he would meet with Mar personally whenever he stopped by Gemini, and this time was no different. The plan would be to enjoy some dessert and sometime during, slip away and read the letter. That would certainly work. Off in a daze, his mind continued going over who could have written the letter.

On autopilot, he greeted the king and his wife.

Gemini's wife, Queen Gemini, was a caramel-complexioned, beautiful woman who wore her jade crown at all times. She had silver hair and a thin yet attractive frame.

The castle was the same one that Mar had been to a lot as a child. His father would often take him there, because the two kings were close, and he wanted Mar to be close with King Gemini. Mar had practically grown up with Gemini's twin daughters, who were not there at the current feast, for some reason. Perhaps they were being courted, just as he was courting Capricorn's daughter. Whatever the case, he decided not to ask. If Gemini wanted him to know, he would bring it up. He didn't have long to ponder to himself before his thoughts got interrupted.

"Mar, please tell the beautiful young lady about your first time seeing the battlefield," King Gemini said as he put his silver chalice of Univine down on the emerald table.

"You have seen combat before?" Catalina queried with shock in her tone.

"No, not officially." He looked up from his food. "My father's friend here likes to jest and make fun of me. I know the story he is talking about. I suppose it can't hurt to tell you."

"That hurts, dear Mar, I thought we were family," Gemini said, pretending to catch an arrow in the heart.

Everybody at the table laughed.

Mar leaned toward the middle of the table. "OK, before I start this story, I want you all to keep in mind that I was only ten years old at the time. I had just discovered my powers a few days before, and I wanted to show off. I wanted to make my father proud of me. I figured I would hunt something, some sort of creature, nothing too extravagant, just an animal I could bring home before my father and show him, like, 'Look, I killed this.'

"I didn't want to get lost, so I went to one of the only areas I knew that I could walk to and from easily, the oceanfront near the castle. A lot of fire horses from Aries would drink water at this particular oceanfront. It must have been because our castle was near there, and my father's men most likely would let their horses out to drink. Anyway, so I get it in my head that I'm going to kill one and bring back the body to my father to impress him.

"Being young at the time, I did not know that almost everything is immune to fire on Aries. Also, I was unaware of the fact that fire horses are the fastest creatures on the planet, aside from royalty. Back to the story: so I saw a pack of them there by the water. I thought about what was the best way to get one cornered and by itself. I wasn't sure if I wanted to contend with all of them at once. After observing for a little while, I noticed that one was drinking by itself. It was a little smaller than the rest of them, so I figured that would be the one.

"I came up behind it." He lowered his voice and leaned in even closer to the center of the table, ducking his head as if he was sneaking up on the horse at that very moment. "I got real close to it and bam! Threw a fireball in its face while it was still drinking the water. The horse didn't even flinch, it didn't react at all at first. At this point in time, I realized my fire was ineffective. Not long after, the small one made a loud neighing sound, and another much larger horse, most likely its mother, ran over and began neighing as well, then the bigger horse got up on its two front hooves and—Mar raised his hands over his head like they were hooves—"I don't know if I froze up because I was scared, or if something was wrong with me, or if I even knew how dangerous it was, but the next thing I knew, I heard a whooshing noise. I had been saved by my father. And I was picked up and brought back to the castle just before the horse's hooves came down on me. My dad was never a man of many words. I was still worried he was going to yell at me, or worse. I wasn't sure if he was really angry with me or not."

"He didn't seem upset at all, though. He sat me down, looked me in my eyes, and talked to me. 'I'm not sure what you were planning, but if it was to kill one of those fire horses, that certainly isn't the way to do it. You must never hesitate when you make a decision like the one you just made. You cannot back down or change your mind when your enemy strikes back at you. However, I can understand your shock, you're probably not used to using your new powers, or even aware of when you should use them, and for what purposes. Naturally, mistakes are bound to happen in your lifetime. Even I, after all these years, make mistakes. However, there are certain types of mistakes that cannot be undone once they happen. What you almost did, or what almost happened to you, rather, would have been one of those mistakes that couldn't be undone. Try to pick your battles more wisely.'

"I sat there and thought about what he said, and figured maybe I could have tried to kill a smaller creature or not have tried to do it at all. Maybe there was no need to impress my father. After that, I figured I would make my decisions not based on impressing him or attempting to artificially gain his attention, but I would do what I felt was right, and eventually he would be impressed with my efforts if I did the right thing. Safe was another thing I felt then, because I realized that my father had been watching over me the entire time. Ever since that day, I felt as though I would never get too badly hurt, because he would be there to watch over me, before anything too bad happened."

They were all quiet, staring at him at that table. Gemini's wife had genuine tears coming from her eyes, despite the fact that she had heard that story many times before.

"Why did you make me recount that story?" Mar asked. "Now I feel embarrassed in front of the ladies."

"Mar, I assure you, ladies like stories in which they get to know about you." Gemini smiled from ear to ear. "That story was very revealing, and what it revealed was good. There is truly nothing to be embarrassed about."

"Was that sincerely the last time you saw action?" Catalina asked whilst staring at her food.

"Believe it or not, dear lady Catalina," Gemini chimed in, "not all princes have seen combat. In some kingdoms, it seems that fathers wish for their royal sons to play an active role in combat, and some others."

"Like mine," Mar interrupted, taking over the conversation again. "Don't believe in their sons fighting in battles or leading soldiers. My father tells me that I will see combat someday, he is certain of that, but he would rather I be thrust in headfirst. That way, I won't have any doubts or worries or fears from past battles. All I will have is my gut instincts and abilities. 'I didn't have a chance to practice any battles or fight in part of a battalion or royal force or with any brotherhood,' he would always say. 'When I first fought, all I had is my gut and my abilities, which is what you'll have.' That's what he always tells me. I'm lucky he even spars with me he says. He also said that my older brother had no combat practice before his first battle that he fought on his own. My brother has been off successfully expanding the empire for quite some time. Just knowing that makes me feel better about my father's opinions. I'm sure when the time is right, I will be ready."

It was then that he remembered he still hadn't read the letter, so he decided to make his escape.

"If you would please excuse me, I have to make waste." Mar dabbed at his face with a napkin and then stood up.

"Of course, I trust you remember where the facilities are." Gemini looked toward him.

Mar simply nodded.

He knew where almost everything was in the castle because he had been there so often. He was actually relieved that he had decided to go to Gemini and that Catalina had agreed. He was unsure there was any other place where he could enjoy such great food, friendship, and get the chance to find out the contents of the letter all alone.

The bathroom was designed to fit two people. The king liked most things in twos. The full body mirror doubled as an aqua communicator, and the bathroom was fashioned with fine white and black stone covering nearly every corner, aside from the toilets, which were covered by a soft substance and were split black and white straight down the middle.

Unable to sit down, because of his anxiousness, he dug the letter out of his pocket. Opened it up as fast as he possibly could, yet carefully so as to not endanger the message.

He nervously read it. To his dismay, it revealed that his worst nightmare had come true. It was exactly as he thought it was.

The letter read: "I know your secret, a secret you thought only you and the princess of Taurus knew. Pretty soon, everyone from every kingdom will know."

"That's it! The letter doesn't even say what they want. Oh no! No! No! No! This is even worse than I thought." He balled up his fist but fought the urge to punch the wall.

He began pacing around the bathroom. Was he powerless against whoever this person was? No, he still had options. He could tell everyone himself, first. That would take all the power from whoever this coward was. That couldn't be a good idea, though, after his father worked so hard to set things up with Catalina.

If the Taurus were the way his father painted them, they would certainly take it as disrespect, and would possibly even lash out at the Aries, for his secret relationship with Diantha. Not to mention, King Capricorn would be infuriated, along with Sagittarius, whose son Ranger was already arranged to marry Diantha. Further, he had grown somewhat fond of Catalina, she was extremely beautiful, and her company was more enjoyable than Mar had initially thought it would be.

The only solution he could think of was to find out who the person was, what the person wanted, and try to give it to them. But he didn't even have any clues, not a single thing to go upon. A couple of ideas came to mind, though.

Regaining his composure, he prepared to face his host and his date. Separating from Catalina on pleasant terms would have to be his next move. Improvisation was always his thing, though, so he figured he would wing it, and he walked out of the bathroom with nothing on his mind but fixing the problem.

***

Knock, knock.

"May I come in? This is Stone from dyad management."

"That is rather formal of you. I sort of thought you would just barge in whenever you wanted to. Please enter," Leon said from his chair.

"It's best to practice good manners whenever possible," Stone said as he walked in and shut the door behind him. "In fact, good manners is what keeps Aquarius as such a highly regarded kingdom-planet. However, if there ever were any sort of emergency, I would be forced to barge in. I have come here for a specific reason." He remained standing by the amethyst-colored door. "I would like to tell you all that the dyads of Piscean decent should be here very shortly."

"Great, then that should mean that more like me will arrive here," Arkin said. "That's good. Although I appreciate it, I'm unsure why you felt the need to tell us directly."

"I figured you would all want to know. You have a rather large group of diverse individuals. My king is fascinated by your group, because you are all from different planets and seem to be getting along so well and he told me to keep you all abreast of any new developments to your living situation, or of any cohabitants."

"That's very considerate of him, so far he is shaping up to be far more considerate a leader than our old king, we are all very fortunate," Pierce said, looking at all the others from his alabaster chair, which stood out as all the chairs did against the black background of the rest of the room.

"I will now be taking my leave," Stone said, and he did a swift one eighty and exited.

The men all sat in their new dorm, which was similar in design to the Aries dorms but lacking a few things like a holographic display system, and colored differently.

"I can't believe Gwen still isn't here," Arkin said, staring at the door as if she would pop in at any moment.

"Maybe that's a good sign," Rudolph said with an easy shrug and optimistic smile.

"We cannot be too certain of that. I would say if we don't see her very soon, that must mean that we won't see her at all tonight, just like last night. Come to think of it, I'm surprised that Stone guy came and talked to us so late in the evening," Leon mentioned lightly.

"He's a strange fellow. Perhaps he wasn't necessarily supposed to work this late or deliver the message at this time, but he just brought it upon himself to do so," Arkin suggested.

Gwen finally showed up at their door. She was by herself.

"Took you long enough. I thought the fact that you were gone so long meant you would come back with someone else for sure. I guess you really weren't able to recruit anybody then," Arkin said.

"Nobody from your people wanted to join our noble cause? Wait, what is our cause again?" Pierce asked everybody and looked around at them all for an answer.

"Our cause is overthrowing the unjust kings and putting an end to their tyranny," Arkin said.

"Nobody from my people wanted to join your cause." She shook her head. "In fact, some were even trying to persuade me to not spend any more time with your group." She laughed a small, harsh laugh. "I told them that your group is much more appealing than you all appear because of what is going on inside your minds. They still didn't believe me. I gave up on convincing them and decided to just come back and let you all know that I couldn't persuade a single one of them."

"Maybe that's for the best. Now we don't have to worry about any more ladies screwing up the plans," Pierce joked with a smirk.

Gwen glared at him.

"I was only joking, I'm sorry."

"I'm going to go back to my room for sleep. I will see you all tomorrow." She turned back around to leave out the front door.

"Wait, don't you know that you can sleep here with us now, in the same room?" Arkin asked.

"Stone said it is OK for us all to sleep and spend time together in this dorm," Leon added.

"First of all, I don't even know who Stone is, and I don't care if it's OK or not. I do not intend to sleep here with you all."

"Nobody will violate your body. You have my word. I will crush whoever so much as tries to." Pierce stood up and balled his fists.

"There is no need for that, you can lock yourself up in your own room when you go to sleep and nobody will even be able to touch you. You guys are forgetting, we don't all have to hang out and sleep in the same room," Leon countered.

"Fine, then I pick this room, all of you leave at once, so that I may slumber."

"Gwen, please give me a second. I actually wanted us all to talk. We have plans to make." Leon stood up "Things to discuss. Gwen are you aware that the Piscean half bloods—"

"Don't you mean dyads?" Rudolph interjected.

"Whatever, Piscean dyads"—he looked at Rudolph—"are on their way here. They should be here shortly, possibly even by tomorrow."

"Wait, I thought you were part Piscean, Arkin."

"I am half, but both planets, Aries and Pisces, have Pisces-Aries mix and Aries-Pisces mix. I am the variant from planet Aries, obviously. How did you not know that? Aren't there Gemini-Cancer and Cancer-Gemini mixes that you have come across?" Arkin asked her.

"That was the next question I was going to ask you. Do the Pisces-Aries mix and Aries-Pisces mix have any different physical characteristics or abilities or anything? I ask because as far as I know, all Gemini-Cancer and Cancer-Gemini hybrids are the same, more or less."

"Oh, OK, I see. As far as I know they all have the same abilities as me and look similar, whether they are from my planet or from Pisces."

Pierce took his turn. "Same with all the half bloods I know of my variant."

"I believe the same could be said of all those of my classification as well. More or less, anyway. Some have differences in fur color and some, like myself, don't have overly pronounced Leo or Virgo features, but I think all of us have the same abilities," Leon related.

Everybody began staring at Rudolph and Sage.

"You are all curious about our dyads? If I'm not mistaken, all of our variants are the same as well, in both physical appearance and ability. Wait, no, that's not exactly true. On Sagittarius, some of the dyads have traditional Sagittarian lower bodies. I'm not sure what that's about, but I'm certain that I never seen someone from planet Scorpio who was mixed with Sagittarius who had that. Honestly, it's pretty uncommon, though. Most Sagittarius-Scorpio mix or even Sagittarius-Capricorn have normal legs."

"Maybe Sagittarius are different, somehow, than all the other dyads," Arkin commented.

"Maybe the horse lower body is just a dominant feature of Sagittarius blood, so it is passed down even to some of those with only half blood," Leon added.

"Is that all you had to say, because I want to go to sleep now," Gwen said, tapping her feet and remaining impatient.

"No, I'm sorry, I just found our discussion interesting," Leon said.

"Leon wants to discuss our next big move," Arkin chimed in.

"Next big move?" Gwen asked.

"Yes, the whole reason that we are all gathered. I'm sure that we all lost loved ones before and even after the consequences of the final Battle of Orion on Bellatrix. I have a burning desire to bring justice to those kings," Arkin said with particular disgust for the word *king*. "Leon agrees with me wholeheartedly."

"I'm not sure I'm all that into revenge," Gwen said, backing away closer to the door.

"Count me and Sage in," Rudolph said. "I can't stand Sagittarius royals, the king or any of the other ones."

"I seek revenge as well," Pierce volunteered.

"Not only revenge, this will be our chance to improve the lives of the commoners and dyads of all planets. If we can overthrow the unjust kings and replace them with righteous ones, we will improve life for all the planets and kingdoms and bring them to another level. I know some of the commoners may hate us and think that we show no allegiance to our own homes, but we have to forgive them for their ignorance. The commoners merely go off what their kings, their royals, and the puppets that are in between the two tell them. In fact, even now the rebellion on Leo has cooperation between the Leo dyads and the commoners. Proof that we don't need to be at odds. If we can improve our situation, we can improve theirs as well," Arkin declared, proud of his vision.

"Well, I suppose there is only a few who live the lives they want. It would be nice for people to be able to live in peace, no matter who they are or where they are from. I suppose it can't hurt to listen to what you have to say, and chime in if I feel at odds with your aim." Gwen stepped further away from the door.

"Thank you, Gwen." Leon picked up the conversation and moved into the forefront. "Because believe it or not, I feel that Arkin and I could not make real progress without a diverse group of dyads who believe in helping others, too. Our tactics will have to be harsh, but sometimes one must be cruel and swift and strike without warning in order to get things done."

"That's a rather peculiar expression, where does it come from?" Gwen wondered out loud.

"It's an ancient Leo proverb," Leon said matter-of-factly.

"Very good, well, now it's time we got down to business. Leon, who would you say would be easiest to strike right now?" Arkin cut back in and asked.

"I would have to say my former king and one time tormentor, King Leo."

"That's exactly what I was thinking, with the rebellion, he has the weakest kingdom as of now. Further, his natal day is fast approaching even as we speak. I think it may be the perfect opportunity to do something. Wait, but will he even celebrate his birth, given the current circumstances?"

"I know what you're thinking and you're right, Arkin, he wouldn't go on with the celebration if the rebellion was still happening. He wouldn't even be able to. But I'm certain that the rebellion will end in time for his natal day celebration. Leo cares far too much about his own glorification and praise to let the festivities get canceled. Why, in fact, I'm certain we will lose contact with our rebels on Leo within a few days."

"Well, that's terrible."

"No, Arkin, a rebellion cannot go on forever. You should already know that. This was mostly just to show the weaknesses in Leo's forces. I have already acquired a ton of information."

"It was you guys? You guys are the reason there's a rebellion on Leo?" Gwen was shocked.

"They apparently also had something to do with us coming to live here on planet Aquarius," Pierce added casually with a shrug.

"What! You two have to explain yourselves to me right now, or I'm walking out. Is all of that true? And you have the nerve to say that you're helping dyads and commoners. I have heard word of the horrors that happened on Leo since the rebellion began. If anything, the commoners and dyads have been the main ones suffering."

"And what would you have us do?" Arkin debated. "Let Leo continue going on with his lion's den, where he forces the weaker Leos to fight for their lives for sport? This way, communications will be opened up and Leo commoner and Leo dyad deaths will no longer serve as amusement for the king, his royals, or the other commoners who are too stupid to know that they are not above being forced to participate themselves. Truth is, the rebellion was guaranteed to happen with or without our lead."

"What about the other kings? Are you planning to kill the other kings as well? You cannot tell me that King Aries, or King Sagittarius, or any of the others force commoners to fight for sport."

"No, you're right about that, but the other kings are cruel in their own way. Did you know that King Scorpio used to send commoners on a death quest through the desert to try to fetch an item for him? I heard Virgo experiments on people. All the kings are capable of evil. Nobody should be as powerful as they are. I understand they are that way because they have too much power, most likely anyone with as much power as them would behave in a similar manner, but just because I understand their mentality doesn't mean I condone their actions, or that I can allow it to continue. Now, are you interested in helping us or not?" Arkin was frustrated and invaded Gwen's personal space when he spoke.

"I don't know. I'm not sure that I can get behind murder plots. You make a persuasive argument, and I understand why you think you must take them out of power, but I wonder if others just as evil and powerful won't just step up to replace them. Maybe there is a better way. Have you ever stopped and thought of that?"

"There is no other way. In this universe, power is the only thing anyone respects," Arkin replied.

"Whatever, I'm walking on this one. Find yourself another one. I don't want to be involved, but don't worry, I won't tell anyone."

Gwen walked out swiftly, ignoring anyone who tried to talk to her or stop her as she walked out.

"What do you think we should do about her?" Arkin was worried and looked to Leon immediately.

"Don't worry, it will be fine. There's a ninety-five percent chance she will be back. And as far as her telling, I trust her, she won't, and even if she did, who would believe her? At worst, Stone the manager guy would probably just watch us more. There would be nothing to prove. It's not like we are even out there doing anything. Technically, we are here on Aquarius, in a way, we have no ties to anything that's actually happening on Leo."

Leon paused to catch his breath. "What I'm saying is that everything will be fine. I earnestly think that she will be back and join us again shortly. And if she doesn't, then that means that she was not really for the rise of the half bloods, don't you correct me, Rudolph." He glared at him, feeling that the words "don't you mean *dyad*" would come from Rudolph's mouth. "Moving right along, we have to think of something. It's imperative that we don't miss this opportunity. King Leo's birth event will be one of the only chances we get to catch him completely off guard. Especially because the rebellion will have just ended, and he will be relaxed, thinking that everything is under control in his kingdom."

"You seem to know a lot about King Leo," Rudolph said.

"Yes, of course, I am from there."

"I thought you were from planet Aries."

"No I'm from Leo, born and raised. I just don't have strong Leo characteristics, and I kind of lied my way onto Aries during deportation once the final Battle of Orion was over. Odder than that, I'm missing the V imprint from my forehead that is common among Virgos and Virgo half bloods."

"You are truly a rare breed, is what that means," Pierce observed. "You all are doing a lot of talking and that's fine and everything, but it bores me, so I'm going to go to sleep." Pierce stood up and stretched.

"Wow, seriously, you can't just go to sleep. You don't want to plan this out with us? All we need to do is discuss ideas a little while longer, and we will have a plan in no time, I'm sure. Planning is the most important part of anything in life. Tell him, Arkin."

"I don't know about that. That seems like a very strong statement about the planning thing, and truth be told, I don't see why Pierce has to be here. He doesn't seem like the long-winded, planning all day, thinking before taking action type anyway. I mean no offense by that, of course."

"None taken. It's decided, then, I'm off to bed. Late night planning isn't for me." He smiled at everyone as he began walking toward the door. "And now I'm hungry. I think I will see if I can access the common area during after-hours and get a snack." Pierce left.

"What about you two? Do you two want to leave, too?" Leon asked, a little disheartened.

"No, we are fine here. We always had to listen to all sorts of military planning during our time with the Sagittarian Royal Army."

"Oh, that's right, so you guys should have some very valuable insight, then. You two will be useful because of your royal army experience. I guess we don't need those other two after all," Leon replied.

"Don't worry Leon," Arkin said. "You know how you made your prediction about Gwen, well, I'm going to guarantee you that Pierce will be there for us when we need him. When the time is right. He's just not a big talker. I could tell, and it's always important to let people do what they are strongly suited to and not to force them to do things that they are weak at. That's why I cut him loose. This will actually make this conversation easier to have."

"I suppose you're right Arkin." Leon still looked disappointed. "I hadn't considered that. I was just enjoying our group being as large as it was."

"You think our group was big with Pierce and Gwen, just you wait, we are going to have even more people soon, I can feel it." Arkin quickly clapped his friend's shoulder.

Leon smiled, then looked directly at Rudolph. "Now, please tell me a few military strategies that you guys have overheard or seen implemented. I feel this will be good for the brainstorming process."

Chapter 9

"**D**own with the tyrant, King Leo," the large group yelled as they marched down the fiery streets as if they owned them. It was a diverse group of common lions, some were orange, others brown, and a few red and even some yellow. Not to mention the mob had various half-beast Leos, the Cancer variety having slight greenish tint to their fur.

The streets of Leo looked as if they couldn't take much more of the rebellion. Buildings were burning, factories destroyed, houses ruined, devastation was abound.

Zemar was happy to have met up with Llewellyn when he did. Now it was the two of them to face off against the rebels.

"Situations like this almost make me wish that our pride carried around weapons," Llewellyn said, his dark brown fur still showing damage from his recent scuffles, and red with fresh and dried blood in various spots on his coat.

The two friends laughed as if it were the funniest joke they had ever heard. They had to in order to feel sane while dealing with such a crazy situation. Both were worried. Neither had ever seen a rebellion this scale. They hadn't been there during the rebellion on Bellatrix, but they were sure even if they had been that it couldn't have been as chaotic as this.

Zemar had been lucky. The one altercation he had before meeting with Llewellyn must have been after another royal lion had fought the rebels, because he only fought against five rebel lions and two half bloods in his fight earlier. His orange reddish fur had a few nicks here and there, but he was in pretty good condition. In other words, he was in much better shape than Llewellyn.

"You know, if any more rebels attack, I can try to hold them off myself," Zemar offered with a smirk.

"Nonsense. I have more combat experience than you and have served under the king for more years," Llewellyn retorted.

"Exactly, which means that you're much older and slower than me."

The two laughed again.

"Shhh, do you see that?" Llewellyn suddenly straightened up and became serious.

Off in the distance, there was a mixed group of common Leos and half bloods carrying torches that moved toward them, just like what happened to Llewellyn earlier. The flames burned into their eyes, demanding more attention than the common folk and half-beasts carrying them, especially in the darkness of night.

"I never fall for the same trick twice," he growled, and turned and grabbed a lion with a short sword who was right behind the navy-blue trash sorter machine, preparing to stab him.

"It seems that our ambushers have been using a certain tactic to trick us." He looked to Zemar to show him and explain. "The ones with the fire off in the distance would catch your eye, and a smaller lion with a short sword would stealthily close in on you, and stab you in your back." He lifted his would-be attacker up by his neck, and pulled him in real close to his face. "Just out of curiosity, what sort of half beast are you?"

"The kind that will bring you and the king death."

"I know, judging by your sneaking skills, you must be half Cancer, and I'm afraid you are the only one who is going to die here." Llewellyn snapped the greenish-orange half-Leo, half-Cancer's neck and dropped his lifeless body.

By the time he finished killing the half beast, the ambushers descended upon them. This time, the odds were in his favor. When he entered the brawl to take on the twenty plus Leos, Zemar was already engaging seven of them.

"How about we have a competition to see who can kill more?" Llewellyn said. Sizing up his opponents, he took a battle stance.

"OK, I'm game," Zemar said, taking a much looser and more relaxed battle stance than Llewellyn, "but just to be fair, the one you just killed, the backstabber, doesn't count."

"Fair enough," Llewellyn said before engaging.

The two men began brawling with confidence and bravado. It was no wonder the Royal Pride never felt the need to use weapons. Zemar was a mad man, flinging and tearing smaller lions left and right. Whereas Llewellyn was like a tank, absorbing damage and focusing on one lion at a time and destroying him completely. Llewellyn grabbed a small lion by the head and crushed it in his bare hands. The next one, he gouged the eyes out. Another, which took particularly long, he choked to death just to make the other lion suffer. It seemed like the two Leos were untouchable. Until they saw another much larger group of lions approaching.

"I think we need to leave now. We will not survive an onslaught from that many at once. It doesn't matter how much stronger we are than them. They outnumber us too greatly," Llewellyn concluded.

"Are you sure? I was just starting to have fun," the younger Leo joked before he slashed the throat of one of his earlier ambushers.

"We leave now, or we die, I'm sure of it."

Zemar began running and Llewellyn was shortly behind him. Zemar didn't doubt that Llewellyn knew what he was talking about. He had a lot more years of combat experience than Zemar did. These rebels were very good at striking together and working as one. Llewellyn was barely able to take out the lions from the group they just fought. If it hadn't been for Zemar, he wouldn't have fared so well, but because he had fewer targets, he was able to do his brutal kill moves.

"You know, I hadn't thought about this until just now." Llewellyn looked at Zemar as they ran. "But I'm not sure of where we should go. I don't think the king will allow us back to the castle, if we could even make it in there, past the rebels, and all of the spots where our pride used to convene have been taken over by them."

"Are you serious?" Zemar gazed back at him, disbelieving. "The king won't let us back in, even though we are in danger? How do you know?"

"I was given strict orders not to come back until the rebellion is over, but he also said that he's working on a solution." Llewellyn began to search the area ahead, trying to figure out a safe place to go as they ran.

"Damn him and his solution. He may as well have sent us out here to die. All we can do out here is fight until our last breath. As you said before, they outnumber us far too greatly. We won't win every fight. Do you know where our remaining brethren have gone to?"

"If I knew, I would have suggested going there a long time ago."

"True, well, I don't know what to do, then." Zemar faced forward as well and the two continued sprinting.

They finally reached what appeared to be a dead end. Ahead of them was a very large group of rebels littered with Leos, Leo-Cancers, and even Leo-Virgos. Behind them was the group of rebels who had chased them to their current place. On both their left and right sides, they faced similar opposition. Not only that, but it seemed as if the original group that chased them had grown in number. It looked as though they had reached their final standoff with the rebels. They finally stopped running.

"It looks like this is it. I am still on the fence about whether we should fight to the very end or whether we should try to strike a deal with these clowns."

"We have to fight until death, of course." Zemar gave his elder a stern look.

"Here we have them," a rebel who wore orange robes said, he led the line as he pointed his torch at them, the red fur of his face glowing under the light of his torch. "The royal pride, they don't seem so prepared to take life today." It even seemed as if the moonlight of the night sky gave him a spotlight.

There must have been over one thousand lions with torches surrounding them, even more if you counted the ones not carrying anything, but they were all quiet as the one lion spoke. There wasn't anything particularly special about the lion, he just looked like an average commoner aside from the fact that his robe and his fur color weren't seen all that often. Llewellyn and Zemar both didn't recognize him, but why should they? They had never had to deal with commoners on such a level before as they were now on this day.

"What shall we do with them?" The rebel leader looked around at some in the crowds when he asked.

"We should fight against them until they die, just like they always do to us in the arena," someone said.

"Now, now, the point of this exercise is to show them that we will not stoop to their level," the leader said, focusing back on Zemar and Llewellyn with a smirk. "Besides, I wouldn't want them to defeat a few of us and get the wrong idea and think they had any chance of leaving this alive."

"Hang them," another yelled, and a few joined to repeat that with him. "Hang them!"

"That's not a bad one. Maybe we should do that. I'm not sure, there are so many ways we can kill them, just like we did their comrades." A smile formed at the corners of his mouth.

Did that mean that all the others were dead? Zemar and Llewellyn both thought in their heads. That would mean there would be no help to show up, and that this really would be the end for the two. The last stand. If it were that bad, then surely the king himself would have stepped in and handled it personally. The leader of the rebels must have been exaggerating.

He wants to teach us true fear, that's the only reason he said that, Llewellyn imagined. *This still is an impossible situation, though*, he also noted mentally, and briefly considered giving up for a moment, because he wasn't sure that he wanted to take on a group of more than one thousand Leos and half bloods. He thought maybe if he asked they would give him a quick death. Tuning out the leader of the rebels who was still talking, he continued thinking. No, surrendering and dying without a fight was not a real option. Especially not in front a younger comrade. He had to make some sort of stand.

"I still can't decide. Gentlemen, please tell me how you want to die." The rebel leader stared at them.

***

Cancer came down to his study to greet his guests. He saw three lions from the royal pride. They weren't the biggest or strongest Leos he had ever seen, but he was certain that they would do just fine for his purposes

His study was a simple area that consisted of books, holographic librarian aides, a visual scenario simulator, holographic versions of books that would display the story in 3D, and chairs and tables. It was a ruby-red-colored room, with brown shelves, tables, and chairs, reserved for learning, planning, plotting, and developing strategies.

The three Leos stood, which made it easier for him to size them up. They were still much bigger than any commoner from Leo. Their brown fur was partially covered by half-body armor made from leather and metal, like most royal Leos liked wearing. Curious as to why they didn't have any weapons or even full armor, he decided just to ask.

"I think I may already know the answer to this, but why don't you three have full armor or any weapons?"

"Members of the pride do not carry weapons nor do we wear full armor. This is for a few reasons. One, without armor slowing us down, we move swiftly, uninhibited. Two, our hand-to-hand combat is the greatest of any royal of the twelve, because we do not rely on weapons. Three, we like the feeling of destroying our enemies with our bare hands. Finally, our king never favored the use of traditional weapons and armor, so when a few of our pride insisted they be given weapons, he strongly admonished them. This is why we lack combat gear, sir, but I assure you, we have done well in all of our fights without weapons and the fact that we fight barehanded makes us stronger and more capable than anyone."

"I figured as much, so your group never uses weapons. I guess I made the right decision picking you all, then," he said with a smile. "I have a very simple thing to ask of you three. All you have to do is protect me. I'm sure that Leo may have told you bad things about me. I don't think I have ever met any of you before, because he usually uses different Leos for a lot of his operations. It is no matter. I can tell you that whatever he said about me is a lie or exaggeration. I am not a bad guy, despite what everyone would have you believe. I will be needing protection relatively soon, and I thought you all would be the best."

"Can I ask how long this detail will be for us?" the shortest one of the group asked.

"I myself am not sure yet, but I can tell you this. You will need to earn your right to leave. I am doing a great favor for Leo, which is why he is allowing me to borrow your services. My own elites will be busy performing tasks for me so they will be unable to help you protect me. You can all sleep here and use the facilities my elites would typically use. My lovely assistant, Adeline, shall get you set up. From now until I release you back to Leo, make yourselves at home."

"Adeline." He looked for her right after he called her name. She was immediately at the door of the study as soon as he called for her in a long white-and-red robe with a red flower adorned near the midriff of the robe. The robe went down to just above her shoes and was tightly tied and was complimented by the red flower in her tight hair bun.

The beautiful green woman was immediately on the move once her king called her, escorting the Leos out of the study and giving them a partial tour and explaining to them the things that were for them to use and the things that they were not to use, and so forth.

One lion jokingly made a comment about getting a chance to use her. The other two laughed, but she quickly put him in check by calmly saying, "None of that would be allowed and if any such thing happened, relations between Cancer and Leo would be horribly diminished to the point that the two would be enemies. I'm sure your king wouldn't want that."

Slowly, Adeline's and the Leo's voices faded out. Cancer waited until they were completely out of range, and began finally talking to his men who stood before him no longer invisible.

"How are things progressing on Leo?" he inquired, speaking a little low.

"We have found the responsible parties for the rebellion. We know who the leaders are, and we have a plan to effectively crush their rebellion," one of his elite said in a similarly low voice.

"Very good, very good." Cancer lowered his voice even more and leaned into his soldier and said, "Don't crush the rebellion right away. I want King Leo to feel the consequences of this rebellion for a little while longer. I will give you word before I speak to Leo, and once I do, then you can stamp out the uprising. I have his soldiers, so there isn't as much of a rush for you to stifle it completely yet. You're doing very good, Cyrus, keep it up, and maybe you will be as respected as Maestro one day," he said, speaking very close to his servant's face. "This is a good opportunity for you to continue to impress me, Cyrus. Maestro and Gregorio are tied up doing something else for me, so I no longer have them assigned to Leo, so I'll be relying entirely upon you."

"Of course, I understand, sire. I won't let you down," the tall, thin, expertly groomed blue man said to his king.

"I know you won't. You better not," Cancer said with a flash of a smile. "OK, you all have your orders, you're dismissed. Do not come back to me until everything is finished."

The six Cancer Elites disappeared from the king's sight instantly.

Everything was going according to plan.

"Master, I'm back," Adeline said as she swiftly appeared behind him.

He turned to face her. "That was fast, I take it our Leo guests must be occupying themselves right now."

"Yes, they found our recreational facilities to be rather stimulating, and they are utilizing them even as we speak. It seems that they will be busy for a while."

"Very good, and how are things going with the three Aries who are fetching those items for me?"

"I have not heard from them in a day or so, the last time I did, they were more than halfway through with the list of items you asked for."

"Wow, that's impressive. They may finish ahead of schedule. I can't believe how well everything is going. One more question: Where are Maestro and Gregorio?" he said. His entire tone changed when he brought up Maestro and Gregorio. "I had actually thought that they would be back by now."

"They said they are on their way. They just finished gathering the items for the next task you set them out to do."

"OK, I understand. Thank you, Adeline, keep an eye on our guests, of course. Keep them from looking around too much, and away from all the areas I told you about earlier. I am going to relax for a while, you know where to find me."

"Of course, sire," she said before making herself scarce. Adeline always knew that when the king said he was going to relax near his study that meant he was going to his multipurpose room. The room was so important to him that only Adeline and his wife were allowed in. Not even his elites were permitted entrance. The room was top secret, and it was where Cancer plotted some of his moves. He always felt more creative when safe and relaxed.

This is too easy, Cancer thought.

"I am the most fortunate of all the kings, to be in the position that I'm in. Now all I have to do is wait for everything to fall into place," he said as he walked to the bookshelf that secretly hid his multipurpose room.

***

The downtime was refreshing for Croix at first, but now he was ready to get back to business, itching to finish his initiation into the brotherhood. Relaxing was fine and all, but he felt restless, on edge. There had to be something constructive he could do with his extra time, but what? Suddenly a stroke of genius came to him, he could master his new powers, using the abilities the ring he wore gave him, but where would he train?

Leaving Aries probably wasn't a good idea, after all, the other initiates might finish the sand dragon task at any moment. But he also wasn't sure that his powers would be useful on Aries, or at least as effective as he would like for them to be.

There had to be something he could do. He decided to contact Brother Eames to see if he could leave his home planet. He felt as though his new talents could be really tested on somewhere like Sagittarius, or possibly even Gemini or Taurus, basically anywhere but Aries, where nearly all beings and things were immune to fire, but he knew he didn't want to go back to Scorpio either.

"Eames, I wanted to ask you something," he said when his instructor appeared on the aqua communicator.

"Go ahead." Eames prompted him, but looked distracted and didn't give him eye contact, but was looking off at something.

"I was wondering if I had enough time to leave Aries for a little while."

"What?" Eames finally gave him his full attention. "Why?

"I just have a few things I wanted to look into."

"That's fine, but you're going to be leaving soon anyway," Eames said, looking tense in the water screen; his grim expression made him look even more serious than usual. "Actually, one of the other recruits just dropped out. Now it's just you and one other guy. Bear with me for a little while here, and just stay on Aries for the time being. I will be giving you your next mission very soon, whether or not this other candidate finishes."

Croix had his answer, he wasn't happy with it, but now he knew. It still would be cool just to look at his powers and see how they worked one more time. He went outside with the intent to test them out some more.

Aries was beautiful during mating season. There was always a reddish hue to the planet, because of all the fires, volcanoes, fire creatures, and other fire-based things, but the color of Aries was a little different during the mating season. The whole world seemed to be a lighter pinkish red everywhere.

He wasn't really sure how he missed it before. It could be that he was too focused on his latest goal. Whatever the case was, mating season made the planet a lot prettier than usual. Still unsure of how he could properly test his abilities, he stared up at the pink sky above him.

His eyes followed a trail of smoke that was coming from a nearby volcano. There was a volcano within close proximity. For a moment he reflected on the vision that he had when he first put the ring on, and if he wasn't mistaken the ring had given him the power to absorb energy. Volcanoes were tremendous sources of energy. He could stock up and store vast amounts of power. Then again, maybe it was too risky. To his knowledge, his uncle had never dived into a volcano. While it sounded potentially beneficial, he wasn't sure if he would make it back out alive; he heard there were deadly flesh-eating fish that lived in the lava of the volcano.

Another idea came to him. Why not race some of the fastest people he knew? That wouldn't make anybody suspect him of having the ring, because he was already known for being fast. Also, the ring was from Scorpio, there was a strong chance that nobody even knew about the ring on Aries, his first time hearing about the ring was when he spoke with the guardian at the temple. That reminded him, he had never given the ring back. It wasn't a big deal, he was sure he could just bring the ring back after he finished his trials. At least he hoped so. He didn't mean to lie to the temple guardian but he had forgot and he knew it would come in handy for the rest of his brotherhood tasks. The thought crossed his mind to return the ring right away. But he was told to stay on Aries for the moment so he dropped the issue entirely. He hoped it would be fine. He decided that the next time he was on Scorpio he would return the ring.

Mar and Ram, his cousins, were both away, so they were out of the question for a race. His father and mother were still on Taurus, so they weren't available, either. Racing his uncle and beating him or matching him would probably tip his uncle off to the fact that he had an unfair advantage. There was always a chance, even if only slight, that his uncle knew what the ring was.

The king. He wondered if he was actually faster than his uncle now. The more he thought about it, the more he figured he would probably just race one of the other royals. At least two of the royals were supposed to be about equal speed to Croix before he got the ring.

It was time to test just how fast those royals really were. Plus, it would be a subtle way to test his new speed without anybody suspecting anything. He arrived at his uncle's castle in milliseconds. The servant at the door let him in without saying a word.

"Uncle? Uncle, are you home? I would like to ask you a favor." He didn't hear a thing, so he zipped around a bit to find the king.

Whirling through the house at less than a one hundredth of his speed, he found his uncle, just sitting in his throne room, on his throne, lost in thought.

The throne room was huge. It had countless paintings, mostly motion paintings that depicted great battles that King Aries and his closest friends, Gemini, Sagittarius, and Leo, had fought. Aside from the motion paintings, there was just the throne, the paintings that lined the walls and floors, and a board with figures shaped in the likenesses of different kings; different areas of the board were designated to represent the different planets. It looked as though King Aries did not use the board much, because all the figures were in their own respective planets, with their armies there also in the same place that they had started at. It took a while, but his uncle finally looked up at him.

"Croix. What are you doing here? I thought you were going through the initiation to become one of the brotherhood."

"I am Uncle. I finished the first task early, and Brother Eames allowed me some spare time."

"Why is it you chose to come here? You should probably be out training. Your next task may be harder than the first."

"I hope it isn't. Defeating the sand dragon really took a lot out of me."

"Sand dragon? Interesting. I did not know they were running it like that. Last time I heard, the first task was catching one of those spiny rodents."

"Do you mean the explosive quillbacks?"

"Yes those things." He made eye contact before continuing. "They really stepped it up for the first task. Maybe I was wrong, maybe your next task will be easier. I still don't understand why you came here to my throne room of all places, unannounced. Neither of your cousins is here, so if you're looking for them, you're out of luck." Aries leaned back in his throne made of diamonds.

"Actually, I was hoping I could race some of your fastest men."

"Race them? To what end? Unfortunately, my three fastest are gone at this very moment, so that's impossible. I'm sure you could probably race a member of the brotherhood. I give this recommendation because of the fact that all my other men have more pressing matters than racing you for your entertainment."

"It was really supposed to be for training so I could measure my speed."

"Don't lie to me." His lip stiffened. "All Aries men, especially of royal blood, know exactly how fast they are and how to use their speed by the time they reach your age."

"It is no lie. I know how fast I am, but I don't know how fast I am compared to members of the brotherhood or your personal men."

"Hmmm, OK, I suppose. Still, I have nobody here for you to race. That is, of course, unless you would like to race me?" he proposed, leaning forward in his throne and staring Croix in the eyes. "Even though I'm your uncle, I won't show you any mercy."

"No thank you," Croix said with a smile. "You are the fastest in the kingdom. I will pass for now. Perhaps once I have finished all of my tasks, I will race you. I guess I wasted your time. Sorry, I will take my leave now. Farewell."

Aries just looked at him for a moment, gave a slight nod, and went back to his focused daydreaming stare.

That was close. Croix was tempted to race his uncle, but he wasn't sure if it was a good idea for his uncle to know that he was as fast as him. If that were even the case. There was a chance that he wasn't as fast as he thought, but if he was, he knew that his uncle would figure something weird was going on.

His uncle was the fastest in the kingdom, still even faster than the young prince Mar, who was still growing into himself, the way the king put it, and equal in speed to the older prince Ram who was expanding the Aries empire.

If Croix raced either of his cousins, it wouldn't raise any suspicion because they always competed as children and sometimes he would even win back then. But he was certain he would have raised a degree of skepticism and disbelief with his uncle if he took him on, and he wasn't sure if he would have been able to hold back. His uncle was extremely competitive and would have tried to antagonize him until he felt the need to go all out, and then his new abilities would have been discovered, and maybe he would have had to fight his uncle.

"No way, that's crazy," he argued with himself, interrupting his own thoughts. "There's no way I would end up fighting my own flesh and blood, especially over something so trivial."

The trip to the castle had been fruitless. He was on his way back to think of new ways to train, but before he could, he was contacted. Eames appeared on the water screen of his mobile communicator when he opened it.

"Hey, Croix." Eames was in better spirits than last time. A faint smile could even be seen on his face. The first Croix could remember ever seeing. "Are you ready? Whenever you're ready, come on back to the brotherhood house. We are going to give you your newest assignment."

"Wow that was faster than I thought it would be. OK, I will be there in a little while."

At least there wouldn't be any more time lost. The thought gave him comfort as he headed for the brotherhood house. Training would have to be something that he did in between missions. If he did things here and there on other planets, he was sure his new abilities wouldn't be discovered until he was ready. When he arrived to the brotherhood house, he only saw one other recruit, Archer. *That's right, Brother Eames did tell me that one had quit during the first task,* he thought.

Brother Eames stood in center of the room and waited for Croix to sit. "Now there are only two of you. This is usually how these sort of things go, so I can't say I'm surprised. You both fought long and hard and took out the sand dragon, which is an impressive feat. It's no small undertaking to defeat a dragon, especially a sand dragon of Scorpio. You both deserve a round of applause."

He clapped his hands for the two recruits, but only for a short moment.

"OK, that's enough. You two still have quite a ways before you become men of the brotherhood. Let me ask you, recruit Archer"—his focus was only on Archer at that moment—"what was the purpose of the task we just had you complete?"

"The last mission was designed to measure our power and courage."

"Well, you're partially correct. It was also used to measure your resourcefulness. That's right, the last task was designed to measure your resourcefulness, strength, and courage. This next task will be simply about measuring your wit, nothing else. We are headed to Gemini. I'm sure you both have most likely been there before."

It was true Croix had been there quite a few times, so he nodded his head slightly, as did Archer. Croix felt that Eames himself was only partially correct. It seemed to him that the last goal also tested his wits; if it hadn't been for him acquiring the ring, he would not have been able to defeat the dragon, he was pretty sure about that. It made him stop and wonder how did the other recruit, Archer, defeat a sand dragon. He would have to ask him later, if he got the chance.

I'm sure Archer wouldn't feel the need to keep it secret from me, but then that means I will have to tell my secret of how I defeated my dragon. No, I guess I would just have to make something up. He sat there, lost in thought for a moment, but figured he should bring his attention back to his current goal, which was this new task. The sand dragon was behind him. What did it matter, anyway? But still, burning curiosity consumed his mind. It didn't make sense that Archer was able to defeat the sand dragon with no assistance. Unless, that is, Archer knew something that Croix did not. Croix looked at Archer, who had his attention glued to Eames, but then felt guilty, so he began focusing on what Eames was saying, too.

"The thing is, we aren't going to the kingdom of Gemini, not even near it. What would be the point in going to the kingdom? Instead, we are going to the wilds of Gemini. A place where they say all things are as equally treacherous as they are magnificent," he asserted.

"You may see beauty on this next quest. You may see death, if you're not careful. I have to warn you, despite this current task's outward appearance, there is a chance of death. Again, the point of this one will be to measure your intellect. Despite what I said a moment ago, another point will be to measure your communication abilities, because today, gentlemen"—he pointed at both of them—"you will be talking to a two-headed troll. Talking him into letting you have some treasure from the cave he guards and also into becoming your friend. I'm not sure if you already know this, but the troll doesn't actually have two heads, and was named such because it has two very different personalities.

"Some say that the trolls on Gemini have two souls rather than one, and that this is the reason for the diametrically opposed personalities. I'm not really sure of that. What I do know is that you both will have to communicate with one. There is only one particular troll that the two of you are set to deal with, so that means you will both go one at a time, as opposed to last time.

"Obviously, because there is only one troll and you both are tasked with friendly communications with it, this should go without saying, but I will say it anyway. You cannot kill the troll. In fact, no harm or as little harm as possible is to be inflicted upon the troll.

"This particular troll, who we call the guardian, is currently guarding a large cave in the wilds southeast of the kingdom of Gemini. This cave is said to host some of the finest treasure on Gemini. Only the treasures of Taurus, with all their splendor, can compare to the treasure of this Gemini cave, or so I'm told. To make things interesting, you both will have a time limit. You may think that you can run right past the troll, and truthfully maybe you can, but I assure you it is in your best interest to talk to and communicate with the troll, and that is your mission."

"Croix." He turned all of his attention to him. "Because you completed the last task in record breaking fashion, you choose the order. Would you like to go first or second?"

Croix sat there for a minute, going over the benefits of both. If he went first he could get it over with and would be guaranteed a troll who wouldn't be that irritated because he would be the first stranger it would have to deal with. Also, maybe if he did it fast enough, as he did with his last task, he could possibly get the chance to rest and relax in between this task and the next mission. Furthermore, and most importantly, he would get as much treasure as he possibly wanted. However, if he went second, he would get a chance to try out his new powers some more and maybe he would be able to get tips on how to complete the task, even. Although, it was unlikely there would be a chance for him to ask Archer for tips, and discussion between recruits was most likely illegal, given what Eames said before the first mission. Croix was usually fast to make decisions, but with something this important he didn't want to rush right into it.

"Having trouble deciding? I can flip a coin for you if you would like." Eames produced an Arien copper from his pocket, flipped it once in the air, and caught it.

"No, I got it all figured it out. I'm going to go first," Croix finally confirmed.

"Very well, whenever you two are ready, meet me back at the ship, at the same place as last time." Eames walked away instantly.

Croix hadn't noticed before but there were no longer any other full-fledged members of the brotherhood in the house. As a matter of fact, there had not been any since he got there in the morning. Maybe for the rest of the recruitment process, only Eames was responsible. He was fine with that, but the glyphs seemed to glow a little duller and the room seemed to have a lot less energy without all the other members. Eames seemed to be a fair and impartial judge of the recruit's abilities, though, so Croix figured it would be fine. The tasks were given directly by him each time, anyway, so far at least, but he did find it a little strange that the men of the brotherhood were not available to race the other day and were not there now. *I guess it is like my uncle said,* he thought as he headed toward the rendezvous point to meet up with Eames, *they must be too busy.*

Planet Gemini always looked interesting from an aerial view. It was perfectly split into two separate but equal parts at night. Half of the planet was relatively bright for night and vibrant, and the other half was extremely dark.

The place they arrived at was on the border of light and darkness. Huge wet leaves were everywhere and noises from all sorts of wild creatures were, too. Light from the light side reached the place that they were at, but only barely, almost romantically, so they could still see a little. The romantic beauty of the light touched the darkness and ever so slightly it touched the wet, hot, jungle. The trees varied in all manner of size, from really tall trees down to three-foot-tall trees. *Different than what I expected,* Croix felt about his current environment.

"Is there a reason why we came here at night?" Croix continued looking around at his environment.

"Yes, of course. There is always a reason for everything in life, Croix," Eames replied with a nod of his head and a friendly smile.

Croix rolled his eyes, a bit peeved that Eames didn't directly answer his question.

"Before I tell you the reason"—Eames became serious again—"I want you to guess. Why do you think you were brought here at nighttime?"

"Because we have to speak with the troll at night," Croix guessed.

"Exactly, pretty simple, right? These tasks are designed to be hard, and it is said that all Gemini trolls generally have a tendency to lean toward their darker side at night. I'm not sure why. I suppose all trolls are morning creatures, but they must guard the cavern day or night, and thus he will be there waiting for you to talk to him. Well, that's not what he's waiting for. I'm sure you both know what I mean. I'm going to leave you both right here. The cavern is directly that way." Eames pointed forward. "Do not stray from the path or go in other directions."

Croix looked around and was shocked that everything looked about the same in all directions. He would most likely get lost if he went any other way. The two recruits had been told that they would not need anything this time, except for an empty backpack that Eames gave them on the ship, supposedly to carry back treasure. That being said, Croix had no choice but to simply trust Eames and go in the direction he pointed.

"I will be waiting here. Only one of you is permitted to head toward the troll and the cavern at a time. Like I said before, don't deviate. Head exactly in the direction I'm pointing at right now," he said, raising his arm to point in the same direction again.

"How will we find our way back when we are finished?" Archer asked, peering into the forest as if trying to find a path.

Eames relaxed his arm, feeling more questions might be coming. "Reasonable question. The answer is, you won't. You will have to ask the troll for directions back. Most likely, the troll will point in one direction and tell you to run straight along that path until you reach our ship. The troll will know where the ship is. The trolls always know of any disturbances to their living area. Although we are not intentionally destroying anything or doing anything wrong, we still constitute a disturbance to the living space of the troll.

"Actually, that fact alone will likely set you both off on the wrong foot with him, but no need to fear. It's not something so terrible that he won't get over it. You have to talk the creature into being your friend, letting you pass to get the treasure, and giving you directions to come back here.

"I want to reiterate one of my points to you one last time before you begin. Do not assume that you should just run back in the direction you think you came from. This jungle is disorienting. You may think you came from left"—he turned his body left—"but it turns out you really came from the right." He continued facing left but pointed behind himself. "You may think you should head north"—he finally turned to his original position and pointed north—"but the ship is located south. In other words, it is imperative that you listen to the troll's instructions at the end. Now, I believe that is all the advice I can give you two. Whenever you're ready Croix." Eames fixed his gaze on Croix and lifted his finger once more to point.

Without saying a word, Croix dashed with a small burst of speed, into the dense forest. It was a good path indeed, it was almost entirely clear. Croix had fast enough reflexes to dodge anything that would have come up in the path, but he was happy that he didn't have to. It didn't take long before he reached his destination.

As soon as he got out of the thick patch of woods, he saw a grassy area with fewer trees. The troll was leaning up against the right side of a green leafy one. The troll was a massive, hairy, two-legged creature. It had coarse black hair covering its armpits, chest, and legs; the private parts had so much hair that it was like clothing. The troll had a large club in its hand and had its head down, almost as if it were asleep. Croix couldn't tell if it was asleep or not, but he knew he didn't want to say anything yet, so he continued to look around for a bit.

Directly behind the troll was a bridge made of wood. Two lamps were at the top of the front of the bridge. As well as two lamps were positioned, in a similar fashion toward the back of the bridge. This made the bridge well lit. Croix stood there, trying to think of what his best move would be. The troll was sleeping. Maybe that was a good thing. Then again, he wasn't sure if he should wake it up, because he had to talk to it eventually.

"Well, are you going to explain yourself there? Why are ew here?"

The voice seemed to come from the troll.

It's probably not the troll. Croix dismissed the thought, but he did seem to be the only creature capable of talking in the area.

The troll's head suddenly snapped up and he bellowed. "Answer me when I'm talking to you!"

"I'm sorry, I didn't realize you were awake." Croix jumped and stammered, fearing he had already gotten off on the wrong foot.

"What's it matter whether I'm asleep or awake? That doesn't have anything to do with my question. What I want to know, what I need you to tell me, is why you are here?"

Croix wasn't ready for this to happen for some reason, he hadn't even thought of the most basic answer to give to the troll.

"I'll know if you're lying," said the troll, and he stood up with his body in front of the bridge.

Croix continued to think of what to say. A thought popped in his head. Maybe this was going to be a simpler task than he had originally thought. Tell the truth. As crazy as it sounded, it was worth a try. It worked for him back on Scorpio at the temple.

"I'm here for the treasure that lies beyond you."

"Now that's an honest lad." The troll smiled and gave a quick laugh. "Go on right ahead and claim your prize. An honest answer deserves a proper reward."

The troll stepped to the side slightly to clear the path for Croix. The troll was still blocking most of the bridge, though. He was about twelve feet tall and at least eight feet wide. Croix figured it would be safest to run a little but not jet past the massive creature. He made a slight dash toward the right side of the bridge, which was the open area of the bridge the troll wasn't blocking, but before he could reach his destination, the troll moved his club in his path. Smashing his club into Croix's face he then lifted slightly, which made Croix fly backward through the air.

The troll laughed. "You think I'm guarding this here treasure to just let anybody in who says they want it?" The troll lightly tapped his own head with his club. "Not very bright are you?"

Croix's head was rattling, his vision blurry, but he felt lucky to still be alive. The troll most likely could have killed him with the one blow if it wanted. It seemed as though the troll was holding back, as if to be playful. *This must be like a game to him,* Croix figured. While he continued to try to get his bearings together, he heard what sounded like two voices arguing, but all that stood before him was the one troll.

"You could have killed him. That's not nice. He was only being honest with us. So many lie and say they wish to be our friend. I appreciate his honesty," the new voice cried.

Dang, why hadn't I thought to say that? It was such a simple answer to the question he was posed a few seconds ago, and it was at least partially true because he was tasked with befriending him. He sat up straight and looked up at the troll who was moving his head left and right, as if to get a better look at himself. Each time his head moved to the other side, the voice and opinion changed.

"Nonsense, I twasn't trying to kill im. I was just having fun. If he would have died from that hit, then he would have deserved it."

"That's it, right there, that's the reason everybody hates you. Not all things that are weak deserve to die, and not all things smaller than us are weaker than us."

"Everybody hates you just the same as me." He nodded to himself to add weight to his statement.

Croix interrupted the conversation the troll was having with himself.

"I'm sorry, maybe he's right," Croix said as he got to his feet.

"See, he agrees with me. Weak things don't deserve to die."

"No, I meant I agree with the other one."

"Ha. He agrees with me, and I almost killed him. See, I told you before, you're too soft for anyone to like or respect you. You're the reason we have no friends, not me."

"OK, OK," Croix said, stopping them again. Putting his hands forth to garner their attention. "You're both right. Well, what I mean is that I was wrong to assume that you guys would let me get to the treasure without doing anything for you both and helping you out first. I can do you two a favor, and in return you could let me get the treasure."

"Favor? For us? What could you do for us?" The troll loomed over Croix, breathing on him.

"Whatever you need. I'm not sure if you noticed, but I'm very fast." Croix stepped back and began stretching.

"Yes, fast enough to run into my club." The troll threw his head back and laughed.

"That's not fair. I'm sure he wasn't running at his full speed, and with the amount of space you gave him it would have been impossible for him to make it past our club."

"Stop sticking up for him," the troll demanded, stamping his foot, hurt in his voice.

"He's right," Croix interjected again.

"Well, of course I'm right. You literally ran into my club."
The first voice laughed again.

"No, I meant him, not you. That wasn't anywhere near my full
speed. I only ran that slow because I thought it would be the safest
way past you." Croix stared at the bridge behind the troll, still thinking
of running past.

"So you're fast, eh? I think I might have the perfect way to
test that. I just might let you pass, if you succeed." The troll picked at
his teeth with his thumb.

"No, don't make him do it." His left side shuddered at the very
mention of the test.

"It's the only way to be sure that he's worthy." The troll
turned his back to Croix to have the rest of his conversation with
himself in private, but was still very audible. "If he can successfully
complete this, I will admit that he's an honest and true person who is
fast. It's a win-win for you and me."

"I don't know. You always say that. I don't think I trust you
anymore. 'Aye, it's a win- win for you and me,'" he said in a mocking
voice.

"All I know is that you want me to be nicer to him, and I will
be, if he does this. He might even be our friend after. Friendship is
something that is earned."

The two turned back around slowly and looked skeptical about
the words their other self just uttered. Then somehow the two voices
said at the same time, "Shake on it."

Croix witnessed the most awkward handshake he had ever
seen in his life, a right hand with a left hand.

"I have just the assignment for you, my boy," the two voices
said in unison, leaning over Croix.

Croix stared up at the towering troll and thought about the
similarities between this mission and his last mission and how
annoying it all was.

To his surprise, the task was actually simple. The trolls just
wanted him to fetch them a rabbit and make rabbit stew. He didn't
know much about the animals on Gemini, but he imagined they
wouldn't be immune to fire, like the majority of animals from Aries.
In other words, he would be able to get to the treasure fast. He paused
for a moment for reflection and realized catching and killing a rabbit
wasn't really a good test of speed. He figured they must be judging
him on how long he'd take to prepare the rabbit stew and other sorts of

things. Croix at first had thoughts of setting a simple trap to capture the rabbit. But with his super speed he figured it would be faster to catch the rabbit with his bare hands. All that he needed was something to bait a rabbit, or to spot one by luck. He wasn't sure if rabbits were abundant in the area, but he was a bit worried about getting lost so he decided to set bait for a rabbit. Croix looked around the area, and saw twigs and leaves and gathered that into a pile that he thought would look tasty to the creature. A rabbit could find the same twigs and leaves anywhere of course, but luckily a rabbit actually ran in his eyesight and Croix caught the rabbit and made short work of it. He made them the rabbit stew and took a break to eat some himself.

"You know, just so you know, I would have let you in to get the treasure without the rabbit stew," the troll said in between bites.

"I don't believe you. I think you're just saying that to sound nice after the fact."

"I'm seriously telling you, I would have let you in if you had insisted, right after I hit you with the club, because this guy over here made me feel bad."

"You should feel bad, that wasn't right," the troll's other voice said.

"Why would you have let me through? The challenge altogether wasn't very difficult, but now I'm curious." Croix stopped eating and shifted against the tree to get more comfortable. Staring at the giant next to him.

"I was going to let you through because I felt sorry for you. It is a sad thing to be a virgin." The troll had pity in his eyes when he finally made eye contact with Croix.

"A virgin? I'm not a virgin. I'm a man of the brotherhood." Croix tried to laugh off the accusation.

The troll laughed. "Seriously, don't lie to me." His expression changed instantaneously back to solemn "I used to procure virgins for a living, male and female. I can smell it on you. You're a virgin, all right"—he nodded—"just as sure as my name is Lance Pierre Armstrong Bernard Shaw Timothy Remulaude."

That's right, he never did catch their names until now.

"My name is Croix. It's nice to meet you, Lance Pierre Armstrong Bernard Shaw Timothy Remulaude. That's a really long name, may I call you Lance?" Croix and Lance put their food down and stood up for the formal introduction.

"Why would you call me Lance? Everybody always calls *him* Lance. You can call me Remulaude."

The troll reached out both of his hands in a friendly gesture. Croix shook the right hand first, which somehow seemed furrier than the left.

"Why does he get to shake your hand first?" Lance asked. Lance was the voice of the nice one.

"Oh, well, Remulaude was just closer to my favorite hand."

"You have a favorite hand aye? Like to play favorites do you?" both voices said at the same time.

"I didn't mean it like that."

"Don't worry, we are only joking." Both voices laughed together. "OK, now the item you want, the item you are allowed to take from the cave, is a ruby-red pendant on a platinum necklace. It should be one of the most beautiful things in the cave. If you give the necklace to a lady friend that you want to be intimate with, she won't be able to resist you. It's a powerful aphrodisiac," Remulaude said as he took over all the talking again.

"Made from the heart of a succubus. It is said that all of the lust of the feminine beast was sealed away in the beautiful stone, and that the woman who wears it becomes overwhelmed with lust until she can't control herself and goes after the first man she sees. This will cure your women problems, for sure. One thing, though. No, never mind, I guess I can explain everything else once you get back. Watch out for me pet, Snarkles, he's in there and likely sleeping. I suggest you try to not wake him up."

"What's a Snarkles?"

"I just told you, it be me pet. I think you people refer to it as a dragon."

Croix's eyes got wide as he took in the statement. Wow! Only his second quest, and he had to deal with another dragon already.

"You said it's sleeping, right? Is it a heavy sleeper?"

"Snarkles does enjoy his sleep very much." The troll smiled to himself. "Yes, you should be fine as long as you don't run into him, like you ran into my club earlier." This time, he seemed serious about the mention of his club. "If you can avoid running into him, you will have no troubles at all."

Another dragon. The young Aries man sighed deeply; he already had to deal with another dragon. The last one was supposedly sleeping as well. All he could hope for was that this time the dragon stayed asleep. The dragon probably was the reason the trolls told him to only get one item. *Best not to get too greedy,* he figured.

He slowly entered the cave. It was much smaller than the caves he ventured in back on Scorpio. It actually made Croix wonder how the troll himself fit inside. *The troll must not come in here often,* he rationalized.

Then again, how could a dragon even fit in here comfortably? All he knew was that the size of the cavern gave him some strange sort of feeling of security. It got brighter the closer he walked toward the center, the opening being dim and dark. Trekking his way through, he finally reached the center. Everything finally made sense to him.

"The dragon is a baby!" he said aloud, pleasantly surprised.

He caught himself right after and from then on he was as quiet as possible. Even though the dragon was a baby, he still didn't want to disturb it. The dragon was red and scaly and the size of a full-grown wolf. It had a crown on its head and jewels on its claws, its tail was curled near its face. Apparently, this dragon loved treasure. It was sleeping on a pile of it. It seemed like a good idea to focus only on what the troll told him to get, so he scanned the treasure center.

There it was. It had to be the necklace the troll told him about. The pendant was such a deep, rich, red that after he spotted it, he could hardly focus on anything else. The pendant sparkled as if somebody had just polished it, as did the necklace around it. The pendant was a few feet to the right of the dragon.

I guess I have to come a little bit closer to the Snarkles to reach the treasure. Tiptoeing near the slumbering Snarkles, he quickly went to the right before he got too close. Bent down, reached for the necklace, and grabbed it slowly, pulling it up from the ground. Looking over at the dragon, he checked to see if it was still asleep.

"I don't think you will be needing this anymore, Snarkles," he whispered jokingly as he kissed the necklace and made his escape.

It appeared everything went well without any sort of snags. Pendant in hand, he continued to sneak around, just in case. Finally, he reached what he believed was the entrance to the cave and walked right out. Somehow, that all felt too easy, but he was grateful all the same.

From the cave entrance, he could see the troll's back and the bridge he had crossed earlier. He walked across the bridge again.

"I see you made it out all right without waking Snarkles. Very good. If you would have woken him, I would have been forced to eat you." The troll stared down at him with a menacing look.

Croix looked the troll in the eyes to try to gauge whether or not he was serious.

"No, I'm only joking, of course. It's a sad thing for a man to be eaten when he's still a virgin."

"A sad thing indeed," Lance chimed in, and they shook their head.

Croix didn't say anything but was slightly annoyed that the two kept bringing it up.

"At any rate, if the girl accepts it as a gift, you will be good to go. She'll be yours. You want to be the first thing she lays her eyes upon, though, that's important."

"OK, I think I got it. Farewell, Lance Pierre Armstrong Bernard Shaw Timothy Remulaude." He put his hand up to say goodbye and nearly sprinted off.

"Wait, I imagine you be needing directions before you go. Furthermore, I just wanted to say that we feel that you're our friend now, and we will help if you ever need it and you're back on this here planet. You're not from here, right?"

"I'm from a planet not too far, but yes, you're right, I'm not a Gemini."

"Indeed, I know what the locals look like. Well, if you ever need our assistance and you're here, we will be more than willing to help."

"Anything you need," Lance added.

"That's as long as you find someone to guard the treasure"— the troll looked back toward the cave—"or basically just come back here and bring your enemies right here. As long as I can see the entrance to the cave, I will feel that it is safe and secure, and I will gladly help you crush your enemies." He finally looked back to Croix.

"That's good to know. I'm not sure I could find a replacement for you guys, though. Would it have to be another troll?"

"Troll? What's a troll?"

"I never heard of a troll either," Lance agreed, scratching his head, trying to figure it out.

"What do you guys call yourselves?" Croix gave up.

"We are treasure guardians," they stated proudly in unison.

"Oh, OK, well, would your replacement have to be another treasure guardian?"

"I don't know, just somebody tough enough to protect the treasure. I'm not really sure I've seen a lot of fellas like us running around here. Don't worry, I'm sure if you come back here, you'll figure something out if you ever need our help. So you're just going to run straight down that way."

The troll pointed one of his hands in the direction that appeared southwest. It was strange, Croix felt as though he remembered coming from the exact opposite direction, but he knew he could not deviate from the path the troll indicated.

He gave the troll a final farewell and headed down the trail the troll pointed him to. It was definitely the right route. It wasn't long before he reached the ship.

"Good thing I listened to the troll," he said, thinking out loud.

"Ahh, good, Croix, it is good to see you back in one piece and so soon." They had started a fire when Croix was gone. Eames walked away from it. "Please show me what treasure you acquired," Eames said as he stepped closer to him, genuinely interested.

Croix held out the necklace he just got from the cavern.

"Wow, that's quite a sight to behold. What does it do?" Eames inquired while staring deeply into the pendant.

"What do you mean?"

"A good number of items in that cavern are magical, or so I understand. I hear the troll only lets anybody who goes in have one item, and that if they try to take more he kills them and eats them. I also heard that the item is different for each person and is something they need or want. This pendant looks powerful so what does it do?" Eames was still staring at the pendant.

"You have never been in that cave before?" Croix eyed him suspiciously.

"No, back when I was initiated, the process was completely different, the tasks were different. Some of the tasks are the same each year while others rotate. Both the tasks you two just completed were not from previous years. There's no need to be embarrassed, please tell us what the necklace does. That might even inspire Archer to try harder when he takes his turn." Eames finally looked up at Croix. Tired of him not answering.

Would it be suspicious to tell the truth? Lying was beginning to be a thing he was forced to do regularly. If he told them it would make him faster, which was a feasible story, then they would expect him to wear it all the time. He could say though that he was fast enough because he was the king's nephew, so he gave the necklace away. The truth might not be so bad either, though.

"The necklace makes the wearer faster," Croix heard himself say out loud.

"Really, that's pretty cool. You lucked out on that one." Eames clapped his shoulder. "I would have thought that you were fast enough, given that you're directly related to the king, but I guess it can never hurt to be faster. It looks a little feminine to me, though. I can see why you're not wearing it now.

"Oh, well, I guess you're up, Archer," he said, looking at the other man, who stared at the ground blankly. "Just do whatever it is that Croix did, and you should be fine. You know the routine, run in the direction I point to, don't deviate."

Archer jumped straight up to his feet, and clapped his hands. Consumed with boredom while waiting for Croix, he had played in the dirt a little. Now he was ready.

Eames extended his arm in the same direction he had earlier with Croix.

Croix was so excited about the necklace that he fantasized the whole time Archer was gone about what was going to happen once he gave it to Ava. Quite a bit of time passed until, Archer returned, just as the sun was beginning to rise. A beautiful medley of colors were in the sky, welcoming the morning. Purple, red, orange, yellow and blue were all displayed in the strange but beautiful sunrise of Gemini. Archer had a pair of silver pants in his hands.

"I'm not even going to ask what the pants are all about," Eames said, and shook his head.

Archer didn't seem to be bothered by it and just shrugged his shoulders.

"Back in the ship, guys, it's time to go home."

They left planet Gemini to head back to Aries.

Chapter 10

In similar fashion to the last time he completed a goal, heading straight to Ava's house was the first thing that was on Croix's mind. Even more so this time, because if what the troll said was true, then he was going to get to participate in the mating ritual with her ahead of schedule. It felt like his lucky day. Just the thought of finally getting to be with her physically and not having to go through with all the other trials she made up for him, or that shock and amazement nonsense, made him feel great.

When he arrived at her place, it was almost like she was expecting him. She opened the door almost immediately.

"Back so soon?" She leaned on the door a little playfully. "Did you even stop by your home after the task to bathe and relax?"

Croix just laughed a little and didn't even answer. He should have bathed after the mission, but maybe with the pendant it wouldn't matter, he thought, and it's not like he stank, it's just that he could have been fresher. She backed away in order to let him in.

"I came straight here. I was very excited to give you this gift I got for you," he said as soon as he walked in.

Holding the necklace out lengthwise to show its beauty, he smiled at her as he offered it.

"Wow, this is a very lovely necklace. I hope it didn't set you back any. Did you buy it with the reward earnings from completing some of your quests, or perhaps you got it from Taurus? I hope it didn't cost too much. I would feel too guilty to accept it." She never touched it as she spoke. She stared at it as it remained in his hands.

"Oh, no, it was free, I assure you. In fact, I got it during my last quest."

"Is that a fact? Then why don't you give it to the brotherhood." Her gaze finally lifted from the necklace.

"It's not for the brotherhood. They could never appreciate the kind of beauty this necklace has."

"I find it somewhat interesting that they have you collect items." She stared into his eyes. "For example, the head of a dragon, a beautiful necklace, and they allow you to keep the items. What do they benefit from that?"

"I think the point is to see if I'm capable of getting the item, not for them to keep it themselves. And the reward I get is the pride and satisfaction of knowing I have completed a difficult task, and I'm to keep the item as a reminder of my past successes."

"I suppose," she said lightly while frowning and looking back at the necklace.

"Would you mind trying on the necklace now?" He smiled again and held the necklace out as if he were going to put it around her neck.

"Where is this coming from all of the sudden?" She somehow seemed surprised.

"It's just the pendant will compliment your beautiful complexion, and the necklace around it will look amazing against your skin."

"Yes, I'm sure you're right. But I don't know. What's the occasion?"

"I just want to see how it looks on you."

"I appreciate you bringing me the necklace, and I will graciously accept it as a gift, but I'm not sure I want to wear it just yet. I'm not even properly dressed. I would rather wear it when you're taking me out somewhere and courting me properly." She took a few steps back from him.

"I feel as of now you have just been bringing me stuff and showing it off. Like, 'look at this.' You get one point for amazing me, but only barely. I must warn you. You cannot simply keep bringing me things from your tasks and hoping that I accept them as shocking and amazing. That won't always work. I want you to work harder for me than that."

Croix was downtrodden and didn't know what to think.

"Are you sure you can't just try it on for a few seconds? You might not even like how it looks, and then I can bring you something else even more beautiful, and get rid of it."

"No, I'm sure it will look good on me. Maybe you're right, though. It can't hurt to wear the necklace for a few seconds. I'm going to go find a mirror to put it on for you." She looked toward her hall that led to the bedrooms.

"No need for that, my lady. I will put the necklace on you."

Quickly, and without a word, she turned around so her back was facing him and lifted her hair so he had clear access to her neck. Before he got the chance—

—a woman swiftly burst through the door.

"Hey, sis, what's going on? I was just going to tell you—Hey, wait, what are you two doing? Did I interrupt something?"

"No, not exactly. Croix just gave me a necklace and wanted me to try it on. Croix, this is my little sister, Acadia."

Ava had completely moved away from where she was a moment ago, and it seemed as though the window of opportunity had closed for him, at least for the moment.

"Hello, Acadia, it is nice to meet you."

"Nice to meet you as well, Ava has told me all about you," she replied with a wink.

"Acadia!"

"What? But you have!" Acadia laughed.

I guess that's a good thing, Croix reasoned about the fact that she spoke with her little sister about him. Acadia had a strong smell, not a bad one, but her fragrance was powerful, much heavier than Ava's. The powerful fragrance forced Croix to direct his attention to Acadia, and when he did, he realized she looked familiar. There was no mistaking it, she was clearly Ava's sister. The two women both had large, almond-shaped eyes the color of green grass, which complimented their ruby-red skin very well. Jet-black hair and full lips, with noses that slightly curved up near the nostrils. The resemblance between the two was uncanny. But there was something else, aside from her looking like Ava that reminded Croix of something. Finally, to avoid feeling any more frustration, he decided to ask.

"Do I know you from somewhere Acadia?" He interrupted whatever conversation she was having with Ava.

"No, not that I know of." She met his gaze inquisitively. "I have never met you before personally. Unless, of course, you mean you recognize me from the mating ritual dance. Ava and I both danced before the fire that night," she said in her smoky voice. She sounded more dramatic for a moment. "But you chose her," she finished flatly. "I hope you two have been enjoying each other." She winked and gave her sister an elbow nudge.

"Oh, OK, I see, you were the other woman in front of the fire."

"Yes, it was I. Unlucky me. I still haven't found a suitable mate, and Father insists that I find a brotherhood man. He always says it's not enough for me to find royalty, it has to be a man of brotherhood status. 'Those are hard workers,'" she said in a stern voice, mocking her father, "or some other nonsense." She physically dismissed her father after her impression of him with her hand.

Ava's sister, she was the other woman who danced in front of the fire. Come to think of it, why did he choose Ava? That's right, it was her dancing. Obviously, it was a dancing ritual, after all, so it only made sense. Ava was a better dancer than her sister. However, after meeting her sister, he got the vibe that maybe he should have chosen her instead. Maybe he would have actually gotten to mate already if he had.

I can't believe my luck. I must have chosen the only woman on Aries who wouldn't have actually mated with me that night, Croix had a brief conversation in his head.

"Croix, not to be rude, but I need to talk to my sister," Ava mentioned after making eye contact and touching his arm. "Would you please give us some time? Come back whenever you finish your next task. Thank you again for the necklace. I won't try it on until you and I get a proper chance to spend time together." She let go of his arm with a gentle squeeze.

Just as I suspected, my chances are blown with her again. I'm not mad. I should have suspected it. At least she isn't going to wear it without me being present.

"Sure thing, Ava, I'll see you later. It was nice meeting you, Acadia."

He left empty-handed again. Lance Remulaude would have probably laughed at him if he saw. It seemed as if the two sisters were having an argument just as he was leaving, but he didn't care, he was still upset about not getting to copulate.

Oh well, maybe it won't be hard to finish shocking and amazing her, he thought, walking away more defeated than the first time he spent the night over her place.

* * *

"Cancer, you have some nerve showing your face here, in my throne room, unannounced, and you still haven't even brought me any results. The revolt is still going strong. My men are out there dying." Leo slammed his fist on the left hand rest of his throne.

"Then why don't you join them in the fight?"

"I have been advised not to, and I think it may be a bad idea." Leo stood up and stared out the window. "I don't want to kill too many of them at once. One of my closest advisors said that may be the reason the revolt started in the first place, because I killed one of their leaders." He threw a glance over his shoulder before looking back toward his window.

"Sure, whatever excuse you need to make." Cancer cut his eyes to the side and fought off a laugh. "I have actually come to speak to you about that. I can have the entire rebellion over within a day or so. In just enough time for you to prep for your special day. I need you to do something first. The people of your world have spoken. They no longer wish to see the bloodshed of their fellow commoners and half bloods in the deadly lion's den. You need to announce to the people that no longer will those suspected of crimes be forced to fight for their lives to prove their innocence."

"I am not going to let any foolish, undeserving, common blood weaklings dictate my life and my decisions. I run this kingdom," Leo said through his teeth, his full attention directed toward Cancer.

"Relax, it doesn't matter whether or not you actually stop having them fight in the arena. I'm just saying, for now, you need to reach out to all the people of your kingdom and tell them that you will no longer be having these exhibition matches in the ring for the accused. They don't think it's fair, or that it proves anything. With the death of that martyr being the catalyst for the rebellion, their making a statement loud and clear. They won't fight for you in the arena anymore for trivial reasons. They would rather die in the streets, fighting for what they believe in. You must tell them that from now on, they will receive judgment some other way."

"There is no other way to solve this, other than me yielding?"

"Ha, that's just the start of it. Honestly, there may still be more things that need to be done. On your end, this may be the only thing you need to do, perhaps. But I'm just telling you that I know the solution to your problems, and one of the ways to stop this rebellion, before things get even worse for you, is to admit that you have been wrong this entire time. Your people think of you as a tyrant and as the worst king, which is why you had the rebellion in the first place. I'm not trying to insult you." Cancer's tone lightened. "I'm genuinely trying to help you. If you do this for me, well, really more so for yourself, I'm sure you won't lose too many more of your pride. Speaking of which, I hear two of your finest are missing. That would have never have happened had you loaned them to me."

"How dare you joke at a time like this, while my royals are being slain?" Leo's spittle landed on Cancer's face, and he got aggressively close.

Cancer didn't flinch, but wiped the spit from his face. Calmly, he continued. "I'm not joking. At any rate, if you make the statement as I'm telling you, then everything should work out fine. The people will be divided among themselves and some will no longer wish to oppose you, since their strongest motivation was to end the thoughtless slaughter of the arena."

"I did not force them to fight to the death strictly for entertainment. Does no one talk about the great deeds I do for the people, or my generosity? I give to them copiously, so when they steal or commit crimes in my kingdom, I have them punished publicly to dissuade others from doing the same. I still believe there is nothing cruel or evil about having them fight publicly."

"That may or may not be true, but what if they aren't guilty and they die in the ring? Combat doesn't always prove who is right or who is honest."

"I will make the announcement." Leo turned away and moved swiftly to sit back in his throne. "You do whatever else on your end you need to do to bring this to a close. You still owe me, and I still haven't seen any results. You still have my men." He turned toward Cancer.

"Yes, I know. Anything worth doing always takes time, remember that."

Cancer disappeared.

Leo had a device that allowed him to project himself out to all the lions that were outside. The holographic image displayed King Leo's face in the sky. He appeared as though he were talking from the heavens to his people. He had never had a reason to use the device, but he felt confident that his message would get to everyone who mattered.

Zemar and Llewellyn had fallen to the rebels and were being strung up to be hung. After all the fighting the crowd had settled on that option.

"Attention, all Leos and half-beasts, royalty, and everyone else. It is I, your king, Leo. I would like to let you all know that from now on, the guilt or innocence of those accused of a crime, will not be determined in the lion's den. From now on, guilt or innocence will be determined by other means. The arena will no longer be used in trials. If that is the reason you all wish to wreak havoc on our fair planet, I ask you to stop at once, and consider that you are destroying the very areas that you all live in. I am more than happy to negotiate with you to find other solutions that may help for other issues you suffer from as well. Please, let's start to rebuild Leo and bring an end to this violence."

Some people from the crowd started walking away immediately following the announcement.

"I guess there's no point in continuing if he's going to give us our way," a random Leo said.

"There has been so much destruction caused by this rebellion, maybe we should stop all this," another voice cried out.

"I hope my house didn't get burned down, so much chaos, I feel like I don't even know what to do anymore," a female voice from the crowd added.

"What are all you talking about? They are still our oppressors, are they not? King Leo is still a selfish, self-serving, worthless joke of a king. We can't believe a word of what he just said," the rebel leader announced, once again pointing his torch at Zemar and Llewellyn. "I say we still kill his two henchmen. Even if we do call a truce and find peace. These two bastards have killed enough of us to empty out a small village."

The Leos who held Zemar and Llewellyn stood there frozen for a moment, still trying to process everything that was going on. They wore steel masks commonly worn by the king's executioners. The masks covered everything but the eyes, and the design was so ferocious-looking, it usually kept victims from begging for mercy. It was odd that the rebel lions had the masks, though they didn't seem to help. The would-be executioners seemed unsure whether they should hang the two royals.

Suddenly, a fist burst through the chest of the crowd leader. He instantly coughed out his own blood and dropped his torch.

Unseen forces snapped the executioners' necks.

"Cancers!" a Leo-Virgo woman yelled, and the crowd panicked and fled.

"They can't kill us all," some said as they dispersed, a lot of them dropping their torches.

The Leo commoners were afraid of the Cancer Elite. The destruction of their leader, which only took a moment, and the death of the executioners was all it took to send the already thinned crowd in a panicked frenzy.

"We got saved by the skin of our teeth," Zemar said, only able to see from one of his eyes. "Our king is amazing."

"Yes, I can hardly believe what just happened." Llewellyn touched a wound near his stomach to check for damage and recoiled at the pain.

The two royal Leos were in such pain, and still exhausted form the battle they had just lost, so they stood there for a moment catching their breath.

***

Callum wasn't going to see his mom for a long time and he knew it, so he decided to make his goodbye meaningful.

"Momma, I won't be home for a while. I'm leaving to join the Capricorn Royal Cavalry," Callum said as soon as he entered the kitchen, a black bag slung over his shoulder.

"How is that even possible? I thought everybody that joined the Cavalry had to be royal blood," his mother said, and she turned to face him, tucking a thick strand of her pure silver hair behind her ear. His mother had aged gracefully, she remained a breathtaking Capricorn woman and the source of Callum's good looks.

"They opened it up for nonroyals just recently," Callum said, looking away.

"How long are you going to be gone for?" she asked, stopping all motion and giving him her complete attention. Cleaning the house was her main concern until she realized how important the conversation was.

"I'm not sure. I imagine for a very long time." He stared at the ground and dropped his bag.

"I'm not going to try to stop you," she sighed. "You always did have to have everything your way, just like your father who raised you, and you seem to have your mind set to this. I just hope it will be everything you want it to be. Not everything is always as nice as it sounds, and not everything is always what it seems. Be safe. I love you. If it gets too hard, or you can't carry on, just come back home. I'll take you in anytime you ever come back, because I love you." She held her arms out to hug him. Deeply, tightly she gripped her son.

She loosened her grip and looked him in his eyes. "Don't worry about all the chores I'm going to have to do by myself when you're gone, and don't worry about me making a living without your help or bringing back food," she said, looking away for a moment. Then she looked back at him after her statements to see if she had made him feel guilty.

They shared a laugh together at her exaggerations.

"Mom, I know it may be hard when I'm gone, but I will try my best to come back as soon as I can. I think I can return after training."

"Even if you can't, you should still go. Maybe you'll even get to meet your birth father."

There she goes again, claiming that the king is my father. Feeling the statement didn't dignify a response, he rolled his eyes and moved on.

"Yes, OK, Mom, I will go and make a new life. When I return, you will no longer have to live in this tiny, cramped shack. I will come back with riches from Taurus and other great and wondrous things you have never seen."

With that, he took his shoulder bag, slung it over his shoulder, and left from his mother's house. Tears streamed down her face as she saw the only child she had left leave. Right outside his door, his two royal escorts waited. The emotionally driven goodbye between mother and son wasn't long. He didn't want to be rude, and so he hurried out to them.

"Are you ready?" Caleb inquired.

"Yes, I think I have everything."

"Are you able to ride a horse? What was your name again, Kullen, right?" Caleb stepped away from the door and walked to a horse.

Callum was confused, when the prince had made his speech earlier, neither one of them had horses.

"It's Callum." Callum followed suit, strolling through the brown-yellow grass of his front yard.

"OK, Callum, do you know how to ride a horse?" Caleb said as he mounted his black horse.

"No, I have never even seen a horse before today." Callum admitted. "Where did the horses come from?" He stared at the animals looking from Caleb's horse and then back to Cassius's.

"It's all right, he will ride with me," Cassius, already seated on a brown and white mare, concluded.

"Somebody brought the horses over for us, so that we can get to the prince faster. When the prince is meeting new people for the first time and any other royal of lower rank is present, the lower-ranking royal is not allowed to ride a horse, unless, of course, we are in battle or during times of war. This is so that the prince may stand out more gloriously. It's actually his father's rule, from what I understand." Caleb finished with a shrug.

"That seems a bit strange, considering that these horses aren't the same type as his horse from earlier. Wouldn't he have still stood out just for the simple fact that his horse was a different color?"

"I know you are young, and the prince wants us to welcome you, so I'm not going to be mean. I want to be as nice as possible. Please listen to me when I tell you this," Cassius warned with a strong gaze that he directed at Callum. "It's best not to question decisions royalty makes. The prince may have seemed nice back there when you met him, but he's very strict about the rules. The rules were set for a reason, as far as he's concerned. You will get hurt questioning his rules in front of him, no matter how silly you think they are."

"I won't ask anything else, then."

"Good, let's go."

Cassius helped Callum up onto the horse and gave him simple instructions. "Just hold on as best you can."

Caleb had already taken off. Callum was amazed at how far the castle was. They rode past desolate areas in Capricorn, and even some nicer areas with rich green grass, bigger houses, and stables of animals.

Not everybody has to be royalty to live a better life, Callum reasoned to himself with a smile. That's what he liked about his planet. He heard that some who weren't of royal blood on Capricorn still lived good lives. They passed by a marketplace with small wood huts holding a vast array of items from all over. They passed by metal-and-silver-encased shops and houses. The further they went, the nicer the houses were. Eventually they came to an area with mansions and small castles.

This had to be where royalty lived, judging by the enormity and gorgeous exterior of the castles and homes near them. The two men he rode with did not say anything, but the horses slowed down to a walk. Before he knew it, they were directly in front of a huge castle shaped like the rook chess piece. There was also a bigger castle not too far behind it that was more rounded, but somewhat similar in shape and a lot taller.

"We are here." Caleb tugged on the reins to make the horse stop entirely.

"Wait out here, Callum. I will go up and get the prince," Cassius told him, while dismounting.

Cassius entered the huge castle by himself and was gone for a while. When he finally came back out, the prince was with him.

"You're lucky, Callum, you're the last recruit for the day. Let's go," the prince said. His garments were even fancier than before and looked more comfortable, and were dark blue in color with a white cape.

Caleb and Cassius tied their horses up and they all began walking toward a large grassy field, not too far from the prince's castle. It was a massive, open, expansive area. Far from where they entered, the opposite end of the grass field was littered with machines and other equipment, and even further out it looked like there was a small forest area. Callum saw what he believed to be at least five hundred Capricorn men in common wear. They truly did have a lot of recruits. Callum really did feel lucky.

"Please join the group," the prince said, and waited for Callum to blend in with the others. "Hello all, I am Cicero. I have gathered you here, as you all know, in order for you to join the ranks of Capricorn Royal Cavalry." Some men began clapping.

"Please hold your applause." He folded his arms behind his back and planted his feet, standing front and center. "Now, I'm sure you would all like to be leaders, at least I hope so, but unfortunately, some of you will have to follow. This is precisely why we are here right now. You will all be competing today to determine your rank and duties.

"There will be exercises designed to test your strength, overall endurance, your combat skills, and listening skills. Some of these tasks will be more difficult for some of you than others, but I assure you there will be things far more difficult in store for you if you actually become a member of the Capricorn Royal Cavalry. This is a once-in-a-lifetime event, because traditionally only royals are chosen for the positions you will be competing for. However, there is great need to protect our wonderful planet from a number of potential threats, so our forces will be open to any who wish to join and successfully complete these endeavors.

"I will say this now, even if you find you aren't scoring as well as you would like, still try your hardest to finish. If you finish, even if you finish last, I assure you there will be a spot for you in our cavalry. I am just here to deliver the speech and as such, I cannot be here to watch the completion of all your assignments. But I may show up for the second or last competition. Until then, I must say farewell to you all. Good luck to all of you. May the best Cap win. Cassius, Caleb, and Cyd"—he indicated the three selindium-clad men to his left—"will be here to assist you in any way that you need."

Callum hadn't noticed until then, but there was another royal Capricorn standing there near Cassius and Caleb. The slimmest of the three, Cyd stood straight with perfect posture, having even more presence than his fellows and yet somehow bearing a sunnier appearance than his two counterparts.

Callum prepared himself mentally as he thought about his goal. He knew this wasn't going to be easy, but all he would have to do was keep his eyes on the prize.

Cassius took center stage. "I know you have all heard of how successful the Capricorn Royal Cavalry has been in past battles. I'm sure you have all heard the legends of our king. I want to tell you, at least most of that is true," Cassius said, as he walked before the group, one side to the next.

Some recruits laughed.

"All jokes aside. The thing that separates the Capricorn Royal Cavalry from all the other royal forces from all the other planets is perseverance, dedication, and endurance. All the Capricorns I know aren't extremely fast like the Aries, they aren't expert archers like the Sagittarius, not invisible like the royal Cancer. What is true about all the Capricorns that I know is that they are the toughest, most dedicated in all the universe. None of you were forced to come here. None of you are forced to remain here. You can all quit, whenever you want, and we, the Cavalry, will be all the better for it. We don't need quitters. I know the prince told you that you would be challenged here today, but he didn't tell you how hard we are going to push you. I assure you that I will do all that's in my power to make sure that you all push yourselves to your mind's and body's end. The same will be true of Caleb and Cyd. Feel free to exit now, if you cannot handle it."

"With all due respect, sir, I know we are all grateful for this opportunity and nobody wants to leave," one of the recruits spoke up.

"Ohhh, OK, so you speak for everybody in this group, is that it? Is he your leader everybody?" Searching for an answer, Cassius studied the crowd.

"I think he was just trying to speak positively, sir," another recruit said.

"OK, so *you* have all the answers now? I see. I apologize. Perhaps you two should be doing this instead of me, and you should be up here in my place speaking to them. Royal blood doesn't mean anything, neither does experience. I don't know what I'm talking about. You two can go ahead and come on up here and replace me whenever you're ready," Cassius continued.

Nobody moved.

"OK, so you're not ready to take the lead then. I suggest you all do a better job listening from now on," he said to the entire crowd. "You two, step forward."

The two Capricorn men were a light brown, similar to Callum, and of average height. Nothing seemed to be remarkable about them.

"There is a time to talk and a time to listen. It should be clear to you all by now"—he directed his statement toward the crowd— "that this would be considered a time to listen." His attention came right back on the two. "You two personally will have the hardest tasks, I'm going to make sure of that. Furthermore, you two have already failed one of your exercises, an exercise in listening, that was supposed to come later."

His attention went to the crowd again. "Good news for everybody else who didn't speak, is that you are guaranteed to out rank these two. Now I'll say this again. Anybody who wants to leave is free to do so. Nobody will judge you here, and even if they do, I certainly won't. None of you are royal blood. Royal blood on Capricorn is both a gift and a curse. At least for the males, that is." He paused briefly to signal for the two who interrupted to speak with Cyd, who quickly took their information and had them return to formation.

"I was born into this. I was made to do this. I am genetically superior to all of you, unless you have royal blood that both you and I don't know about. I did not have a choice to join the Cavalry, as you all have here today. Feel free to exercise your right to leave if you see fit.

"You will also have the chance to leave during the tests if you feel that you cannot go on. As long as it is safe for you to leave, you can leave at any time. I will not make another announcement like this during any of the trials. You'll know if you need to go.

"With that being said, I would like to describe how this is going to work. You will all begin by competing directly against one another. What I mean by that, is that two of you will go up against one another one on one for this first trial. Later, as the trials proceed, it may be more than two of you competing at a time, or you may even be timed and perform a task by yourself.

"Obviously, we won't be in this area for the entire time. We will have to migrate occasionally to new areas. There will be no breaks aside from the time it takes us to move from one place to the next. You will not be given any water. Water is nice, but you will not always have water on the battlefield. You may go on for days without any nourishment at all while you are engaged in a battle. I'm telling you this because I'm giving you another chance to quit. This is really the last time I offer you the chance to quit."

A few laughed in the crowd.

"You do not laugh unless you are told to. I did not tell a joke. Joking time is over," he said stopping to stare at the recruits.

Everybody in the crowd stopped laughing.

"Your first task will be very simple, extremely simple. You will run from this point right before me and back to that other point over there, over and over again, until you can't run anymore. You will be in direct competition with one person, who will also be running."

The rookies looked out at the two points he was talking about. It was very simple. There were four rocks in two pairs. One pair per runner.

"Who would like to volunteer to go first? If I don't have any volunteers, I can pick from certain parameters I will set. In fact, I have to set parameters for choosing the order you all will go in for future exercises." Cassius stopped for a moment to look to his fellow instructor. "Caleb, do you mind?"

Caleb quickly stepped to the center, and Cassius walked to the side. "It looks like I will have to take over now. It really doesn't matter whether it's me or Cassius or Cyd or anybody else, we may as well all be the same person, we are equal parts to this, and you will still have the same outcome when you are judged and your performance is measured. That being said, I am waiting for volunteers. I will pick the first one of you I see if none of you volunteer."

Finally, the two men who had spoken out earlier stepped forward.

"I would like to volunteer."

"I would like to as well."

They looked at each other and started talking. "Haven't you gotten into enough trouble with our leaders?"

"I just figured, might as well get it over with, because I'm already in trouble. That was my logic."

"I was thinking the same thing." They laughed together.

"Gentleman, please, enough with the chitchat. Nobody cares if you're fast friends. I will count the amount of times that you on the left run back and forth."

"My name is Raff—"

"I don't recall asking for your name. As of now, your name is useless until you prove yourself otherwise. As I was saying, I will count how many times Useless over here on the left runs back and forth." Caleb pointed to Raff. "My associate Cyd will count for you on the right. Lastly, it doesn't matter who begins first. Start whenever you're ready."

The two men both began running at about the same time. Back and forth, back and forth. For the longest time. Finally, they reached over one hundred laps.

"OK, since those two are still running, I think it's safe to say that one hundred times back and forth will be a benchmark. I expect you all to go out there with that as your minimum goal in mind," Cassius said, making his way closer to the contestants. "Also, I have figured out the order in which the rest of you will compete. Age. Each of you will go according to how old you are, oldest to youngest. Now that we have that settled, that will be how all competitions go from now on unless we have volunteers."

Cassius noticed the two men were still running laps. He walked over to his two colleagues to see how many laps the two men had done.

"One hundred twenty-five! Not bad for commoners. I think. That's almost impressive. I feel it's important that I remind you all that this is only one of the tasks that you are to complete. I understand that none you want to stop until the person you're competing with gives up, but you should be mindful that this is the first and easiest task. It is designed to be easy so that you don't waste all your energy on it. As I said before, we will not give you any traditional breaks during any of these tests. I'm glad you two feel the need to use so much energy. It's good to see you have so much spirit," he said, turning to the two men.

Callum was eager to go, so he began to stretch, preparing to volunteer next. One of the contestants began speaking to him, a short older man.

"I don't know if I would volunteer, if I was you. This may be one of those tasks that it would most likely be best to just sit back and watch, to be honest. I know they didn't say this earlier, but the Cavalry are known for their patience. Patience is probably another thing that we are being tested on. Maybe not right now, but it will most likely come up. I'm not trying to tell you what to do, kid, I'm just saying, offering my opinion is all."

Callum stopped stretching and sized up the other man in an attempt to appraise the worth of his comments. He was a hairy and diminutive Capricorn.

"I suppose there isn't any huge, obvious benefit to volunteering. I'm just eager to go."

"Understandable, but look at everyone else. What do you see them doing?"

"Nothing, just watching."

"Exactly, a crowd this large, I'm sure plenty of them want to get this over with, but there are merits to going first and merits to going last. I seriously think maybe sit this one out for a while, and then later, you can go first if you feel that going last wasn't the best strategy, or is counterproductive to a certain task. Only later will you know if going first or last is best. It's early now, so you can afford to go last on this one, trust me."

Callum didn't say anything to the man, he just nodded his head. Waiting wasn't so bad. He would just wait.

Chapter 11

Valera finally arrived on Aries. It wasn't exactly what she expected, but it was still nice, for the most part. The plants and trees around her weren't very green or colorful. Everything had a reddish- orange hue to it, which reminded her of a sunset on Virgo. It was the afternoon, she was sure of it. Maybe the world just always had the look of a sunset to it.

That's just wonderful, she thought to herself about the beauty of the foreign world.

The ground beneath her, however, wasn't so beautiful. She was standing atop black grass that somehow still seemed alive. This was no time to criticize, so she decided to embrace all that she saw on Aries. The place she had landed was odd. She'd aimed for an area with regular citizens, but this region seemed underpopulated.

"Perhaps Aries has a smaller population than the other worlds I have been to," she said to herself. "Maybe I just chose a bad area. I'm already here, so I might as well continue to look around."

She took a few more steps forward from her ship and saw a great ball of light on the ground. The ball of light alternated between multiple colors. Green, blue, red, orange, yellow. All these colors flashed in the ball of light. The light kept growing stronger. It felt as if the ball was getting closer to her, although she wasn't moving.

"You may want to watch out," a nearby female child's voice suggested.

"Are you talking to me? Whatever do you mean?" Valera asked, still mesmerized, staring at the ball, unblinking.

Suddenly, Valera fell to the ground, she didn't know what hit her, but somehow she ended up behind a rock.

"What happened to the ball of light?"

"That was an exploding spike ball, not a ball of light."

"Who are you? And what are you talking about?"

"My name is Apple, and I just saved your life," the little Aries girl said.

"Apple?"

The little girl was the color of red licorice and had a smile as big as her face and little black twin pigtails in her hair. She looked very friendly, and was dressed in a green dress and shoes with a ribbon that matched.

"Yes, my parents said that they wanted me to be one of a kind despite being a commoner, that's why they named me that." She stared at Valera with her green eyes.

"What is an exploding spike ball?" Valera had really been more curious about that.

"It's the creature that almost killed you." The little girl sat on the rock. "I heard them called other things by other people, but I can't remember the other names they're called right now. Basically, they are little furry creatures that have prickly things that come out of their backs. They can make these prickly things change colors, dazzle, and sparkle, which attracts prey as well as distracts its predators. Then it shoots all the prickly things out, like *pewww*, out of its body, and if those things land in you, you're in trouble," the little girl said, putting her hands to her face in feigned distress.

"Prickly things? Do you mean like the ones shrews have?"

"Yes, I think that's what those little fur balls are called." The girl smiled at her.

Kaboom! A small bright explosion nearby shook the ground. They both took cover behind the rock.

"Wow that was crazy. We would have both died from that explosion. That's insane it was such a small creature. They have creatures called shrews on my planet too but they aren't nearly as dangerous."

"Yes, I guess that makes sense. I could tell you're not from here. I have never seen someone from here stare at one of them before. Plus, you don't look like anyone I've ever seen before."

"You sure do speak a lot for a child."

"Yes, I have to." She got serious. "My dad always says 'if you don't speak up, nobody will listen to you.' I don't know what it means but it sounds true."

Valera's curly brown hair bounced as she laughed. "Perhaps you wouldn't mind bringing me to your parents."

"I don't know. I'm not really supposed to talk to strangers. I just did that to save your life because I could tell you were a foreigner."

"Excuse me, I suppose I have been rude." Valera stood up to introduce herself. "My name is Valera. I am from Virgo. I am actually the queen of Virgo. I have come to Aries on peaceful terms to learn more about your land in its purest form outside of the kingdom." She offered her hand to the little girl for a handshake. Apple stood up but ignored her hand.

"There's no way you are royalty." The little girl's eyes squinted as she stared even harder.

"Oh, and why's that?"

The little girl paused to give it some thought. "I heard Virgos are geniuses, especially the royalty. You almost got killed by a glowing fur ball just now. If I hadn't come by, you would have got shot and exploded. I don't think royalty travel alone, either."

"You are a smart little girl, but I assure you I am royalty. I have chosen not to have an escort, so I can travel as I please and get into fun adventures on every planet I come to. Have you ever seen anything like this before?"

Valera showed Apple her bracelet, which contained stars shining in pitch-black darkness, the same color as the blackest of night skies.

Apple stared at it, wide eyed. "That looks nice, but still doesn't prove anything." Apple quickly dismissed the evidence, averted her eyes, and began squinting again at Valera.

"I don't know if I would call myself a genius, but I am capable of some things, and the shrew was unlike anything I had ever seen, so I wanted to enjoy looking at it for as long as possible. Here, I can show you that I'm royalty. Do you see that rock over there? I will lift it with my mind."

"What do you mean?"

"Just watch."

Valera stared at a large dirt red rock that wasn't very far from the two of them, and within a few seconds, it was floating toward them.

"Whoa, that's cool. I guess you really are royalty. I don't even think the king can make things float. Make something else float, please." She jumped up and down.

The rock fell down a few feet from the two of them once Valera looked away from it. Valera began staring at Apple and suddenly, the little girl began floating.

"Whoa, now you're making me float. Cool. Higher please."

The girl began to float higher and higher, and then she was moving faster and faster back and forth, higher and higher. The little girl stuck out her arms like a bird and began giggling.

"I can fly now," Apple said. "Higher, higher."

"Now, now, if you fly too high it will be hard to get you down."

She set the girl down, who was still giggling.

"Haha, that was so cool. You're my best friend now. I used to have a friend named Alfred, but he's gone now. I think he moved. That was so cool. I really felt like I was flying. I want to know all about your planet."

The little girl took Valera's hand in hers.

"Are all people from where you're from able to do that, or is it because you are the queen?" Apple stared up at her.

"As far as I know, only me and one other Virgo are able to do that." She shrugged.

"Who is the other person?"

"My husband."

"Wow, that's so cool. My mommy and daddy are going to be happy to meet you. They've never seen royalty before."

They were walking toward one of the small huts in the area.

"Careful, Queen." She removed her hand from the queen's.

"Why is that? Is there another exploding fur ball around?" Valera looked around in anticipation.

"No, ash bugs," Apple whispered from the side of her mouth.

"What's an ash bug?" Valera matched her whisper and leaned to be closer to her.

"They look just like ash from a fire, but they fly around and try to land on your tongue or get into your body some other way because they are pamatites."

"Do you mean parasites?" The two continued whispering.

"Yes, that, no more talking."

They closed their mouths as they moved through the black grass, continuing toward the small hut. It did in fact appear as though ash was floating in the air all around them, but upon closer inspection, the wings of the ash bugs could be seen. Quietly, the two trekked on until they were out of the field.

"I think we are OK now." Apple's voice returned to normal. "If they land on your tongue, they can do all sorts of things. It's really scary. You're lucky you had me with you today." She pointed at herself and closed her eyes while boasting. "You could have died twice. You owe me, Queen."

"This whole time I thought we had become fast friends. I would say we are, especially considering I showed you my abilities earlier."

"That was amazing. Apple laughed. I was only joking. We are finally here."

They arrived before a small, brown hut.

***

All I have to do is improvise. Mar worked hard to focus himself on his way back to the table. *All I have to do is improvise.* Just like that, a brilliant idea came to him.

"Hey, Mar, welcome back," Queen Gemini said. "I was starting to worry about you. I was going to send my husband in looking for you." The king and queen laughed.

"Yes, I'm not feeling so well." He stood near his chair.

"Was it the food? I will literally kill the chef if his food made you sick," King Gemini said, gripping his fork in one hand, knife in the other, and looking toward the kitchen.

"No, Gemini. I'm not so sure it was your food. My date and I ate earlier on Libra. Something hasn't been sitting right with me since I left there." He held his hand over his stomach.

"That is true, he has been acting weird since we finished at that restaurant," Catalina confirmed.

Mar could barely hold back his smile. It was a clever lie he had thought of, in his opinion. Catalina herself could attest to his strange behavior upon departure of Libra.

"Although it didn't seem like he was sick, and he said that he was just deep in thought, because I do remember asking him multiple times if he was OK. Now that I think about, it seems strange for him to have not said anything during the meal or even after, when I asked him about it."

His happiness instantly faded. He wasn't sure if she was trying to call him a liar indirectly, but it certainly seemed like it.

"I wasn't sure of it at the time. I didn't know if I had eaten something bad, or if the food wasn't sitting right with me, or if something else was the matter. It seemed that the princess here was enjoying her food, so I didn't want to ruin the mood."

"I find it interesting that neither of you are directly talking to each other anymore," the king noted, his eyes glancing over each of them in analysis.

"Haha, that's funny, very good observation, very interesting," Mar said. "At any rate, I guess we'll be heading out now. I would like to thank you for your hospitality."

"Of course, Mar, anytime. It was lovely meeting your bride to be. I understand you two are to be wed soon, is that correct?" the queen asked, eyes lit with excitement.

"Nothing is written in stone," Catalina said in a nonchalant tone.

Mar couldn't put his finger on it, but he felt as though maybe he had made Catalina angry. He also felt as though she didn't believe him. *My lies are certainly believable, she has no reason to disbelieve me, he reasoned to himself. It must just be my imagination.*

The two young people were escorted out by the same twins who had brought them in.

The two walked together to the ship in silence.

"Well, at least I'll finally get to see where you are from, right, Mar?" Catalina ended the silence when their ship took off.

He hadn't thought about that. Being sick meant he was heading home. There was no way he could justify not showing her his place.

"In fact, I can even nurse you back to health, probably." She gave a smile. "My father always says I can be very nurturing when I want to be."

"No, no, I surely couldn't allow you to. I have servants for that sort of thing, and my family's love and support. I would not want to take up too much of your time. Aside from that, I would say this sickness isn't too bad. It may pass on its own after a few days of rest."

"Surely you are quite sick." She nodded. "If you were not, you would not have stopped the lovely conversation we were having with the Geminis that you are so fond of."

This wasn't going well. He had almost been caught in a lie. She could be quite pushy when she wanted to be, he realized.

"I'm sorry. You're right, I just didn't want to make you to feel obligated. I do feel quite sick. I suppose if you insist, then you can watch over me for a little while, if it makes you feel better. Maybe you could even help me fall asleep," he urged playfully.

"I'm sure I could," she replied evenly.

He wasn't sure if she meant the same thing he did. One thing he was sure of, was that she wasn't going to leave as easily as he thought she was. *Maybe that's a good thing, he thought optimistically. This must be one of her traits; stubbornness. I'm not sure if I find her equally attractive or more attractive because of her being so difficult, but I know I like it, somewhat. This could be a fun challenge. I have to make sure not to anger her too much, though, because this union between me and her means a lot to my father.*

"I'm really looking forward to seeing your home, Mar. I have heard such great things about your kingdom."

Diantha and the letter would have to wait. As long as Catalina did leave eventually, everything would be fine, and he would be able to go to Taurus to sort through all the clues. Catalina would surely leave as soon as he pretended to be asleep, and he would slip out when she was gone. Diantha was always ready to see him, no matter how short the notice.

"Did you know that you do that a lot?" Catalina asked, staring at him again.

"Do what a lot?"

"Go deep into thought. You're making the same faces and you seem to be just as deep in thought as you were when we were on our way to Gemini. If I didn't know any better, I would think that there was nothing wrong with your stomach, but rather your mind. You don't look like someone with stomach pain to me."

Dammit, I need to be more cognizant of what's going on. I have to quit getting so lost in thought. This woman, Catalina, keeps trying to read me, and I don't like that. I have to keep everything together.

"I apologize," he said with the whisper of a smile. "I have a lot going on. Not only is my stomach bothering me, but I was thinking of some things that are going on with my father, in terms of our planet."

"Oh, really, what things?"

What is she, an investigator? Mar was getting angry about her not accepting his lies and simple answers, but he had to keep it in. He was growing tired of her questioning him, but he didn't want to blow up at her, because that might as well be a confession to the fact that he was lying about something.

"For one, my father has sent away all the half bloods from our planet. That has him stressed because the half bloods were a vital asset to our world, and we all treated them with respect."

"Interesting, I thought when we spoke about it earlier you said that you felt they were mistreated, which led me to believe you meant on your own planet."

"No, I actually meant generally speaking, among all the other kingdoms."

"OK, I see, well, I'm sure it was in their best interest for them to get sent to Aquarius. I've only been once, but it's a lovely place, and the king is a kind man."

Finally, she seemed somewhat content with the answer he had just given her. It was mostly the truth, after all.

"Prince Mar, we have arrived," his chauffeur, a hornless bald headed Aries-Pisces man, said.

The ride back from Gemini seemed much longer than the ride to Gemini. All he had to do was keep things going with his lies until Catalina left.

This shouldn't be too hard, I hope, he said in his mind.

***

"Magnus, it's about time you reported back to me. How are things going, working for that snake of a king?" King Aries asked his royal.

"As of now, my lord, Cancer has only been having us gather items. So far, we have traveled to seven of the other planets in search of the items. It's strange, he gave us rules like not to engage with other royals or to let others know what we are up to."

"Have you given him any of the things that he has asked for?"

"No, not yet. He said not to report back to him until we had acquired everything on his list. I just wanted to report to you, in order to see what your thoughts were on the task at hand."

"I'm not really sure what to make of it. You three are the fastest, aside from my brother, myself, and my sons. It actually makes sense that he would have you gather things. I would say don't worry about it too much for now. Just give him what he wants. At least he isn't having you do anything too suspicious."

"Understood, Master. I am almost finished with everything. I will contact you as soon as we finish up with Cancer, before we head back home."

"Indeed."

The image of his trustworthy brotherhood man quickly disappeared from the water screen. What could Cancer be planning? Knowing the treachery he was capable of, Aries felt uneasy. Whatever he was up to, it couldn't be anything good, but Aries didn't want to have an unnecessary war. Especially not against Capricorn, or Taurus, or possibly even Sagittarius.

"What I'm doing is right, it's the only way," he reassured himself.

***

"Finally, it's about time you brought the specimens in." King Virgo said.

Vernon brought a humongous metal cart that had the bodies of five orange, red, and brown common Leos.

"This should help further all of my experiments. For once, I'm almost impressed by your efforts, Vernon." Smiling wasn't usually Virgo's thing, but a quick one formed on his face in Vernon's direction.

"Thank you, Master."

"Yes, yes, now get out. I will call you when I need you." Virgo shooed him out.

Virgo finally had everything he needed to conduct his newest experiment, splicing of DNA. He had attempted it before, but this time he was going to create his own creature nearly from scratch. Beginning with pregnant Libras, he would use the DNA from the kings and see if he could mix it with the baby Libra and its mother. The baby was still in the pregnant patient's stomach, and Virgo decided to begin there.

"Hello, mother," he said to the Libra woman who carried a baby boy in her stomach.

The mother was in a glass tube with green fluid and bubbles floating all around her. Green also became the color of her skin, temporarily, a leaf green, just like the fluid of the tube. She was sleeping.

"Let's just get you out of there."

Virgo opened the glass tube to release the woman, and laid her down on a silver table so he could inject the solution into her stomach. It was the perfect experiment. He did King Leo's DNA first, then his own, Aries's, Sagittarius's, so on and so forth, doing all the twelve kings, with Scorpio's DNA being added last. Virgo had finally figured it out. The reason his genetic modification experiments were not working was because he was conducting them on full grown specimens. This time, he was going to only use the fetuses of pregnant women for his experiments.

"Now for the next two."

Virgo wasn't entirely sure if the fetus would be able to take the blood of the kings. King Scorpio's blood was literally poisonous; so were the other Scorpios, but not nearly as lethal as the king's blood. He figured he would try different methods for the other subjects. One fetus would be imbued with DNA from all the various different royals from a multitude of ranks and statures, and the last one with commoner's blood and DNA from the half bloods.

Another specimen would have been nice to inject with the DNA of half bloods only, but it could draw too much attention if too many pregnant Libran commoners were abducted at one time. Libra did so love his people, even those of common birth.

Virgo returned his first Libran specimen to her tube and made sure her vitals were stable. Next, he used the DNA he had acquired from all the other royals on his second pregnant Libran. Lastly, he injected the final specimen with all the DNA of all the commoners and all the half bloods he had before him. Vials covering the widest spectrum, ranging from navy blue to the deepest, darkest red, plus white, black, and everything in between were injected into the unconscious women lying on his operating tables. The needle he used was extremely sharp and long. Still, none of the women even let out a sound, they were too deep in sleep to feel anything. Excitement permeated from all of his being. This experiment would be very fruitful. With all three women secured back in their tubes, his work was finished for the moment. All that was left was to play the waiting game and watch for the results.

"Vernon, come here immediately." Virgo looked toward his cousin who stood near the doorway. Not too close so he wouldn't disturb Virgo, but he also needed to be close enough to fetch anything that was needed.

"Master?" Vernon responded at once hurrying toward the king.

"Thank you for all your hard work. I expect the results of these current experiments will be far more impressive than the last." He extended his hand for Vernon to shake. Firm hand clasp was had between the two, and Virgo looked Vernon in the eyes. "I can't thank you enough. Although I did all of the heavy lifting. I shall give you credit as well, after I reap the rewards of my hard work."

"What is it, exactly, that you are trying to do?" Vernon asked, staring at the women in the green tubes. It was one of the first questions in a long time that Virgo could remember him asking.

"Oh, Vernon, my dear, dim-witted cousin. I am creating the future. The future not only for Virgo, but all of the kingdoms. The future for everyone is looking a lot brighter now," Virgo said as he clapped the larger man's shoulder and resumed eye contact once more.

"What do you want me to do with the leftovers?" Vernon inquired as he looked at some of the dead bodies that were lying around. The corpses offered snapshots of all the races. Not all were dead, though, some were just unconscious.

"Dispose of the dead anyway you see fit. Including any who died today." Virgo looked around his lab at the bodies himself.

"You had me bring in the Leos for nothing?"

"No, it wasn't for nothing. I needed to get a few more samples of common Leo blood. I needed to test the DNA in the same way I tested all the other races, to ensure that all the commoners were similar. I hadn't had a chance to do that yet until today. Not that you even know what I'm talking about. You're lucky I'm in a good mood, otherwise you would be punished for questioning me.

"As I was saying, you can return the ones that are alive back to their home planets, but be discreet about it. I think those two Aries over there may still be alive, along with a few others. Clean up everything and do not touch the three pregnant women in the tubes. I have to go celebrate," Virgo said.

Virgo had a big grin on his face, and he patted Vernon on his back, and Virgo was out of there happier than ever.

***

"I cannot tell you how good it feels for everything to be back to normal, Llewellyn. Nor can I tell you how good it feels to see you and Zemar alive and in good health. It is unfortunate, however, that some of our pride will never come back." King Leo looked away after his statement, out toward the window nearest the throne, as if paranoid and expecting to see the fiery rebellion still brewing. Outside, it was serene; however, damage was still visible on the streets and buildings, but there was hardly a soul running about.

"The loss does hurt indeed, Your Majesty." Llewellyn lowered his head and his gaze. But after a moment, he looked back up. "I am shocked that we were saved by Cancer Elite. What could have happened to make King Cancer want to save our lives, if you don't mind me asking? Does it have something to do with why some of our compatriots are gone? But no matter the reason I just know I'm happy to still be alive, and wish our brethren could have been saved as well, even if it was by Cancer Elite."

"Actually, I do mind you asking. I am still your king. All I will say is that I have found some of others from the pride that are still alive, and that they are already back with us. And that three others, Amra, Gur, and Hari, are definitely still alive because I sent them on a special mission just recently."

"Maybe that means that Abbas and Ari are still alive, just like the others who you sent off."

"No, I don't think that can be the case." Leo stood up from his throne. "I was given confirmation from Corin that they were found dead."

"Lost forever, then. I guess now is an appropriate time to begin mourning them." Zemar hung his head low.

"Yes, but my natal day is still coming up, and we must celebrate. For we have a lot to celebrate. We will celebrate for our lost brethren. I'm sure they wouldn't want us to be miserable without them. That is not the way of the Leo, to sit and dwell in the sadness. I'm happy that the Cancer were able to save you. I'm also happy that the rebellion ended in time. Your birth celebration is coming up also, isn't it, Llewellyn?" Leo wanted to change the mood for his sake as much as for his subordinates.

"Mine actually passed during the rebellion, my lord." Llewellyn tried to remain expressionless while making his statement.

"Indeed, I give you permission to leave my side and enjoy yourself, then." Leo smiled.

"Mine also passed during the rebellion." Zemar made an effort to piggyback on the energy of the moment. "I miss my family. I haven't seen them in a while, because of all of the fighting, and I imagine they miss me dearly."

"That's fine, Zemar. You, too, may take your leave. You two should report back to me after you have celebrated with your families. I will begin preparations for my birth celebration. Llevara, come to me at once. We must plan."

The delicate burnt orange Leo woman appeared, her dress dark red and a small white floral ornament in her hair. She was ready to take her king's orders. She came eagerly with parchment and a beautiful writing utensil to take notes.

"Thank you Llevara, but I will see to all the preparations," the queen of Leo strolled in, her white fur looking even lighter against her golden amber dress. "My poor king has been stressed by all the happenings of the rebellion," she said, standing near her husband. Gently touching his face for a moment. "I will handle all arrangements I want you to rest so you can be prepared for your grand day and they all can see you in your splendor." She made a sweeping gesture with her arms. "I will run everything by you, but there's no need for my king to worry his head. Everything will be magnificent for your special day."

"Thank you, love." He held her hand in his, kissed it softly. "You heard her, Llevara." His gaze turned toward his servant. "You are to take all of my wife's orders and suggestions and use them. My birth celebration must be extraordinary this year. It has to be the greatest one anyone of this world has ever seen. So that they may know how powerful their king is, and that nothing can get me down, not even the disobedience of them all."

"Yes, my love. The queen said. It will be the best that anyone of all the twelve worlds has ever seen. Come with me now, Llevara." The queen and Llevara swiftly left together. The king decided to relax. His wife was right, he hadn't slept right since the beginning of the revolt. Now that it was all over, this would be the best time for him to recuperate.

***

Callum would finally take his turn in the simple yet dreaded first task. The first two men had set the bar pretty high. Luckily, the bar hadn't gone much higher with all the other participants. The way Callum saw it, all he had to do was two hundred trips back and forth. It didn't matter if he won or not. He had learned from sitting back and watching and being patient, as the older man had advised him to earlier. One thing he learned was that it wasn't always a good idea to sit back and wait and watch, at least not for a task where the requirements aren't fixed.

The instructors decided to raise the minimum level of laps required. He continued recapping everything he learned and began running. The more the next two people would score, the higher the minimum amount of laps required went up. For example, the last two contestants who went each did over two hundred, but because they did so many past two hundred, two hundred became the new minimum. It wasn't that you would not be able to join the cavalry at all. It was just that you would automatically get the lowest score possible on the particular task you were working on, if you didn't reach the standard.

Callum had learned one or two other things from observing the other contestants. One of the most important things he learned was that most who were successful did not watch their opponent. The contestants who watched their opponents would often defeat themselves.

On second thought, I have learned quite a bit by watching and observing and waiting to participate in this challenge. However, from now on I think a better strategy will be to compete in the middle of all participants. That way, I won't have the bar raised too high for me when it is my turn to compete. As well as, I won't have to worry about setting the standard. His mind was working hard as he tried to come up with a future strategy for the rest of events. He was so focused on his thoughts that he forgot to count his laps and forgot that he was running.

Randomly, he looked over at his opponent and realized he wasn't running anymore.

"OK, that's enough, you beat your opponent. You will outrank him in terms of test purposes for this event. You may stop whenever," Cassius addressed Callum.

"Losers! Are you ready to move on?" Caleb stepped up toward the front near Cassius. "It doesn't matter if you are, because it's time for the next challenge, whether you're ready or not."

"The next challenge is going to be very different from the last one. In fact, the next challenge transitions into another challenge right after it. Basically, the challenges are back to back. It starts with a mountain. You all are going to climb a mountain at the same time." Cassius pointed to a mountain a little distance away from them. "When you reach the top of that mountain, you will be given a nonlethal weapon. You will then use this weapon to fight anybody else who is on top of the mountain with you," Cassius dictated.

"Wait, but won't we die if we are fighting on the mountain, and we lose our balance?" a recruit Callum hadn't noticed before asked Cassius.

"Part of this training is compassion. Compassion may seem like a useless skill, and truth be told you won't need it much against your enemies. But you all here are supposed to grow to be friends, so now is the time to practice empathy. On to your question, let's talk about the mountain. First I want to say that the mountain is literally designed for you all to fight on the top, so that shouldn't be an issue. The mountain has more than enough space to fit a good number of Caps. No Cap will force you off, because that's against the rules, and

Caleb, Cyd, and I will be watching. Actually, if one of you kills another on purpose, or accident, or any other sort of way, the killer will automatically be disqualified and may have horrible things done to him. Caps should never kill other Caps, especially during sparring, which this qualifies as. I'm sorry, I tend to digress sometimes when I hear something that needs to be expounded upon. Returning to the explanation I was giving a moment ago. All on top of the mountain are expected to fight all others, aside from instructors, of course.

"The first who is defeated watches the next two fight. When that fight ends, the loser becomes the watcher, and the first watcher returns here. And so on until everyone who made it to the top has fought at least once. I hope that wasn't too complex for you all. I will explain it again later, before we all start to climb the mountain, if need be. So if you have any questions save them for later."

Immediately, a young Capricorn put his hand down.

"Let's head toward the mountain. Forward march," Cassius declared, doing a one eighty with one gesture.

It wasn't long before they reached the bottom of the mountain the gargantuan, dark brown mountain had little rocks protruding from every which way. It almost looked like it was Capricorn made and designed to be climbed with all the ridges in it, but that didn't seem possible for something so monumental.

"So, do any of you have any questions?"

"Sir, what happens if more than one of us makes it up the mountain at the same time?"

"Then you will fight, of course. Fight all other people up on the mountain at the same time as you, aside from the instructors. We instructors will have the same swords and piercing weapons that we have now. Cyd had two scimitars and Cassius had a long sword and Caleb had a short sword and dagger. "Furthermore, we will remain dressed as you see us here and now in our selindium. You all will be given weapons very different from ours. Anybody who attacks an instructor is disqualified. As I said before, anybody who kills another contestant on purpose or even on accident will be disqualified. One of your goals is to learn restraint when sparring and practicing with your fellows in the cavalry. I would hope you all have that killer instinct already for real combat. At any rate, killer instinct is not something that can be taught, especially not by simulation. I believe I have explained all of the rules. Any more questions?"

"Are there any aides or devices we can use to assist us in climbing the mountain?" a short Cap asked.

"That is a terrible question," Cassius said. Anger was visible on his face from the comment. "It wouldn't be much of a challenge if there was, now would it? Ask another question like that and disciplinary action will be taken against you. Now, are there any more questions? Please try to keep them questions for which the answer is not obvious."

"You keep saying something about being disqualified. What do you mean by that?" a new Cap asked.

"I mean the Cap who kills another Cap during this next mission and is caught will not be allowed to finish these trials. Any more questions?"

He waited for a moment, looking around at all the enlistees. Seeing that nobody had any more questions, he began the next part of his speech.

"That being said, you all need to wait for us three to climb this mountain first. I will yell down for you all when you are allowed to start. Until then, I expect nobody to put a single foot or hand on this mountainside. If anybody does, they will be disqualified." He grabbed the side of the mountain, but paused.

He let go and turned around. "For this challenge you will be graded on two things. One will be whether or not you win the fight or fights that you engage in. Secondly, you will be judged based on the amount of time it takes for you to climb to the top of the mountain. If you have a hard time climbing the mountain, that is fine. It may be best for you to hang back and try to climb up after a while with hopes that there will only be one or two opponents for you to face when you get to the top.

"Additionally, I want to say that you are not being judged at all on your descent down the mountain after you finish your fight, so once you yield to the opponent who defeats you or you win it all, just climb down the mountain as safely as you can. Also worth mentioning, even though you are being judged on how long it takes you to climb up the mountain, I don't want you to die while climbing, so take all proper precautions as you make your way up, and think of your safety while ascending as efficiently possible.

"That is another thing that this exercise is designed to indirectly measure; how efficiently you can accomplish a difficult task while following all of the rules and procedures. I believe that is everything. Now the three of us will make our ascent. Again, do not begin your climb until I give you the signal." Cassius stared sternly at the recruits. His gaze swept the crowd as he made eye contact with as many of them as possible.

There are a lot of things that they are trying to measure with these exercises. I'll have to put safety as my number one priority for this one, and put my all into my fighting. I don't know how long it will take me to scale this mountain, but I imagine I won't be one of the first, Callum thought.

Without another word, the instructors began climbing the mountain. Rapidly, they ascended, but they looked down occasionally to ensure none followed.

Callum gave the mountain another once over. The mountain had to be at least six thousand meters high. It seemed like insanity to him that they all had to climb with no assistance and even fight when they got to the top. This was going to be difficult.

I definitely must be concerned with safety first and foremost, he reaffirmed with a nod to himself.

It wasn't long before the three instructors disappeared from his line of sight.

"Go now," Cassius yelled down.

Nobody cheated, so they were all on equal ground when the competition began. Callum looked around at the other contestants and at the mountain to evaluate.

It was hard to tell, but it looked like there were certain areas of the mountain that were better suited to climbing than other parts. The area of the mountain that Callum was near did not have an easy path straight up. There weren't many rocks for him to grip. So Callum figured he would ascend on a different side.

Callum could see a path that looked more accessible. And so Callum walked across the bottom to the better path. Some of the others who were still at the bottom raced over to the starting spot that he had seen. Callum continued to take his time getting to his spot.

Finally, he reached the spot where he intended to begin his climb. Grabbing a handful of the giant rock in front of him, he began climbing. His theory had been correct. It was easy to grab the mountain and get a good grip on the new path. Again, the mountain's formation made him ponder its origin. Was the mountain naturally like that, or did some of the royals set up the mountain to work that way? Wouldn't be very surprising; after all, they had apparently altered the mountain's top. Returning his focus to progress, he saw three Caps fall from higher up. They weren't much higher than he was, so he was pretty sure they'd live.

Slowly he made his way up, scaling as if he had all the time in the world. Leisurely making his ascent, he looked to his right after he heard a sharp noise and saw a climber moving horizontally at a rapid rate toward him.

"I don't think I want you climbing up with me. I'd rather not deal with any competition when I get to the top," the other climber said when he was close. A scruffy-looking older man with a gut and a cantankerous look on his face, there was nothing outwardly pleasant about him, and apparently nothing pleasant about his attitude, either.

Callum was suspicious of the other climber as soon as he saw him getting too close. The brutish man tried to punch at Callum with one hand. Somehow, Callum dodged it. Altering his path up the mountain slightly to the left, Callum attempted to get some distance from the other man, and to continue to make progress, but the other climber just altered his path the same as Callum had. This was not good. A fall from this high would possibly result in death or at least a very serious injury.

He must figure the instructors have no way of knowing if we kill one another during our ascent. It couldn't be proven who, if anybody threw another climber down.

The slightly new path Callum was climbing had almost as many parts for him to grip as his original, ideal course, but he still wasn't sure what to do about the other climber. If he fought the man and somehow lost his balance, he would still die, just as if his unrelenting antagonist had got him. Unfortunately, the other climber's pursuit was persistent.

"Make no mistake, I'm going to get you before you can make it to the top."

Damn, why hadn't the instructors mentioned anything about cheating on the way to the top? They must have figured it was useless because they had no way of monitoring it. Perhaps they gave all the participants the benefit of the doubt or too much respect, thinking that they were all honorable men. This older man who was trying to pursue Callum was not honorable at all. It seemed like he was specifically picking on Callum, and ignoring all other climbers that they both passed, who all seemed to be minding their own business.

"I got you now." He had Callum's shirt in one of his hands. It was only the bottom of his shirt, but it was still enough to give him an advantage that scared Callum. Gripping the mountain tighter, he decided to stop moving and just try to maintain his position.

"Thank you for not putting up a fight and dying peacefully." The man laughed.

Callum's actions shocked the man, and he didn't react right away. A split second later, a climber above them fell. The climber was falling so close to Callum's assailant that he reached out and grabbed the man who was holding on to Callum, and began trying to climb him.

"I'm so lucky I grabbed a hold of you. I think I just might live," the young Capricorn man who had fallen from high above said.

"Get off me, you bastard," Callum's assailant yelled as he kicked the young fallen man in his face. The other man wouldn't let go. He just continued climbing him.

Callum's assailant was no longer able to hold onto the mountain with his other hand and eventually he only had a hold of Callum's shirt.

The shirt began to tear. Capricorn fabric was tough, but Callum was a commoner, and it wasn't designed to support the full weight of a Capricorn, yet alone two of them. It became hard for Callum to hold on. He began losing his grip. But then the shirt finally ripped, and the two men who were holding onto Callum fell rapidly down the mountainside.

After that, Callum had a weird dark blue half shirt that covered his chest and stomach somewhat. Luckily, he had been wearing a shirt that was too big for him.

Trying to kill Callum had led to the other man's death. He wasn't sure how he felt about that, but he didn't have time to think on it. The climb was what mattered. No longer deterred or distracted, he climbed faster and faster, not wanting to spend any more time on that mountain than he had to.

The top of the mountain; he finally reached it. As soon as he did, Caleb tossed him a weapon.

Before him stood two other competitors. This battle was going to be harder than he would've hoped for. Metal staff; that's the weapon he held in his hands, the weapon he was handed to take out the two men. Callum realized that he would now have to focus on fighting instead of security, Callum braced himself for battle. The two competitors were both gray in skin tone, about average height, and dressed raggedy.

Callum stood there with the long metal stick. Unsure of what to do. He figured it was OK for him not to join in the fray yet because the other two men were still circling each other.

The Capricorn-created battlefield at the top of the mountain was very big, as Cassius had mentioned. The top was divided into four areas. The division between the areas was significant because therein was where the instructors were waiting. One of the four corners had an instructor Callum had never seen before.

The area for the fighters was made of wood and looked very study. The four corners had some sort of metal. Most likely it was designed that way to discourage people from fighting the instructors. If someone were to slip while fighting and taking a shot at one of the instructors, they would not only be disqualified, but would likely fall to their death. But what about the instructor? What would happen to them if someone attacked them? Wouldn't they fall, too? Would an instructor intervene to save the life of a participant? Callum had his thoughts interrupted once Caleb spoke to him.

"The two fighters have begun engaging with each other. My suggestion would be for you to attack whichever one of them you feel is the strongest while he's distracted. That way, you may only have one other opponent to worry about." Caleb's arms were crossed, and he gestured with his head to the two other combatants. He looked comfortable in his corner.

"Couldn't I just wait for one of them to defeat the other?" Callum asked.

"You don't have enough time for that. A new challenger will appear before one of them accepts defeat from the other." Caleb shook his head in disapproval of Callum's plan.

Callum remained still and weighed out his options.

He assumed the only way to score positively during this exercise was to defeat someone. After all, there was no other way they could be scored, so it didn't matter if everyone came to the mountaintop and ignored him. He would have to fight eventually, if he wanted to improve his rank. Thinking of all these things and about fights he had had in the past, he tried to figure out the best method.

The fact was, he had only fought with people his own age and never with weapons. Renewing his resolve, he reminded himself he'd come too far and wanted this more than anyone, he should just do his best to put on a good show, and not worry so much. If Caleb said it would be best to double team one of his opponents, and the rules did not explicitly state he would be disqualified, he should be fine taking the advice of his instructor.

He held his metal staff firmly in his hands, took a step forward and began analyzing his opponents, and their fighting techniques, looking for his opportunity to jump in.

A new voice boomed behind him, apparently talking to Caleb. Quickly, he looked back to see who the voice belonged to and saw the biggest Capricorn he had ever seen. The man appeared to be a giant to Callum. The man told Caleb he didn't want a weapon, it would be unfair to the others that he was going to defeat, and that he didn't want to kill them. Callum thought it was a good thing at first, but he realized the man had his eyes set on him.

The giant Capricorn had uncombed, nasty-looking hair that appeared just as crazy as his eyes and no shirt. Scarier still was the aggressive expression he had on his face, which was somehow worse than the climber who had tried to pull Callum down earlier.

"You there. Boy. Why aren't you fighting already?" he growled at Callum.

"I was thinking about all my options, coming up with a strategy, and analyzing my opponents."

"You know what I think? I think you're a weakling and a coward and far too small to join the cavalry. I'm going to save your life, boy, by destroying you here and crushing your soul until you're so defeated you never think about fighting again, so you can go back home to your mommy a shell of a man. This is going to hurt, bad, but remember I'm doing you a favor," the massive man said with a smirk.

The man left the mountainous area for the arena portion and suddenly charged at Callum.

Callum set his feet, and moved the metal staff to block his face. The man punched it hard. Which made Callum slide back and almost lose his balance.

"Do you think you can hide behind that? Even though it's metal, I'm going to tear through it and you."

That sounds like the words of somebody planning to kill me, Callum thought. But he was trying to take comfort in the fact that his instructor did not condone the murder of other initiates. He looked over at Caleb for a second. He didn't know what he expected to see, but he saw a slight smirk. One thing was for certain, he could expect no help from him.

"Pay attention, boy." The barbaric Capricorn snuck a headbutt in against Callum. "Look away from me while I'm fighting you again, and I just may kill you for being disrespectful."

A throbbing, terrible headache overwhelmed him. He was surprised he was still conscious, but he knew he wouldn't be able to withstand very many attacks like that. Going on the offensive was his only option. No longer back peddling, he took a fighting stance and held the staff out with one hand and put his other hand behind his back.

"There's some fight in you after all. That's good, it will be all the more meaningful when I crush you." The brute was unfazed.

There had to be a weakness to his opponent. The two circled each other, then once again the huge Capricorn charged at him. Callum saw it in time to sidestep. *That's it! There had to be something with the charge the man kept doing. No matter how big an opponent, they have to have a weakness,* Callum thought as he sidestepped yet another charge.

How would it be possible for Caleb or Cassius or Cyd to take this man out, when they, like me, are smaller than him?

Suddenly, there wasn't enough time to think. The man tackled him and began to punch at his face. Luckily, he was able to block most of it with his staff. But not all of the hits. The other Capricorn punched a lot, so he landed one right on Callum's jaw.

Fighting back the urge to pass out, he somehow stayed conscious and landed a hit himself with the staff to the other man's face. The larger Capricorn's fists were like boulders and Callum couldn't afford to take any more hits, of that he was sure. Still, he was amazed that he even survived that punch, maybe the other Cap was pulling his punches. It didn't matter, all he knew was that he had to fight back, so thinking quickly, he struck his attacker's thighs with a quick thrust to the top part of the man's leg.

He still wasn't sure why the other man hadn't taken his staff from him, but he was glad he hadn't. The blow to his aggressor's thigh was just enough to stop him. Callum wriggled free from the position, with the help of the staff still jammed in his opponent's upper thigh. And when he stood up, he took his time to analyze the other man. Callum spent so much time looking at the man's monstrous form he hadn't realized that his legs were disproportionate to his upper body. *The legs, that's it.* Not wanting the other man to know that he was on to him, he decided to wait for another charge. That's when he would strike.

Aim for the legs, because it seems to be the other man's only weakness.

"I'm tired of this. I'm going to finish you now," the large man said.

With that, he charged at Callum again. Callum sidestepped earlier than before, crouched low, and swung his staff at the man's legs. The Cap fell forward. Callum struck him on the back of the head once and then once more for good measure.

"I was wondering if you were going to figure that out." Caleb grinned at him. "You're lucky he's still alive. That second shot to the back of the head may have killed a weaker Cap. Given his size, though, I would say it was just what he needed. No time to rejoice, though. Another competitor will likely join the ring soon."

"We're not finished yet," the beastly Capricorn yelled as he got back up to his feet.

"Oh, yes, you are," Caleb replied.

"We will see about that," he said. And he then charged at Caleb who sidestepped him so fast Callum thought he'd teleported. He grabbed the beast by the back of his neck and slammed him down hard. Then put his knee over his throat.

"Yes, you are done. I should kill you for your insolence, but this is a holy mountain and killing is forbidden. If you calm down, I won't take your life once we leave this place. "

Caleb stepped away from the downed man who sat up, angry and still catching his breath.

"I will talk to you more once you finish, Callum."

"Why not now?"

Suddenly, he felt a sharp pain in his side. His new competition was very different from his last opponent, it seemed. He swung his staff around quickly, but his new adversary jumped back.

"My name is Calypso. I saw the tail end of your fight with the giant. I was happy you were able to take him down, but I would have done so much sooner."

The new Capricorn that stood before him had a suave appearance, almost the opposite of the man he just fought. Dark gray skin, a thin moustache, slightly above average height, he was thin but very sinewy, with a black shirt that hugged his body tightly and showed off his abdominal muscles and sculpted arms.

"My name is Callum, and with that hit from behind, you introduced yourself like a coward just now." Callum winced in pain, still hurt from the recent attack.

"There wasn't anything cowardly about it. If this had been real combat and I were a Cancer or some other foreigner, you would be dead by now for having your guard down. I'm sure our leader over there is happy I'm giving you such realistic practice."

Callum looked over at Caleb, who merely shrugged his shoulders.

"You should never take your eyes off your opponent, second lesson," Calypso said while driving both of his batons into Callum's stomach, causing him to fold in half. Spitting out blood after the strike, Callum felt disappointed in himself. He should have already learned that supposed second lesson. By this point, he had already had about enough of this Calypso guy, so he began taking shots at him.

Calypso expertly dodged. Smiling. Wearing the expression of a man enjoying himself. "Too slow, too slow. You're definitely an amateur with that weapon, if I've ever seen one."

Calypso stopped dodging and parried Callum's attack and lined up a quick strike that was heading to his stomach again, so Callum put his staff there to protect it, but instead he got a hard baton to the chin at the last minute.

"You're way too easy to read, and you believe I will do something just because you see me feint. You're clearly an amateur. I guess I shouldn't waste any more time with you. I thought you were good because you defeated the giant a moment ago, but I guess I was wrong. Bye."

This time it looked like one baton was aimed for his testicles and another for his chest, so he switched the position of his stick and held it vertically and close to his body to protect the targeted areas. It was another feint, though, and he left his head unguarded again and both of the batons crashed into his temples. Unconsciousness was inevitable this time.

"Wake up. I said, wake up."

Callum opened up his eyes slowly, and finally saw Caleb over him.

"You took quite the hit. I'm impressed you woke up so soon."

"What happened?" Groggily, Callum tried to recompose himself and figure out what was going on.

"The battle is over. It's time to move on to the next stage of testing," Caleb said evenly.

"Where is everybody else?"

"Everybody else is finished. It doesn't matter, though, because unlike this exercise the next test only has two participants at a time. I just wanted to say before we go, your strategy for the brute was good. It shouldn't have taken you that long to figure it out, though. Anybody charges at you like that, you can most likely take them out the same way you did him, especially if they are top heavy, and if you're fast enough. In the future, you have to try to remain on offense and defense at the same time, while also avoiding heavy damage and simultaneously analyzing your opponent. But it's good that you already know the value of patience and watching your adversaries for openings and weaknesses. I'm impressed that a young man such as you already knows those important values, and that you were able to take down that brute who was more of an Aries-Taurus beast than a real Capricorn."

The two laughed.

"Come now, let's go. We can't stay here forever."

The two climbed down the mountain together and headed off to the next challenge area.

Chapter 12

"Remarkable progress," Virgo said, staring at the three women in the glass tubes. Daily, it seemed, his time spent in the lab increased, but it was necessary because this experiment was important to him.

There was a blue digital display before him that showed the vital stats of both the mother and the infant in her womb in great detail, but the mother was so far along in her pregnancy that Virgo didn't need the digital readout to see it. Information including the baby's estimated time of arrival and the size of the fetus and its organs were displayed on the screen.

He had thought that there was a possibility that the infant with the blood of the kings would develop faster than an average fetus, but he was surprised that all his experiments were developing at an accelerated rate. It must have had something to do with the mixing of the DNA, he thought. Good thing Virgo kept all expectant mothers in an artificial state of sleep, if he hadn't, he was sure there would have been ramifications, such as damage to the bodies of the soon-to-be mothers. However, their bodies seem to have adjusted quite fine to the abnormal growth rate of the unborn children. The embryos were supposed to have another twelve weeks at least before their births. Instead, at the rate they were developing, it looked as though they would be born in a few days. Virgo was very excited.

"It won't be long now. My experiments are perfect. Soon, genetically perfect beings will exist. This program was a success. No, it's too early to call," he said, going back and forth between thinking to himself and talking out loud. He began pacing; it was hard to hold his excitement in.

It wouldn't be long before the fruits of his works could be displayed. A thought surfaced that there was a chance that these superior beings would not obey him. A contingency plan would be important.

There's no time and besides, since I am creating them, I will be their father. My queen still hasn't bore any children for me. This way I can raise them as my own. After a time with running tests and learning about them, I'm sure I will know how to keep them in check.

Enamored by his miraculous work, he stood there for a while, staring in awe at what he had done. Visions of beauty; that's what his experiments were to him. Excited as he was, the thought crossed his mind of revealing his experiments early to Scorpio. Only for a moment, though, because he quickly cautioned himself against it. The fruits of his hard labor would be displayed soon enough at a council meeting that he would call as soon as the infants had time to develop, and he had time to run tests on them.

Running his fingers across the glass surrounding the sleeping mothers, he fantasized about it. Unveiling his finest work, his children; the greatest children to be born in all the universe. How marvelous it would be. For now, there was nothing more for him to do but wait. It was not like him to leave his laboratory, but he didn't want to start any new projects until he saw this one all the way through, and he couldn't speed it up more than it already was.

Vernon had the day off, perhaps he would join him. His wife had decided to take a tour of all the planets, so he couldn't spend time with her. It seemed like a somewhat foolish endeavor, but it was most likely because he had been able to travel to all the planets his whole life whenever he saw fit that he felt that way.

Indeed, she is quite young, and it's reasonable for her to explore the kingdoms even if she doesn't have an escort. She'd mentioned to Vernon that she wanted to tour the other eleven planets not very long ago. When it turned out she was missing without a word to anybody, Virgo had some contacts look into it. She was seen leaving by herself by a servant who was sworn to secrecy. The king figured she knew how to handle herself because she was about as powerful as him, a notion he still didn't understand, so he would leave her be. Besides, he didn't have the proper time to entertain such a young queen anyway, especially with all the attention his current experiments demanded from him.

"I suppose I will join Vernon and partake in any endeavors he has taken up today. It feels odd to leave the lab, but perhaps a break is necessary." He turned out the lights and stepped out to join his cousin. Leaving his experiments on their own.

***

"How are preparations going?" The Lioness hovered over Llevara to see what she was working on, her black dress a sharp contrast against her white fur.

"They are going well, my Lioness. Everything is on schedule." Llevara looked up with a genuine smile from the costume she was creating. There were numerous other lady Leos in the room, but generally, the Lioness only conversed with Llevara directly.

"Very good. If possible, contact a few of the other kings and their queens and see if any can attend the celebration or give an offering or tribute of any sort. Also, be sure to note any suggestions they may have to make the celebration as special as possible. If you cannot reach any of the kings or queens, speak directly with their second or any other royals that are available. And ask them to ask their kings and queens.

"If you cannot get a hold of any royalty from a certain kingdom, just tell me about it and I will contact them personally when I can. I am going to rejuvenate myself, so do not disturb me. I will come out when I am ready."

Why does she have to rejuvenate herself? She always looks the exact same after, her servant thought to herself, but merely said, "Yes, ma'am." And Llevara passed the costume to another servant to finish, so she could work on the assignment the Lioness just gave her.

***

The red full moon in the night sky of Aries looked even more beautiful at the top of the king's castle, Mar's home, in the highlands where the royals of Aries lived, at the highest point of the kingdom. The color of the moon that night was typical for mating season on Aries. Mar and Catalina arrived back on Aries in their lightning ship and were immediately greeted by Mar's parents upon landing.

"I'm so happy you two are hitting it off. Are you going to be staying with us for a while, Catalina?" his mom asked excitedly.

Mar was perplexed, and he wondered how his parents had anticipated his arrival. *Perhaps the Geminis put a call in.*

"I don't know. You should ask your son. We didn't come back here to spend more time together. He felt sick, so we left early from the company of the Geminis." Catalina spoke with her gaze fixed on Mar the entire time.

"What's wrong, son? Does your stomach ail you?" the king asked, patting his son on the back playfully.

"Yes, Father, ever since we left Libra, actually."

"Is that so? It's so kind of you to have taken him all the way back here then, Catalina. Don't worry about him anymore. One of our servants will take care of him from here."

"No, really, I would like to take care of him and stick around for a while, besides, I've never seen inside your lovely castle before."

"Excuse my husband," Queen Aries said, standing in front of King Aries. "He forgets that he needs to be polite sometimes, even though he's king."

"I'm terribly sorry, Catalina. My wife here will give you a tour while I talk about a few kingly matters with my son." He immediately turned all his attention to Mar. "Expansion of the kingdom is very important, you know, son. It's a good thing your brother is out there searching for useful planets with abundant resources so you don't have to."

"What? Why are you bringing this up now?" Mar was irritated.

"Shh, just play along." The king leaned close to Mar to whisper, then stepped back and continued to talk about unimportant things with his son until the queen and their guest were out of earshot.

Aries put his son in a playful headlock.

"You old dog, you, things must be going well if she wants to spend the night here and nurse you back to good health. I knew you would come to your senses."

"Let go of me. I'm not doing this for you." Mar pushed his father away.

"Even though you're not doing this for me, I'm happy you're making the right decision to be with this Capricorn woman. So how does she like you so far? How do you like her? Tell me every detail of your date."

Mar was disgusted by his father's smile and overexcitement. It was strange to see the king so animated. "I like her a lot, actually, and things are going well, I believe."

"I would say they are. She has only known you for a day, and she already wants to take care of you." He winked. "Sly fox you. Are you only pretending to be sick so you can have her alone in your room? I'll understand if you are. It is mating season, after all," he concluded with a laugh.

Mar was shocked that he hadn't thought of that sooner. Having her over might not be such a bad idea. He could potentially get the chance to lay with her and get to know her body more intimately.

Then again, maybe she would think he was lying the whole time, and maybe she wouldn't want to do it. But perhaps she already knew it had been a lie the whole time. And she wanted to come over and see his place, so she could "take care of him." He had no clue what she could have possibly been thinking, because he hadn't paid enough attention to her earlier and was only thinking of his predicament and the down sides of her being with him.

With renewed vigor, he ended his conversation with his father and headed to his room. Catalina still wasn't there yet. Touring the castle with his mother would possibly take a while. He got dressed in his night wear, which was simply some elegant blue pants made of soft material, and lay in his covers. After talking to his dad, he was a little excited about having her there. It would be a win-win situation for him. Either he would insult her pride by making passes at her and she would leave, which would make it possible for him to sneak out to see Diantha, or he would get to enjoy the mating ritual with the princess of Capricorn, his potential future bride, early.

Things always work out in my favor, it's good to be a prince. He smiled to himself, finally feeling good about his circumstances again.

"Mar, I have finished showing Catalina around. Your father and I will give you two some space. We are always here when you need us," his mother called from the hallway just outside his door.

"Of course, thank you, Mother."

"May I come in? You're not indecent are you?"

"No, come on in."

"Quite the room you have here," Catalina observed as she walked in. Looking around, she saw various jewels and gemstones on the top of a wooden drawer. Landscape paintings of space, the sky, and some planets that had friendly relations with Aries were painted on the walls and ceiling. A large winged beast was caged in a corner and there was a massive bed, a holographic display system, and an assortment of weapons on a weapons rack in another corner of the room. Lastly there were two aqua communicators and two wall mounted paintings, one of his mom and one of his whole family. "Can I ask you why you don't have your own separate land and castle?" she queried once she finished looking at everything, and she walked closer to his cashmere cream-colored bed.

He lay sideways, facing her to speak. "My father wants me to wait until I have a wife, at least. He thought there was a chance that I might want to leave and expand our kingdom in new uncharted territories, like my older brother, and even now he goes back and forth on whether he should just give me this entire castle. But he keeps saying he doesn't want me to have to wait that long. If I really push it, they would build me a castle of my own right away. I'm still unsure of what I myself want to do, though."

"Oh OK, I was just curious. Are you comfortable? Is there anything I can do to make you more comfortable?" She stood near the side of his bed.

"You could lay down near me," he offered, patting the bed in an empty spot near him.

"Why would I want to do that if you're sickly?"

"It's my stomach, it's not contagious."

"Even still, I don't see how that would make you feel any better."

"It would take my mind off my stomach pain. You asked a question and I simply answered honestly. Of course, you don't have to, but I thought you were here to nurse me back to good health." He looked up at her, directly in her eyes.

"Oh, yes, of course, I am here for that, but I never heard of a nurse laying with the sickly," she joked back.

"There's a first time for everything," he countered with a smirk.

She stared at him for a moment but eventually lay down in front of him. They were facing each other, no more than two inches apart. "Is this helping? Is this what you meant?"

Mar was getting excited. *Father was right,* the little voice in his head told him.

"Yes, I'm feeling better already,"

The two laughed at his comment.

Mar could hardly contain his excitement. The two were staring at each other. Finally, she kissed him on his cheek.

"Despite having our first night out interrupted, I had a good time," she revealed to him.

He just stared back at her. A kiss to the cheek was nice, but he wanted more.

He went for it. Kissing her on the mouth, gently at first, on the lips a few times. When he saw that she kissed him back equally, he began using tongue. Partially surprised that she kissed back with such passion. The two engaged in that manner for a while, until he touched her back and made an effort to bring her body closer to his.

"This is the first night. I don't know you very well, and it's your mating season," she said, stopping him. "I know our fathers want to bring our kingdoms closer, but I don't think I can tonight. I want to be more of a challenge for you than that, and I don't want to do it until after the unification ceremony."

"Come on, you just said it yourself. Our fathers want this. I want this. You want this. Both of our kingdoms want this, and everybody from both. If you won't do it for me, do it for our fathers."

"The last thing I want to think about before giving my body to a man is my father." She pushed herself away from him. "Besides, I thought you were sick. So far, you seem to be rather healthy to me. I'm leaving. You're making a good recovery all on your own." Catalina stormed out.

Mar wasn't sure if he should stop her or be happy she left. He didn't even have to make up any lies to get rid of her. She left on her own free will. Although, he had enjoyed her company and he was sure he would have enjoyed her even more naked. It was definitely for the good that she left.

Patching things up with her would be easy enough when everything was said and done. All he had to do now was wait for a little while longer, and he could see Diantha without worrying about anybody knowing, and he could try to get some answers.

Tiredness swept over him immensely, but he could rest easy. The night was still young and if he fell asleep for a little while, it wouldn't hurt his plans. With that happy thought, Mar rolled over and fell asleep for hours.

Startled, he woke up in the middle of the night. Unaware of when he had fallen asleep. Almost returning because he momentarily forgot why he was up, but after a few seconds he quickly remembered why he was awake.

Perfection, this time of night, everyone including the servants would be sleeping. Mar had to get dressed before he left, so he put on a snug-fitting black shirt, with pants and shoes that matched. Turning on the aqua communicator, he prepared to head to Taurus. Princess Diantha had a secret path to an area where she would meet him most nights. The path between the two worlds was always left open for him. Diantha gave him free reign to visit whenever he wanted. Mar entered the aqua communicator and made his way through the path.

Lighting a torch with his powers, he used it to guide him down the long white stone hallway that led to their secret meeting room. For years, Mar and Diantha met up this way. Not every night, but regularly. Even if she was asleep, the path he was on was directly under her bedroom, so he could just knock until she woke up. He made it to the end of the hallway. Opened the door, to reveal Diantha, who was already sitting in the secret room.

She was bathed in moonlight. Sitting on a pink bench and staring out toward the moon roof as if the night sky had the answer to a question she would die if she didn't get. She had on a beautiful dress that shined as if it was made from pure white diamonds. In fact, knowing Diantha, it was made from pure white diamonds. Their secret room was simple with just a bed, the moon roof, a bench, and an assortment of flowers. Somehow, she looked even more beautiful than usual, her delicate brown skin and small black horns glowing in the moonlight, as he saw a part of her profile.

"I couldn't sleep, and for some reason I just knew you would be coming to see me tonight," she explained, still staring at the moon roof, clearly aware of his presence. "When I had Rufus build the secret path for us and this room, because I threatened to blackmail him to my father, I thought for sure that someday we would be discovered. I just knew that one day he would tell on us and my father would walk in on us."

"But I suppose Rufus is as loyal a servant to me as he is to my father. It's strange, loyalty is. It has its merits, I'm sure, but too often people who don't deserve our loyalty get it. Do you know what I mean?" She slowly turned away from the moonlight and reached for eye contact with her light brown eyes.

Mar wasn't really sure what to say. He felt as though she was talking about her loyalty being misplaced with him, but he had never betrayed her before, in his own opinion.

"I think I know what you're saying. Do you believe I have been disloyal to you?"

"It's too simple to say that I do. I know you were hanging out with that Capricorn girl today. I'm not angry or even jealous. I'm just curious. Do you actually care about me? Is this really something you're doing for our safety, to keep our fathers happy, or do you genuinely want to be with her? Maybe I made everything too convenient for you." Diantha stood up from the bench, but had her back turned to him.

This was the last thing Mar wanted or expected. He didn't have the time for this, but knew better than to brush her feelings aside.

"Diantha, I don't know what you want me to tell you. I have no other alternative than to do as my father wishes, as you must follow your father wishes. I know you love me, but I would hope that you wouldn't do anything to jeopardize my unification with the Capricorn girl."

"What do you mean by that?" Diantha turned to face him.

Maybe she really doesn't have anything to do with the letter, he figured, a bit relieved. But maybe it was Rufus who wrote and sent it. But if it was him, she certainly didn't seem to know. On top of that, if she didn't know anything, his trip to her would be fruitless. But if he ruled her out, maybe he could make sense of this whole thing. Her reaction wasn't enough to say she was innocent for sure, though. Putting her to the test was his only option.

"When is the last time you were on Libra?" he insisted, moving even closer to her.

"What? Why? What does that have to do with anything?"

"I guess I should just show you."

"Show me what?"

Mar pulled the letter out of his pocket and handed it to Diantha who quickly read it and gasped, holding her hand over her mouth.

"Oh, no, this is not good. Who would do this?" she said, removing her hand from her face.

"I don't know. That's why I came to you tonight," he intoned.

"You think I would do something like this to you? Despite how you may or may not feel about me, I really love you, Mar. I would never do something like this to hurt you. It would actually hurt me as well. My father still wants me to marry that Sagittarian."

"I'm not saying you necessarily did it on purpose, or that you even wrote the letter, but maybe you told somebody and they told somebody else and they wrote the letter. Is there anybody you may have told?" He gently put his hand on her arm, softly caressing her bicep, hoping to ease her into the truth.

"Why would I tell anybody? King Taurus's daughter is supposed to be untouched and pure. This would ruin things for me." She lightly stepped away from him, not removing his hand by force, but by motion as she paced a little around the bench.

"You're absolutely sure that you didn't tell anybody?"

"Mar, I swear to you on my heart and all things that I love that I never uttered a word to anyone of any of the things that we have ever done. Maybe someone was in the house with us. Somebody saw us, but we didn't see them." She slowed her pace when she came back in front of the bench and stared at him, making eye contact once again at the end of her statement.

"That's impossible, I sent all the servants away. No other royals were around, and my parents were out," he answered.

"It doesn't make sense, but that's all I can think of."

"Somebody saw us, but we didn't see them. Somebody saw us, but we didn't see them." Mar let her words echo in his brain a little. Then he finally made the connection.

"Cancer. It must have been a Cancer. Maybe even more than one. I hear they are always spying on everyone from every kingdom. What do you know about Cancers?"

"Not much, I'm afraid. My father used to be very close with King Cancer not too long ago, but even still, I don't know much about them."

"I can't ask your father for help. Then he would be suspicious of me."

"You need to do something. We can't have our secret exposed"—she thumped the letter with the hand that wasn't holding it—"not like this. Maybe I should tell my father first on my own, and you should tell yours."

"Are you crazy? That's suicide. Don't worry, I will take care of this." Mar grabbed the letter from her hands. "All of this. Don't tell anybody, not a single person. I have to go, Diantha."

"Wait, what are you planning? Maybe we should try to figure this out together. It does affect both of us." Realizing it was too late and that Mar was gone, she gave up.

There was still hope. Before Mar would go to see Cancer, he decided to go back to the Libran restaurant where he got the letter. In fact, maybe that was his best bet. The voice. The waiter had a very distinctive voice. It didn't help that Mar had never gotten a good look at the waiter. But it didn't matter, he supposed all Librans looked the same to him anyway.

***

"I need to speak to whoever is in charge here," Mar demanded, rushing into the Libran restaurant. This was a different host than the one from last time, this one was a short, red-haired Libran woman, her red hair a reflection of the poinsettia flower in her hair.

"I'm the prince of Aries, Mar, and I need to speak with whoever is in charge here," he added to get a snappier response out of her.

"I'm sorry, this is a bad time, Prince Mar. Although this restaurant never closes, there are only certain hours during which Sir Leif is actually here and available to speak with anyone, princes included."

"Well, where is he? Where does he go once he leaves here? Where does he live?" Mar insisted through his teeth, literally looking around the restaurant as if he somehow expected to see him.

"I cannot tell you that information," she reported, avoiding eye contact for a moment.

"Look, I'm not going to leave here until you tell me how I can reach someone who is in charge of all you servants. I just need to speak with the one in charge of the waiters. It doesn't have to be Leif, if he is unavailable. But if you don't bring me somebody above you in a few seconds, you and everybody else here will regret it," Mar cautioned, fire burning in his eyes.

The hostess met Mar's eyes with a bit of challenge, almost as though she wanted to call his bluff. But instead, she began contacting someone through her desktop aqua communicator.

It took a while for her to get a response, but eventually a tall Libra man appeared before her, sporting a high quality indigo-blue suit and a white hat on his head. The white of his hat bled into the top of his face's palette, and the bottom portion of his face was indigo blue. "What have I told you about contacting me? Never, I repeat, never contact me without permission. I don't care what you are dealing with," he barked at the poor waitress.

"I understand, sir. I'm sorry to have disturbed you, master. I have only done so because I have the prince of Aries here. He needs to ask you something."

"Very well." He gestured for her to leave from his sight, and at the same time for the prince to come before the aqua communicator screen.

"How are you doing, Mar? It has been a long time." Leif gave the slightest of smiles.

"Yes, indeed, it has been too long. I need a favor from you. I will be truly indebted to you if you would gather all the male waiters in your employ at this fine establishment and allow me to question them," Mar stipulated.

"At this time of the evening?" Leif's face and tone were a mixture of disbelief and discontentment.

"Please, Leif, I am in need. I will talk to my father and see what can be done for you once you pay this favor to me."

"But of course, Mar. I will be there in a moment personally, and all males who work for me will be there for you to speak with," Leif related through his teeth.

Mar didn't have time to question Leif's behavior. It was very late. But Leif's insolent tone and mannerisms upset Mar a little, especially considering that he had only married into royalty and would only be called *sir* and *sire* by those who weren't royalty. Whereas Mar was a prince of the first kingdom established.

Pushing the thought of teaching Leif a lesson from his mind quickly, Mar began to relax a little. Now wasn't the time. Besides, his father wouldn't be too pleased at the thought of him disciplining a Libran royal, even if only through marriage. Still, it was a bit disgusting that the Libras were OK with marrying commoners. Royalty should marry royalty. No matter, his personal feelings were of no consequence regarding the situation.

The hostess showed Mar to an empty table a little away from the stage. The left and right tables closest to the stage were occupied.

"Whatever you eat will be on the house. I'm sure my master would want as much. We can't have the good prince wait without any food. Someone will be here to take your order shortly." She bowed slightly before walking away.

"Thank you."

The hostess left his table to return to the front of the establishment. Mar didn't even get a chance to order before Leif and his escorts, a few similarly well-dressed Libra men sporting black suits, came into the restaurant and to Mar's table on a mission.

"Right this way, Mar." Leif politely waited for Mar to get up from the table.

Leif and his escorts led him to the back, to a part of the restaurant that Mar had never been to, a part that most had never been to, he was sure. When they arrived at the back, there was nothing but a plain white wall, clean as if it had never been touched. Mar decided to hold his questions. Leif put his hand against the wall and the wall retracted and moved to the right, out of view.

"Step into my office."

Inside was immaculate. There didn't appear to be anything out of place. There were ten book shelves, on the left and right walls, five per wall. Each shelf had physical books, the right amount of books to appear both useful and as having space for future reads. And a clear desk was in the center of the room. There was an equal match to everything that existed in his office. They walked past the bookshelves and a room that appeared to have nothing but Libran paper currency, all the way to the back to a small sectioned off area with a black desk and a door. The room on the other side of the door was see-through with a glass divider separating it from the area where Leif and Mar stood.

"I have informed all of my male servants that you were coming and that you need to speak with them."

"These are all the servants, then?"

Before Mar on the other side of the glass stood a diverse group of common men from all twelve of the planets, and all the various half bloods. It seemed that Leif still had at least one man from every world in his employ, even after the great migration of all the half bloods to Aquarius. The room the male servants stood in was plain, there wasn't much in there at all. There weren't even any chairs. It was just a plain, French vanilla-colored room.

"Of course not. All my female servants are still out there, serving patrons and hosting, but you said that you only needed to speak with my male servants. And as I said before, this is all of my male servants." Lifting his hand, he gestured toward all the males in the other room. "Take your time speaking with them. You can either speak with them through this room or one by one in person."

"How about you speak to them for me? I want you to have them say, 'Can I take your plates? Is there anything else you need?'" Mar wasn't sure if that's what his waiter had said, but he knew waiters ordinarily said things of the sort and figured it would be enough to guess the waiter after hearing it.

One by one, all of the men in Leif's employ stepped forward, some were from Taurus, some were from Pisces, so on and so forth. Mar wasn't sure if it was a Libra who served him, so he decided to let all from every world speak up. They each took their turn stepping forward and delivering the desired speech. He hadn't seen the waiter's face so he didn't recognize any of them. What was worse, none of their voices meant anything to him either. All their voices sounded vastly different from the one who had dropped the letter.

"This is futile. Are you sure this is all your servants?"

"You have my word. These are all the males of all the races who work for me."

"Thank you for your time. I will be off, then."

"Wait, what was this all about? What about you putting in a good word with your father?" Leif called out to him.

Mar stormed out of the restaurant without so much as a word to anyone. Only one option was left before him.

***

It was the king's big day. King Leo's day to celebrate his life with the people of his land had finally come. Commoner lions carried the king and queen along with Hayder in three litters through a small parade. The king liked for all to be able to enjoy and appreciate his birthday in some way. His royal pride were on foot, set up two around each litter that carried the king and his family, just in case something were to happen. His royals wore yellow-trimmed, steel-plated armor today. It was heavier than their standard armor, but it was only under his wife's recommendation and only for the day, so Leo agreed to it.

Flutes, harps, and other strings played as they were carried from place to place. It had taken the queen a long time to make preparations for her husband's birth event, and so far, it was paying off. Upon finally reaching his throne and dining area, he, his wife, and his son were greeted by a performer. The youngest was allowed to stay home. At the age Aleser was, there was no need for him to partake in these events. To some degree this grand, extravagant birthday was to show the rebels how strong Leo remained. Another celebration with just royals was planned for later in the evening.

The performer was a man from Libra. It was interesting, a lot of planets traded resources. However, Libra would primarily trade people for deals. The Libran performer was exceptionally slender with a slight orange tinge to his appearance, but he also had the innate Libran translucence to him. He wore one article of clothing, which covered his entire body and seemed to have every color known to man, and it gave him a sort of comical look. He began performing when the Leo royal family was seated.

"I just came back from Scorpio and boy, am I hungry. Luckily, on Scorpio, there's no shortage of food."

Brown sand appeared in his hand magically. He opened his mouth and poured the sand in until it was all gone. The king and his family laughed.

"Delicious. I've had my feel of that for now, time for dessert."

A small scorpion mysteriously manifested itself in his other hand. The scorpion dangled from his hand onto his tongue for a moment. Until he ate it, a few seconds later.

The performer continued. "Something is not quite sitting right. Those scorpions are nasty buggers. I should check on my stomach. Wouldn't want to get stung," he said. He began coughing as if trying to get something out. At first, it was a small coughing spell. Eventually he coughed harder and harder until a palm-size glass statue of King Leo was regurgitated from his mouth.

"I believe this is for you, Your Majesty," he offered, looking at King Leo, but handing the statue to one of his royals. This royal then brought the statue to King Leo, who was about to refuse it. This upset his wife.

"My love, I put a lot of hard work into planning for this moment. Please accept the gift, it's from me, not the performer," the Lioness pleaded, placing her hand in his. Her white fur shined luxuriously as she had done extras to prepare for the big day including wearing a sunflower dress that her King had given her for her last natal day.

After that, King Leo accepted the gift with a smile, and the performer continued.

"Wow, I really need to lay off that food from Scorpio. After I left Scorpio, I headed to Aries." He paused for a moment. "There isn't much on Aries, so all I got was fire."

He began juggling a few flame torches as the crowd laughed. "Why go to Aries from Scorpio you ask? Because quite simply, my ship was running out of fuel. That's right, my ship runs on fire."

The torches disappeared behind his back where he threw them, and before him was a miniature lightning ship. The ship appeared to be flying around guided by his hands. He had his hands extended toward the ship as if he were throwing lightning bolts at it.

"I flew around for a while and crash landed here on Leo, the best planet of the twelve. I've never been the best pilot, you see."

The miniature lightning ship crashed and exploded in a glaringly loud and dazzlingly beautiful colorful display." My landing wasn't quite as explosive as that," he said.

"At any rate, I'm happy with the place I have landed at. You are all lucky to live here with a beautiful planet, and the finest king and queen of the twelve. Thank you for allowing me to entertain you."

He bowed and received lavish applause. The Lioness looked over at her king, who appeared somewhat pleased. Llevara stepped toward the space the Libran performer just left to introduce the next act. Llevara's bright yellow dress and flower in her hair were attention grabbing.

"Great ones of Leo and common folk, this is a most joyous occasion, on which our great leader celebrates the day he was born and given that, our next performers will show a day in the life of our beloved king."

A group composed almost entirely of women, except for one male who had extra fur on his head that was supposed to represent Leo's mane, came out. Most of the women had fake beards, goatees, mustaches, and horns.

"Hahaha! I am King Leo," the orange-furred man proudly exclaimed with his paws on his hips, throwing his head back.

One of the women who was supposed to be King Aries (you could tell by the size and shape of the fake horns on her head) said, "Let's begin our meeting."

The council meetings weren't public information, but everyone knew the kings had contact with one another. The queen had told her servant that it was fine for the performers to playact a meeting, just not to give any specific details of any of the past meetings. The ladies all tried their best to give their own take on the other kings, with most simply saying which king they were supposed to be. The meeting was basically all the other kings saying blah, blah, blah and other nonsensical phrases with King Leo being the only voice of reason, talking sense and stating the facts and making decisions and forcing the others to talk sense and make definitive commitments. Then a few legendary exploits of the king were briefly acted out.

Until finally at the end the male lion said, "I have accomplished a great many things again today, and now I'm going to make love to my wife." He picked up the most beautiful light- brown-furred female common lion present, held her in his arms, and they walked off stage. It was mildly amusing, but a bit too restrained, most likely because the characters were too afraid to do certain things, fearing death if they charted taboo subjects too deeply. The performance nearly put Leo to sleep.

The next act was a group of acrobats, and last there was a team of jugglers. Once all the performances were over, it was time for the great feast. There was an assortment of fine dishes from all over. There were a few commoner servants just to serve the king himself and four more servants to serve all the other royals at the table. The queen looked over at Llevara to make sure preparations were made for the finale. Llevara firmly nodded her head, so much so the flower resting in her hair almost flew out. The grand moment was finally approaching.

"Honey, look," his Lioness said as she tried to guide his attention toward the beautiful multicolored explosions in the sky. Leo looked up for a few seconds, but Llewellyn began asking him if he knew where the three missing members of the pride were. Leo couldn't hear him over the cheers of the crowd so he leaned in.

Leaning over, he asked Llewyan to repeat the question. Just then a flash of movement caught Leo's eye. He heard the twanging sound of a bow, three times in rapid succession and a moment later three arrows struck his chest simultaneously. Blood gushed out of his chest and mouth.

"Ahhhhhhh! Nooooooo!" his wife screamed.

"The king! The king has been shot! Find the shooter!" Llewellyn yelled. He and all of the others from the pride rushed from the table to search for the culprit.

"Dad? *Dad?* He's still alive. We need a healer over here, now!"

King Leo's vision blurred until he closed his eyes, unable to stay awake any longer.

***

"Healer! He's finally coming to."

Slowly, the king opened his eyes. Horrifyingly, he found he could hardly breathe. In fact, each breath he took felt more difficult than the one before it. He opened his mouth to speak to his son, Hayder, who was the first one he saw in the room through his blurry vision. But speech was a lot more difficult than he expected it to be.

"What happened?" Leo barely managed to ask.

"You were shot, Dad. Three arrows in your chest. They barely missed your heart. The healer said you're lucky to be alive. Unfortunately, the arrows were laced with poison, so the healer doesn't know if or when you'll be able to leave."

"Arrows laced with poison?" He strained as he inquired, squinting from the white light in the room. His vision was almost back to normal.

"Yes, Mom is out there trying to resolve everything now. Our pride was unable to find the shooter. I can't believe those bastards would try to kill you on your natal day." He clenched his fists. "I promise revenge will be had against the Sagittarius and the Scorpio or anybody else who was involved."

Leo just looked his son in the eye, not sure what to say. Honestly, he hadn't thought three arrows to his chest would do so much damage. He was still shocked to be in a healer's room. *Must be the poison. I'm not so frail to be taken down by arrows,* he thought with an inward smile.

"The good news is that the poison doesn't seem to be spreading that fast." His son's mood and tone became a bit more upbeat as he continued. "Or at least that's what the healer was saying."

The Lioness raced in the room and leaned into him near his bedside.

"My powerful lion. I cannot believe someone was evil enough to do this to you, on your natal day of all days." She grabbed her husband's hand and rubbed it on her face. She kissed the inside of his hand and made eye contact, her green-yellow eyes filled with emotion. "Don't worry, Hayder and I will take care of everything."

"It must be Sagittarius who is responsible, but think carefully about how to fight them. Our forces are still weak from the rebellion." He began coughing uncontrollably.

"Take it easy father. Healer! We need you now," Hayder yelled, standing up and walking to the doorway.

Due to the natural healing abilities of the Aquarius-Pisces, all the healers on planet Leo were of Aquarian-Piscean decent. The truth was, at the end of the day no matter how many half bloods were sent off to Aquarius, there were still large numbers of them on every planet. This particular female healer was a beautiful, dark-skinned lady with long silky blue hair. Blue eyes, deep and mysterious as the water, common of Aquarians, and a friendly demeanor. She was wearing a sky blue long coat that almost covered her entire body, a long sleeve shirt of the same color, and pants to match, standard attire for healers so those in need could easily recognize them.

"I'm happy to see you're awake, King Leo. I'm not sure if your family already went over this with you, but I would like to explain your status." She indicated a black touch screen near the leftmost wall that had a generic green outline of Leo with red areas around the chest and neck. "The three arrows you took to the chest have caused severe damage to your sternum along with your trachea. To make matters worse, you have been poisoned. Typically, Scorpio poison renders victims dead within hours. However, it seems the poison is acting rather slowly. I'm not sure if that's because of how powerful you are or perhaps the nature of the poison. Quite possibly it's a mixture of the two. We have tested the poison, and we are sure it is Scorpio poison. It is not as strong as the poison of the king of Scorpio, we are sure of that, but it might be from a Sagittarius-Scorpio. It could also be poison from a commoner of their race. We merely speculate, but we feel it's probably not the poison of any royal. That's just a theory, though. The good news is, the rate that it's spreading, which is slow as I said before. The bad news is that you will still die at this rate. The poison in your veins, although slow, is still lethal."

"How long until the poison kills him?" Hayder asked, voicing his concern, staring at the screen with his father's readout.

"Your father will only be able to go on like this for a few weeks. A month or two, if he's really lucky." The doctor shrugged, not prepared to give a solid answer.

"Why can't you just heal him?" The Lioness tried to contain her rage.

"Unfortunately, my healing abilities cannot cure poison. Additionally, the affected area cannot properly heal until all the poison is out of his system. I'm sorry to be the bearer of bad news, Your Majesty, but that's where we are at." She stepped away from the screen after pressing it to dismiss it, and gave her full attention to Leo. "I've heard there are cures for Scorpio poison, but I don't believe any of it is here on Leo. And we aren't even sure if it would work because this slow-acting poison may react differently. I will leave you all alone for now." Her eyes briefly landed on the Lioness and Hayder. "I will inquire with my colleagues to see if they have heard anything about a cure for Scorpio poison. If you have any additional questions, please feel free to see me in my office or call me over to your room."

"I'm going to kill all of them for you, Dad." Hayder stood near the door once the healer had already left.

"What? Kill who? Don't do anything foolish. Dammit, Hayder, don't make any premature moves," Leo warned his son and reached out his hand as if to stop him physically.

Again the king had a coughing spell that he couldn't control, it was longer than last time, and at the end of it, he coughed up dark red blood into his hands. Affectionately, his wife dabbed at his face with a napkin to clean him. She couldn't help but to wear a concerned look, but was trying to comfort him.

By that time, their son had already stormed out.

"Lioness, please watch over our boy for me." His eyes finally met hers. "I love him, but I'm afraid he isn't prepared to rule yet. We should ease him into a ruling position. You two should consult with me from time to time and before any big decisions. If he needs to make a decision, please guide him, if you can. Don't let him decide too much yet on his own."

"Of course, my love," she passionately answered, crying and rubbing his cheek. "I will take care of all of it, including getting the cure for the poison." She kissed his hand again and left.

Llevara waited patiently in the hall, black dress and black flower in her hair on display.

"Is there anything you wish for me to do, my Lioness?"

"Just watch over him at all times. I will send other servants to help you with anything you need. For now, just stay in the room with him and be ready to call for the healer."

"Yes, my queen." Llevara advanced into his room.

The queen took off.

Chapter 13

Croix finished two more of his tasks with great ease. The first two were the most difficult, in his opinion. The next two tasks were both done on Aries. Already, he had made it to the fifth task. Archer had as well. The two Aries men sat before Eames, waiting for their briefing.

"Congratulations, you two," Eames said with his back toward them both, staring at a rune-filled wall. "You have both been accomplishing your tasks at a steady, efficient pace." Finally he turned to them. "I can't say this with certainty, but you both seem like brotherhood material. Which is what brings us here today. You have both almost finished phase one. However, the fifth task will take me some time to prepare for you." He began slowly pacing around the room. "In theory, the fifth task is supposed to be a culmination of all the tasks you completed so far. That's not always the case. Each year, the fifth task is different." He stared at one of the early brotherhood founder statues in the corner.

Stepping back in front of them, he continued. "Basically, the goal is for you to use all the skills you learned from the first four tasks. The hunting abilities you learned from killing the sand dragon. The gift of gab that you learned from dealing with the troll. The importance of patience, which often young Aries have trouble with, which you should have learned from gathering ash bugs of Aries. And knowing how to look for weaknesses and openings and how to strike those openings, which you should have learned from taking down the bear and exploding shrews.

"I'm supposed to give you a task that brings the use of all those skills together. I may or may not do so. The fifth task is always the instructor's choice. Believe it or not, I have been consulting with Briccio before sending you out on all your last four tasks. Most of the tasks were predetermined, but confirmed by both of us. For this last one of the first phase, I really want to test you two. This is why it will take me some time to prep everything for your next challenge.

"So as of now, you two are free to go. I will contact you when everything is ready. It shouldn't be more than a few days, but consider it a time for celebration. Celebrate that you made it this far. Even if you fail the next quest, you two will always be royalty. Of course, there are benefits to being in the brotherhood; otherwise, nobody would join. I'm not sure if you two know all the benefits. Maybe you joined because your parents told you to, or maybe it was just a way to challenge yourself or test your abilities. I'm not sure, but either way, once you two successfully finish the fifth task, if and when you do, I'll explain some of the perks. For now, I won't keep you any longer. Stay on Aries, do not leave the planet for any reason. I will find you when I'm ready, enjoy yourselves." He dismissed them, turning his back to them once again.

The two men got up and left the brotherhood house. Croix was sure he knew how he was going to spend most of his break. He was going to spend it with Ava; thinking about that made him smile.

"Hey, what are you going to do for your break, Croix?"

"I'll probably just relax at home, mostly, but I may spend some time with a lady friend of mine tomorrow or the day after," he answered.

"Oh, OK, do you mind if I come along when you go?"

"What?" Croix suddenly became serious, his entire expression changed.

"Well, I don't want to intrude. I only mean if she has like a sister, or female cousin, or royal female friends," Archer lightly added. I feel bored with the woman I mated with for the initiation ritual and I'm ready to get back out there. You know spread my seed some more.

"Yes, OK, no problem I guess. She actually just so happens to have a sister. I will contact you before I go there. I'll see you in a little while."

Croix felt reluctant at first, but the two men were going to both be in the brotherhood ranks soon. They probably should spend some time together. Besides, what could it hurt? So, Croix went to his house and Archer went to his own, with plans to go to Ava's in a day or two, to meet with her and her sister.

***

Valera was welcomed to a small steel home by a radiant smile that belonged to a green-eyed, red licorice-toned older woman, who was dressed nicely, but modestly. Beautiful, but her age showed, it may have been her full head of silver hair or her regal peaceful energy. Either way, she was old, and she had to be the mother of Apple, as she appeared to be a bigger version of her.

The home seemed basic on the outside, but it wasn't even really a hut. Valera found it strange that the home was actually steel on the inside.

"Hello, I see my daughter has made a new friend. Who might you be?" The Aries woman smiled, but analyzed Valera.

"My name is Valera."

"Nice to meet you. My name is Abigail." She nodded her head slightly as an additional greeting.

"She's a queen, Momma. The queen of Vigo."

"You must mean *Virgo*," Abigail helped her daughter.

"Yes, Virgo."

"Wow, well, welcome to our humble home, Queen." Abigail turned from her daughter to Valera and gave an even friendlier smile to accompany her words of welcome.

"I'm so happy that you are not mad at Apple," Valera said, smiling. "She told me you and your husband are always cautioning her against speaking to strangers. I can't say I blame you, though, not all are kind to little ones."

"Oh well, I can't be too mad this time. I know you must be one of the good ones because you brought her back home to us. Her father may have a few words for her, though."

"Momma, I only talked to her to save her life." Apple pleaded with her mother, even tugging on her mom's gown. "

She was going to get exploded by the shrew."

"That's fine, dear. I believe you. Don't worry, we will talk about it later." Abigail patted her daughter on the head. "Anyway, please have a seat. I'm preparing dinner for my family."

Valera noticed all the chairs were made of steel, which didn't look very comfortable, but she didn't want to be rude. The only nonmetallic seat was very small and appeared to be where the child would sit. Valera sat down in the den area and hoped that the dining room would be more comfortable. To her surprise, the chair felt more like sitting in fine leather than metal. She adjusted herself in her seat; she was genuinely impressed. Aside from the table and chairs, the den area was mostly vacant. Scattered on the floor were miniature figures designed in the likeness of various queens from all over the twelve. There was not one in Valera's likeness, however.

"This is a nice chair. It's a lot more comfortable than it looks."

"Yes, these are special chairs. The house is special, too. My husband designed them all from a certain metal he developed." She lightly touched a chair that was near to her and then sat across from Valera.

"What do you mean, *developed*? Metal just exists, right?"

"No, not this metal, it's artificially created." She gave the chair she sat in a tap. "It's designed to be tough but malleable, and it's fireproof. That last part's nothing to brag about, though, because almost everything on Aries is fireproof."

"No, it still sounds very impressive. Speaking of your husband, where is he? I would love to ask him about his special metal." Valera looked around from her seat.

"Oh, so that sort of thing intrigues the queen. I'll call him out here now.

"Honey, please come out here, we have a guest." Still seated, she called in a friendly voice toward the direction of the front door. "Honey?" She turned back toward Valera. "He doesn't like it when I call him honey. He also may be busy working on something and unable to hear me. I'm going to go get him, I'll be right back." Abigail stood up, walked off, and disappeared from sight.

Valera had thought from outside that the house was very small. Apparently it wasn't considering that she hadn't seen the whole house, and the den and dining area were really big she considered, as she patiently waited to meet this metal creator.

A man about the same size as Abigail with an orange skin tone appeared. He had brown horns that were small for an Aries male, that curled a little just behind his ear. He was covered in sweat, and he extended his hand toward Valera. Valera stood up, and they shook hands briefly.

"I'm Arthur. I see you met my wife, Abigail, and my daughter, Apple." He gestured to them both as if to introduce them.

"Yes, I have, they are both lovely. You have a lovely family and home."

"Thank you, Miss—?"

"Valera. No need for formalities. Just call me Valera."

"Daddy, she's the queen." Apple tugged on his pants

"Queen? Queen of what? She's not even from here." He looked down at his daughter.

"She's the queen of Virgo, Daddy."

"Interesting. Is that what you told my daughter?" He looked back up, returning his attention to Valera.

"Yes, it's true. I am the queen of Virgo," she replied honestly, returning his gaze.

"Well, what on the twelve could have possibly brought you here?"

"I initially set out on a journey to see what all the twelve planets have to offer, and to get to know all the people of the different worlds."

"Strange, that sounds very strange, it's not like you rule over us directly. Aries and all the other planets have their own queens, you know, that right?"

"Yes, of course I do. I was curious about all the inhabitants, as I said before, I just want to know more about your world and about the people of the other planets I have never been to."

"You're a far ways off from the kingdom. The kingdom and this place where we live are almost worlds apart in and of themselves. How did you come in contact with our daughter?" Arthur changed his tone and the subject at the same time.

"Arthur, I think that's quite enough." His wife slapped his arm. "We should be welcoming the queen into our home, not interrogating her. I'm sure it's rude to question royalty." Abigail turned to Valera and bowed slightly. "Please forgive him, it's not often that we come into contact with royalty."

"I was just curious." He shrugged his shoulders.

"It's quite all right Abigail." Valera lifted her hand to dismiss any of Abigail's worry. "Your daughter saved my life earlier, and after that, I became curious about her and you two, so I wanted to meet you both. You have a very kind daughter, she is a good girl." She looked toward Apple.

"Yes, we are truly grateful to have her." Abigail beamed, boasting.

"Is dinner ready yet?" Arthur transitioned the conversation to his whim, bringing his attention toward the kitchen.

"Oh, yes, I have to go check on it. Give me a moment. You all sit in the dining area and wait for me."

The dining area was simple, it had the same chairs as the den area. Six chairs surrounded the oval table, which had a large black tablecloth covering it.

Valera waited for Arthur and Apple to sit before she sat. Apple sat next to her dad, who sat on the left side of the table.

"Are you sure you're royalty? I have never seen a royal travel by themselves, now that I think about it. Not to mention, I never seen one so overly polite." He stroked his barely visible mustache.

Valera finally sat on the opposite side from them. "I would not lie about something like that. Something of so much importance is not to be taken lightly."

Arthur shrugged his shoulders yet again.

"So, Arthur, please tell me a little bit about this special metal that you have created." She rubbed a chair that was next to her.

"I don't want to bore you with the details. It's just a mixture of things. Maybe one day I could show your majesty though. However, since it's special to me I would need some sort of guarantee that you wouldn't tell anybody else or use it yourself"

"I would enjoy seeing how it's made, and I can assure you that I would have no use for it. I don't spend any time making anything, and as queen you would have my word that the secret formula would be safe with me." Valera said.

"So what's it like to be a queen?" Apple stared up at Valera. Her big green eyes filled with wonder.

"Well, it's like every day is your natal day." She smiled and leaned toward Apple. "And everybody wants to take care of you and do nice things for you. If you have a decision to make, you don't have to make it on your own if you don't want to. You can ask other people for their advice, and they are sure to give you the best answer, because the decision you make will affect them as well."

"Wow, that's so cool, it sounds great. Daddy, Daddy, can I be queen someday?" She excitedly turned to her father.

Arthur paused and looked at his daughter sympathetically.

"Sure, baby, you'll be the best queen of them all." He patted Apple on the head.

Valera felt like she needed to say something.

"But when you're queen you do miss out on certain special things."

"What kind of things?" Apple asked.

"Things like time with family, like what we are sharing now. Everything you do is watched by everybody, and all your decisions affect people other than just yourself, so you have to think for everybody."

"Can't you just order somebody to make decisions for you, if you're queen?"

Valera wasn't really sure of what to say, but luckily she didn't have to say anything because at that moment, Abigail came out with the food.

All the food looked overcooked. It seemed so overcooked, in fact, that she couldn't tell what she was looking at. Most likely, there was a meat dish, and perhaps something of the plant variety, and some sort of dessert.

"Oh, I'm sorry, this is how some of the dishes are prepared on Aries." Abigail read and understood Valera's facial expression. "I assure you, the food will taste a lot better than it looks."

Sure enough, the food was a lot tastier than Valera expected.

"You're right, this is far better than what I expected. This may even be better than the food I'm used to on Virgo, and I have a professional cook." She joyously ate.

"Thank you, you are far too kind. I'm sure it can't rival that of a chef who cooks for royalty."

Valera stopped eating to look up and say, "I am not exaggerating, this is great."

"Yes, you're right, it really is good. I'm lucky to have such a wonderful cook as a wife." Arthur reached out his arm around his wife briefly.

"Thank you, honey, I appreciate it, but I really think you two are just buttering me up to get more dessert."

Dessert was a special substance Valera never seen before, with a buoyant, light, and fluffy consistency and melt in your mouth texture.

They all finished their plates rather fast, because the food was so good.

"I think I must be going now. It was a true pleasure to meet you, and I really enjoyed the meal." Valera stood up slowly.

"You cannot be serious." Abigail stood up in kind. "You must stay the night with us."

"I really don't want to intrude. Additionally, I wanted to explore this planet more. Besides"—Valera looked around—"not to be rude, but where would I sleep?" It was unclear where they even slept.

"Nonsense, there's no way we can let you leave here right now. You have to spend the night. Aries can be a dangerous place at night, especially for foreigners. You can explore to your heart's content in the morning. Apple and I will even trek with you. And of course, we have plenty of space for you here."

"That's right. You can sleep in my room," Apple offered with a smile, getting out of her chair too.

"No, Apple. We have a guest room. The queen needs her privacy, I'm sure."

"A guest room sounds fine to me, thank you, I appreciate your hospitality, but now there's the problem of me having nothing to wear."

"You can wear some of my clothes, of course. Your shape doesn't seem that far off from mine. I'll get something for you for both this night and the morning."

Valera sensed there was no polite way for her to get out of it, so she just gave in.

"Thank you, I will wait out here, then."

"Actually, how about I show you to your room now, so we can all prepare for sleep?"

"I could show her my room first," Apple volunteered, standing near Valera.

"No, Apple. It's time for everybody to go to bed, and I'm sure this young lady is tired from her journey, and she will need all the rest she can get, if she's going to explore all the planets on her special trip. Don't worry, honey, the three of us will have some fun in the morning, a special adventure."

"Yay!" Apple shouted.

"And you can show me your room in the morning, Apple."

"Yes, it's going to be great," Apple exclaimed as she ran off to get ready for bed.

Abigail led Valera to the middle of the floor, and suddenly she moved a fabric rug to unveil a steel door.

"What is all of this?"

"It's the way to the bedrooms."

"Why are they all below?"

"My husband just thought it would be the safest way, in case anything were to ever go wrong." She looked up while opening the hatch below.

"Very clever," Valera agreed as she descended.

They walked down a set of set of stairs, which were also made of the special metal, but when they got down the stairs, it was vastly different. The area opened up to a much more spacious environment. Something seemed homier about the new area. There was tan brown fabric covering everything, and everything was much softer than the upper area.

Valera's imagination began running away with her. She couldn't figure out why they had all the things on the upper level. Was it just a front? Why was the bottom so much different than the upper area? Something prevented her from asking. It seemed to her that every inhabitant of every world she had met so far had some sort of secret, except for the Capricorn boy. Perhaps even he had a secret, but she just hadn't learned it yet.

Whatever the case, this family still seemed more honest than the sketchy character she had met on Pisces. She still couldn't figure out what was off about him. But something certainly was.

Abigail interrupted Valera's thoughts. "This room right here will be yours."

The room was nice but simple, red-colored, and had a large bed that could fit at least two people of Valera's size, and a decent-size holographic display system. Valera was unsure about what she was seeing, again, she wasn't sure that commoners had things such as holographic display systems. Maybe commoners had more luxuries on Aries than Virgo she considered the idea to resolve how overly nice she felt the guest room was. Other than that, the room was pretty bland, with nothing more than a sink and a sky window for looking up.

"I imagine it may be hard for you to fall asleep with the sky window open." Deep red moonlight illuminated the entire room. "Feel free to close it if you need to. This device controls it." Abigail handed her a small black remote with three blue buttons.

"That other remote over there controls the holographic display system. They were a bit much for my husband and me, but he insisted that we have them in every room, even though we don't get guests that often. He just feels it's the best way for people to entertain themselves, being able to watch old memories, or anything they could dream up, or recordings on the big screen. Anyway, I know this isn't as luxurious as what you're used to, but I hope you will enjoy your stay. Just let me know if you need anything, our room is two doors to the left. Goodnight." She exited with a smile.

"Thank you again for everything," Valera said.

She changed into the clothing Abigail gave her; a simple red gown that fit a little loose, looser toward the bottom and tighter toward the top, and reflected on her journey so far.

***

Croix and Archer arrived at Ava's front door.

Was it really a good idea bringing him here? Croix wondered.

"So this is the place, then, huh? Pretty fancy. I see you have good taste in women," Archer said with a wink and a slick smile.

I guess it's too late now. Hopefully everything will be fine. Croix stood there quietly, not responding to Archer, waiting for Ava to get the door.

Ava came to the door in the finest attire Croix had ever seen her wear. She had a black dress that must have been imbued with magic, given the glow it had. It appeared to float almost like it wasn't even on her body, but just hovering over it, and yet it covered everything except for her left and her right side.

"Wow, you look absolutely stunning," Croix complimented her, his eyes big and transfixed.

"Thank you, Croix, and who is your friend here?" she asked, turning her attention to Archer. Her smile changed slightly.

"My name is Archer. And like Croix over here, I'm going through the initiation process for the brotherhood." Flashing a smile, he reached for her hand and shook it briefly.

"But of course you are." Ava stepped to the side of the door for them to walk in. "Please come in, my sister was just preparing some food. We always make a lot, so there should be more than enough for you two."

Croix was glad that he dressed in some of his finest garments before he came to Ava's house. Croix was wearing a deep black jacket with light white sparkles that shined like the stars in the sky, and under it he wore a charcoal gray shirt. The jacket was special, for only the king's direct relations could get one. His lower body was covered by standard pants that were blue, as he liked his jacket and pants to be a different color for contrast. And he had shoes that were fashioned in the same deep black and white light sparkles as the jacket. At first, he thought it was good idea just to make sure that he looked better than Archer, in case he wanted to compete with Croix. He hoped it wouldn't come to that, but he wasn't too sure. After all, the two men were competing in a sense. Not that there were limited spaces in the brotherhood or anything like that, but as far as Croix figured the trials had something to do with ranking.

"That's quite an interesting jacket you have there," Ava said.

"Thank you, it's just a jacket my uncle gave to me. The shoes are made from the same material, actually," he bragged.

"Oh, yes, I can't say I've ever seen a jacket like that before."

"Yes, it's no big deal, but I think it's rare," he gloated a little more, garnering attention while staring at his shoes.

"Oh, do tell," Ava half-joked.

"Yes, I believe there are only about eight of them that exist," Croix continued gloating and posed. He wasn't aware of her sarcasm.

"Do you find that interesting?" She brought Archer in the conversation.

"Yes, I guess so." His eyes were focused on his own drab clothing. "I have never seen a jacket like that before either. I'm underdressed," Archer said. "With you being so lovely, and Croix with his star jacket, I feel a bit out of place."

"Ha, no, don't worry. Those sort of things don't matter here, not right now. We are just going to have a lunch together. Although, I'm surprised you two decided to show up here unannounced. Luckily, nothing exciting is going on at the moment. I will enjoy both of your company. I'm sure the same could be said of my sister. Honestly, since we are on the subject, I'm actually surprised at how Croix is dressed myself. He normally doesn't come over in such fancy garb."

Croix was used to seeing Ava dressed up, but never like he saw her today, he found it weird also, but wasn't sure if he should mention it. Not believing Ava's story about nothing going on, the thought crossed his mind to ask about her dress lightly during lunch.

"You don't say. Well, he must be trying to keep up with you. You are quite lovely, after all."

"Oh stop, you are just trying to flatter me." She dismissed his compliment with a wave that looked like she wanted more compliments. "Thank you."

"You have a lovely home here also," Archer said.

"Yes, it's one of the nicest places I've ever been to on Aries." Croix felt a bit left out of the conversation.

"Wow, I don't think I've ever heard you say that before. Quite the compliment, especially coming from the king's nephew." Ava brightened even more.

"The food is almost ready." Acadia finally came out of the kitchen to the dining room area. "Oh, well, hello there. I didn't think we would have company. Croix, it's nice to see you again. And oh, you brought a friend this time. Who might you be, Croix's friend?"

"My name is Archer, and I must say you are very—"

"Hold that thought, I have to go check on the food." Acadia abruptly disappeared back into the kitchen.

"Can I ask something?"

"Of course, Croix, what's on your mind?"

"Why don't you guys have servants cook for you?"

"There's a few reasons, really. Where to begin?" She tapped the side of her face with her index finger. "For one, our current servant is away on vacation."

"You give your servants vacations?" Croix was astonished.

"Yes, of course, it is nice for all people to be able to rest and relax and enjoy life occasionally. Anyway, the second reason is that my sister and I genuinely enjoy cooking. It is somewhat therapeutic to prepare your own meal, or even a meal for others. The third reason is that it can be a useful skill to have. What if something happens, and we no longer have our servants to cook for us? I'm not saying anything will, but in a way, that's being too dependent on others. There are other reasons, if you would like to hear them."

"No, that's plenty."

"So you two did the mating ritual together, right? Are you planning on doing the unification ritual together as well?" Archer queried, apparently bored with their conversation topic.

"What?" Ava became uptight, and her body literally stiffened.

"That's a pretty personal thing to bring up." Croix sought to defend her, but most importantly to stay off the subject.

"I'm just asking, just curious." He casually shrugged. "You two seem to have something going on here, so I figured you had mated already, are expecting a little one, and are on your way to starting a new life together." Archer's tone became friendlier.

Croix and Ava blushed, turning royal blue on their cheeks and unsure of what to say. Luckily, the food was ready.

"Here we are, everybody, this is the main course." Acadia brought out a very large meat dish that was prepared Aries style and therefore blackened to a crisp. Acadia was also dressed fancy, especially for there to be no special occasion going on with them. She had an emerald-green dress that gave her an aura.

"Let me help you serve the food, Acadia."

"Thank you, sis. I didn't expect for you to help, but I do appreciate it."

The two ladies brought out a vast array of different meats and plants prepared in various styles; the large feast could have fed at least two more full grown Aries males.

"How are you enjoying the food, Croix?" Ava wondered.

"It's very good, all of it is." He partially smiled. "Hey, I'm curious, but are two expecting somebody else to come over? This sure seems like a lot of food, and you didn't even know we were coming here. You are both dressed so lovely."

"Thank for the compliment." Acadia nodded softly with a smile. "Yes, our father may actually be coming home to visit us tonight, or at least he is supposed to."

"Oh, OK, I see," Croix replied.

"How about you Archer? How are you enjoying the food?" Ava inquired.

"I think it's just OK." Archer played with it for a second, perked his head up and began staring. "Hey, you said your name is Acadia right?"

"That's correct." She didn't look up right away.

"I don't want to be rude, but do you think it's too much to discuss the mating ritual with others? I hope my question isn't offensive, or that the subject is too crude, but I'm just curious."

"I personally don't mind talking about things like that, but my sister does. I don't think it's a big deal though." Acadia's attention finally became focused on Archer, who was sitting next to her.

"Yes, I don't think so either. We are all young here. It's mating season, it can't hurt to talk about it a little. It's not like I was even asking for details. I skipped past that part and went straight to the children and those two becoming one through the unification ritual."

"Don't worry, if your friend Croix or Ava doesn't want to talk about the mating ritual with you, I will be more than happy to." She leaned a little closer, smiled, and laughed.

"You would," Ava muttered under her breath.

"What was that?" Acadia asked.

"Nothing, absolutely nothing. So tell me, Archer, how has it been for you so far, completing tasks for the brotherhood?"

"They have all been extremely easy so far. I haven't broken a sweat yet," he professed. "Now, Croix, on the other hand"—he raised an open palm toward him, pausing to make sure they looked at Croix—"has had a hard time once or twice out there. It's actually quite sad."

"What are you talking about?" Croix was confused.

"I'm talking about how you almost got eaten by the troll. Remulaude told me about that, and how you brought back a glass head of a sand dragon, but I brought back a regular head. I'm actually surprised Eames even counted it, he must have felt like being nice."

Croix was relieved for a second, thinking that Remulaude didn't tell Croix's secret to Archer, but he was infuriated listening to Archer trying to one up him.

"Remulaude also told me another secret about our friend Croix here. Do you ladies want to know what it is?" He raised his eyebrows and grinned.

Acadia edged closer to Archer, with an eager expression.

"I think a man shouldn't tell the secrets of another man. It is not very masculine." Ava said.

"That shouldn't come as a shock to you," Croix said. "There isn't anything manly about Archer. Which is precisely why I finished all our missions before him."

Archer, seemingly unfazed, whispered something in Acadia's ear. The two even laughed.

Finally, Archer looked up across the table. "Is that so? Well, perhaps I would be manlier if I were the king's nephew. Maybe then I would be able to get the help I need so as not to have to struggle to accomplish tasks."

The nerve of him, Archer was accusing Croix of cheating. The two stood up out of their chairs and stared each other in the eye intensely.

"How about we go outside, and I show you just how much of a cheater I am?" Croix suggested.

"Acadia, how about you bring out some more dessert?" Ava tried to ease some of the tension.

"There's already enough dessert here for everybody," Acadia retorted, annoyed at the suggestion.

Ava gave her younger sister a hard look.

"OK, but only if you come with me," Acadia teased with a devilish smirk, winked an eye, and stuck her tongue out.

Acadia must have wanted the two to fight.

Archer helped. "No need to worry, ladies, Croix and I will handle this outside."

Before they moved, Eames called.

Croix had a mobile communicator so the brotherhood could contact him anytime. Producing the tiny water screen from his pocket, he answered Eames.

"I'm ready. Everything is set up. You and Archer can head over here. He's with you, right?"

"Yes, he is." Croix momentarily returned to the staring contest.

"OK, come by the house as soon as possible." Eames ended communication without waiting for a response.

"Well, this has been quite the lunch," Ava said. "It's been fun. Croix, I'll walk you out. Acadia, will you see to it that Archer makes it to the brotherhood house. Some fresh air can really benefit us all, I'm sure.

Chapter 14

"Finally, the time has come," Virgo was pleased to say to himself. "I have so patiently waited. Any minute now, my wonderful patients shall give birth to the future of all the kingdoms. With the birth of these children not a single member of any race will have to go forth and fight anymore. But first, I must get their mothers prepped to give birth." He smiled to himself.

Virgo began taking the mothers out of their tubes. Of course, they were still in a state of sleep, because they had been in the liquid for so long.

"I wonder if I should wake them up prematurely. No, that shouldn't be necessary. I imagine the birth of their children will wake them. Child birth is a forceful event, after all"

Excitedly, he danced about as he set up the areas where the mothers would give birth and began extracting them from their tubes with his telekinesis. He couldn't help but to glide back and forth, as happy as a song bird as he waited to see the fruits of his labor. Unbeknownst to anyone, Virgo had actually been working on learning more about all the people of the twelve for a long time, even before all his recent experiments. He never understood why the physical characteristics would generally lean toward one race, even with half bloods. There were so many things that he never understood. Although this experiment deviated slightly from his original questions, it would likely still reveal a few things regarding the DNA of the twelve races, and what's more, serve an even greater purpose by giving birth to super soldiers and making combat a thing of the past for all, commoner and king alike.

"I should call Vernon in here."

Vernon didn't respond right away, and Virgo remembered that he sent him out to fetch something.

Once each mother was out of her respective tube, he put them on large, soft beds with their feet resting in stirrups, and set them in a position that would be most comfortable. Still unsure of whether they would try to fight or do anything strange, he toyed with the notion of restraining them all, at least partially, so he wouldn't have to worry about interruptions. The conclusion he came to was that it wouldn't make sense for them to try to leave. They were pregnant long before he kidnapped them or began his experiments; he could easily pass for a neonatal assistant or a healer, both of which were typically involved in assisting mothers with giving birth, so he decided not to bother with restraints.

"This calls for some celebratory music."

He cued up a recording he had of a live performance from Libra on his holographic device. Chords, horns, and dark percussion began playing. The dramatic music always gave him a stronger feeling of genius and inspiration than the softer, subtler tunes. He turned off the visual portion of the hologram so it wouldn't distract him from his work.

A glass fell, leaving purple fluids on the ground not far from where he was. Then another glass shattered on the ground violently.

"Is somebody there?"

The thoughts began pouring into his mind rapidly.

The king said to keep my mind clear, Virgo can read thoughts, an intruder reflected.

"I can read your mind. Whoever you are, whatever you are doing here, you picked a bad time. I'm afraid I'm going to have to kill you, no matter which king sent you, this is my lab and nobody comes in here without my permission," Virgo warned.

Laughter was the only response to his threat.

"I know, you must be Cancers."

Virgo wasn't sure how he wanted to handle the situation. He could lift everything in the room with his telekinesis, but his precious experiments would be disturbed in the process. If only there was a way to lure them out. Even when they laughed, the laughter seemed to be from everywhere. It wasn't helpful that there was more than one of them. He was a king, the Cancers wouldn't be a match for him, so he decided he would take them out one by one, thus ensuring the safety of his experiments

Virgo began floating. Using his abilities, he lifted himself up in the air, and then created a push-pull field (a telekinetic sphere that covered Virgo and both pushed against and pulled on objects and created a sort of gravity field in which he could control objects that penetrated his sphere) of at least his own weight, as a shield to protect him from the Cancers. The Cancers would have a hard time attacking him through his field. It took a lot of concentration but was important to help him get a better idea of where his assailants were in the room. Closing his eyes, he maintained his levitation field and began to follow a trail of thoughts from one of the intruders. The words took physical form, and he followed the trail to find his first victim.

"There you are."

Virgo pinpointed the intruder's location very well from the thought trail and focused his energy at that point. Sure enough, he was able to lift something that seemed to weigh as much as a Cancer man should.

"Goodbye." He brought the invisible man up and floated him to eye level.

"I wouldn't be so fast to do that, if I were you." Virgo opened his eyes to look down.

"Put him down, or I'm going to kill this woman."

One of the pregnant Libra woman was being held up in a standing position and had a knife to her throat, with nobody attached to it, of course. Although invisible, at that moment he knew where the other man was.

Damn them. The bastards, using my patients against me.

"I don't care about her. Your friend is still going to die," Virgo guaranteed.

Virgo squeezed the Cancer man with his mental grip until he saw blood gush from the invisible entity. The man screamed. Virgo squeezed harder, and the man went silent. Virgo dropped the bloodied corpse, invisible no more, to the ground.

"You forced my hand," the Cancer man informed him, but instead of her throat being slit, she disappeared.

"What?" Virgo was stunned as he witnessed his experiment vanish before his eyes. The Cancers weren't capable of making other people disappear, unless it was some sort of teleportation.

The shock of what he saw caused him to lose a bit of his concentration. The next moment he felt a twinge of pain as three knives grazed his body. His protective field was weak because he lost some focus. Before he could recover, another of his other experiments disappeared just as suddenly.

His confusion became overwhelming as he witnessed the last patient disappear as well.

He couldn't focus at all anymore. King Cancer should have been the only Cancer who could teleport, and it didn't make any sense for them to be able to make people disappear.

Virgo dropped his field entirely and nearly plummeted straight down, letting himself go instantly and rushing over to where his last patient was. Was it King Cancer? He had to investigate, curiosity overwhelmed him. Aside from that, he could no longer feel the intruders' presence and thought they may have gone. Just to be safe, he maintained a light telekinetic field around himself at first, just in case the intruders were still about, but he had to let go of that too, briefly, so he could investigate. He moved to the area where his experiments had once lain, and he reached where the last expectant mother was laying and put his hand out, to his surprise he felt a warm body.

"Invisible?" Virgo questioned right before he felt the last sensation he ever felt in life. Virgo felt a mind-numbingly painful, burning feeling in his throat. The distraction worked. He cared too much about his experiments. He thought that killing the other Cancer man would show them that he wasn't bluffing. They still called his bluff, and slit his throat.

***

"Master, the deed is done."

"Very good, so Virgo is out of the picture, then?"

"Yes, sire."

"Good work, Maestro. Report back to me once you are finished there." Cancer, the blue devil, smirked.

"And what should I do with the Libran women he was experimenting on?"

"Just move their bodies somewhere safe and far. Clean up the lab somewhat. I need for it to be entirely free of bodies, aside from Virgo, his doesn't matter."

"One more thing." Maestro requested his King's attention.

"What is it?"

"Should I do anything else? These women appear to be pregnant, in fact, they seem as though they are about to give birth right now."

"No." Cancer lost his patience. "I just told you to move their bodies to a secure location."

"Understood. One last thing: Cyrus is dead. Virgo killed him."

"That's unfortunate, but I had already suspected that we would take a loss. Just do everything as I said, then clean up there and come back to me as soon as you can." The transmission was over.

Cancer laughed, amused with himself. *Pisces thinks he can boss me around. I'll show him. Soon, I should have everything I need to use them against him and everybody else. I grow so weary of him always thinking he has everything in control. He doesn't seem to be fulfilling his end of our promises. It's a good thing I had those Aries men working on that list. Pisces, you fool. You may be the next one I kill, you self-righteous bastard.*

Maestro did as his master ordered, but something in his gut told him to ignore the orders and kill the Libras and their babies, too. He knew there would be consequences if he didn't obey so he just left it alone, and moved the bodies of the mothers to be, as he was told. Witnessing the babies in the stomachs of the three women still kicking gave him knots in his stomach, and he felt apprehensive as he and Gregorio transported the bodies and left King Virgo's lab a bloody mess.

***

Callum watched as two participants competed. This newest competition seemed strange. There was a small building, broken into two sections that had glass in the front, back, and both sides for each separate section. Each participant also had a glass window that faced the person he was competing against. The two Capricorn men were building something, but Callum had no way of being sure what it was.

"This is an exercise that tests memory as well as listening skills," Caleb explained, staring at the competing men as well.

"What are they building?" Callum asked.

"It doesn't matter. It's not always the same thing each time. In fact, they could be building two different things, or they may be building the exact same thing. The point of this exercise isn't what you build, it's how you follow the instructions you are given on building."

"That doesn't sound challenging at all."

"It may not be if you remember everything you're told by your instructor before you begin," Caleb agreed.

"They don't repeat the instructions if you need?"

"It depends, but generally speaking, I would say they don't."

"What do you mean, *it depends?*"

"I mean, it depends on the instructor and a few other variables. The main factor however is the level of complexity of the design. The more complex the instructions the higher the likelihood that the instructor would repeat it. Anyway, that's all I'm going to tell you for now. Anything else, you will have to find out while you're actually trying your hand at completing the exercise for yourself. I'm not sure how many are left to go, but I'll signal you when it is your turn."

Caleb walked away and met with the other instructors, and they shared a few laughs.

The Capricorns looking to join the cavalry were all lined up around the two boxes, watching the other men building whatever it was they were building. One looked like he was building a large replica house and the other looked like he was building some sort of vehicle.

Callum patiently watched; one thing he was sure of, after all the tests he had taken, was that the Capricorn Royal Cavalry expected patience out of all their troops, just like the older man had told him. There was a lot of waiting involved with all the trials he made it through so far.

"Callum, come here." Caleb waved Callum over to him. Caleb had walked away from the other instructors.

Cyd and Cassius walked into the glass rooms with the two men; apparently they were finished. "I got you going up next. I will be your instructor for this. Listen to me very carefully: I want you to build a replica of the castle," Caleb instructed.

"The castle?"

"Yes, don't you remember? We were there earlier today."

"Oh, yes, OK, I understand." Callum nodded, slightly unsure of himself.

"Here's your instructions: You can build the castle with the parts in any order, except for the drawbridge, which must be assembled last, and the right wing, which must be done before the left wing. Additionally, you must always build from the ground up. This means you must start from the bottom and work your way to the top. You cannot start on the left or the right wing until you have built up around both of them in the middle. Here is a picture of what the castle looks like, in case you haven't committed the image to memory.

He paused for a few seconds, holding up the scrolled image at both sides so that Callum could fully see it. The castle had three portions that had three tops, the middle portion led to a circular top, the right side led up to a top that was square, and the left portion had a top that was triangular. There was also a drawbridge. This didn't seem anything like the prince's castle or anything Callum had ever seen before, but it didn't matter. Maybe he just missed all these details last time he looked at it.

"Do you have any questions? Please build the prince's castle exactly how you see it here."

"How long do I have to finish?"

"Honestly, the time isn't the most important factor. There is technically a time limit, but it is more important that you complete this according to everything I just told you a moment ago. So, do you have any questions about my instructions, the image, or anything else I told you?" He made eye contact with Callum.

Callum gave his instructor an affirmative nod to say he was ready.

"The clock begins ticking as soon as you enter your respective box. You will be on the left. Take your time. The man in the box across from you will be assembling the same thing as you. I recommend that you don't look at him or focus on what he's doing. You will construct your castle by using small pieces that interlock into one another. I must warn you, however, that just because two pieces seem to fit into each other, doesn't mean that they necessarily are supposed to be locked together. OK, that is all, try your best." Caleb walked away.

Callum walked inside the glass box and was surprised by how cold he felt. On the solid white floor in front of him was a piece of paper that also had instructions. This troubled him. Caleb hadn't said anything about any written instructions. Should he follow these instructions written on the paper or ignore them? He figured for now, he would at least read these additional instructions and see if they conflicted or confirmed everything he'd been told earlier. Then from there, he could make a determination as to whether he would follow through with the new instructions.

The paper read:

The goal of this exercise is to test both memory and listening ability. You have been instructed to put together a castle using simple interlocking pieces. All the interlocking pieces are in the right corners of the room toward the rear and toward the front. You are only to grab pieces from the front of the room first and use them all before you grab any of the pieces from the rear. However, you can use the pieces to build up the castle in any manner. The pieces from the front right side of the room don't need to be used for the right side of the castle, for example. You should start with a strong foundation first, only arranging pieces toward the bottom to build up the castle in a manner that will make it as sturdy as possible. Also, it is important that you build the castle in the center area of the room. Lastly, you are not allowed to ask your instructors any more questions. Begin when ready.

Callum looked up at the light brown man in the other room and saw him putting the paper down at the same time Callum finished reading his instructions.

Let me see. The paper didn't seem to contradict anything my instructor told me. I also just saw the man in the other room finish reading his paper, too. Maybe instructor Caleb just forgot to tell me about the paper. I suppose it can't hurt to follow the paper's instructions as well.

Callum looked over at the pieces in his front right corner first, and then he looked over at what he believed was the rear right corner and saw that there were many more pieces on that side than the side he understood to be the front right corner.

They really could have given us more instructions outside.

He decided to go with his gut and to assume that the area he suspected of being the front right corner was exactly that, so the next thing was for him to start gathering pieces from there. He moved over to it and brought back some of the pieces, as many as he could carry, over to the center. The pieces were mixed colors, all were a few centimeters in length, width, and height. Then he went back and forth, carrying pieces from the front right corner back to the center until he had all of them. There must have been at least three hundred pieces, most of them being peach- colored, some brown and some black. Glancing up briefly, he checked on the status of his competitor. To his horror, the other man was working at a breakneck pace. Stunned for a moment, he almost panicked and began rushing, but he remembered his instructions.

I don't have to rush, this has nothing to do with speed. I was told to take my time, and I should do so. Now all I have to do is build this castle from memory.

There were a number of square pieces, and they all appeared to be interlocking and compatible with one another. They had no apparent differences, aside from color, so Callum began rapidly building the foundation.

I think I understand how my competition was able to build so fast.

Callum built most of the center of the castle. It was now time to start on the building the wings, but for some reason he couldn't remember whether the left wing of the castle, or the right wing, or if the center of the castle was supposed to be built first. It must have been the strain of also learning and trying to remember all the other rules, including those written on the paper.

How should I make my decision for this?

Callum figured it would be best to build the left wing first. He had already begun building around the center and the left wing, so it would be easier to complete. He took another glance at the other man, who was building the first wing of his castle.

That's strange, a while ago, he was ahead of me, but now he's only on the same part I'm on. Does that mean I did something wrong when building the foundation?

There was no time to worry about that. Caleb had said that there was a time limit. Although it wasn't the main concern, it was still a concern.

Callum quickly completed the left wing. He ran out of pieces, so he had to get the blocks from the other corner of the room.

Why are there still so many pieces left if I'm supposed to only build the right wing and drawbridge? He wondered once he brought all the new blocks over.

Perplexed, he looked up again at his opponent's castle, which somehow was completed. Shocked, Callum began working rapidly. He finished the right wing, and he did all the top portions of castle. Then he completed the drawbridge. As soon as he was finished, Caleb entered with a clear holographic notepad before he even had time to look for him.

"I have a few questions for you. My first question, why didn't you take all of the pieces over with you from the beginning? The piece of paper you read said that you had to gather pieces from one side first, but that didn't mean that you couldn't have gathered them all before you started building. So why did you gather the pieces from one side at a time?"

Callum didn't take long to think of the question, because he already knew the answer.

"I wanted to make sure that it was clear that I gathered all the pieces from the side I was supposed to before I moved on to the next side, so it would be easy to tell."

Caleb made notes on his holographic notepad by tapping on the see-through screen.

"My next question is, why did you follow the instructions on the paper?"

Heart dropping from his chest, Callum swallowed hard. It must have been a trick, all the instructions on the paper. That was why Caleb didn't mention it in the first place.

Caleb must have seen the fear in his frozen pupil's face, so he helped by repeating.

"Why did you follow the instructions on the paper? I'm just asking a simple question. It's not necessarily right or wrong. I'm just curious. Technically, the exercise was designed to test your listening and memory capabilities, not your reading capabilities, reading comprehension, or ability to follow written instructions. However, I want to tell you honestly, this test measured much more than your listening and memory abilities. Please give me an answer. At this point, it can't harm you. I am just curious. The test is already over and as I said before, following the instructions on the paper is not inherently right or wrong."

"I followed the instructions on the paper, because..."

He paused trying to find a good answer.

"I read the paper and felt that it didn't contradict anything you told me earlier, and that maybe the instructions on the paper could better help me complete the task. All the statements on the paper seemed to be doable instructions and I thought maybe additional guidelines would help me to complete my task. I thought maybe you had forgotten to mention it to me."

"That's a reasonable answer. Is there anything else?" Caleb didn't make any notations on his notepad this time, but rather peered harder at Callum. "Any other reason that you may have followed the instructions on the paper?"

The boy remembered that he had also seen the other Capricorn read the paper before he began, and debated with himself whether or not he should tell his instructor.

"Yes, another reason is that I saw the other man in the room across from me read the instructions on his paper."

"Thank you for your honesty. I truly appreciate it." He took more notes on his holographic notepad, and then looked back up at Callum. "That's the exact answer I was looking for. I'm glad you remembered that we were watching you. I already knew that you had looked over at the other man, and I figured that was one of the reasons that you followed the instructions written on the paper. OK, that does it for this test. You only have two tests left."

Two more tests. This whole process had been exhausting for Callum; he had already lost consciousness once, almost died, climbed a mountain, and built a replica castle, and now he had another test, no, actually, two more tests before he would be done.

"How did I do on this test? How am I doing so far?"

"You did about average on this one. You didn't listen to all of my instructions, and you didn't remember everything I said. What's more, you didn't complete the castle."

"What do you mean?"

"You didn't finish the moat around the castle."

"I didn't realize that I had to."

"I told you to complete the castle exactly how it is in the image. In the image, there was a small portion of the castle surrounded by water. I have the image right here if you want to look again. Also, another thing is you didn't build the prince's castle. I lied to you when I said the castle in the picture was the prince's castle. You were there today, you should remember it didn't look anything like the castle from the image at all."

"What are you talking about? You're my instructor. How was I supposed to know I couldn't trust you, and furthermore, how was I supposed to build a moat when there weren't enough pieces left?"

"There may have been even more pieces than the ones before you that you didn't notice. And as far as the prince's castle, you were supposed to call me out on it and say that doesn't look like the castle we were at earlier. Believe it or not, as ridiculous as it sounds, that was a part of the test, for you at least. All you had to do was question me to get that part of the test right. Essentially there were two possibilities, you could have completed the prince's castle from earlier from memory, or put together the castle from the image. You didn't do either to completion, in this case."

"What about my competitor?"

"What about him?" Caleb folded his arms over each other in front of his chest.

"How did he do?"

"Honestly, he did very well." He unfolded his arms, softened his tone, posture, and stance a little. "Look, kid, the point of the exercise was to measure your listening and memory capabilities, not to see how well you can copy somebody else's work. I told you that from the beginning. You didn't really need to read the paper at all, technically." He shrugged. "In fact, not reading it may have helped you, because apparently you were so focused on the paper's instructions that you missed the other pieces that were in the room, right over there."

Sure enough, there were other blocks directly behind Caleb.

"It's OK, not everybody always scores high on this test. This test is designed to trick you up and be difficult, so don't be too hard on yourself, kid. The other man who you were referring to had different instructions than you did. Also, you began building the left wing before you began building the right wing. I told you earlier to do it the opposite way, but I guess maybe your instincts told you to build left first. I don't know, whatever the case it was another mistake, but a small one.

"I know you saw the other man, who was building up the left wing first. You were smart enough to know that his starting on the right wing was actually him building the left wing, but again he had different instructions from you. We don't have much time. We have to go and prep you for your next challenge. We're moving on now. If you have any concerns or feel that you could have done better on any of the challenges or that you didn't fully understand anything, you can voice any of your concerns at the end of these last two at the honoring ceremony, where you all will receive your ranks. For now, let's go." He turned his back to Callum. "I won't say it again."

Caleb walked out of the glass room, and Callum quickly followed, not wanting to upset him. They walked to another large field area, this time it was littered with a number of machines, devices, and obstacles.

"Welcome, children, to your penultimate challenge, the obstacle course. This one is simple, just make it through all the obstacles, machines, and devices as quickly as possible. You will be broken into groups of ten and compete in that manner. Then, after the first run through, you will run through it again with nine other people that you didn't compete with the first time, and so on and so forth, until you have directly competed against every other initiate level Cap," Cassius said. "Can I get some volunteers?"

This time, ten Capricorns eagerly volunteered, including Callum, who was eager to make amends for his last performance.

"Go!" Cassius yelled.

"Stop! Cassius was joking with you all." Cyd said quickly speaking up before the recruits really got going. His brownish-gray skin glistened in the sun, as did his jet-black curly hair, as he commanded the recruits' attention for the first time all day. "I know jokes aren't his strong suit so you all probably couldn't tell. It's actually my turn to instruct. Now it's time for the fun part." He rubbed his hands together. "This is my favorite part. The dreaded obstacle course. I say dreaded because you will die, literally, if you fail at this one." He became serious and straightened up. "At times like this, one must ask oneself, is it worth it? I know Cassius said you can all leave whenever you want to and that he would not offer it to you all again. Well, I am going to. You can leave now if you're afraid to die, or you think joining the elite segment of Capricorns is not worth it. So, does anybody need to leave?"

He paused for a moment, looking around at the ten volunteers and the much larger remaining group.

"OK, so I'm going to assume that you are all as dedicated as me, but I'm not impressed yet." He stopped and raised an index finger. "It's one thing to say it and another thing to do it." He dropped his hand. "With that said, I would like to explain the obstacle course to you all." He raised his voice so everyone could hear him.

"First, you will have to run, grab a rope, and hold on for dear life because if you let go, you will fall into a pit of Capricorn-eating fish, dangerous little bastards." He grimaced.

Caleb whispered something in Cyd's ear. Cyd looked surprised. Then he shrugged and spoke to the recruits again. "I just heard that they actually eat all sentient beings in our known galaxy, from the Taurus to Scorpio back down to Pisces. I say that to say you will die, literally, if you fall in that water with them.

"Next, you will do the same thing with another rope. Swing across again, but this time, the pool of water you will jump over has lightning in it. If you fall, you will die." Cyd began acting out all the motions the recruits would have to do, but he mostly did so with his upper body, and stood in place.

"Once you make it to the other side of the lightning water, you will have to climb a large wooden structure we around here like to call the board. If you make it to the top, but fall on the other side, that's right, you guessed it, you're gonna die. Instead, climb to the top and stand up straight, there's enough room for you to do that, then you want to jump into the pool of water. The pool of water is surrounded by spikes on both sides, spikes directly below the board, and spikes on the other side past the water. You don't want to jump too far or too short.

"Once in the water, swim to the bottom and grab a bottom feeder, the one we all call a gruber. You should recognize it immediately; it is the only gray fish down there. Swim back up with it and make sure you keep it far from your face, it will bite. And from there, you can climb out of the pool on either the right side or left side, because neither side should have any spikes. Walk around the front spikes and you will see a straight and narrow path. Sprint down that path and at the other end, you will see a Capricorn in royal battle attire just like we three have on. You will hand him your gruber, which can be dead or alive, it doesn't matter, and he'll ask for your name. Tell him your name and then wait for the others recruits to reach that final point. At the end, when all ten of you are there, or however many survivors are left, you will be given instructions by the aforementioned Capricorn man. He will tell you how your final task will work. His name is Calvin, by the way." Cyd finally stopped moving and acting out the obstacle course.

"Again, I'm going to ask, does anybody want to leave? We are playing for keeps, so I'll understand if you feel that you can't do it and would rather not risk your life."

He paused, waiting even longer than last time.

"You're sure none of you want to back out?" His voice was much louder than the first time he asked.

Nobody left.

"Seems we have a brave group of Caps here. Remember, you have only two objectives while completing this. One, is to make it across as fast as you possibly can. The other is to just make it across alive. I shouldn't need to tell you which objective is more important. The speed at which you finish this course will be measured. But that won't matter if you're dead. Therefore, you should take your time if you need to. Any questions?"

Nobody raised their hands.

"I love all your attitudes so far. You may begin when ready. Timer is starting now." He stepped back from the forefront, closer to Caleb and Cassius.

Callum ran as soon as Cyd finished speaking, but then he stopped dead in his tracks in front of the water. The option to leave was still there. His mother still loved him and would still take care of him.

No, I can't go back to my old life. Not after all this.

"I no longer want to be a burden to my mother," he reaffirmed in a whisper.

All he had to focus on during the task was not dying. He decided he was going to finish when he could, but he wasn't going to try to do it so fast that he ended up dead.

Like Cyd said, running the fastest doesn't matter if you are dead.

Callum looked over at his competition. To his surprise, only two of the others had actually gotten any sort of start. Five other competitors swung back and forth on the rope. And two more were still at the starting point, sizing up the obstacle course like him. He wasn't going to let anything discourage him, so he ran back to get some distance, and then ran forward again and jumped and reached out to grab the rope.

***

Hayder and his mother landed on Scorpio. They had come to speak with the king. As soon as they disembarked they headed straight for the king's castle.

"So this is what Scorpio looks like. Can't say I care for it much," Hayder said with a frown, as he wiped some sand out of his light yellow fur. Luckily, he wore brown robes for the trip, as advised by his mom, so not much sand would get on him. His mother wore similar clothing. The robes were simple and would shield them from some of the power of the Scorpio sun, which was exceptionally hot during the summer.

Despite being a prince, he hadn't seen a few planets, Scorpio being one of them. It's not that he couldn't, of course. He simply never had a need or desire to.

Scorpio's kingdom was engulfed in sand. In the marketplaces on their way to Scorpio's castle, they saw numerous young women standing around everywhere, soliciting their services. Most of them had stingers, and some did not. There were some desert plants here and there, and a few horses were walking around untended.

There were multiple palaces all throughout the kingdom, but most likely they were for some of the king's royals, because there was one palace that stood out from the others. It was the tallest, for starters, but also it appeared to be made of pure gold. It shined and shimmered beautifully in the sunlight. Even the sidewalk leading to the path to the king's castle was lined in gold.

"Make sure you don't criticize the kingdom in front of the king." His mom disapproved of his comment. "Remember, we are here to ask him for a favor."

"Wait, what are you talking about? I thought we were here to ask him what he knows about the attempt that was made on my father's life."

"That doesn't make any sense. Even if he knows something, there's no way he's going to tell us. Why would he openly admit to knowing anything? We are here to ask if there is a cure for Scorpio poison."

"Of course, I wasn't going to come out and ask him directly. I was going to allude to it. I was going to subtly get him to indirectly admit to it."

The Lioness stopped dead in her tracks.

"The answer is still no. Don't do it. Hayder, it's most important that we get your father better. For now, our focus is not on whether Scorpio had anything to do with the assassination attempt. We will have to assume Sagittarius was working alone for the moment. Additionally, I will call forth a council meeting as soon as we are finished finding the cure for your father."

"Well, don't you at least think that things should be sorted out with our kingdom? One of us should be there right now to keep everyone in line."

"There's no need to worry about that. Our pride can take care of that, of course. Llewellyn and Zemar are more than capable, as are the others. I have given them instructions. With the rebellion over, everything should be fine. If anything, this might make all the commoners sympathetic to our plight."

"I really feel our priorities are mixed up at a time like this," Hayder softly argued.

The two continued walking down the golden road.

"Well, feel free to go back to Leo then." The Lioness began walking slightly faster.

They finally reached the entrance. The large golden door had detailed carvings of what appeared to be a giant scorpion being worshipped by humanoids.

"Halt, who goes there?" one of the guards who stood before the door demanded. There were two other identical guards standing before the entrance to Scorpio's castle. The black armor they wore covered every part of their body, aside from their eyes and their stingers.

"It is I, the Lioness, queen of Leo"—she pulled back her robe's hood—"and my son, Hayder, the prince, next in line to the throne after my husband."

"Is Master Scorpio expecting you?

"No, he's not, but we need to speak with him at once. It is urgent," she said.

"I must inform him first. I'm sure he will be pleased to see you, but I must always tell him beforehand who it is that requests his audience before any guests may speak with him."

"That's fine," she answered.

The Scorpio royal ran and disappeared into the massive castle. The doors were partially open.

"I cannot believe they don't have a more efficient way for the guards to communicate with him. They don't even have a looking glass so Scorpio can just see that it's us out here," Hayder said.

"King Scorpio likes to hear in person from one of us when somebody has arrived." The guard on the right side of the door replied to Hayder's comments without looking at him, still staring forward.

It wasn't long before the first guard returned and without a word began opening the door to the castle even wider. The first guard took position to the left of the door and spoke again.

"Step inside. King Scorpio is ready to see you."

Inside, the castle was even more glamorous than the outside. The walls were made of gold but not only that, there were diamonds in spots all over the interior. The roof was ridiculously high, and the floor sparkled with the same polish as the walls.

The prince and his mother walked down a long hallway by themselves and began to feel weird.

"Isn't it strange that nobody is meeting us or bringing us to the king?" Hayder queried as he looked around at various decorated pillars that lined the inside.

"Yes, I suppose it is, a bit. I guess it's not the customs of the Scorpio to have a servant bring you directly to the king."

"No, ordinarily I would have had one of my servants come out to meet you, but I heard you need my help, and it's something urgent so I decided to meet you near the entrance," Scorpio answered, and stepped from a pillar to the side of them.

"Forgive me, you startled me Scorpio," the Lioness said and took a step back.

"What is it that brings you all the way here? How can I help you?" Brown skin and a handsome face, Scorpio was one of the most feared kings of the twelve. Not only because of his fearsome appearance, but also because of his abilities. Scorpio stood on two feet, but like a scorpion or any of the other full-blooded inhabitant from his planet, he had a stinger that came from his back all the way to the front and hovered just above his head. His stinger was the biggest of all Scorpios. He was much taller than both Hayder and the Lioness. He had an extremely muscular physique and only wore a thin black silk robe, open to reveal his chest and stomach, and he wore similar silk pants to cover his lower body. He was usually shirtless most of the time. Around his tail and part of his lower body, he had an exoskeleton like that of a scorpion.

"Your Highness. We come humbly to ask a favor of you." The Lioness lowered her head to appear humble, her white fur almost entirely covered by her dark brown cloak. "You see, my husband is dying from poison." She raised her head. "Scorpio's poison and we seek a cure."

"Scorpio's poison? Wouldn't he already be dead?" Scorpio sincerely inquired.

"The healer isn't sure why, but she said the poison is slow acting. We figured if anybody would know anything about it, it would be you." The Lioness caught his gaze, which was fixed on her for analysis.

"Why would I develop a cure for my own poison?" Placing a hand just below his chin, he waited for an answer.

"I'm not sure, maybe as a safety precaution," the Lioness guessed.

"Hmm. There may be a cure. If I'm not mistaken, Virgo was developing one. I'm not sure if he completed it, though. In fact, he and I were talking about creating a version of my venom that would be slow acting. I'm sure he would never use it on your husband, though."

"Yes, I know that he wouldn't. Our kingdom and his have never been at odds," she said.

"I suppose your best bet would be to see if Virgo finished perfecting the cure and has it in his lab. Now that I think about it, how do we know the cure for my poison will work for another Scorpio's poison? I have more than one kind of poison I am able to produce naturally, but none of them are slow acting. Virgo once told me that essentially my poison and that of all other Scorpios are very much different."

"The healer said that all poison starts with you. She led me to believe that your poison is the strongest. I imagine that if the cure can work on your poison, it can work on any other poison, even if it acts in a different way," the Lioness suggested.

Hayder silently watched them both as they spoke.

"You have no way of knowing that yet. Honestly, as I said before, we aren't even sure if the cure works on my poison. Even if Virgo finished creating it, I'm sure he hasn't begun testing it. It might be deadly to use an untested antivenom on your husband."

"We have to try. Please," she pleaded. "You know Virgo the best and as his close friend he will be more eager to help if you come along with us. Let's go to Virgo's lab and check it out. We can speak to Virgo, and he can tell us everything he knows. I'm sure he would have a good idea of what to do." Virgo often got so lost in his work that he would ignore any and every one while working on a project, sometimes even Scorpio.

"Say no more. We will leave at once. Bartell," Scorpio called.

"Sire." A dark and handsome Scorpio man appeared.

"Prepare the ship for the three of us to depart at once."

Hayder finally jumped into the conversation. "Can't we just use an aqua communicator? You and Virgo are friends, right? I'm sure he would open it up for us to travel directly there."

"Virgo is a hard one to contact. He's always so focused on his work that generally speaking, I just have to show up and talk to him. He doesn't like being disturbed, but if we are there right in front of his face, which is how I always communicate with him, then he has no choice. Now let's go. Time is of the essence."

Hayder and the Lioness began following Scorpio who walked with a brisk pace in the direction Bartell went, deeper into his castle.

"I want to ask you a question." Scorpio looked directly at Hayder.

"Yes?"

"How long does your father have to live at this rate, with this slow-acting poison in his system?"

"The healer says that he has a month at the most, but more than likely he only has three weeks or so." Hayder solemnly said the words, trailing off some toward the end.

"That's good that he has that much time. I can't understand why anybody would want poison that takes that long to go into effect."

"Then why were you and Virgo developing such poison," Hayder asked, stepping up his walking effort to keep up.

"The purpose of our slow-acting poison wasn't going to be to kill. Our poison was going to be used for the extraction of information from enemies and it wouldn't have worked as slowly as that," Scorpio explained.

They finally arrived at the ship.

"Bartell, take us to Virgo immediately," Scorpio commanded as he and the Leos strapped themselves in.

Without so much as a nod, Bartell fired up the ship, and they were on their way.

It didn't take long to arrive at their destination, lightning ships were always fast. Not to mention, Virgo wasn't far from Scorpio.

Virgo had a pad on his rooftop for ships to land, so they were already at his home.

King Virgo's castle wasn't much of a castle. It was very different stylistically from the other kings' homes. It was simple and emphasized technology. Everything was designed to look futuristic. Glass was the main component used for most of the construction for Virgo's mansion, along with a variety of metals.

From the roof, it wasn't hard for the three to make their way straight to Virgo's laboratory. They walked down a series of vertical stairs, then a set of stairs that wound in a circle, until finally they reached a long hallway.

"Right this way." Scorpio walked ahead of them.

Finally, they reached the room at the end of the long hallway, and when they walked inside, they saw a terrible mess. Blood was everywhere and broken glass with purple, green, blue, and red liquids covering the entire floor. Glass was everywhere. On the floor, King Virgo lay face up, surrounded by dried blood. Not far from him was another large pool of blood. Standing above him was his cousin Vernon with a deeply pained face.

"What? This is impossible. Who could have done this?" Scorpio demanded.

Vernon's eyes were teary as he stared at Virgo's lifeless corpse and muttered to himself.

"What happened here, Vernon?"

Scorpio touched Vernon on his shoulder to get his attention.

"I don't know," he cried. "I'm not sure. I was gathering tools for my king and when I came back, he was like this. His latest experiments are gone, too."

"His latest experiments? What was he working on?" Scorpio stared at Virgo's corpse even while speaking to Vernon.

"What does that matter now? He's already dead," the prince interrupted.

"Be quiet." Scorpio looked at Hayder to make sure he turned silent. "What was he working on, Vernon?" Scorpio pressed for more, giving his full attention to Vernon and moving closer.

"He had a couple of pregnant Libras, and he was trying to create soldiers using the DNA from all the kings and the royals and even commoners and half bloods."

"That's crazy, he'd already begun conducting those sort of experiments? He told me recently he still didn't even fully understand the DNA sequence of any of the kings, or royals for that matter, and yet he'd already moved on to those levels of experiments? Leos"—Scorpio looked in their direction—"I think whatever Virgo was working on last got him killed."

"Scorpio, I don't mean to be rude, but what about the cure for the poison?" The Lioness remained focused on what she wanted.

"What about it? Feel free to look around. I doubt you'll find anything useful, whoever did this destroyed a lot of his lab, his experiments, and his work. The antivenom should be clearly labeled. Vernon," Scorpio said, turning his attention away from the Lioness and her son and back to the king's cousin. "Is there anything else you know? Where are these experiments? You said there were three pregnant women. I don't see any women here. Do you know what happened to them?"

"I don't know. I'm telling you, when I got back here, everything was exactly how you see it."

"We can't find anything. Would you mind letting—Vernon, you said his name was, right? Would you mind letting Vernon help us look through the lab for the cure?"

"I'll do you one better. I'm going to call a council meeting. I'll find out who is behind this and before I kill them, you can ask if they know what happened to the cure."

"But that doesn't—"

"I'm leaving."

Before Scorpio disappeared out of sight, he turned back to the corpse of his dear friend and closed his eyes.

"I will see you in the next lifetime my friend." Scorpio patted Virgo's chest firmly, and his eyes watered up.

After that, he immediately walked out without looking back or saying another word.

The Lioness asked Vernon if he knew of a cure for Scorpio's blood, but Vernon seemed to know even less about Virgo's experiments than Scorpio did. Hayder searched around the laboratory for quite a while until he gave up. Either the cure had been destroyed during the altercation between Virgo and his attackers, or his murderers took it. It didn't matter. The fact was, neither Hayder nor his mother could find the supposed cure for Scorpio's poison.

"Let's go, son. Scorpio was right, we aren't going to find any answers in here." The Lioness stood near the doorway, ready to leave.

The two left Virgo through his aqua communicator almost as swiftly as they had arrived, and they headed straight for Libra.

"This council meeting should take place soon. When Scorpio wants something done, he gets it done." The Lioness cued her son in to why they needed to be on Libra.

"Yes, but what if all the other kings are busy?"

"Something this urgent should make them all put this meeting as their number one priority. At this point, no matter what else they are doing, there is nothing more important," the Lioness maintained.

"Hello, Lioness, and you must be the prince of Leo. I take it King Leo can't make it." Lucian, a Libran royal servant to King Libra said.

"You must not have heard what happened. Lucian, my husband, the king…" She paused. It was still hard to say. "Is in critical condition."

The bald-headed Libran man solemnly shook his head before responding.

"I'm so very sorry. You have my deepest condolences. My position doesn't require me to know all the details, so my master does not tell me everything." Lucian frowned. "I was merely informed that a council meeting was going to be called. I do not wish to take up anymore of your time. Please come in."

The Libra man opened the door to the council meeting hall. Inside the hall, there were paintings of numerous battles won long ago by various planets in the region. Also, former kings from all the kingdoms were depicted in motion paintings throughout the room. Libra, Scorpio, Capricorn, Pisces and Aquarius were already seated at the table.

"Lioness and young prince Hayder, welcome. I thought for sure you would still be looking for the cure at Virgo's lab, but I'm glad to see you're not," Scorpio said.

"No, of course not. This meeting is as important to us as it is to you."

"Indeed. Please have a seat. Everybody else has been informed and should be here as soon as they can." The Lioness and Hayder sat next to each other in the Leo section. The first king of Leo was painted on the wall behind them, and the section was gold.

"I refuse to wait for everybody to show up for this." Aquarius stood up. "I know that you both have something to say, Scorpio and Lioness, but I also have a few things to discuss." He sat back down.

"Is there any chance that you could start talking about it now, while it's just us, so we can have an idea of what to expect before the others get here?" Capricorn asked Scorpio directly.

"No, I want everybody to hear this. I'm not sure that the things I'm going to say are things that can or should be said more than once," Scorpio replied firmly.

After Scorpio's words, the other men sat there, waiting quietly and patiently. A Libran female with violet-colored hair and matching flower brought them some refreshments. It took a little while but eventually Aries and Gemini showed up around the same time, followed shortly by Cancer and Taurus. Aries asked something similar to Capricorn in terms of getting on with the meeting, but Scorpio said that he wanted to wait for Sagittarius.

Time passed. "Come on. I don't think Sagittarius is going to show up," Aries said. "It doesn't seem like it. Honestly, this meeting is somewhat out of nowhere. You should tell us your agenda, so we can begin discussing everything. Despite Virgo's and Sagittarius's and Leo's absences, I believe we have enough of us to make a sound and fair decision on whatever matters are at hand."

Scorpio breathed in deeply, sighing out loud, exhaustion and hurt visible in his expression. The day had taken a toll on him.

"Why are they missing?" Capricorn asked, looking to all at the table for an answer.

"Obviously, the Lioness and prince can explain why Leo is missing," Gemini replied. "As far as the others, we will have to try to figure it out." He shrugged slightly.

"Let's not get sidetracked here." Scorpio stood and spoke loudly to focus everyone's attention. "I suppose I may as well get to my point. Everybody that I want to speak with personally is already here. Gentlemen." He placed his hands on the white marble council table, looking at them all, but at no one in particular. "Virgo is dead. Somebody"—his eyes scanned the room toward his suspects—"one of you here, is responsible."

"What?" a few of them said at the same time.

"Why would somebody do such a thing?" Gemini looked around at the others.

"That is, of course, why I have brought us all here, to find out that very answer." Scorpio held his eyes closed tight for a second. "I personally promise you all that I'm going to find out who killed Virgo and I'm going to kill them. I'm going to kill all parties responsible for his death. Anyone that I find had a part in it." He redirected his gaze for a moment and then looked each of them in the eyes.

"I say it like that because I believe more than one person may have played a part in this. I have no way of knowing yet, of course, but it is a possibility.

"I am going to investigate you"—he looked at each of them briefly—"all of you. None of you can stop me. I just wanted to let you know that I'm going to be doing it so none of you will be surprised or upset when you notice that I'm looking into you all.

"I also want to be as upfront as possible and say that I already have suspects. I haven't ruled any possibilities out yet and I won't, but I already have prime suspects. Aries, Gemini, and Cancer." He looked over the three respectively. His gaze remained fixed on Cancer. "Given the nature of your abilities and the abilities of your subordinates, I can only imagine that you three had the most capability to do what was done to Virgo."

"This is ridiculous. I should not be suspected of anything just because of my abilities and those of my subordinates. Besides…" Aries looked surprised by his own words as he stopped himself.

"Besides what, Aries?" Scorpio's gaze intensified as it moved to Aries.

"Nothing. I just don't think it's fair that we are suspected because of our powers or those of our royals."

Cancer smirked as if he imagined he knew what Aries may have almost said.

"I have to be as logical and methodical as possible in order to get to the truth about what happened to Virgo," Scorpio said, "and logic dictates that you three and your men would be in the best position to kill him the way he died. There were no signs of quakes nor horn marks, so that leads me to believe that Taurus is innocent. There was no sign of an arrow penetrating his flesh, so that leads me to believe that Sagittarius is innocent."

The Lioness stood up. "I hate to butt in, but like Scorpio I believe that one of the council members has wronged a king. My king. My husband. I believe Sagittarius is guilty—of attempting to assassinate my husband! We were hoping that Sagittarius would be here, but unfortunately, he's not. I'm not sure if all of you are aware, but my husband, King Leo, was attacked and is still fighting for his life at this very moment. An assassin attempted to kill him on this very day during his birth event. I want to fully support Scorpio in finding Virgo's killer, because he may have the cure for the Scorpio poison that was used on my husband."

"What? Why don't you just ask the Scorpion?" Gemini scoffed and folded his arms.

"I already reached out to him, and he was not even familiar with the poison that was used, nor did he have the cure." She sighed to herself and slumped.

"I didn't have anything to do with the failed attempt to kill Leo," Gemini confessed, unfolding his arms. "Neither I nor my men ever use arrows for fighting."

"Of course you would say that. No killer would ever fess up to such a foul deed," Cancer chimed in.

Gemini gasped and stared at Cancer, clearly taking the comment as an insult.

"Look, we all have a few problems. For one, we no longer have a king representing Virgo. Secondly, Leo was poisoned and shot by arrows, and Sagittarius is missing from the meeting. Additionally, we don't have a cure as of now, and if we don't find a cure, we may have another vacant seat on the council soon. We should go through the list of problems and try to find a solution for each one," Libra said. "Who is next of kin to King Virgo?"

"I know he doesn't have any kids. He has a wife, and though she's young, she's supposed to be as gifted as him. She wasn't there when we found the body. I will find her, and we can appoint her to the Virgo throne temporarily and as council member," Scorpio replied.

"Virgo doesn't have any brothers, uncles, cousins, anybody else? What about the viscount?" Taurus didn't mean to be rude, but ordinarily the throne was passed down to males.

"He does have a cousin, but his abilities are nonexistent. All the other royals who were under Virgo weren't from his direct bloodline; the ones who were, weren't very gifted. No, it definitely has to be the queen, as I said before," Scorpio reaffirmed, even more certainty in his voice than a moment ago. "I will find her and bring her here, and she will make decisions in Virgo's stead from now on. We have no other choice. There has to be a royal representative from Virgo sitting on the council, just as we here represent our planets."

"Scorpio is right, it's important that everything remains fair as possible," Libra agreed.

"OK, that solves one of the problems, but what will we do about King Leo?" Taurus looked to Scorpio for an answer.

Aries caught all their attention by standing. "No offense, everyone, but I feel that's between Sagittarius and Leo. Sagittarius did not even feel the need to show up. I'm not sure, but I would say that's an open act of defiance, and I know I would go to war if I was Leo, but that is not a decision to be taken lightly. I do know that it's a decision only Leo can make, though," Aries concluded.

Everybody seemed satisfied by that answer except for the Lioness.

"What about the cure? Will none of you help at least find and develop the cure?" the Lioness looked to all of them for an answer.

Aquarius looked up and finally responded. "I think this would normally be easier for Virgo, but I will look into it. Now, I would like to bring up my point, the reason that I want to speak here." He stood up and dusted off his amethyst-colored attire. "Not all the dyads are in my custody. I understand you are all busy, but I thought we had an agreement that they would be on my planet for their own safety and happiness."

"I need my half bloods. I'm not going to give them all away to you. They are often quite useful, sometimes even in my dealings with other kings," Libra answered.

"I understand that, but we already talked about this. Any dyad that does not work directly for you or under your royals should be brought to my planet. I'm sorry Lioness, I know this is a bad time to mention this. With everything going on right now. But I don't think I have any of your dyads from your planet in the living area I designed for them either. Take your time of course. But please send them over when you can.

"OK, no worries, Aquarius. I will send them today. I was actually prepping them before my husband got shot"—she stared at the ground—"but it's been a tumultuous day. With everything that's been going on, I didn't get to finish."

"I'm sorry and I understand, Lioness. I will be looking forward to their arrival on my planet, whenever you get around to it." He smiled at her, trying to lighten her mood. "The rest of you know who you are. Please don't back out on our agreement." Turning back to all them, he finished his speech.

"OK, are we done?" Capricorn asked.

"Yes, we're all done for the moment," Scorpio told them. "Gemini, Cancer, and Aries, remember I'm going to investigate the crime scene and whatever Virgo was working on, and I'm going to investigate you three and your men personally." He looked at each one after he finished speaking.

"Pisces, you've been awfully quiet." Libra started a new conversation as the others prepared to take their leave. Libra stood close to Pisces, and they conversed.

"Yes, I've just had a lot on my mind, that's all. Thank you for your concern." He looked at Libra for a brief second.

Hayder raised his hands to stop everyone. "Wait, who is in charge of Leo in my father's absence?" His eyes darted around the room at the others.

"Wouldn't that be you?" Aries asked.

"I think it should be you, of course," Scorpio added. "Unless, of course, your father said he wanted your mother to run everything." Scorpio's eyes scanned them both, looking for an answer.

"No, he never said any such thing."

"So then you have your answer," Scorpio finished.

Hayder smiled for a moment.

"Actually," the Lioness interjected, "my husband is still well enough to talk. My son, the prince, and I will still meet with Leo and ask for his advice before big decisions. This is why we haven't yet decided if we are going to war with Sagittarius or not. Also, because we still don't know his involvement in the event."

"It is such a terrible thing to happen, especially on a man's natal day." Gemini shook his head.

"Yes, it is. The responsible parties will be brought to swift justice I'm sure," the Lioness reconciled.

"I believe that is all. I will see you all later," Scorpio said, already on his way out.

Scorpio decided it would be best to speak with Queen Virgo alone to tell her what happened to her husband. After the council meeting, he went back to Virgo to figure out how he could find her. The last time she was spotted, she was leaving Pisces.

Scorpio figured that if she was visiting all planets, she must have at least made it to Aries. From there, he deduced that she didn't visit the kingdoms of Pisces or Capricorn, so she most likely avoided that region on Aries, too.

Lightning ships have a special pattern that can be detected by a machine that Virgo developed. Scorpio headed to Aries and used the machine. It didn't take long before he found a rural area with a lightning ship signature, so he searched for the queen in that area. Scorpio had only seen the young queen of Virgo on a few occasions, most of which were brief, aside from the unification ceremony, but of course she stood out while walking in a rural area of Aries with a little Aries girl and woman.

"Hello, Valera."

"King Scorpio. What a pleasant surprise. It is nice to see you. What brings you to this area of Aries? Did my husband ask you to look after me?" She asked him with a curious smile.

"No. I actually have something I need to speak with you about at once. Alone. Please accompany me to my ship." He gestured toward his ship, sweeping left a little, indicating the path.

"But what about mine?" She pointed to hers, which was in a grassy field some ways away.

"One of my men will take care of it and bring it with us to where we are going."

"Well, where are we going?"

"Libra. Please come now, every second counts. I understand you must have a lot of questions, but don't worry, I will answer everything I can for you, but for now we must go." He reached out a hand for her.

Valera looked toward Apple and Abigail. She had grown quite fond of them.

"Forgive me, I must be going," she apologized. "This is King Scorpio, a dear friend of my husband's, and he has something urgent to speak with me about."

"Wow, more royalty, how exciting."

"Calm down, Apple."

"Can we spend time with the Scorpion King, Momma?"

"No, baby, they have to go and so do we." She took her daughter's hand in hers and looked her in her eyes.

Apple, Abigail, and Valera said their goodbyes.

"OK, would you please tell me what's going on Scorpio?" she demanded when they were alone.

"We will talk on Libra." He began walking. "I have a lot to tell you, and I'd rather not upset you here, so far from a place of comfort."

"Just tell me now. I'm already getting upset." She didn't budge.

"OK." He stopped walking toward his ship, turned to her slowly to make eye contact, and said, "King Virgo"—he looked away for a moment and then back to her—"your husband...is dead. He was murdered."

Scorpio paused to watch her reaction. She wasn't one of his main suspects, but he still hadn't ruled her out. After all, she would be the supreme ruler of all of Virgo now, the first woman to boast such a thing. At first, she didn't seem to react, she was frozen, almost as if she didn't hear him, but eventually she put her hand over her mouth and screamed and began crying uncontrollably. Her face filled with deep pain.

She began whispering to herself right after.

"How could this have happened? Why? Why? Why? Why? No. My love, my sweet love. I wasn't even there for him in his time of need. This is my fault.

"It has to be something that I did wrong." She shook her head to herself slowly. "On this stupid, useless journey. All I learned is how much I don't know, and now my poor husband is gone." she said through tears.

Scorpio grabbed her and looked her in the eyes again, this time with empathy. "I promise you, I will find who did this and kill them, whoever they are. I know you're going through a lot right now, but I need to ask you an important question." He let go of her arms, but maintained eye contact. "Do you know anything about the last experiment your husband was working on? I think it may have something to do with why he was killed."

"I don't have any idea what my husband was up to." She wiped away old tears just for new ones to appear. "He was always secretive about his tests and experiments. Never wanted me to see them unless they were already finished and perfected."

"He didn't let you in on anything he was working on at all?" Scorpio's eye contact became an intense stare. He was checking for a lie again.

"No, he never did." Her voice shook, her hands quivered by her face. "I'm not sure if he figured I wouldn't understand or—I don't know why, but he never showed me anything before he completed it."

"Maybe I know more than you, then." Scorpio dropped his gaze, and took a step back. "I think the last thing he was working on had something to do with the blood of all the kings of the twelve. He showed me one experiment in which he mixed some of my DNA with some of his own. I still don't know for sure because of the way his lab was left. We will have to go back to Virgo and his lab so you can see for yourself, but for now, I'd like for you to come with me to Libra."

"Wait," Valera said, halting her tears for a moment. "Who even has the capability to kill a king like my husband? Wasn't he powerful, like you and the other kings?"

"Your husband was very powerful in his own way, but still, I don't know of any kings that are immortal. I can name a few beings who would be capable of killing him, and they are all royalty. I feel the three with abilities most suited for the type of thing I saw would be Aries, Gemini, or Cancer. I'm personally going to look into it, and as I said before, kill all those responsible for his death." He clenched his fists by his side, fighting back tears and his anger.

"Thank you." She paused and gave a faint smile through her still sad face.

"This should be expected of me." He put his hand on her shoulder. "Your husband was a dear friend of mine. I'm not sure if this is the best time to mention this, but since he's gone and there are no male heirs, you are solely responsible for the kingdom of Virgo now. In fact, the other kings and queens will most likely start calling you Virgo as opposed to your name and eventually, I may do the same. Your subjects will refer to you as they had in the past. Also, as I said before, you will be in charge of all decisions that Virgo makes in context to the rest of our galaxy. And this is why we need to go to Libra now. I have something to show you."

"Do you think whoever killed my husband may be following us now?" She looked around.

"It's hard to say. Even if they are, if my theory holds up, there wouldn't be anything we could do to know that, not right now, anyway. Let's just head to Libra. We will talk more there.

Chapter 15

Callum gave it another try. He ran, leapt forward, and grabbed onto the rope with all his might, held on tight as he swung over the pool of water, and let go when he was over the grass on the other side. After making it past the first pitfall, he still had momentum going. He hit the ground running and did the same thing immediately again for the next part.

This must be one of those things that becomes more dangerous the more you hesitate, he thought.

Making it past the lightning water proved to be as easy as making it past the first pit.

He was tempted to look at the others in their own similar obstacle courses but quickly disregarded the thought. Now wasn't the time to worry about something such as speed.

Looking up at the board he had to climb, he felt disheartened for a few seconds, but realized that climbing was actually the easiest thing in the entire obstacle course, so he quickly changed his attitude and embraced the challenge.

Climbing it was still very difficult. His dug his feet onto the wooden board, climbing steadily. Pacing had become the most important thing to him, so he didn't rush. He grabbed the top as soon as he made it, and climbed up slowly.

This part was very important. He didn't want to fall on the spikes on the other side. Finding his balance wasn't difficult once he stood on the top. Cyd told the truth, there was space on the top of the board. Not only was that true, but there were indeed spikes below him, and he could see more spikes off in the distance in front of him, with only a bit of space between the two groups. Taking a deep breath, he tried to prepare himself mentally for the jump and could no longer resist the urge to look over at the other Capricorn competitors. He saw that the one on his left was in fact dead, lying face up on the second set of spikes with blood covering his mouth.

That was a bad idea; it was hard for him to stay calm after that.

Should I close my eyes before I jump? No, even if I do that, I still might die. In fact, it might be worse that way.

He had to jump as far as he thought would do the trick. He had an idea though. At the height he was standing on the board, he wouldn't have to jump too far. The front spikes didn't extend out as far as the second set of spikes, he realized, so all he would have to do is try to land closer to the front side. He continued to survey the area that he was about to jump to, until he noticed that there was a small patch of grass in between the first spikes and the water hole that he was supposed to jump into. That had to be the trick.

He leapt just right, and he cleared the front set of spikes, but landed awkwardly only an inch in front of the water ditch, so he stood on his tippy toes and seconds later lost his balance and fell in. After the plunge, he swam deep down into the water with his eyes closed.

I cannot close my eyes in here. I have to be alert. There could be dangerous fish down here or something else I don't even know about.

Swimming wasn't his forte, but he was managed pretty well. Soon, he reached the bottom. Scanning the sea floor wasn't easy. For one thing, it was dark down there, but after a time he saw a gray fish.

Reaching out, he grabbed for it, but missed it by a few inches. The fish was fast, he realized he hadn't missed, the fish moved. The fish then lunged forward, bit and held onto Callum's finger before he could try to swipe at it again.

The pain started off as mild, but the longer the fish held on to his right index finger, the more the intensity increased.

I should be fine, the instructors never said anything about the fish being poisonous.

Prize in hand, he quickly swam back to the top. Coming up for air felt so exhilarating, but the danger wasn't over yet. He still had to be careful of the spikes on either side of the hole he was swimming in.

While up for air, he examined the left and right path, both were clear of spikes. He chose to go right. He navigated around the second spike pit that was north toward the goal line, and reached grass. Beyond the grass was a dirt road that had separate lanes. In the distance, he saw a Capricorn male. He took off in a sprint.

That has to be the guy Cyd was talking about, Calvin.

Heart pounding in his chest, fatigue and exhaustion from the day's events caught up to him in that moment. But he would not be stopped. He put it out of his mind and focused on his run. Closer and closer the next instructor got as he ran toward his goal, and finally he made it.

His new instructor was a brown-skinned Capricorn with brown eyes and brown hair cut short. His facial features not as sharp as Cassius, Caleb, or Cyd. And he was dressed somewhat similar to them, but his selindium armor looked lighter.

"What is your name?" the new instructor asked, staring down at a holographic notepad, not concerned with looking at Callum.

"Callum."

"OK, please hand me your fish, Callum." He raised his head.

Callum tried to hand over the fish, but the fish still wouldn't let go of his finger. He didn't realize it until he tried to pry it off.

"Ha, he got a hold of you and you never took him off your finger, very funny." Calvin stared at his finger, genuinely amused.

The instructor removed the fish by grabbing it on both the bottom and the top jaws and pulling hard.

"There we go. You're lucky those things aren't poisonous, otherwise you would be dead, my friend." He held the fish in his hand, and somehow it appeared lifeless even though a moment ago it seemed alive when gripping Callum's finger.

"What now?"

"What do you mean, what now? Didn't Cyd tell you what happens after you give me the fish?"

"Yes."

"And what exactly did he say?"

"He told me I have to wait until all the others who ran with me finish."

"Then that is what you are to do right now."

"That doesn't make any sense, though, nobody is here."

"I'm here and you're here. You finished first. Just wait for the others to get here."

Callum was a little bit shocked at the notion of being the first one to complete the obstacle course. He hadn't come in first in any of the other events so far. His shock was quickly replaced with excitement however. It wasn't long before the others started showing up. In the same fashion as he greeted Callum, Calvin greeted each runner as they came in. Eventually there were eight other Capricorn men there. Two had died.

"All right, gentlemen, bring it in close." The recruits formed a tight circle around Calvin and awaited instruction. "During your next task, you will either lead or follow. You will be in a battle simulation. Throughout the battle simulation, you will have opportunities to strike your enemies, who will be the next group to finish the run.

"Here's how it works: if you lead, then you may be chosen for a leadership position for the ranking ceremony if you do well. However, if you lead and your soldiers don't follow you, or they don't succeed, you automatically will be disqualified for a leadership position. Another thing is, you can be a follower as many times as you want, for as many groups as you want, so if you want to follow in this first group and then lead in the next group, that is open for you, you can do that.

"Obviously you can't all be leaders, so you will all have to come up with a way to determine who the leader is, if there are any quarrels over the matter.

"If you are all planning to keep following with the hopes of becoming leader with a bunch of experience under you, I want to let you know a few things first. One, the more times you follow, the more points I will subtract. Two, the larger the group of Caps, the more points I subtract. Another thing to keep in mind: there may be limits imposed on the size of the group, so you may not be able to compete again as a follower even if you wanted to, or you may have a longer wait to compete again.

"The last thing I want to say in terms of scoring is that your team doesn't need to win this challenge. The fact that you all made it this far alive means you automatically pass this last test just by participating, but if your team losses that will obviously affect your rank. So if one wanted one could win one battle simulation against the other team as a follower and then stop right after that and receive a rank."

"That is all I have to say for now. I hate repeating myself, so I'm going to tell you all the rules for the battle simulation when your competition shows up. One last thing, I want you all to decide your leader later. Don't do it right now. Wait for me to finish giving all instruction, including the rules for the battle. That's it for now. Hold tight, boys." Calvin patted a smaller Capricorn who stood next to him on his back.

Callum excitedly stared off in the distance toward the direction the other Capricorns would come from.

***

Scorpio brought Valera back to Virgo to see her husband and let her mourn. Once she was finished mourning Virgo's dead body was cast into space in a rocket ship, as was written in his will. He loved science and discoveries so much that he hoped that he would be a discovery for a distant race of alien people. Perhaps he would somehow find new life in distant space Scorpio thought after sending his friend off and then he searched the lab for clues. Scorpio instructed Vernon to preserve the lab, so that if he missed something on his first sweep he may find it on his next. Then they left to go to Libra. While on Libra, Scorpio showed Valera around briefly and described everything to her.

"I'm not sure if I already told you this, but this council was designed for decisions that are too big for one planet to make on its own. Basically, if the decision affects more than just the inhabitants of any one world, then generally speaking we all come together and vote to make a decision." He pointed to the portraits of the kings on the walls. "You just missed a few big decisions earlier today, actually."

"All twelve kingdoms make all decisions together?" She raised an inquisitive eyebrow.

"No, actually only eleven. One member has to sit out of all decisions made for a year, and we rotate so each of us sits out for a year, every twelve years. This is done to avoid any ties, so that all decisions have a clear majority. I brought you here so that they don't assume they can exclude you from the decision-making process because your husband is gone. They should all be here shortly."

"I thought you had more you wanted to say to me? I thought we were going to talk about my husband. I have more questions I need to ask."

Scorpio turned his attention toward the lilac-colored door "Don't worry, we will talk later. I think they are here."

Aries came storming in first. Everybody else followed shortly after.

"Again, Scorpio? I barely left here a little while ago after our last discussion," Taurus questioned with disappointment oozing from his very being.

Interestingly enough, all the same members attended this meeting. Aries, Gemini, and Cancer were all present, the three council members that he actually told beforehand the purpose of the meeting.

Scorpio thought the guilty party would have a hard time going to a meeting, and seeing the face of a widowed woman, considering they killed her husband. But then again he thought something like this might happen. He figured he would have to do his investigation. The guilty king may have sent his royals to do the deed rather than have done it personally, or just may have known that it would look incriminating to not show up.

"I'm sorry this may seem silly, but I brought you all here for her sake and her sake alone." He gestured to Valera.

"I'm not sure if all of you are familiar with her. I know not all of you were at Virgo's unification ceremony, and she hasn't been queen very long. So I wanted you all to get better acquainted with her, and for her to get to know you all better as well. Show the new face of Virgo. And I felt this is the proper place for us all to show our sorrow and offer condolences for her late husband."

"I'm sorry for your loss, queen." Taurus stood up and walked over to her chair. "Virgo was a brilliant man. Different style of fighting than me. If you can even call it that"—he chuckled—"but I admired that about him. He had his own ways and stuck to them."

One by one, the other kings followed suit, coming up to the queen and saying something nice about her husband.

Except for Pisces, who came with his right-hand man, Pim. Pisces leaned into her, real close, handed her a gift, then he whispered something in her ear. A small hug was how Pisces ended his conversation with her.

Scorpio wasn't sure why, but he found everything Pisces was doing somewhat suspicious. But he was certain that Virgo more powerful than him.

I'll just look into him later after I finish with Aries, Cancer, and Gemini, he reconciled. Pisces can see the future but maybe he had a reason for not telling everybody that Virgo was in danger. No, there was no good excuse. If he can see the future as he says he can, then we were all owed a warning that Virgo was in danger. Come to think of it, he never mentioned Leo being in danger either.

In fact, the more I think about it, the more suspicious Pisces becomes. I need all my facts first. Throwing around accusations without evidence won't get me anywhere. Scorpio stopped himself from questioning Pisces right away. The truth would come out, that was for certain, but nothing needed to be rushed. The investigation could possibly be a long one, but all avenues would have to be explored. Scorpio would have his wife take care of things at his kingdom, and that would free him up to investigate.

Once Virgo was finished speaking with all the other kings, she returned to Scorpio's section where he had stood and watched everybody. "Scorpio, thank you for showing me all this, and for telling me everything, and just for all the things you are doing for me." A warm smile appeared on her face.

"Of course." He flashed a smile. "As I said before, these things are to be expected of me. I will accompany you back to Virgo if you're ready to go home." He put his hand gently on her back and led her to the door.

"Yes, thank you, I am. I would like that very much." A nod and a modest smile accompanied her statement.

The two left first, then all the other members left shortly after, aside from Cancer and Pisces.

"I know what you did, Cancer." Pisces glared at him. "You are foolish to not have listened to me."

"You are not in control of everything, Pisces. In fact, you're in control of nothing." Cancer added a quick and dismissive laugh. "It was high time I showed you that."

"You haven't shown me anything. Remember, I'm always one step ahead of everyone."

"Ha, you and I know both know that's not true. You're the weakest and youngest of the twelve, and you will pay for your arrogance."

"Cancer, you already—"

Pisces stopped talking as soon as he realized that Cancer was gone.

"Thinks he can make a fool of me? I'll show Cancer and all the rest of them. Fool. He should be more worried about his own mistakes," Pisces said low to himself. "Come now Pim." Pisces's sea green cape fluttered as he shifted quickly and walked out of the council room.

Pisces and Pim made their way out of the council hall and began whispering.

"Do you think the queen noticed me?" Pim asked.

"Hardly, you look completely different from how you did last time you saw her, and besides, she was clearly too grief-stricken to think of anything but her husband and his murder and everything Scorpio had told her."

"Yes, master." Pim nodded excessively for an instant. "I still don't understand why I had to show up to this meeting. Aren't these meetings only for kings and queens?"

Pisces began talking slower and louder. "I thought I already told you I want all the kings and queens to be familiar with you for the future. There will be a time when I need you to make moves for me."

"What about Priscilla, your wife?"

"Pim. No more questions, let's go."

"Yes, master." Scampering behind his king, Pim walked in silence the rest of the way.

***

Croix returned to the brotherhood house and saw that Archer was already there, seated, waiting for Eames's instruction.

"Welcome, Brother Croix."

Brother? I'm not sure what happened to make Eames start calling me brother, but I think I like it.

"Are you two ready?"

"Yes, of course," Archer answered.

That's odd, he's not giving us more information.

"I'm not going to tell either one of you anything else right now. Croix, you will be going with me." Eames glanced at him. "Archer, you're with Briccio." Eames pointed to a shirtless Briccio, who leaned against the black wood door. "Archer, you two will be going first. Any questions, please save them for Briccio, he's just as good at this as I am, and he's been doing it longer than me. Croix, just sit tight. We are going to wait for a while here in the brotherhood house, until we are sure that Briccio and Archer are gone. Save any questions you have for me until we know they've left. Enjoy your leisure time however you want. Leisure time won't last long, but feel free to do as you please."

A few minutes passed. While waiting, Croix played Catch the Shot, an old Aries game where participants would stand a little less than a foot away from a dart board, launch a projectile at it and then move in front of the dart board to catch their own projectile. It was a game that tested and improved reflex. However, Eames called it right, his wait was momentary. Before he knew it, Eames was standing at his side. A dart was still in Croix's hand, and he was just about to throw it.

"Aren't you going to wait for Briccio to contact you?" Croix continued to stare at the board with only one eye opened, he saw Eames in his periphery.

"No, there's no need." Croix could feel Eames's stare directed at him, so he put the dart down. "We didn't really need to wait for them to leave, honestly. I just really wanted to make sure that neither of you heard the mission the other was assigned. For now, all I'm going to say is this next challenge is designed to measure your judgment along with all the other skills that were tested during the course of the other trials."

Eames gestured for Croix to follow him and began walking. Until the two were out of the brotherhood house.

Eames continued to move forward in silence the entire time until they made it to the lightning ship. In front of the ship, he began again.

"Your next mission is actually so difficult that some people who have completed it have said that it is the most difficult trial of all." He stopped and looked Croix in the eyes and made sure he had eye contact. "The next task is for you to kill a royal," he said, expressionless, emotionless.

"What are you talking about?" Croix laughed and waited for Eames to join. On the contrary, Eames's expression began to look even graver. "Are you joking?" Again, Croix stared at Eames and looked for some sort of sign, some indication in Eames's face, that he didn't mean it. "Kill a royal? *That's insane!*"

"Calm down. Of course I don't mean any Aries royalty. I mean a royal from another kingdom."

"Still, won't that be like an act of war or something?"

"That's why this trial is so critical. You have to do it in such a way that nobody catches you or finds out. Also, you have to bring back an important keepsake from the dead royal."

"What do you mean by *keepsake*?"

"Just something that was important to the deceased when they were alive or something that you think was important to them, a necklace or a trinket that they wore or a ring will do just fine."

"I see how this might test my other skills, but how is killing a royal from a different kingdom testing my judgment skills? How on Aries will I even be able to get a royal from another kingdom, another planet, all alone to kill him secretly?"

"That's all part of the testing. Now tell me, where do you want to go? What planet shall you go to in order to kill your royal born, or would you have me choose? You could always quit if you don't like the trial that lies before you, or if you think I'm being unreasonable. Quitting is still an option, especially for you because you're the king's nephew. What's it going to be?" Eames questioned Croix.

Croix was flabbergasted by everything Eames was saying to him. It wasn't that he was actually against killing someone. But to kill someone for such an inappropriate reason, someone he doesn't even know? It didn't make sense. Ridiculous, outrageous, those were the only words that came to mind to describe the mission. Just didn't make any sense. Could initiates from all the years have been doing this the whole time?

"Croix!" Eames disturbed Croix's thoughts. "Which option are you choosing?" he pressed.

"I guess I want to go to Capricorn," Croix mumbled unenthusiastically.

"If you try killing a Capricorn with that attitude, I can absolutely guarantee that you will die."

Croix had only picked Capricorn because as far as he knew, they didn't have special powers like all the other royals. He wasn't one hundred percent sure on that fact, though.

"Don't worry, I'll be fine." He continued, head low, still disheartened, and the two boarded the lightning ship.

There had to be a way to pass this challenge without killing a life form. Croix wasn't sure how yet, but he had to think of something.

I know. I can probably talk a Capricorn into giving me his keepsake. That's probably all I have to do. I don't want to kill for a nonsensical reason. In fact, that must be what this test is all about. Judgment, he said this test was about judgment. It must be a bad judgment call to kill a foreigner on their own land. Eames must think I'm stupid enough to just run off and kill someone without a thought. Even I know enough to know that's bad judgment.

"We're here Croix. Make us proud," Eames said. Standing near the door, Eames lifted a latch to open the airlock because there was no pilot for the lightning ship that time, Eames piloted it. He gave Croix a solemn nod.

Croix hopped out of the ship and hit the ground running. As usual, Eames had taken him to the middle of nowhere to begin his mission.

This is going to work out fine. I can't panic. Everything is going to be fine.

Croix jetted toward Capricorn civilization, not even sure where to start.

***

As Callum waited, he weighed the pros and cons of being the leader of the first battle simulation. There was merit to being first, but like the older Capricorn man had told him earlier there was merit to watching and observing as well.

"You again? I'm glad to see that you're not dead." Callum looked up to see the man he'd fought earlier, Calypso. Odd, that meant he hadn't noticed Calypso when he finished the run.

"It's good to see that you're still alive, Callum." Calypso smiled, revealing pristine teeth.

"Thank you, you as well," Callum said.

"I mean, I didn't think you would die from the run. You're a pretty tough kid, after all, but it's still nice to see you. Sorry I was so rough on you earlier, but you understand."

"Yes, I understand. No problem at all. I have no ill feelings over it." Callum forced a quick smile. "Simply a life lesson for me to learn, that's all that fight was. Nothing more, nothing less."

"Very good. You're a student of life. That's what it's all about, learning any and everything you can from any and everywhere you can. You're still very young, so you have a lot of potential."

The two didn't finish their conversation because they noticed that Cyd had come back to the area where they were all waiting. All the Capricorn men who were waiting for their next task grew silent when they saw Cyd.

"No need to stop talking on my account. I'm merely here, waiting for your competition to arrive."

Even after his statement Callum, Calypso, and the other Capricorns remained silent. Not long after, the first of the next group arrived, out of breath. Seeing that made Callum wonder, how it was that Cyd got past the obstacle course, in full armor, so easily without running. *He must be a pro at it, he probably trained a lot of people here.*

Then again, there could be a secret path or some sort of way to cheat that only the instructors knew, like a shortcut. It didn't matter. All Callum knew was that he was ready to get started. Calvin took the first runner's information and fish as he had everybody from the original group. Not much later, another runner showed up and gave his information, until eventually, the entire second group was there. The major difference between the first group and the second group was the number of survivors. Only eight people existed in the first group, whereas the second group somehow had all ten.

"All ten made it back, impressive. Looks like you guys have your work cut out for you," Cyd said, looking at Callum's group with a smile and a laugh.

"All right, are you ready?" Cyd asked.

"You know it." Calvin nodded his head.

"OK, you all from the first group, you're with me. I'm going to brief you on your next goal with more detail than I did earlier. Follow me."

Cyd led the second group away, and Calvin led Callum and the others to a jungle area. Lush vegetation abounded, vibrant plants of all colors decorated the scenery. The purple plants were the most beautiful and even looked inviting. One of the plants in the area was formed in the shape of a busty green-and-brown Capricorn woman and had a great smell. It appeared to move and sway and actually call for attention.

"Don't go anywhere near the beautiful lady plant. It's a creature eater. It gets all of its nutrients from living, breathing organisms. Capricorns like you and me are its favorite," Calvin stated seriously. Calvin must have read everybody's mind, or he was used to recruits falling for the plant.

Callum had never known that his people had so many predators and threats before all these trials he went through. The whole thing was very enlightening to all of the dangers he could possibly face.

"OK boys, your objective is to defeat Cyd's group. The way you win is to knock them all unconscious. This isn't a fighting match though like you had before, so I'm going to give you all guns to accomplish your goal."

Calvin pulled small black-and-white guns from his bag. They had long cylindrical barrels that were white, and the other parts of the guns were black, sleek, and oval-shaped with small triggers. He handed each of them their own gun.

"Boys, I must warn you." His hand remained in the bag as he continued. "These weapons use concussive force and will knock you out cold if you misfire. Do not use them on your own team members. There is no reward for the amount of people you put to sleep. The only thing being measured is the execution of your battle plans and whether or not you can defeat all of your opponents as a team. I have another present for you."

He pulled out small, round, black insects from his bag and handed them to all the recruits.

"These aren't real insects." Finally, he set the black bag down. "They are used as communication devices. They only work short range, by short range, I mean only within this jungle. They are very effective. Just put it near your ear, the bug attaches itself to your brain in a nonlethal and easily removable way, and you can hear the surface thoughts of any of your team members no matter how far away they are. As long as they're within this jungle, you will able to communicate telepathically. These are some of our finest communication devices. No worries about the enemy hearing what you tell your team members, because you can all hear each other's thoughts, so you should avoid speaking out loud at all costs. Try them out and see how it feels."

Like this, one of them thought for everybody to hear after placing the bug near his ear.

Wow, it really does work, another one thought.

I can't believe this. Can you all really hear my thoughts?

"Believe it, mister. Now, you all should know that I can hear your surface thoughts, too." Calvin continued speaking out loud. "I will be spying on you. I have eyes in the sky." Gesturing up with two fingers, Calvin further illustrated his point by indicating a small group of insect camerabots flying just above them. "I will be watching at all times, so I will know who wins immediately after it's over. Your competition has a base location similar to this and are being briefed there right now. Their base is just a few nanodes east of here.

"Overall, there are two generic strategies you can employ. One, make them come to you, and the alternative is you guys going to them. If they come to you, the advantages are obvious, you will know your environment, because I'm going to describe your environment in detail in a moment to give you more helpful information. Conversely, going to them gives the advantage of being on the offensive and potentially catching them off guard."

A Capricorn raised his hand.

"Please save your questions until I'm done with my explanation. Anyway, there are about two ways to find them. You can either A, set up a howler plant perimeter around yourselves, or B, if you are searching for them, you can use the life detector machine. I'm not sure if you are all familiar with the machine, but basically it emits a signal with a large number of frequencies that picks up the heartbeats of living creatures, supposedly all living creatures. I'm not so sure about that myself, but they are generally very effective.

"OK, now for plants, you all have the lovely lady plant over there, I call her the seductress. Then there's the howler plants I mentioned before, good for warning you when your enemy is trying to sneak up on you. There's the pricklers over here, which sting pretty bad, which you can arrange like spikes for your enemies to step on. Then there's the suckerpunchers, those little plants over there. Every other plant in the area is more or less neutral, and probably won't help for this match."

He paused for a brief moment to give the recruits a chance to look around. The howlers looked like little green mouths, not like plants, but they were buried in green and coming from the ground. The pricklers were fashioned similar to porcupine quills, and the suckerpunchers were beautiful orange multiple petal plants.

"The suckerpunchers release a concussive gas, but only when they are uprooted." Calvin's explanation continued. "They spray their gas instantly. That's it for interesting plants, and that concludes my explanation. Now, do you have any questions?"

He looked around at all them.

Calypso didn't bother with raising his hand but asked his question just the same.

"When you say the concussive gas is released when the plant is uprooted, do you mean only when it's picked up by hand?"

"No. I mean if the plant is forced out of its soil, period," Calvin confirmed. "Any more questions?" No one else seemed to have any, so he continued.

"OK, so you all need to pick your leader and then come up with a strategy. From there, I will give the signal to Cyd to let him know you are all ready, and then you start." Calvin backed away from the circle of Capricorn enlistees.

A rainbow of colors exploded in a light flash in the air, east of their location.

"That was Cyd's signal. His group is ready, but I know you guys are not. It is important that you pick a strong leader and form an effective strategy. The leader can appoint anyone under him to perform in any capacity he sees fit. Let me know when you all are ready so I can give him the signal. Take your time. This is very important."

"We should decide by competing with each other," an athletic Capricorn suggested while stretching.

"A competition?" a wide-eyed Capricorn asked.

"There's no time." Calypso quickly dismissed the idea.

"We should pick by luck," yet another Capricorn offered.

"What do you mean," Calypso asked?

"Like maybe Instructor Calvin can pick a number and the one who guesses it right wins or something like that."

"That's not a good idea either. We should go by how well we all placed in our previous tasks," Calypso decided.

"That doesn't make any sense. This is very different from the previous tasks," the same athletic Capricorn argued.

"OK, then how about we do a combination of placement and luck?" Calypso compromised.

"What do you have in mind?" the athlete asked.

"The three who placed highest in all the last tests should play a guessing game. Instructor Calvin?" Calypso's gaze settled on the instructor.

"Yes," he answered, not looking back at Calypso.

"What is a fact that you know about this jungle, that none of us would know?"

"How many trees are within a twenty-foot radius? How about that one?"

"Yes, that question should do just fine. OK, the three that compete have to close their eyes and will only have five seconds to guess the answer. First then, we need to figure out how everybody placed so far on the previous tests."

"OK, I will tell you all then, because I already know." Calvin pulled out a holographic notepad and tapped it a few times. "We instructors have our ways of communicating."

"Calypso is doing best all the way around. Callum did well because he came in first on that last task. Cormac is doing third best."

"What system are you all using to judge?" another Capricorn voiced.

"None of you others have won or done as well in any of your respective tests. I assure you, we know what we are looking for and judge well," Calvin answered, his anger hard to conceal. But he let the question slide all the same.

Callum wasn't sure about the rankings. How was it that he was able to compete in the top three? He didn't even want to be leader. Oh well, it wouldn't be right to turn them down. Plus, he still had a chance of losing if he made a bad guess.

"Callum, Cormac, you two are with me."

Calypso was already acting like he was their leader. May as well have made it official, but maybe it was all in the name of fairness that he was doing this competition.

"Are you guys ready?"

Cormac, a curly-haired Cap, and Callum nodded.

"Close your eyes. Don't worry, I will let you all know if one of you opens up your eyes early. I will also countdown the seconds for you," Calvin said. "Five. Four. Three. Two. One."

Callum wanted to use a bad guess on purpose so he yelled five, knowing that there was definitely more. This was a jungle, after all. Calypso and Cormac seemed to take it more seriously. Cormac guessed thirty-eight and Calypso guessed fifty-two.

"Well, which answer was closer?" Calypso asked when he opened his eyes.

"Yours. The correct answer is sixty-five."

"All right, then, it's decided."

"What was the point in that?" The athlete once more asked a question.

"That was to measure our intuition, Calypso said. None of us are familiar with this area save for Calvin. He told us everything he plans to tell us, and I still feel that's not enough. So intuition will be important. Since I have performed the best on all the tasks so far, been the most assertive, and proven I have the best intuition, it's only natural that I be leader. I could have taken it by force, but I prefer diplomacy, so we can all be on the same page. Now, are we all on the same page?"

"Yes, sir!" everyone yelled.

"Good. Here's the plan: We make them come to us. I need four people to remain here and enclose themselves around howlers and suckerpunchers twenty yards out in every direction, and hold a tight perimeter. I also need one person to go out there with a life detector. This person will lead our enemies to believe that we are going after them and will serve as a decoy. They should also be able to take out one or two of them, with any luck."

"Won't they be using a life detector machine also, which will make them suspicious because they will see it's only one person coming at them?" the shortest and grayest Capricorn asked.

"You're right, but it won't be one person, it will be four. Three more will be behind the one using the life detector.

"What is your name?" Calypso swiftly moved on and pointed to one of the recruits.

"Tristan," a skinny brown Capricorn with jet-black hair said.

"OK, Tristan, you're going to be our final shooter in the center. I'll give you more instructions later as things progress, same to you, Callum, and you, Cormac. The next most important one to me will be my runner, the first one to go out. Decoy, decoy." He scanned the group. "You."

This time Calyspo pointed to the skinniest Capricorn who was there. He was tall and lanky and was even skinnier than Callum.

"You look like you're the fastest to me. You're going to be the decoy, but also try to get as many of them as possible while you're at it. It will also be your responsibility to figure out their location. Just think about it, and we'll know since we have these special bugs in our brains. You're going to be one of the most important parts of my plan so I'm counting on you, at the very least to find out the location of our enemies. Do you understand? Do you think you can do that for me?"

"Of course. I will do my best." He nodded.

"What is your name?" Calypso asked him.

"Hunter," the smoke-gray Capricorn, who was the tallest out of the group, said with a smile.

"OK, Hunter, are you all set and ready to go?"

"Yes."

Calypso turned to the three men not already assigned a position. They were all about the same height. One was dark brown, another dark gray, and the other a grayish brown. "OK, so just you three are left. Not to be rude, but I'm not going to ask for your names. For now, I will call you all *the three*. You three will follow behind Hunter, not too close, not too far. Stagger yourselves so that you're all close but appear far from each other. This may trick them into thinking that there are more of you.

"Try to learn something about the enemy, anything, and possibly lead them back here. My hope is that you guys take out a few. Do your best, you guys, that's all I ask of you. Let's go everybody get into position."

They all began setting up their equipment and formations. Hunter had the life detector, and the three just had their weapons. Calypso, Callum, Cormac, and Tristan set up their perimeter. It took a little while, but there didn't seem to be any holes in their setup. Everyone was in position, so Calyspo looked at Calvin.

"Are you ready?"

Calypso looked to all the others, who all nodded.

With that, Calvin fired a glowing red beam of light into the air. The light beam illuminated the night sky temporarily, giving them floral pink skylight to admire for a moment. Hunter used the life detector once right away, and then he and the three sprinted east toward the enemies.

"OK, all we have to do for now is pay attention to the thoughts of those four. If things seem to be going a different way than we want, we may have to adjust our plans. For now, remain in this circle with our backs to one another. The perimeter we set up should effectively allow us to take out at least two of them."

"Uhh, shouldn't we be paying attention to Hunter's thoughts?" Tristan worried.

"I've been paying attention the whole time, multitasking. His first thought was that all ten of them were heading toward our base. He somehow managed to take out two before falling unconscious," Calypso replied.

After that, all four men grew silent and began focusing in on to the thoughts of the three soldiers.

Eeeeeeeerrrrrrrr!

Green light flashed briefly. They felt a strange pulse and like their hearts skipped a beat. It must have been the life detector machine used by their opponents.

We took out two, but I'm not sure of where any of the rest of them are, Callum, Calypso, and the others heard in their minds.

What if they are sneaking up on us? One of the three thought.

Oh no! They're here!

Their minds went blank.

Our comrades must be unconscious, Calyspo thought to his teammates, finally switching to thoughts only. *Brace yourselves, they are on their way. Luckily, we only have six to deal with because our boys did well. Tighten up the circle now.*

They came closer to one another to make the circle stronger. At this point, they were all back-to-back, as close as possible, facing all directions, preparing for the onslaught. Suddenly, multiple howlers went off. They each took a shot and heard two groans. That should leave four. Shots came back at them, but missed.

"Only four left. Just shoot a volley of shots until they drop. Rapid fire now!" Calypso yelled.

Everybody began shooting, and so did their opponents. Tristan got hit. Calypso knew one of his shots connected with another one of them. Callum took out one himself. They saw one Capricorn approaching slowly.

Does that mean that there is only one left?

Calypso shot and hit the straggler.

Doesn't this feel a little bit too easy? Callum projected to his group.

Pop!

Another shot was fired. This one took out Cormac instantly, leaving his body limp like a ragdoll just outside of their circle of Capricorns.

Where is it coming from? Callum projected, looking all around him in a panic.

Instinctually, Calyspo hopped out of the circle. Right after his agile side leap, he saw Callum lying there, unconscious.

Where were the shots coming from?

Another round from the concussive gun came dangerously close to Calyspo, but had much less accuracy. He jumped back even further.

It doesn't make any sense, only one approached us from foot. If any had been walking toward us, I would have noticed it. That's it, he must be above somehow.

As if the other guy could hear his thoughts, he then began speaking.

"Ha, I'm sure you thought you had it all won. It's just me and you now. I've had the upper hand this entire time."

He had to be bluffing. He couldn't have the upper hand, otherwise he would have dealt the final blow. There were only two of them left, that part sounded true, but if he could have shot Calypso, he would have done so already.

Calypso looked up to the trees, but couldn't see anything. The light from Cyd's gun had extinguished a long time ago. The moon was barely visible, giving the trees above a light silhouette.

"Don't worry, I'm quite sure you'll have a hard time finding me, Calypso. Isn't it funny you were able to defeat me in the mountaintop fight, but in the end, you'll still have to take orders from me?"

A shot came at Calypso, then another one, but he saw both and dodged in time.

One thing is for sure, wherever this guy is, it has to be somewhere above the circle I was in a few moments ago. It doesn't seem like he's moved any at all, because his accuracy is only getting worse the farther out I move. It could be that it is difficult for him to aim while hanging in the trees. Maybe he's upside down, his accuracy is so terrible.

Another inaccurate shot missed. This time, it gave away his position. Calypso took a shot.

"Close, but no," his opponent taunted with a mocking laugh.

Dammit, he really does have the upper hand. I thought I could figure it out from listening to his voice, but it almost seems to be moving. What do I have to lose? I might as well go all out.

Calypso began running back toward the circle and shot up in the sky at random. He sprinted past, jumped, and shot. He could tell he was missing, but the fact that he was sprinting must have thrown his opponent off, because he didn't even shoot back, and when he did, it was horribly inaccurate.

He began another sprint. He ran, jumped, and saw a shot close to his leg. He looked up toward the tops of the trees, and in a small gleam of moonlight, he caught an extremely brief glimpse of something white. It had to be his opponent's gun.

Got him.

He ran across one more time and shot toward the white object hanging in the trees, until he couldn't shoot anymore. Six shots in rapid succession. Seconds later, he heard a loud thud. And he saw the body of a grizzled man who had given him a hard time on the mountain, but had lost, because he talked too much.

"Again your mouth was your undoing. You don't need to talk down to me in order to feel stronger. If you hadn't hesitated, you could have won," Calyspo taught the unconscious Capricorn.

"Congratulations, your team wins."

Calvin began walking to all the unconscious Capricorns one by one, holding a vial directly under their noses. They all woke up instantly. He gathered them into a line of eighteen men, with Calypso standing just outside the line.

"I hope you all slept well, now that you are all awake, you have two options. You can either keep on going, try to learn more and do better, or you can accept the rank for the way you just performed.

"It is important for you all to know that if you won, and you try this again, and next time you lose. It will only be counted as a loss. In other words, only one score can be given and that's for the last time you compete. That said all of you from the losing team have nothing to lose by trying again. Winners, I suggest you all go and wait for the ranking ceremony. There will be some downtime, and you can relax for a while."

He immediately turned away from Calypso and his team, and focused all of his attention on the remaining ten Capricorns who had lost.

"Losers, you can either accept your rank or you can compete again in the same exercise. If you choose to compete you will be divided amongst the next two competing teams"

Three from the losing team immediately left, perhaps thinking it wasn't worth it.

"Which way do we walk to get to the ranking ceremony?" Callum asked.

Calvin simply handed him a dark blue device that had one black button on the top. Callum clicked the button and a light blue path became illuminated on the ground. They all began walking down that path with the assumption that it must lead toward the ranking ceremony grounds.

Calvin continued talking and explaining the competition.

"Hey. I'm surprised that none of you are going to try again," Calypso mentioned as all the members from the winning team walked down the blue path.

"Why should I? I stand to lose a lot more than I stand to gain. Besides, it's been a very long day," Callum answered, looking like a burden was placed on him after just hearing the suggestion.

"I think you could pull it off," Calypso responded.

"Maybe I could, maybe I couldn't. I just know I'm not going to try. It really isn't worth it," Callum insisted.

"This decides our rank in the Capricorn Royal Cavalry. How is it not worth it?" Calypso was still concerned. Stopping dead in his tracks, he looked around at all of them and continued speaking. "In fact, all of you should try again. You could be the leaders next time. We won because we were a better team than them, not because of my plan, but because of how well you all performed."

"Look, I'm sure they all feel the same way I do. It's not worth it," Callum repeated.

They all kept walking toward the ceremony grounds in silent agreement.

"I'm sure there will be another chance for us to prove ourselves again later, and move up in rank. We won. I'm happy enough with that for now. There is no need for me to be the leader yet. Besides, I'm the youngest Cap here. You might be OK with that, and everybody in our group might be OK with that, too, but even if I were able to somehow become the leader during another battle simulation, there's no way of telling whether anybody would even listen to me. "

"You're going to let something so simple hold you back? Even if they don't listen to you, there is a lot to gain and learn by trying to lead soldiers during a stressful situation."

Callum and the others just kept walking.

"It's OK," Tristan said. "Like Callum said, there will be other chances to prove ourselves in the future. It will only be a matter of time before we can change our ranks, I'm sure."

Calypso sighed and shrugged finally dropping the issue. "I'm sorry, you are all right. And it's none of my business how ambitious any of you are or aren't."

Callum smiled at him. We may be more ambitious than you know. However, I have learned a few things over the course of these trials. For one, patience is extremely valuable, highly valued within Cavalry ranks. As long as any person is alive there's always time to achieve and strive for more." After Callum said what he felt he continued walking and so did the others.

The rest of the trip they were all silent, until they reached the green grass of the ranking ceremony grounds. The ceremony grounds were very simple. There were over one thousand chairs, divided into two equal parts, and a large stage. Callum's team was the first to arrive at the grounds, so they all sat down close to the front.

It wasn't long before another group joined them by sitting down, and then yet another team. Eventually almost half of the chairs were filled. There was soft chattering among those ready to receive their ranks. Cyd, Cassius, Calvin, and Caleb silently moved to the sides of the stage and stood, two per side.

"Quiet everyone," Cassius said, holding out a closed fist. "Listen to this."

A glowing luminescent holographic image of the prince stood before the new recruits. Even though it was a hologram, his golden hair somehow still seemed to shine luxuriously. It was easy to see because it was dark outside.

"Hello to you all. Welcome to the Capricorn Royal Cavalry." His image scanned the audience as if he were actually looking at them. "You have done well to get here, completing the trials and competing with one another. For those who couldn't make it, the Capricorn Royal Cavalry isn't for everyone. It is unfortunate, though, that some may have lost their lives during the course of the trials." He paused in a moment of self-observed silence, presumably to honor the dead.

"But none of you did, so let's move on to the good news." The hologram produced a politician's smile. "You will have certain benefits for being a part of the cavalry, such as royal pay, free living quarters, reduced cost of food and beverage no matter where you are on the planet, and also other incentives such as being able to travel to other planets and see other things. I'm sure you're all curious about the other planets in our galaxy.

"Anyway, you have all done well, and I know you will all serve our kingdom to the fullest. You are the first of your kind, because never before have there been this many commoners in the cavalry, so congratulations." He quickly clapped his hands together once. "I'm sure you're all eager to get on with it, so I'll turn things over to Cassius."

The image disappeared immediately, as if it never existed.

"Well, you heard your prince," Cassius said, stepping to the stage and walking to the center. "The other instructors along with myself would just like to second everything he said by saying congratulations and that you should all be proud of yourselves. No matter what rank you get or how many people are above you, what you all have done is no small task.

"On that note, I would like to begin ranking you all. When you hear your name, come forward to the stage, and I will present you with an award, which also has the rank that you will wear in the future. Do not wear it now. Once you leave the stage, sit back in your original seat and wait for further instructions," Cassius said.

"Whether you're happy or not with your rank, doesn't matter you will all have plenty of time and opportunity to move up the ranks with us as you serve and work for the cavalry. If you would like to voice your concerns about the competitions however, please wait until the ceremony is over before you speak up.

"Nobody ask questions. There are too many of you present here and we don't have time for questions. Q and A will be after everybody is given their rank, during the same time as the objection to the rank period is taking place. We will begin now."

Cassius stepped back, and Caleb stepped forward to the front of the stage and began calling names. Callum wasn't sure if it was a good or bad thing that his name wasn't called for quite some time. Then again, Calypso had performed very well on everything and he was still sitting right next to him, so it must not have been a big deal. In fact, maybe it was better not to be called first. Just when he stopped worrying about it, his name was called.

"Callum, fifth battle commander."

The walk to the stage felt long, as if the grassy field kept extending under his feet. Eventually he made it to the stage, received his award package, which included the bug he had used earlier to communicate telepathically with his comrades and the staff he had used during the fight, along with the castle he had assembled and a digital plaque that said his name and rank. It was a surprisingly thoughtful package that would commemorate everything that he had done during his trials except for the run. Inside the package was also an orange-colored hat and a small reddish-orange handkerchief. Callum assumed the hat and the handkerchief must have something to do with his rank, so he didn't even bother asking.

He turned and left the stage.

When he reached his seat he sat there thinking back on his long journey to get to where he was at that moment. It was only a day ago that he was with his mother back in his village. His life had changed rapidly; he'd met a queen and after that, he became a royal himself, well, a royal of sorts.

He was sure that he and all the other Caps who joined with him would not get the same respect as royals, but it was sure to be better treatment than they had before during their regular lives.

Some time passed before Calypso's name was finally called. Calypso was given the position of first battle commander. It was appropriate, given the fact that he had performed so well during the demonstration match earlier against the other team.

As soon as he sat back down, he looked over at Callum with a smile, waved his orange hat and handkerchief and said, "I wonder if that means we will be working together."

"Yes, I wonder, too. I also wonder where Tristan, Hunter, Cormac and the three are."

"I don't know. I haven't seen any of them in quite a while, even though we originally all sat in the same area together. Strange."

Caleb called a few more forward until he was finished.

"OK, newbies, you are all set to go." Caleb stood center stage with his arms folded behind his back. Somehow, his brown skin still glistened under the artificial light, as if it was daytime. "It should be self-explanatory, but if you got a position like strategic commander, that means you probably won't take part in any of the fighting, but rather help out with strategies. If you got battle commander, than you battle and you're a leader for your soldiers, showing them the correct way to fight on the battlefield and guiding them to victory.

"Any further explanation of your ranks, positions, and functions within our system will be given later. You have one week to spend at home, after that you'll come back to the castle and from there, you will be brought to your living quarters. Your housing is not finished. It took quite a bit of time to set this competition and ranking system, so the housing is behind schedule. Keep all the things you were given, and bring all of it with you when you return in a week, even the plaque.

"All right, anybody unhappy with his rank, you are now free to speak your mind to me directly. Everybody else disperse, go home, and take the week off. Be here exactly seven days from now at this exact time to start your training for your new position. If you need help getting back to your homes, see one of the ushers to the left or right side."

Callum was shocked, even a little disappointed. It's not that he wasn't going to be happy to see his mom. It was just that he was ready to get his new life started. Having to go back to his old life was so depressing. It almost made him feel like all the hard work was for nothing.

Calypso read his facial expression. "Don't worry, we will all be back here a week from now, well rested. You should be happy to have the time off."

"Easy for you to say. I'm not really looking forward to going back to my old life."

"At least you get to see your parents. Look, I need to get going, I plan to enjoy my week. I'll see you in seven days." Calypso walked away with purpose.

Callum asked one of the ushers to help him get back home. It didn't take long for him to get back. Back to square one, it felt like.

But it would only be for seven days. He wanted to come back to his mom with more to show for himself, but she would still be excited to see him, he was sure. The door was unlocked when he got there so he walked right in.

"Hey, Mom, I'm home.

Chapter 16

"**D**o you know what happened? Did you hear about what your buddy did?" Arkin asked, pacing around a stunned Rudolph.

"No, I haven't got word back from him yet," Rudolph replied softly.

"King Leo is still alive. I thought you guys from the Sagittarian Royal Army were supposed to be the best. What is the point in a failed assassination attempt?" Arkin complained, getting a bit too close to Rudolph.

"Calm down, Arkin," Leon calmly stated, sitting not too far away with his eyes closed. He looked like he was in a meditative trance. "It's fine. I already thought about this possibility. Everything should be fine."

Knock-knock-knock.

"Who is it?" Leon and Arkin called in unison accidentally.

"It's me, Gwen. I've been thinking a lot about everything and I want to talk. Can I come in?"

"Yes," Leon said happily. He looked over at Arkin with a wink, as if to brag.

"Hello, Gwen, it is nice to see you again." Leon closed the amethyst-colored door behind her and kept talking. "Have you changed your mind?"

"Yes and no. I've been thinking that maybe I can help you guys come up with alternatives for solving the problems with the kings in the future. If you guys have enough power to do all the things that you say that you are doing or planning to do, then there may be a peaceful way to improve life for all beings, if we force each king's hand."

"We have a lot of important things to discuss right now like, namely, what to do now that the assassination attempt on King Leo has failed," Rudolph said to her.

Stone was told to inform all groups of dyads that the remaining half bloods from the planets were arriving today. He was just outside Arkin, Leon, Pierce, Rudolph, and Sage's door when he heard them speaking loudly and excitedly.

"I was told to keep an eye on them anyway, so it can't hurt to be nosey," he whispered to himself and put his head closer to the door.

"What? That's crazy. *You* guys? *You're* the ones who tried to kill King Leo? I can't believe you guys did that."

"What do you mean? We told you we were going to strike out against King Leo. What did you think we meant when we said we were going to plan our strike against him? The only problem is, Rudolph's guy missed," Arkin answered, anger leaking from his voice.

"No, it's not a problem," Rudolph said flinching at first from Arkin's words and finally relaxing again. "You heard Leon. He figured that this was one of the possibilities and it is fine. I'm not sure how, but that's what he just said. How is it fine, Leon?" Rudolph turned to Leon for an explanation.

"Don't you all see? The Leos will take it as an act of war from King Sagittarius himself. It's beautiful, because now we don't have to plan to take down the Leo Empire personally."

"You would have never been capable of that anyway," Gwen snidely remarked, folding her arms across her chest. *Arrogant*, that's the main word she would use to describe her new companions. But she was trying to remain patient.

"You don't know that. But now we don't have to even worry about that. Everything should fall into place and work out for us without us having to even lift another finger toward King Leo. Downfall and misfortune for that king and his family are imminent. It doesn't even matter that he's still alive," Leon concluded with a smile.

"What about all the other kings? I thought you wanted to make things better for all the common people and for the half bloods of all twelve planets. Isn't that what you told me before? This sounds just like a personal grudge against King Leo," Gwen snapped again, visibly frustrated.

Stone felt that he had heard what he needed to hear, so he immediately walked away toward the king's chambers.

"That is important as well, of course. In fact, I think we can continue to recruit more forces and expand. And you might even be right. Maybe we don't have to kill all or any of the kings." Leon sat down calmly.

"What? But I thought you guys were trying to kill…" Gwen's brow furrowed.

"Well, yes, that's what I thought, too, but maybe we can just set elaborate plans to force the kings into certain compromising positions just like you were saying a moment ago, and so that way they have no choice but to do what we want. And this means we don't have to kill them." Leon clarified.

"How is this forcing King Leo into a position to do what we want?" Pierce asked.

"Leo will most likely have a change of heart after this near-death experience if he happens to survive, and be a changed man, prepared to do better by his people. Is that what you're saying, Leon," Arkin asked?

"Wait, are you two lying to me? I feel like you're both making this up as you go," Gwen said.

"No, this is no lie, I promise." Arkin gave his most sincere and genuine smile.

"I second that. Leo surviving the attack is the best thing to have happened, it seems," Leon added.

"OK. Well, in that case, I suppose I can meet with you guys in the future to help you all come up with peaceful ways of reconciling things with the kings and the common people and the half bloods so that we can all go back home. Now it's time I tell you the real reason that I came here."

They all looked up at her, perplexed.

"All the half bloods from all the planets have arrived now, even the ones from planet Leo."

"Really? Wow, I'm surprised they got here so quickly," Leon said.

"Anyway, I'm going to go. I will see you all later. Don't hide anything from me or keep any secrets or lie to me at all as we go forward. If you can keep true to those conditions, then I'm all in for helping you."

"Sure," Arkin and Leon said at the same time.

Pierce, Sage, and Rudolph simply nodded their heads.

Gwen walked out.

I'm not so disillusioned to believe that they were completely honest with me, but my presence can only be a cause for good during their meetings, she reasoned with herself. They do seem to be the only ones here who want to affect any change, so that's good, in a way. Even if their methods are questionable. All I can do for my part is try to steer things in the most positive direction, and try to guide their group toward peace. I really need to do some recruiting myself, Gwen concluded mentally as she walked away.

***

"Master, master." Stone walked into Aquarius's aquamarine-colored laboratory.

"What is it Stone? I'm quite busy setting up to research a cure for the Scorpio's poison. It is such delicate work that I myself am even going to help the research department, so I can't be bothered with anything. Please go. I will speak with you later." Aquarius didn't look up from the small blood slide he examined.

"No. It's about that."

"About the research?" Aquarius perked up and looked toward Stone. He took off his deep purple gloves, placed the slide down on his black worktable, and got up immediately and walked over to Stone, who was still near his door.

"No, it's about the attempt made on King Leo's life. I know who was responsible."

"Who? How could you possibly know?"

Stone lowered his voice significantly and leaned in very close to Aquarius, near his ear.

"I was telling all the dyads here about the arrival of the other dyads just like you told me to when I finally made it to the group you found interesting."

"What group is that?" Aquarius spoke at standard volume, but he hadn't pulled away from the whispering Stone.

"The group with the Aries-Pisces, Aries-Taurus, Leo-Virgo, and two Scorpio-Sagittarius dyads living together."

"Oh, yes, that's right. It's good that they are still getting along and getting to know one another." Aquarius nodded to himself.

"No, it's not," Stone quickly uttered, his voice just above a whisper. "Because they're the group responsible for the assassination attempt made on Leo's life," Stone said.

"No, no way. That's not even possible. How could they pull off something like that?" Disbelief and confusion were written on Aquarius's face, but only for a moment before being replaced by a smirk, as if he might laugh at the allegation.

"I'm not sure, but they were talking about it in their quarters just now."

"Why would they do such a thing?" Aquarius seemed to take the information more seriously.

"Revenge. One of them is from Leo, and to most of the people, Leo is still considered a tyrant."

"I'm not exactly sure what to do with this information as of yet," Aquarius said gravely. "Thank you for reporting to me. I still find it hard to believe. After all the hard work that I've done bringing them here."

"Appreciation for a favor is a rare find." Stone shook his head in quiet disapproval.

"Nonsense. You appreciate everything I do for you and you're a dyad. Don't speak of your own people that way." Aquarius switched to a more jolly state and patted Stone on the back once.

Stone rolled his eyes. He was a dyad, of course, but none of them were the same kind as him. Not to mention, he was just making a general statement, he wasn't even implying anything because they were dyads. Aquarius either didn't notice him rolling his eyes or paid it no attention.

"Anyway, for now I just want you to keep a close eye on them. Do not make any moves against them. Don't let them know that you overheard them. Go to their room and speak with them on friendly terms, if possible. Did you tell them that the other dyads have arrived?"

"No, I didn't get a chance to tell them. I rushed straight here after hearing their conversation."

"OK, go back, and tell them about the arrival of the others. If possible, even befriend them. If they are capable of doing such a thing from here, they may be formidable. I don't want to do anything to them without more evidence. I will look into it on my end. I'm happy with my decision to put you in charge of dyad management." Aquarius turned from Stone and headed back to his work table.

"I just realized something, though." He turned around full circle. "I gave you some fancy quarters and items and a little higher position in the kingdom, but that's not enough. This project is huge and it means a lot to me. The proper placement and care of the dyads is important. Therefore, I'm going to give you some men of your own under you. In order for you to get what you need done, I'm going to give you direct charge over my royals, five of them. Go back to doing what you were doing. I will send them to your office by morning. It is very late."

"Are you sure about this? Is it really a good idea?" Stone humbly asked, even doing a partial bow reflexively.

"Of course, I trust you dearly, Stone. You're one of my most trustworthy men. I don't care about things like lineage or even the fact that you're a half blood. None of that matters. All I care about is loyalty and you seem to have that, so I'm promoting you."

"I understand that. I mean, do you think it's a good idea putting royals under me? What if they don't want to take orders from me because I'm a dyad?"

"It doesn't matter if they want to. I'm their king and I command it. You really need to have more confidence in yourself and more faith in me." Aquarius smiled. "Now get out of here and do as I said. Expect to see your new men in the morning."

"Thank you, sire. It is always my pleasure to serve you." Stone kneeled before him.

"Get up and go." Aquarius shooed him away. "I've never been a fan of the whole kneeling thing anyway, but you're welcome."

Stone walked out, very pleased with himself. He never knew that this dyad management thing would get him this far. He was able to speak directly with the king whenever he needed to, and now he was being given more trust and royals under him.

"If what he said is true, I have to verify it. It's unfortunate to take time away from finding the cure though. This shouldn't take long, and it's necessary, I have no other choice," Aquarius noted to himself as he moved toward his aqua communicator that rested in his chambers. When he attempted communication with Sagittarius, nobody answered for quite a while. He would not be ignored this time. He kept calling and calling and calling. Finally, someone arrived before him on the other side of the water screen.

"I'm sorry, but my king is unavailable," the brunette queen of Sagittarius said, barely dressed. Oddly enough, both she and her husband didn't have the lower body of a horse that was typically a dominant gene of all born of Sagittarius descent on the planet.

"No, this is an emergency, he has skipped out on far too many council meetings, and he might even be in danger at this point." Aquarius was putting his foot down and his face told her that he was all business.

"He's not even on Sagittarius at this moment," she pleaded, almost whining.

"I know you know how to reach him, please put me through," Aquarius persisted.

The queen sighed deep and heavy, it seemed as though Aquarius had disturbed her sleep. He had forgotten how late it was. It wasn't long until the king of Sagittarius was actually on the other side of the communicator looking back at him wearily.

"I told her repeatedly not to patch anybody through at all," the golden-haired, golden-eyed Sagittarian said.

"I told her it was an emergency and that your life could be in danger. She simply wanted to help. Why haven't you been coming to any of the council meetings as of late?"

"I'm sorry, I can't always drop everything I'm doing on a whim and go to those meetings." Sagittarius looked away from the screen. "I had other, more pressing matters I needed to tend to with my men and other situations."

"Oh, yes more pressing matters, right, like trying to have Leo killed?"

"What are you talking about?" Instantaneously, Sagittarius became alert. He met Aquarius's gaze, concern and confusion both on full display within his face.

"A Sagittarian sniper put three arrows into King Leo, poisoned arrows mind you, not long ago."

"King Leo is dead then?" Sagittarius eyes were still wide.

"No, just in the care of a healer."

"Why are you telling me all this, Aquarius, as opposed to the Lioness or her son? I believe the prince is of ruling age, is he not?"

"I am telling you this because I wanted to find something out for myself. I have an answer from you already, so don't worry, I have no questions. I think the Leos aren't sure whether they want to go to war with you or not. And I also want to say that one of your men may have been responsible for trying to kill Leo, whether you ordered him to or not." Aquarius was reasonably certain by judging Sagittarius's responses and expressions that he wasn't involved.

"Of course I wouldn't try to kill Leo, I actually think of him as one of my closest friends." Sagittarius took legitimate offense to the comment.

"Then why didn't you attend the council meetings?"

"It's not like somebody came out and told me that's what the meetings were about. Besides, I've been busy." Again, Sagittarius looked away for a moment from his fellow king. "Thank you for reaching out, Aquarius. I now have more things to take care of, but at least now I know what's going on."

They both ended the transmission.

Stone was most likely right. I still don't want the dyads to know that I'm on to them right away, though. I should get some definitive proof. Perhaps an example does need to be made of troublemakers after all. Aquarius thought on how to deal with the potential rabble-rousers.

***

Meanwhile, somewhere on Virgo, three children had just been born. Not just any children, though. These were children whose mothers died during delivery. Out of the freshly dead bodies the three children rose, much bigger than the average Libra child is at birth. They had no home, no food, but they had each other.

***

"Not interested," the yellow-furred Leo-Virgo Victor said. Not even looking up at Arkin and Leon, he pretended to be too focused on what he was eating.

"You didn't even hear us out," Leon exhorted.

"I know you." His gaze lifted toward them. "Both of you, Arkin and Leon. I know what you two are trying to do. I'm not interested in helping. You two weren't there"—he paused and looked back at his food—"on Leo, during the rebellion. Do you know how many commoners and half bloods died?" He stood up abruptly. "Of course you don't, you two only care about your plots and schemes. I saw a fist burst through the stomach of one of the leaders that I handpicked." He stared off as if he were watching it again. "That was only a small group of Cancer Elites and a few from the king's pride, and they killed so many of us. I don't want any more blood on my hands for a battle we can't win." Sitting back down, Victor returned his attention to his tray of food.

Leon's friend was being stubborn.

"I understand, but you haven't seen everything we can do as a whole, all of the half bloods united." Leon leaned over his friend's table.

"Oh, you mean the failed assassination attempt on Leo? Yes, that was really impressive," Victor said sardonically.

"It was a lot more than we were ever able to do on our own, and it shows that the kings aren't invincible. I hear even now that King Leo is fighting off the effects of the poison," Leon said excitedly.

"You two should try keeping it down," Arkin whispered. "We can't have anyone realize our plans."

Leon lowered his voice. "All I'm saying is, we will always just be pawns to them. If they are so mighty, why don't they fight all their battles themselves?"

"We will always be pawns during times of war," Victor corrected him. "Now we are in a time of peace, and I hear Aquarius is working toward making it so no commoner nor half blood will be forced to fight anymore."

"Aquarius isn't even capable of such a thing. Not for all twelve kingdoms."

"Maybe you're right." Victor gave an unconcerned shrug and look of indifference. "All I know is I'm not interested, Leon. And I don't think you'll even be able to unify all the half bloods. I'm pretty sure that's impossible. Now, please go away and allow me to finish my meal in peace." Victor once again gave the better portion of his concentration to his tray before him, and took to slurping a soupy-textured food.

All the other half blood lions shook their heads at Leon and Arkin, clearly not interested in the proposition either. Then a large-scale fight broke out between some Aries-Pisces, Cancer-Leos, and Gemini-Taurus, as if to prove that it was impossible to unify the half bloods. All their furry, V-imprinted Leo-Virgo faces turned away from Leon and Arkin.

"See my point," Victor said, eyes fixed on the fight.

Leon held his finger up as if to say something maybe, but instead just walked away, and Arkin followed suit.

"I thought it would be good to have all the half bloods together, but now I'm not so sure. I don't know if we will ever be able to unite them all," Arkin noted as they walked past the brawl and out of the food hall.

"Most likely we won't, but we can't let that discourage us. Just because Victor and all the other Leos wouldn't join, that doesn't mean we should lose heart. We can at least continue to grow our small group. We did almost take out one of the kings, after all," Leon said optimistically.

***

"It is good to see you again," Aries said from his diamond throne to his most loyal servant who kneeled before him.

"Same to you, my lord. It wasn't fun being Cancer's errand boy," Magnus said, rising to his feet.

"Well, you say all he had you do was fetch an assortment of items, and if that's the case, then that's fine," Aries said and looked away for a moment.

"King?"

"It's nothing. It's just now that Virgo's dead, Scorpio is doing an investigation."

"And our kingdom is somehow suspected?" Magnus questioned. "What right does he have to investigate us, or you, for that matter?"

"Scorpio was the closest to Virgo," Aries sympathized, "and if I don't cooperate, it will look suspicious. It's fine, anyway, I'm not guilty of doing anything or plotting anything against the Virgos, so everything should be fine. Scorpio suspects us because of the power that all royal Aries possess, but it doesn't matter. Scorpio's investigation of Aries will come up empty-handed because we are not guilty of anything. And you didn't do anything while you were working for that conniving Cancer, so everything will be fine." He adjusted himself in his throne and made sure he made eye contact with Magnus. "I know I already asked this, but you promise all you did for Cancer was gather items?"

"Do you no longer trust me, my lord?" Magnus kneeled again as if to make amends, then looked back up at Aries.

King Aries paused and just looked his servant in the eye. Magnus was his most trusted servant, and would surely never lie to him.

"No, it's not that, of course I trust you. It's just a lot of what's been going on lately has been troubling me. How come it took you so long to get back from Cancer? The last time you contacted me was some time ago, and yet you just got back today. Why such a large gap in time?"

Magnus rose and smiled, a bit more chipper at the new topic of conversation. "Oh, well, King Cancer felt like being a gracious host. I felt it would be offensive to turn down his offer, especially since I was still under his command, so we stayed on Cancer for a while, as per request, and dined on fine foods and enjoyed ourselves." Smiling a wholehearted smile, Magnus's eyes lit up when he told his king about his stay on Cancer. "That is, of course, once we had already finished retrieving everything from his list."

"Oh, is that so? It's not like Cancer to be gracious, at least not in my experience. Although I'm sure he really needed the miscellaneous items you brought him. Perhaps you got on his good side. I hope you enjoyed yourself on Cancer. Thank you for your loyalty and for serving him when I needed you to. I apologize for making you do such a thing, but I'm afraid he had me in a compromising position."

"Of course, sire. I would do anything you commanded."

Magnus bowed before his king again.

"Yes, yes. Thank you again. One more thing: Do you have a copy of the list of items you obtained for Cancer still?"

"Of course. I actually have it right here."

Magnus handed Aries the parchment.

"Thank you. You may go."

It really was not like Cancer to be so hospitable, especially to Aries men. In fact, there was something odd about it. Suspicion would fall on Aries, or at least his men, if Scorpio found out that they were on Cancer under the control of King Cancer during the time of Virgo's death.

There was nothing that could be done about it. Not now, anyway. Another worry for another time. Besides, it's not like Aries was afraid of Scorpio, he just didn't want blame for something he didn't do. That, and he heard Scorpio was seasoned in the art of fighting. But he wasn't guilty of anything. All he had done was try his best to protect his youngest son, and clean up after one of his mistakes. Done his fatherly duty, and there was nothing wrong with that.

***

It was a long shot, anyway. Mar had barely paid attention to his waiter, so it was his own fault that he wasn't able to ID the one who left the note. Not to mention, he wasn't even sure if they would know anything useful. He was sure that it wasn't a Libra that caught him in the act with Diantha, or at least somewhat sure. His only choice would really be to talk to the snake known as Cancer. The problem was, he wasn't sure of how to do that without his dad finding out.

"Hello," the beautiful green-skinned woman known as Adeline answered.

"Please get King Cancer over here so I can speak with him."

"He is busy as of right now. Do you have a special message that you would like me to relay to him?" Adeline replied nonchalantly, as if she always responded that way to that request.

"No, I need to speak with him personally. Is he there or not?"

"Yes, he's not far from here, but as I said, he won't be able to see you right now."

Mar ended mobile communication immediately. It didn't matter what she was saying. He was going to show up and wait in Cancer's castle until he saw him. Back at home, he prepared to travel through an aqua communicator and try to find his way to Cancer, but instead King Cancer contacted him.

"Prince Mar of Aries, to what do I owe the pleasure?" Cancer received him on the screen with a smug grin. It was as if he had been waiting for Mar to attempt to make contact.

"I need to talk to you."

"Yes, I believe we are doing that now."

Mar leaned his head nearly through the water screen of the communicator. "In person."

"Oh, OK, one of those sort of things. I can't say I ever recall you wanting to visit me before."

"Well I don't exactly want to, I need to," Mar elaborated.

"Very well. You can come by right now if you like. You have my attention. Just come through to my side, if you want."

Cancer stepped away from the communicator's screen so that Mar could step through it.

"Welcome to Cancer, young prince. Would you like something to drink, perhaps some food?"

"There's no need. I just need to ask you something."

"No pleasantries for you, then, just like your father. I've never been a fan of that. What do you need?"

Mar looked around for a moment.

"If you're looking for my servants, I can assure you none are here at the moment." The blue man smirked, clearly amused at Mar's useless efforts.

Mar continued to look around, even swiping at the air.

"OK, even if I didn't send my servants away, let's say they are still here, hypothetically. You won't find them. And if I know something, they pretty much know it. So please, cut to the chase. There's no time, as you said before, right? I must admit I find your distrust of me a bit painful, but I suppose trust must be earned. Please tell me what ails you. I will try my best not to disappoint."

"First, promise me you won't tell my father." Mar quit looking around and finally gave Cancer his full attention.

"I can't promise something like that." He laughed. "It depends on what it is, but he may already know."

Mar gave Cancer the coldest look he was capable of. He looked around again as if he still felt he was being watched, but continued anyway. "I've been seeing Princess Diantha of Taurus—intimately—for quite some time now."

"Yes." Cancer slowly nodded his head at the comment.

"You're not surprised? So it really was you?"

"Really was me that did what, exactly?" Curiosity was roused in Cancer, but only a little.

"The letter on Libra during my meal with Catalina."

"Actually, neither I nor my men have been to Libra for anything other than council meetings for a while now. What does the letter say, exactly?"

Mar reached in his pocket and produced the letter and handed it to Cancer, staring at him the whole time to try to read him.

Cancer laughed out loud after reading the letter.

"This letter is not from me or anyone under me. It seems someone else knows your secret."

Mar gritted his teeth, trying not to get too angry at the lack of concern Cancer was showing his very serious problem.

"How can you be so sure?"

"This letter doesn't even say what the writer wants. Whoever wrote this either wants to scare you, or ruin the unification of you and the princess of Capricorn. I would never reveal that I knew such information without having a well-thought-out plan that would benefit me or my family. My men also know better than to write such a useless letter. Besides, there's nothing you have that I want. You're still but a mere prince. Now, your father, on the other hand, I wouldn't mind having the upper hand on him. Leverage is important when dealing with other kings, after all. If I knew your secret, and I wanted to use it I would use it when dealing with you father," he smirked.

Mar's heart sank. His father already knew. He must be so disappointed. Why hadn't he said anything already? That backstabbing Cancer; even if he hadn't written the letter, he still screwed over Mar and even his father, it seemed. Cancer must have been able to read Mar's disposition.

"Before you get angry and do something that both you and your father will regret, I implore you to speak with him. You shouldn't keep secrets from your father, my dear boy, especially when he cares for you so. Goodbye." Cancer's harsh stare didn't match his words, but were level with his tone, and said that he was done talking.

Rather than get mad, Mar simply left Cancer. He already had enough problems, a quarrel with a king couldn't help him in any way. Maybe once he spoke to his father, he would find some way to condemn Cancer and could even talk his father into annihilating him.

Back on Aries, he thought about ways he could approach his father. It all started with the letter, so that's where he would start. He was already in big trouble, so he decided to be honest about everything. *Just tell the truth about everything. That's all I have to do.*

"You knew all along and you didn't say anything," Mar asked?

"Lower your voice when you talk to me, son, first of all. Second, what are you talking about?"

"I just got back from Cancer. I think that snake played you, Father. What kind of a deal did you make with him to keep my secret? Well, everybody's secret now, because it's so widely spread, I'm not even sure if you can still call it a secret. How long have you known? Why didn't you tell me?"

"I wanted to protect you, of course. I thought once you saw that Capricorn girl, all your foolish thoughts about Diantha would vanish, and you would be ready to start your new life. I figured I could hide your past indiscretions, and we could all move forward as if it never happened. As far as the deal I made, it's already done. I'm sure Cancer wouldn't have soured on our deal unless he had something substantial to gain. Not once has he tried to contact me since we struck the deal, so I feel confident that it wasn't him. What did Cancer say when you saw him?"

"The same thing as you, that it wasn't him. We have no way of knowing if we can trust him, though."

"How did you find out that Cancer knew, or that anybody else knew?"

"From this letter." He read it out loud to his father.

"Is that it?"

"Yes, that's all they wrote."

"That definitely doesn't sound like Cancer. I don't know who knows, but I know this, that letter is trouble. War might be coming for us. I've been thinking about this for a while, since I was actually told by Cancer about your tryst with Diantha, and I think I'm going to call your brother and ask him to come back home, as well as your uncle and aunt. We will need the whole family here. Matter of fact, call your mother in here."

"How do you know there's going to be a war?"

"It doesn't matter. If there isn't a war between the kingdoms, then your brother Ram and everyone else can leave and go back to wherever they came from, for all I care. If there is a war, then we will need the whole family. The brotherhood even. Your cousin, Croix, we will probably need him, too. I'm going to try to assemble the Aries royal family. You can help by contacting the brotherhood, if you want."

His father was always a bit rash, in Mar's opinion, but maybe war really was what the author of the letter had in mind. One thing was certain, whoever wrote the letter hadn't told King Taurus, Capricorn, or Sagittarius anything yet.

***

"Has a cure been found yet?" Leo sat upright in the healing bed to look upon his healer.

"No my lord. If there is a cure for Scorpio's poison, I am sure that none of my cohorts nor anyone in their circle knows how to find it," the healer was saddened to say.

"That figures. Don't worry yourself over it. My Lioness is looking into it," Leo said to her before taking a slow deep breath to pace himself and rubbing a hand over his stomach bandage.

"Thank you sire. One more thing, there's somebody here to see you."

He nodded.

A centaur from Sagittarius appeared, sporting a neatly trimmed black goatee, a long, equally dark ponytail, and wearing a silver crown that most Sagittarius who were of direct relation to the king wore to symbolize their status.

"Shaw, what are you doing here?"

"My lord has sent me to check up on you," the horse man said. His black tail on his lower body moved as he walked closer to Leo's healing bed.

"I am in critical condition. Your king is supposed to be one of my closest allies, why doesn't he visit himself?" Leo eyed the man.

"He is currently looking into whoever might be responsible for your current condition."

"So he's saying he had nothing to do with it?"

"Of course he didn't." Shaw's eyes landed back on Leo.

"And why couldn't he say that to me himself, in person?"

Leo looked up at Shaw skeptically.

"Top priority is to find out if we have a traitor in our midst among the Sagittarian Royal Army. Once that is sorted out, if we are in fact harboring a traitor, we can bring you the one responsible for this and you can kill him personally. That may even lead to finding the cure for your poison."

"Oh. So now you're also saying that Sagittarius doesn't even have a cure for Scorpio's poison?" Leo could no longer hide his disbelief. "You expect me to believe that Sagittarius doesn't have a cure for Scorpio's poison when he deals with it daily?"

"Scorpio himself doesn't even have a cure for his own poison. Does he?" Shaw added the comment pointedly. "Additionally, slow-acting poison is not what Sagittarian soldiers are issued, so we are even less familiar with it."

"What did you come here for, exactly?" Leo grew tired of the exchange. "To apologize for your treacherous king?"

"Yes I am here to apologize for my honorable king. He wanted for me to present you this gift."

Shaw handed Leo a jar with small red and black slugs in it. There were at least twenty slugs in the jar, climbing all over each other.

"What am I supposed to do with this? How is this a gift?"

"It should help with your affliction. These are bloodsuckers, called vampires on Sagittarius. You may not be familiar with them. I believe they may be natives only to Sagittarius. Anyway, they suck your blood and in some cases, can even suck the poison from your wounds."

"Thanks, I guess. You can go back to Sagittarius whenever you want. I appreciate this"—Leo closely scrutinized the slugs in the jar—"gesture."

Shaw left from Leo's bedside to return to Sagittarius.

"I'm not really sure which one of you tried to kill Leo, but I will find out. I still can't even say I know why. Maybe you thought it was time I expanded my empire. Maybe you wanted to test out the slow-acting poison. Whatever your reasons, I don't approve. Whether we go to war with Leo or not, I most likely will kill whoever I find was responsible for trying to kill him. Make no mistake, I will find out who it was. Now leave my sight. Just your very presence is disgusting to me, all of you." Sagittarius turned away from the balcony where he spoke down to his field of soldiers and captains.

"My lord," Shaw said as he bowed and entered his cousin's golden quarters.

"How did it go with Leo?" Sagittarius sat down to his luxurious chair and picked up his chalice.

"He was displeased."

"I know that. It would be foolish to think he would be anything but. Did he take the vampires?"

"Yes." Shaw nodded lightly.

"Well, that's good, at least. It's unfortunate that it had to happen this way, but at least we will get to see how this new poison works and if it can do for us what we want it to. Has Scorpio said anything of his progress with the cure?"

"He's not working on the cure, sire, Aquarius is."

"That's right, Aquarius is doing it. It's going to be interesting to see how all this plays out." Sagittarius put his chalice down and rapped his fingers on his desk.

"Sire?"

Sagittarius stopped all his hand motions and looked to his cousin. "Well, even if we do have to go to war with Leo, what do I care? They are weak. That was made clear by the rebellion and by whichever insubordinate half blood almost took his life. But I want to wait. I don't want to make any moves against him. Certainly not yet. I wouldn't want another kingdom to come to his aid." Sagittarius stared off at a corner that had maps and replicas of the other kingdoms made of plastics. "All I'm saying is the traitor who did it may have done us a few favors."

"What do you mean, *insubordinate half blood*?"

"Obviously, it was most likely one of them who did it. I can't think of a single full-blooded Sag who I feel is untrustworthy."

"Do you want me to look into it personally?" Shaw offered.

"No. I already have some of my finest doing an investigation. It shouldn't be too hard to find out who did it, only a few of our men were on Leo at the time it happened."

Sagittarius made a slight hand gesture. Shaw picked up his cue and bowed out.

***

"I can't believe it. What insolence. I should kill him myself. I'm sure that I can kill him myself if I can get past his soldiers." The Lioness's eyes were dangerous for a moment. She truly considered trying to kill Sagittarius singlehandedly.

"Lioness, calm down please." Cough, cough. Leo held a fist by his mouth to partially block whatever may have come.

"I'm not sure why he sent Shaw instead of coming himself, but it's important that we don't overreact. With me here, and our forces still weak from the aftermath of the rebellion, I don't think it's a good idea to do anything overtly aggressive. I have an idea, though. Have Zemar and Llewellyn and a few of our other lions go to Sagittarius. Not to fight or do anything, but just to see what's going on around there. If possible, contact Cancer and see if he will offer help in gathering information."

"We don't need Cancer's help. It's probably his fault, somehow, that you are in the position you're in now."

"Cancer is the best at getting information. A necessary evil," Leo said evenly.

"No. Let's just try to see what Zemar and Llewellyn can gather. I'll even let Sagittarius know beforehand that they are coming. That way, if they get spotted, it won't be as hard to explain why they are there."

"What information will they be able to gather if everybody already knows they're there?" Leo's puzzled expression matched his tone.

"They will be able to watch the Sagittarian Royal Army personally. I can't think of a better way to find out what Sagittarius is up to than watching him upfront in his face. He won't suspect anything. Trust me. The same way he sent his cousin to see you, it will be just us checking up on things on Sagittarius. We are still on good terms, I don't think it will hurt." She was proud of her idea and her face showed it. She stood up straight and dusted her golden dress.

"Run it by Hayder, see what he says."

"Since when does the Lioness take orders from her son?"

"I'm merely saying mention it to him. He may have some useful input. We have to start taking him seriously. He's going to rule in my place someday, and he needs experience thinking about complex situations such as the one we are now facing with Sagittarius. It will be his duty to be king someday, and he will be ill equipped if you make all his decisions for him. Like I said, just run it by him. Obviously, you don't have to listen to him. I just want to know how he thinks, and prepare him for the future by having him think on important issues."

"Oh, well, I actually already have him doing something of the sort." She smiled wryly.

"Oh, yes, and what might that be?"

"At this very moment, he's setting up the new system for determining guilt of those suspected of criminal acts. I got the idea from the Libras for this new system. Did you know that they have honorary royals?"

"Honorary?"

"Commoners who have proven themselves useful in one way, shape, or other to the Libra royal parliamentary board. They also have a theory that the different races should have a say in the guilt or innocence of one of their own. Half bloods have involvement with cases pertaining to half bloods of the same type etc."

"I suppose that sounds reasonable. I certainly can no longer be blamed for the deaths of commoners."

"Ha, but you still can, actually."

"How's that?" Leo leaned upward in his bed toward her.

"Depending on the severity and nature of the offense against the people of Leo, those found to be guilty can be forced to fight in the lion's den."

"Why would you do that? The lion's den is what caused the entire rebellion. It may even have something to do with the assassin who tried to kill me."

"Don't worry. I assure you that there will be no blood on your hands, but only on the hands of the commoners and half bloods who condemn their own. We needn't forget that the lion's den was useful to us financially. This way, we can keep our commoners happy and foreign royals will continue visiting Leo for entertainment."

"Isn't that a lot of power to give to the commoners? They don't have the wisdom or insight to properly make these sorts of decisions."

"I've already thought of that as well. Two of our weakest from the pride have the ability to override some of the honorary royals' decisions. And Hayder will be able to look over the decisions they make."

"That's good. That boy needs more responsibility. But even with that I still want you to listen to his input about dealing with Sagittarius."

"Why does a Lioness need to tell her cub what she's doing?" She pouted a little bit. "You wanted him to have more responsibility; before you even said that to me, I had already given him more responsibility."

"Just mention it to him. You don't have to listen to his suggestions, but we should bring him into the fold. That's clear to me now, after everything that's happened. The three of us need to work together. Decide things as a family. That way, we will all be on the same page." He reached out his hand for hers.

She took his hand in hers and continued. "But he has no experience making these sort of diplomatic decisions."

"Exactly, that's the problem." He pulled his hand out of hers and sat up. "We may have already crippled him that way. But no more. From now on, he has to actually be a part of what you and I do. Not just appear to be for the sake of outsiders. Look, I just need you to do as I say, woman. Argh."

He coughed up thick dark red blood into his hand, his cough worsened each passing day.

"I'll get the healer in here for you."

He nodded, still coughing.

As soon as he caught his breath he stopped her. "One more thing. Don't worry about Sagittarius. I will speak with him personally about the arrival of our soldiers on his planet. It's a conversation that needs to happen between two kings. Wait for my word to send them and make sure you run it by Hayder first."

The Lioness looked him in his eyes but didn't respond.

"I really mean it."

She simply nodded her head. And then immediately walked out to find a healer.

***

"How have things been going with the new system?" the Lioness asked her son.

Hayder looked and felt a bit awkward in his royal robes, orange and yellow in hue. His father seldom wore them, but everyone thought it would be a good idea for Hayder to, so others would take him more seriously. "Everything has gone well thus far. The citizens seem to be pleased with having commoners determine the fate of other commoners, even if that means more Leos will be a step above them. Additionally, there is a rotation of honorary commoners we added."

"Enough about that, Hayder that seems to be quite fine. I'm sure the new system will work. I have come to speak to you about another matter entirely." She sat down next to her son on the fine onyx bench of their conservatory. "Deployment of two of our soldiers. These two did well during the rebellion, and I'm sure they will make us proud again. The plan is to send them to Sagittarius to have them try to figure out whatever they can. To make a determination as to whether or not King Sagittarius had something to do with the attempt to kill your father."

"Why are you telling me this?" Hayder frowned, appearing more bothered than shocked.

"You are not a child anymore. You will be king someday, and it's important for you to think about these sort of things, so you'll be prepared when the time is right to make these decisions on your own. I'm mentioning this to you to see your take on it, and if you have any suggestions or thoughts you would like to add." The Lioness put her hand under her chin and waited for him to answer.

"OK, well, my first thought is, why not have the Cancers look into it?"

"Not a terrible idea. But I can't say it's necessarily the best idea either. Giving any Cancer that much trust, is too risky, especially at this point."

"Well, why not have both the Cancers and our two men go? I heard it was King Cancer himself who helped us quell the rebel forces."

"Again, that's not a bad idea, but we are still indebted to Cancer for that very reason. Whenever Cancer does something, he expects something in return. We can only ask of him so much, before it's too much."

"Well, I guess if Cancer isn't an option, then we should just send the two, like you were already planning." Tired of thinking on the situation already, he shrugged and was ready to move on.

"I have an idea." The Lioness stood up from the bench excitedly. "You're finished with the preparations for the new system we came up with, right, Hayder?"

Hayder stood up as well. Raised an eyebrow and answered, "It's basically all the way there. Why do you ask?"

"I want you to meet with some of our allies personally to try to rally them toward us."

"Rally allies? To what end?"

"In case we have to go to war with Sagittarius. I will oversee everything here on Leo, correspond with Zemar and Llewellyn, who will be on Sagittarius investigating. And you can speak with some of our allies and see if they will fight for us when the time comes. I would say try Aries, Gemini, and lastly Libra, just for good measure. If you want, you can also ask Cancer and see what he says. This will be good experience for you, dealing with the kings. You know our strong selling points, don't you?"

"Of course I do. I was schooled for years on the trading points of Leo." Curtly he answered his mother, insulted by the question.

The Lioness did not care. "Good, but truth be told that shouldn't matter. If any of the kings agree to help, they should tell you what it will cost. Good luck to you."

"To you as well, Mother. I'll be available for you to contact me at any time if you need me. What did Dad have to say about asking for help?" Hayder figured it was a good idea to double-check before completely agreeing.

"It was his idea, of course."

"Oh, OK." He nodded his head thoughtfully. "I see. Farewell for now, Mother. I'll be off to negotiate."

Just as soon as she saw her son depart, she headed to her chambers and called Zemar and Llewellyn in.

"You two did very well during the rebellion. Now I have something else to ask of you."

"Of course, Lioness, anything you need us to do," the two lions said, bowed on one knee.

"You two are going to Sagittarius."

***

"Gregorio, I have an important task for you, which is why I have called you here." King Cancer was generally a serious man, but he was somehow even more somber than usual.

"Sire, would you like for me to get Maestro?"

"I would have called Maestro if I wanted him here. This is a task for you and you alone. I need you to go to Virgo and look after some things for me."

***

"When I begin investigations I would like for you to be there with me for support, if you don't mind. You can read people's minds, right?" Scorpio asked Valera.

"Not always. It's not that simple, some people are able to hide their thoughts from me. I've met at least two people who were somehow able to do it."

"Well, other than when circumstance prevents, you can ordinarily read thoughts, right?"

"Yes, usually, but mostly surface thoughts. If someone is really trying hard to hide something, they can, unless they are panicked or in some sort of altered state of mind."

"Oh, OK, I see. Well, tell me if somebody seems like they may be hiding something that is still suspicious, and should be noted. Come to think of it, I think your husband once told me something like that. I guess you two really do have the same powers, and they work the same way. Please accompany me, if you don't mind."

"But what about Virgo? Who will take charge of things there in my absence?"

"I'm sure there are a few able-bodied royal Virgos that you can put in your place as a proxy temporarily."

"Why can't we just have some of our royals do the investigation? Is this really the sort of thing a queen, the queen of Virgo, who now has no king, and the king of Scorpio should be doing personally?"

"If we were investigating commoners or half bloods or even just some royals, that would be fine, but these are kings. It wouldn't be wise to have anything less than a king investigate a king. The other kings would most likely not take it as seriously or would take it as a sign of disrespect, if I sent my underlings to their kingdoms to breathe down their necks."

"OK, that makes sense I guess. I suppose I hadn't thought of that." Valera adjusted herself in her seat. Flying around during her tour and now all the flying she had been doing with Scorpio was starting to make her dislike lightning ships. Soft as the seats of the lightning ship were, all the sitting was still becoming a bother for her.

"Relax. All you have to do is try to get into the thoughts of Gemini, Cancer, and Aries, while I talk to them. I will do all the talking. We will go to Virgo first so you can appoint someone to temporarily act in your stead, and then we will go to Aries to begin our investigation."

***

"Vernon, where is the viscount?"

"I will fetch him at once, my queen." Vernon left from Virgo's lab, where he still spent the bulk of his time, to get the viscount.

The old and wise viscount entered Virgo's lab, his beard white and long, extending to his stomach. He was much older than Virgo was and was his second cousin.

The viscount was much too busy to directly serve his king's needs while he was alive, but Valera felt he might be more easily persuaded since he would now be in charge, even if only for face value.

"I am going to be off for a while. I need you to head up things. You'll be in charge until I get back." Valera regarded the viscount, telling him about his new duty as soon as he entered Virgo's lab.

"How long will you be gone for?" The viscount was fine with getting right to the point.

"Not sure," Valera answered honestly. "At all times, I will be in one of the twelve kingdoms, and I will try to contact you each time I move to a different planet, in order to let you know where I am, so I can keep up with Virgo and you can contact me if an emergency occurs."

"And I'm in charge of everything, the whole kingdom, the whole planet?" Stroking his beard, he seemed to have a lot going on in his head.

"No, only in face value. Just keep things flowing the way they are. Do not make any new decisions. Do not meet with any kings or foreign royals. Do not do anything, except for whatever needs to be done to keep things as they are."

"I suppose that's for the good then. I won't have to abandon any of my duties as the viscount." He quickly let his beard free of his hand.

"Yes, of course. It shouldn't detract from your standard day-to-day duties. Additionally, I just want to remind you that you will have Vernon available to assist you in any way that you may need." She pointed to the silent and sullen Vernon, who stood quietly near the door.

The viscount of Virgo agreed to the honor of being in charge of Virgo while the queen was away. With everything settled on Virgo, Scorpio and Queen Virgo left for Aries.
'

***

"Things are going to get very interesting around here soon, Pim. All our hard work will pay off then. Priscilla, come here, my love," Pisces called to his wife. The voluptuous, silver-skinned

Piscean woman with long black hair appeared in his meeting room wearing her favorite fish-skin skirt and stockings. The room was simple. It had a few tables with a few chairs and maps of all the worlds spread about and lists of creatures and things found on each planet. The left wall was entirely windows. Pisces loved looking out to the seas while planning and thinking.

"A lot of good and bad things are going to be happening in the near future," Pisces said, finally lifting his gaze from one of the many floor-to-ceiling windows and looking his wife in her silver eyes. "I will need you and Pim to work hand in hand to do everything I say, exactly how I say it."

"Of course. Pim and I live to serve," she said.

"Everything is going according to plan. And I need to keep it that way for a while. Our journey won't be without its hardships, though. I just want you two to remember that no matter what you see, good or bad, it's either according to plan, or I saw it coming. I will let you two know when to worry. Other than that, there's nothing to fear, take anything that you see happen as fitting in with my vision," Pisces said and returned his stare to the nearest window, into the darkness of the vast ocean. From his meeting room, the view was so intense, it was as if he was riding on the waves into the darkness that he stared out at.

"Love. Please don't bring us all down. Let's celebrate. As you said before, everything is going according to plan. And what a clever plan it is indeed."

"Yes, everything is going according to plan," Pisces said again to reassure himself.

There were still so many things out of his control, but at least he knew, more or less, what the future was going to bring.

www.ingramcontent.com/pod-product-compliance
Lightning Source LLC
Chambersburg PA
CBHW072124250626
47159CB00007B/2561